"Happy Anniversary," Ty murmured.

"A few years back, right here in this house, you told me something that I have never forgotten. You said, even though you could ride like a man and work like a man, that didn't mean you didn't like flowers and candy."

It was then that Jessy noticed the small, beribboned box of expensive chocolates, placed next to one of the settings. Completely lost for words and too choked with emotion to utter them anyway, Jessy could only look at him.

Eyes swimming with tears, Jessy stood there for a long second, more touched by this simple gift than words could express. But she had never been good with words. By nature, she was a woman of action.

Her feet didn't feel as if they touched the ground as she crossed the space and into his arms. His mouth came down, claiming hers in a kiss, filled with that slow, deep-burning warmth that had always been between them. It was the kind that steadied rather than shook, the kind that strengthened rather than weakened, that brought boldness rather than hesitancy. That was the magic of it, and the power.

He lifted his mouth a fraction of an inch, to murmur against her lips, "Dinner won't be ready for another twenty minutes."

JANET DAILEY

Green Calder Grass

ZEBRA BOOKS
KENSINGTON PUBLISHING CORP.
http://www.kensingtonbooks.com

ZEBRA BOOKS are published by

Kensington Publishing Corp.
119 West 40th Street
New York, NY 10018

All Kensington titles, imprints, and distributed lines are available at special quantity discounts for bulk purchases for sales promotion, premiums, fund-raising, educational, or institutional use.

Special book excerpts or customized printings can also be created to fit specific needs. For details, write or phone the office of the Kensington Sales Manager: Attn.: Sales Department. Kensington Publishing Corp., 119 West 40th Street, New York, NY 10018. Phone: 1-800-221-2647.

Zebra and the Z logo Reg. U.S. Pat. & TM Off.

First Kensington Books Hardcover Printing: July 2002
First Zebra Books Mass-Market Paperback Printing: June 2003
ISBN-13: 978-1-4201-4180-1
ISBN-10: 1-4201-4180-5

10 9 8 7

Printed in the United States of America

PART ONE

Montana green grass is what done it.
It brought that first Calder here.
He staked a claim
In the Calder name.
But there's an area where the title ain't clear.

Chapter One

〜

The grass ocean rippled gold under a strong summer sun. The dirt track that cut a straight line through the heart of it was a small portion of the mile upon mile of private roads that crisscrossed the ranching empire of the Calder Cattle Company, better known in Montana as the Triple C.

It was a land that could be bountiful or brutal, a land that bent to no man's will, a land that weeded out the weak and faint of heart, tolerating only the strong.

No one knew that better than Chase Benteen Calder, the current patriarch of the Triple C and a direct descendant of the first Calder, his namesake, who had laid claim to nearly six hundred square miles of this grassland. Its size was never something Chase Calder bragged about; the way he looked at it, when you were the biggest, everybody already knew it, and if they didn't, they would soon be told. And the knowledge would carry more weight if he wasn't the one doing the telling.

To a few, the enormity of the Triple C was a thing of rancor. The events of recent weeks were proof of that. The freshness of that memory accounted for the hint of grimness in his expression as Chase drove the ranch pick-up along the hard-packed road, a rooster tail of dust pluming behind it. But the past wasn't something Chase allowed his mind to dwell on. Running an operation this size required a man's full attention. Even the smallest detail had a way of getting big if ignored. This land and a long life had taught him that if nothing else.

Which was likely why his sharp eyes spotted the sagging wire caused by a tilting fence post. Chase braked the truck to a stop, but not before the pickup clattered over a metal cattle guard. He shifted into reverse, backed up to the cattle guard, stopped, and switched off the engine.

The full force of the sun's rays beat down on him as Chase stepped out of the truck, older and heavier but still a rugged and powerfully built man.

The sixty-plus years he carried had taken some of the spring from his step, added a heavy dose of gray to his hair, and grooved deeper creases into the sun-leathered skin around his eyes and mouth, giving a crustiness to his face, but it hadn't diminished the mark of authority stamped on his raw-boned features.

Reaching back inside the truck, Chase grabbed a pair of tough leather work gloves off the seat and headed toward the section of the sagging fence six posts from the road. Never once did it occur to Chase to send one of the ranch hands back to fix the problem. With distances being what they were on the Triple C, that was the quickest way of turning a fifteen-minute job into a two-hour one.

With each stride he took, the brittle, sun-cured grass crackled under foot. Its stalks were short and curly, mat-ting close to the ground—native buffalo grass, drought-tolerant and highly nutritious, the kind of feed that put weight on cattle and was a mainstay of the Triple C's century of success.

The minute his gloved hands closed around the post in question, it dipped drunkenly under the pressure. The three spaced strands of tightly strung barbed wire were clearly the only thing keeping it upright at all. Chase kicked away the matted grass at the base and saw that the wood had rotted at ground level.

This was one fence repair that wouldn't be a fifteen-minute fix. Chase glanced toward the pickup parked on the road. There was a time when he would have carried steel fence posts and a roll of wire along with other sundry items piled in the truck bed. But on this occasion, there was only a toolbox.

Chase didn't waste time with regret for the lack of a spare post. Instead he ran an inspecting glance along the rest of the fence, following its steady march over the rolling grassland until it thinned into a single line. In that one, cursory observation, he noticed three more places where the fence curved out of its straight line. If three could be spotted with the naked eye, there were undoubtedly more. It didn't surprise him. Fence mending was one of those never-ending jobs every rancher faced.

When he turned to retrace his steps to the pickup, he caught the distant drone of another vehicle. Automatically Chase scanned the narrow road in both directions without finding a vehicle in sight. But one was approaching, of that he had no doubt.

It was the huge sweep of sky that gave the illusion of flatness to the land beneath it. In reality the terrain was riven with coulees and shallow hollows, all of them hidden from view with the same ease that an ocean conceals its swales and troughs.

By the time Chase reached his truck, another ranch pickup had roared into view, coming from the west. Chase waited by the cab door, watching as the other vehicle slowed perceptibly then rolled to a stop behind Chase's pickup. The trailing dust cloud swept forward, briefly enveloping both vehicles before settling to a low fog.

Squinting against the sting of dust particles, Chase recognized the short, squatly built man behind the wheel as Stumpy Niles, a contemporary of his and the father of Chase's daughter-in-law. Chase lifted a hand in greeting and headed toward the truck.

Stumpy promptly rolled down the driver's side window and stuck his head out. "What's the problem, Chase?"

"Have you got a spare fence post in your truck? We have a wooden one that's rotted through."

"Got it handled." Stumpy scrambled out of the truck and moved toward the tailgate with short, choppy strides. "Can't say I'm surprised. Just about all them old wood posts have started rottin'. It's gonna be one long, endless job replacin' 'em."

And expensive, too, Chase thought to himself, and pitched in to help the shorter man haul the steel post as well as a posthole jobber out of the truck's rear bed. "I don't see where we have much choice. It's got to be done."

"I know." Already sweating profusely in the hot summer sun, Stumpy paused to drag a handkerchief from his pocket and mop the perspiration from his round, red face. "It ain't gonna be an easy job. The ground's as hard as granite. It's been nearly forty years since we've had such a dry spring. I'll bet we didn't get much more than an inch of moisture in all the South Branch section."

"It wasn't much better anywhere else on the ranch."

Like Stumpy, Chase was remembering the last prolonged dry spell the ranch had endured.

Stumpy was one of the cadre of ranch hands who, like Chase, had been born on the Triple C. All were descended from cowhands who had trailed that original herd of longhorn cattle north, then stayed on to work for the first Calder. That kind of deep-seated loyalty was a throwback to the old days when a cowboy rode for the brand, right or wrong, through times of plenty and times of lean. To an outsider, this born-and-bred core of riders gave an almost feudal quality to the Triple C.

Chase shortened his stride to walk alongside Stumpy as the pair tracked through the grass to the sagging post. "Headed for The Homestead, were you?" Stumpy guessed, referring to the towering, two-story structure that was the Calder family home, erected on the site of the ranch's original homestead.

Chase nodded. "But only long enough to clean up before I head into Blue Moon. I'm supposed to meet Ty and Jessy for supper as soon as they're through at the clinic."

"The clinic." Stumpy stopped short. "Jessy's all right, isn't she?"

"She's fine." Smiling, Chase understood Stumpy's fatherly concern. "Ty was the one in for a checkup."

Stumpy shook his head at himself and continued toward the rotted post. "It's them twins she's fixin' to have. It's got me as nervous as a long-tailed cat in a roomful of rockin' chairs. There's no history of twins bein' born in either side of our family. Or at least none that Judy and me know about," he said, referring to his wife.

"It's a first for the Calder side, too." Chase looked on while Stumpy set about digging a hole with the jobber. "Although I can't speak for the O'Rourke half."

The comment was an oblique reference to his late wife

Maggie O'Rourke. Even now, so many years after her death, he rarely mentioned her by name and only among the family. This belief that grief was a private thing was one of many codes of the Old West that continued to hold sway in the modern West, especially in Triple C country.

"Twins," Stumpy murmured to himself, then grunted from the impact of the twin blades stabbing into the hard dry ground. He scissored the handles together to pick up the first scoop of soil, then reversed the procedure to dump it to one side. "Look at that," he complained. "The top two inches is nothin' but powder. It's dry, I tell you. Dry." It was a simple observation that was quickly forgotten as he reverted to his original topic. "According to that ultrasound thing the doctor did, it's gonna be boys."

That was news to Chase. "I understood the doctor was only positive about one."

"Mark my words, they'll be boys," Stumpy declared with certainty, then chuckled. "If they take after their mother, she's gonna have her hands full. They'll be a pair of hell-raisers, I'll wager—into everything the minute you turn your back. Why, from the first minute Jessy started crawlin', she was out the door and into the horse pens. She dealt her mama fits. If you ask me, it's only right that she gets back some of her own." He glanced at Chase and winked. "It's for sure you won't be complaining anymore about The Homestead bein' too quiet since Cat got married and moved out. By the way, how's the little man doin' since . . . things quieted down?"

The thwarted kidnapping of his five-year-old grandson Quint was another topic to be avoided from now on. But Chase knew it had left him three times as wary of those outside the Calder circle. After all, not only had the security of his home been breached, but Calder blood had been spilled as well.

"Kids are pretty resilient. Quint is doing fine."

"Glad to hear it."

"With any luck, Ty will finally be able to throw away that sling today and start using his arm again."

The twin spades of the jobber *whacked* into the hole. Stumpy rotated the handles back and forth to carve out another chunk of hard soil. After it was removed, Stumpy took a look and decreed, "That should be deep enough." He laid the jobber aside and took the steel fence post from Chase. "I thought the doctors originally told Ty he'd have to have that arm in a sling for six weeks. That bullet he took totally shattered his shoulder. Them surgeons had to rebuild the joint from scratch."

"True, but Ty figures four weeks is long enough. We'll see if he manages to convince the doctor of that."

Stumpy grinned. "He's probably *hopin'* he'll persuade Doc to split the difference and let him take it off in another week."

"Probably."

"That reminds me." Stumpy paused in his securing of the post. "I ran into Amy Trumbo at noon. She tells me that O'Rourke's bein' released from the hospital today. Is that true?"

"Yeah, Cat went to get him. She should have him home before dark."

Chase remembered much too vividly that moment when he realized one of the kidnappers had shot his son. He saw again, in his mind, the brilliant red of all that blood, the desperate struggle to stop the bleeding and the gut-tearing mixture of rage and fear he'd felt.

But his son Ty hadn't been the only one to suffer at the hands of the kidnapping duo; Culley O'Rourke, his late wife's brother, had also been shot—in his case, multiple times.

Stumpy wagged his head in amazement. "I still don't know how in hell O'Rourke survived."

"He's got more lives than a barn cat." Chase couldn't honestly say whether he was happy about it or not. There had never been any love lost between the two men. At the same time, he knew that O'Rourke lived only for Cat, Chase's daughter and O'Rourke's niece. Maybe it was Cat's uncanny resemblance to Maggie. And maybe it was just plain love. Whatever the case, O'Rourke was devoted to her. And like it or not, Chase had O'Rourke to thank for his part in getting young Quint back, unharmed.

"I guess O'Rourke will be stayin' at the Circle Six with Cat and Logan." Stumpy scooped dirt around the post with his boot and tamped it down.

"That's Cat's plan anyway. But you know what a lone wolf O'Rourke is," Chase said. "My guess is that it'll only be a matter of days before he's back on the Shamrock."

"Is he strong enough to look after himself?"

"Probably not, but that means Cat will burn up the road, running between Circle Six and Shamrock, making sure he's all right and has plenty of food on hand." Noting that Stumpy had the job well in hand, Chase took his leave. "I'd better get moving before Ty and Jessy wonder what happened to me."

As he took a step away, Stumpy called him back, "Say, I've been meanin' to tell you, Chase—do you remember that young bull Ty sold to Parker from Wyoming last year? The one he wanted for his kid's 4-H project."

"What about it?"

"He walked away with the grand championship at the Denver stock show."

"Where'd you hear that?" Chase frowned.

"From Ballard. He hit the southern show circuit this past winter, hirin' out to ride in cuttin' horse competitions and doin' some jackpot ropin' on the side. That's how he happened to be in Denver. He saw a good-lookin' bull with the Triple C tag and started askin' questions." Stumpy's grin widened. "It was grand champion, imagine that. And that bull was one of our culls—a good'n, but not the quality of the ones we kept." With a wave of his hand, he added, "You need to tell Ty about it. As proud as he is of the herd of registered stock we've put together, he'll get a kick out of it."

"I'll tell him," Chase promised.

The high drone of a jet engine whined through the air, invading the stillness of wind and grass. Automatically Chase lifted his head and scanned the tall sky. Stumpy did the same as Chase and caught the metallic flash of sunlight on a wing.

"Looks like Dyson's private jet." Stumpy almost spat the name. "Coal tonnage must be down, and he's comin' to crack some whips. You notice he's makin' his approach over pristine range and not the carnage of his strip mines."

"I noticed." But Chase carefully didn't comment further.

"That's one family I'm glad we've seen the back of."

Chase couldn't have agreed more, but he didn't say so. Ty's marriage to Dyson's daughter Tara had been relatively brief. Looking back, Chase knew he had never truly approved of that spoiled beauty becoming Ty's wife, although Maggie had. To him, there had always been a cunning quality to Tara's intelligence, a quickness to manipulate and scheme to get what she wanted. Thankfully Tara was part of the past, another subject to be put aside, but not forgotten.

Yet any thought of Tara and that troubled time always aroused a sore point. Chase had yet to obtain title to those ten thousand acres of government land within the Triple C boundaries. The memory of that hardened the set of his jaw, a visible expression of his deepening resolve.

Without another word to Stumpy, Chase walked back to the ranch pickup, climbed in, and took off in the direction of The Homestead.

A cluster of old buildings crowded close to the shoulder of the two-lane highway that raced past them. A roadside sign to the south of them, its face pockmarked with bullet holes, identified the unincorporated town of Blue Moon. Long gone was the grain elevator that had once punctuated the horizon. It had been bulldozed to the ground years ago—as had the dilapidated structures that once occupied the back streets. In their place were a few modern brick buildings, a scattering of new houses, and a trailer court to house the employees of Dy-Corp's nearby strip-mining operation.

These were the changes Chase always noticed when he drove into Blue Moon, like the fresh coat of paint on the exterior of Sally's place. The combination restaurant and bar had long been the sole watering hole for the surrounding area. In his youth, the site had been the home of a roadhouse complete with whiskey, women, and gambling. Prior to that, it had been a general store and saloon, established by the town's first settler, Fat Frank Fitzsimmons.

Fat Frank was also the man who nailed up the first sign, dubbing the location Blue Moon. Local legend had it that the name was a gift from a passing cowboy who predicted failure for Fat Frank's fledgling establishment, declaring that people came this way only once in a Blue Moon.

Blue Moon was still a place rarely visited by strangers, as evidenced by all the local license plates on the vehicles parked in front of Sally's. Chase found an empty space and pulled his truck into it.

Sally Brogan, the restaurant's proprietress, was at the cash register when he walked in. Her face lit up with pleasure the instant she saw him, a special light shining in her blue eyes, one that was reserved especially for Chase Calder. A widow of a Triple C ranch hand, Sally had fallen in love with Chase years ago and didn't bother to hide it anymore, even though she knew friendship was all he offered in return.

"You're late." Self-consciously she smoothed a hand over the front of her apron, as if the years hadn't added a few pounds to thicken her waist and turned her copper-red hair to a striking snow-white. "Ty and Jessy were just about to give up on you and order."

"I got on the phone and the call took longer than I expected."

Over the years, Sally had come to know Chase in all his moods. That hard, preoccupied look to his eyes was one she instantly recognized.

"Trouble?" she guessed instantly.

As if catching himself showing his feelings a little too plainly, he threw her a quick smile, his dark eyes lighting up for the first time. "Nothing that I haven't been dealing with for years."

"Old troubles are always with us." Sally came out from behind the cash register. "It's when new ones come along that I worry."

"You're probably right." Chase waited to let her walk him to the table where Ty and Jessy waited.

Out of habit, Chase ran an inspecting glance over his tall, broad-shouldered son, seated next to Jessy. The unmistakable stamp of a Calder was there in his dark hair and eyes, and in the hard, angular cut of his features. On the green side of forty, Ty was a man in his prime. Best of all, except for the sling holding his left arm, Ty was the image of robust vigor. Chase could no longer detect any trace of the sickly pallor that had lurked below the deep tan of his son's face. There was a sense of genuine relief in that.

Beside Ty sat Jessy. As always, when Chase's glance fell on this slender woman with honeyed-gold hair, he experienced a mixture of satisfaction and approval. As slim and long-legged as a boy, she possessed a subtle beauty that went beyond simple good looks. There was a strength and a steadiness about her that radiated an aura of calm. Jessy wasn't the kind of woman to lead a man—or be led by him. But she would stand tall at his side. More than that, Jessy had been born and raised on the ranch. Like the rich tough grass that was the Triple C's wealth, her roots were sunk deep in Calder soil.

A better mate Chase couldn't have picked for his son. Or a better mother to his grandchildren, Chase thought as he took note of the protruding roundness of her stomach, made all the more obvious by her boy-slim figure.

"It's about time you got here," Ty declared as he slid a possessive hand across the back of Jessy's shoulders. "Jessy was ready to faint with hunger."

"That'll be the day." Skepticism riddled his response. With a nod to Jessy, Chase pulled out a chair on the other side of his son and sat down.

"I'll get you some coffee." Sally started to move away from the table.

"Better take our order first. I wouldn't want Jessy keeling over for want of food."

A small, answering smile curved Jessy's mouth at the twinkling glance Chase sent her direction. But some shading in her father-in-law's expression told her that he had more serious matters on his mind. She doubted that a direct question would elicit a direct answer. In that she knew her father-in-law well. Whatever was on his mind, he would get around to telling them about it in his own good time.

Instead, she waited until Sally had taken their food orders then asked, "What kept you?"

"I got tied up on the phone," Chase replied, a telltale grimness coloring his words. He leaned back in his chair and began pushing around the silverware in front of him.

"With who?" Ty asked curiously.

Chase grunted at the question, his mouth twisting in a smile that was without humor. "Which time?" He correctly interpreted the question in Ty's raised eyebrow. "I called to find out what progress had been made in getting title to that land—and ended up getting the runaround."

"They're no closer, then," Ty concluded.

"Nope." With that said, Chase made an effort to throw off the dark mood and flicked a finger in the direction of Ty's sling. "I see you still have that contraption around your arm."

"It'll come off next week."

"Actually," Jessy inserted, "Ty informed the doctor that if it didn't, he was taking it off."

"And I meant it," Ty stated, on the irritable side. "Four weeks of going around with a wing instead of an arm is long enough. It's time I started using it again."

"The doctor said he'll need at least two months of physical therapy," Jessy told Chase.

"Getting back to work is the only therapy I'll need," Ty replied.

"We'll see." Wisely Jessy didn't argue the point.

Ty flashed her a look of annoyance. Then his eye was caught by the serene calm of her expression. Just the sight of her seemed to be enough to smooth everything inside of him. Almost against his will, a smile twitched at the corners of his mouth.

"Okay. I admit I'll need some therapy," Ty conceded, "but not two months' worth."

Most times it was hard to tell what Jessy was thinking. She had always had a man's way of hiding her feelings. But not this time. The glance she slid him was alive with a mischievous sparkle.

"You're just cranky because you hate not being able to cut your own meat at the table."

The teasing jibe was all too accurate, and brought a fresh surge of irritation. "It makes me feel like a damned child," Ty grumbled.

Jessy couldn't resist another little playful dig. "That's why he ordered Sally's meatloaf instead of his usual steak," she told Chase.

"What about my meatloaf?" Sally returned to the table with their dinner salads and coffee for Chase.

Ty shot a warning look at his wife and replied, "Jessy was just telling Dad that's what I ordered."

Taking the cue, Jessy changed the subject. "Have you told Chase your news, Sally?"

"What news is that?" Chase glanced from Jessy to Sally, a mild curiosity showing.

Sally hesitated, then proceeded to refill Ty's coffee cup. "I wouldn't exactly call it news." But she was careful not to look Chase's way. "It's just that I've put the place up for sale."

"For sale." A stunned stillness gripped Chase.

"It should hardly come as a surprise." Secretly Sally was a little pleased by his reaction. "I've been talking about selling out for a couple years."

"Talking about it is one thing." Chase declared with a frown. "Actually doing it is something else again. What in heaven's name will you do? You're too young to retire." Then another thought hit him. "Where will you live? That apartment upstairs has been your only home for years."

"More like decades." Sally finished the thought with a sigh. "To be honest, I haven't decided where I'll go or what I'll do. And I probably won't until I actually receive an offer. Finding a buyer for a place like this out in the middle of nowhere won't be easy, you know."

"I know, but—why list it for sale now?" Chase argued, struggling with a sense of loss he couldn't name.

"Because I'm tired," she replied. "Tired of working fifteen, sixteen hours a day, sometimes more. I'm tired of never having a vacation. And the clientele—it isn't the way it used to be, Chase. Most of the people who come in now are rougher, coarser."

His expression darkened. "Has somebody stepped out of line?"

"With *me?*" A laugh bubbled toward the surface as she glowed at the implied compliment. "Chase, I'm not a young redhead anymore."

"Just the same, if someone isn't showing you the proper respect, I want to know about it."

"Of course." Suddenly this entire discussion was becoming painful and Sally couldn't explain why. "Would you like more water, Jessy?"

"Please."

But Chase wasn't about to let her slip away so easily. "Are you sure this is what you want to do, Sally?"

She paused. "Chase, when you don't like your work anymore, it's time to quit. With any luck, one of the guys working for Dy-Corp has a secret dream about owning a bar and will take this place off my hands. Lord knows they get paid high wages out there."

"If this is what you want, Sally," Chase began, clearly unhappy with her decision, "I'll spread the word around that you're looking for a buyer. But—it won't be the same here without you."

She could have told him she wasn't necessarily leaving the area. She could have told him a hundred different things, but the words wouldn't come. Something in his remark had a ring of finality, and it knifed through her. At that instant, Sally knew that she had always secretly feared that if she ever sold the restaurant, she would never see Chase again, that he wouldn't come see her elsewhere because that would start talk. His comment had all but confirmed it.

"I appreciate your help, Chase."

When Sally moved away from their table, Jessy wondered if she was the only one who noticed the sudden welling of tears. Every time Jessy observed Sally and Chase together—and the love for the man that shone in Sally's eyes—it tugged at her heart. She had loved Ty from afar for too many years not to understand and empathize with the ache of that.

The memory of those times prompted Jessy to reach up and caress the strong hand resting on her shoulder, simply because she was his wife and she could. Tara was gone now; no longer did she have Ty caught under her spell.

The front door to the restaurant burst open, followed immediately by the *bang* of the screen door slamming shut, as loud as the crack of a rifle. Jessy jumped in her chair and half turned in her seat, her glance racing to the entrance.

Something inside her froze at the sight of a slender woman with sable-dark hair. It was Tara, chicly dressed in some blue concoction that looked straight off the pages of a high-fashion magazine.

Maybe it was the old fear that made Jessy dart a look at Ty. She observed the flash of surprise on his face— and something more, something like the pull of attraction. The anger of old resentment and dislike knotted Jessy's stomach.

Chapter Two

～

Like a Texas whirlwind, Tara Dyson Calder swept up Sally the instant she spied the older woman.

"Sally. Thank God, you're here." Relief quivered through her voice. In the next second, her dark gaze bored into Sally, a kind of frantic distress in her expression that was totally alien to her nature. "Is it true?"

Startled and confused, Sally drew back, "Is what true?"

Tara dragged in a quick breath as if trying to gather her scattered wits. "Ty. I just heard. I've been in Europe the past two months—in Tuscany, then the South of France." She shook her head, realizing none of that was important. "Someone just told me there had been a kidnapping attempt, and Ty was shot. Was he?"

"Yes—"

Tara never gave her a chance to say more. "How badly was he hurt? I demand you tell me. His arm, he isn't going to lose it, is he?"

"No. He's fine—"

"Are you certain? I heard—"

This time Sally interrupted her. "I can imagine what you heard. But Ty has almost completely recovered. Don't take my word for it. You can see for yourself. He's sitting right over there." With a wave of her hand, she gestured in the general direction of their table.

Turning, Tara went motionless for a full second, her velvety-dark gaze drinking in the sight of him, her soft lips parting in pleasure and relief. With a practiced grace that had become as natural to her as breathing, Tara glided across the room to the table, clearly blind to anyone else.

Manners, too deeply ingrained to be ignored, brought both Ty and Chase to their feet. But Tara had eyes only for Ty. She was still a stunning woman. Time hadn't dimmed at all the allure of her dark beauty. Ty could feel the animal pull of it. In some ways, it was all too familiar and, as a result, easier to resist.

"Tara. This is a surprise." Without thinking, Ty extended a hand in greeting, and felt the smallness and softness of the one she placed in it.

"Ty." Her voice was all silken emotion, caressing and low, and her dark eyes were bright with promise.

She let her hand stay in his a fraction of a second longer than propriety dictated. An instant later, she noticed the sling, and her expression clouded with a concern that made Ty oddly uncomfortable. "Ty, your arm." Tara reached a hand toward it, then hesitated as if reluctant to touch his arm in case it might cause him pain.

"The sling comes off next week; then I'll be good as new."

"Thank God," she declared with feeling, a hand theatrically fluttering to her throat. Belatedly Tara noticed Chase standing there. "You are looking well, Chase," she said in greeting then tilted her head at a coy angle, striking a provocative pose that Ty recognized all too well. "Or isn't it proper for me to address my ex-father-in-law by his first name?"

"It was good enough in the past; it's good enough now. How are you, Tara?" Chase inclined his head, but didn't offer his hand.

"Much better now that I have seen for myself that Ty will be fine," Tara replied then deigned to acknowledge Jessy's presence with a glance of cool challenge. "As I'm sure you feel, Jessy."

Jessy responded with a cool look of her own. "Calders have always been quick to recover."

But Jessy might as well have been talking to the wall for all the notice Tara gave as she switched her attention back to the two men. "After spending the last two months in Europe, then coming back to hear about the kidnapping attempt—it was such a shock. And when I learned Ty had been wounded—" Tara paused, leaving the sentence dangling to slide him a chiding look. "Honestly, Ty, hasn't anyone ever told you that ex-husbands are only supposed to be shot by their former spouses?"

Her remark attained the desired reaction as his mouth quirked in a hard, familiar smile. "I guess no one has."

"Then you need to remember that from now on," Tara informed him, her eyes sparkling. "Your grandson," she said to Chase, "I understood that he was unharmed?" The lilt of her voice made it a question.

"That's correct." Chase nodded.

"How very fortunate. Poor Cat, she must have been in agony. Is it true that she's married to the local sheriff? Echohawk, I believe they said his name was."

"Acting sheriff," Ty corrected and half waited for Tara to make some slighting comment about either his occupation or native ancestry.

But Tara was too wise to make that kind of mistake. "Well, you can tell Cat for me that my feelings are hurt that she didn't send me a wedding announcement."

"I'll pass that along to her."

"On second thought, don't bother," Tara declared with an airy wave of her hand. "I'll call and tell her myself as long as I'm here. It's awful the way we have managed to lose touch these last few years after we were so close."

"I'm sure Cat would like that," Ty replied evenly, aware that his younger sister had always been fond of Tara.

"We were about to have dinner. Would you care to join us?" Chase motioned to an empty chair at their table, the invitation intended to prompt her departure.

It backfired.

"How kind of you to ask, Chase. I think I'll pass on the dinner, but I would love to join you for a cup of coffee and catch up on all the family news."

Tara took perverse satisfaction in the flicker of irritation that passed so briefly across Chase Calder's expression. She had no illusions about his opinion of her. Regardless of her welcome—or lack thereof—she had no intentions of leaving until *she* was ready.

When Chase moved to pull out the empty chair for her, Tara turned away so she could make it appear she hadn't noticed. Instead she swung around one of the chairs from a nearby table and positioned it so that she could sit between Ty and the loathsome woman he married. Tara hated Jessy. She always had. There wasn't any doubt in her mind that, if it weren't for that she-bitch Jessy Niles, there would have been no divorce and she would still be Ty's wife.

Admittedly she and Ty had encountered some problems in their marriage, but none they couldn't have worked out. Given enough time, Tara would have seen to it. That's why she had strung out the divorce so long.

In truth, Tara had ultimately agreed to the divorce only when it became clear that the harder she fought Ty over it, the more determined he became about it. It was hardly surprising. The grass always looked greener in forbidden pastures. Now that he had had a chance to graze on it for a few years, Tara wondered just how much Ty still liked the taste of it. Surely he had wearied of Jessy by now.

After all, the woman was common as dirt, the daughter of an ordinary ranch hand. It was true that the bone structure of her face was quite good, classical in its line. Makeup would have done wonders to enhance it, but one glance had revealed to Tara that Jessy was totally devoid of any, except, perhaps, some lipstick. That same glance also told her that Jessy still didn't wear the sort of clothes a Calder wife should. Cowboy boots, tan twills, and a sloppy white shirt were hardly suitable attire. Nor did Jessy know how to take care of her skin. Tara had been quick to notice all the feathery lines etched around Jessy's mouth, nose, and eyes, lines emphasized by the golden tan that came from a failure to use protective sunscreen.

It was beyond question that Jessy suffered greatly in contrast to her. With the two of them sitting side by side, Ty was bound to notice the disparity. Tara was counting on it.

"So how have things been at the Triple C?" Tara angled herself toward Ty, effectively excluding Jessy from their conversation as Chase signaled for Sally to bring a cup of coffee for her.

"Fine." Ty's one-word answer was deliberately cool, almost as cold as the accusation in his eyes that seemed to convey he knew what she was up to.

Fully confident of her abilities, Tara was undeterred. "I'm glad some things have gone well for you." She let her gaze slide to his shoulder sling, paused a beat while she summoned a subtle welling of tears, then gave an expressive little shudder. "Every time I think about that horrible moment when they told me you had been seriously wounded, I"—she lifted her head, letting him see the moisture in her eyes—"I was worried out of my mind about you, Ty. Crazy, isn't it, after all this time apart."

His glance fell from her face. "I appreciate your concern—"

"Concern?" Her low laugh was soft with mockery. "I was frantic with worry. Poor Sally must have thought I had taken leave of my senses over the way I grilled her about you when I first arrived. Thank heaven you never saw it. That would have been too embarrassing. Why, the way I was carrying on, a stranger would have thought we were still married."

"Our divorce was final six years ago," Ty reminded her smoothly.

"True. Six years, one week, and two days. But who's counting?" She kept her smile light and playful, but the look in her eyes was something more serious. Truthfully Tara had no idea of the exact date of their divorce, but she doubted that Ty knew it either. "Look." She raised her left hand, showing him the black opal ring on her finger. "I'm still wearing the engagement ring you gave me. I told you I was going to keep it. Even with the problems we had, we also had some very good times."

"Dammit, Tara." He pushed the words through gritted teeth, checked some further angry retort, and ground out instead, "It's long past time you took that ring off."

"Now you sound like Daddy," Tara chided.

"How is your father?" Chase inserted, regarding her with an impenetrable expression.

"Daddy, he's—"

"Doing quite well, thank you." The male voice with its distinct Texas twang came from E.J. Dyson. Dressed as usual, in an expensive Western-cut suit and familiar white Stetson, he came to a halt beside Tara's chair and cast an indulging smile at her head.

She glanced up in surprise. "What are you doing here, Daddy?"

"Looking for you, of course," he replied then nodded to Chase. "Good to see you again, Calder. And you, too." His encompassing glance included both Ty and Jessy. "It's been a while."

"Yes, it has," Ty agreed. But it was the worn and weary look about the older man that had Ty narrowing his eyes to make a closer inspection. The man looked every bit of his seventy years and more.

"As you can see, I still have trouble keeping track of my daughter. Some things never change, I guess. Truthfully, I'm not sure I want them to." E.J. laid a hand on Tara's shoulder in affection, then turned a smiling glance on Ty. "I understand congratulations are in order for both you and your wife."

Before Ty could respond, Tara looked up in confusion. "Congratulations? For what? Have I missed something?"

"Jessy is expecting," E.J. informed her.

For the space of a heartbeat, Tara didn't react at all. Then, slowly, she turned to look at Jessy. "You're having a baby?" There was nothing, absolutely nothing, in the brightness of her voice that reflected the hatred that blazed in her dark eyes.

Inwardly, Jessy recoiled from it, but outwardly she maintained a calm composure. "Twins, actually."

"Twins," Tara repeated. "How wonderful. And when is this blessed event to be?" She directed the question to Ty.

"Early December."

"In time for Christmas. Isn't that perfect timing?" Tara declared then gave Ty one of her patented, side-long looks. "Papa Ty," she teased. "I can see you now, passing out cigars. Daddy, we really must remember to send Ty a box of Cuban cigars, so he can celebrate the birth of the twins in style." Graceful as a doe, Tara rose from her chair and tucked a hand in the crook of her father's arm. "Daddy's come to drag me off to some dreary dinner with his mine supervisor, so I might as well leave willingly. Please give my love to Cat in case I don't have time to call her this trip, will you, Ty?"

"I will." Ty made a brief show of rising then settled back in his chair when the pair moved away from the table. There was a vaguely preoccupied air about him as he sent Jessy a half-apologetic glance. "With any luck, it will be another six years before we see her again."

"We can only hope." Few things ever unsettled Jessy, but the look of pure hatred in Tara's eyes had.

"That reminds me," Chase began, "I ran into your father this afternoon."

He went on to explain about the rotted fence post. After which the conversation moved into a general discussion on the overall condition of the fencing on the ranch, replacement costs, and the massive man-hours the task would require. The subject of Tara wasn't raised again.

A three-quarter moon on the wane rode high in the night sky. Its bright glow dimmed the sparkle of the blanketing stars. But the multitude of them was still awesome, stretching from horizon to horizon, from infinity to beyond. Barefoot and clad in a tan sleeper-tee that outlined the growing roundness of her stomach, Jessy stood at the second-floor window of the spacious master bedroom and gazed at the vastness of the Montana night sky.

Below her line of vision was the sprawling collection of outbuildings, barns, storage sheds, commissary, and housing that comprised the headquarters of the Triple C. In size, it was that of a small town, something a stranger might marvel over, but Jessy was too accustomed to it to notice. It had not the mystery of the starry sky.

An intermittent flash of light made a track across the studded blackness, catching her eye. A second later she recognized the red and green glow of navigation lights and knew it was an aircraft banking southward, not a shooting star. Too few planes flew across this empty stretch of the state. At that altitude, logic insisted that the aircraft had to be Dyson's corporate jet—with Tara on board.

The view somehow marred, Jessy turned from the window just as Ty entered the room. He saw her by the window and paused briefly in mild surprise.

"I half expected you to be in bed."

"I was headed in that direction, then stopped to do a little star-gazing. It's a beautiful night out there."

"To be honest, I'm too tired to care." He crossed to the brass-edged bootjack and used it to pry out of his boots, one foot at a time. "It feels like it's been a very long day."

"Mmmm," Jessy made an agreeing sound, then she watched while Ty began the laborious, one-handed task of shedding his clothes, something he insisted on accomplishing without assistance. It was a case of male independence and pride.

"You know, I've always known we had an exceptional herd of registered Red Angus, but every time I think about one of the bulls we bred walking off with the Grand Championship at the Denver show—" Ty stopped and shook his head, as if the feeling it gave was beyond description. "I think I'll look up Ballard in the next day or two and make sure he wasn't feeding your dad a line."

"Why would he do that? The facts are much too easy to verify."

"And I'll do that, too." Ty scooped his jeans off the floor and tossed them over the arm of a plush chair upholstered in gold damask. "Everybody knows Ballard has shown a tendency to exaggerate in the past."

Jessy hid an amused smile. "You never have liked Dick Ballard very much, have you?"

Her smile deepened at the way Ty took such pains to avoid looking her way. "I wouldn't say that. He's a good hand, fast and sure with a rope, steady and reliable, willing to turn his hand to any work, and sits deep in a saddle." Ty ticked off the man's good points, but in his mind, he kept remembering all the times he had seen Ballard sitting at Jessy's table in the past. "But he's too quick to chase anything in a skirt."

"You still hold it against him for making a pass at Cat at the Christmas party a few years ago, don't you? Good heavens, the man had been drinking, Ty."

"I know. Just the same, Ballard has always been a little too full of himself."

"He was that way when he was young," Jessy agreed. "But all males are in their youth."

Ty stripped off the last sock and added that to the pile of discarded clothes, then arched her a skeptical look as he stood there in his shorts and undershirt. "Really? I don't ever recall being that way."

Her wide mouth curved into a smile. "That's because

you were too busy trying to figure out what it took to be a Calder."

Ty chuckled in remembrance. "You've got that right."

"At least you finally got the hang of it." Jessy crossed to the four-poster, canopied bed and began folding back the satin coverlet into a neat bundle at the foot of it.

Ty stared at the flashing gold material for a second, then flicked a glance around the rest of the room. The line of his mouth thinned with displeasure at its look of sleek elegance. "Next month when you and Cat go to buy all the baby things, you need to pick out some different furnishings for in here. It's time we got rid of all this slick satin and gilded furniture."

"That suits me," Jessy replied, and wondered if Ty had noticed she had already removed some of the daintier feminine pieces. But the rest of the master suite was much the way it had been when he and Tara had shared it.

After their separation, he had moved back into his former bedroom and the master suite had sat empty. But with the twins coming, it was clear they were going to require larger sleeping quarters, hence the move into the master suite. But Tara's hand was visible everywhere Jessy looked. She was never more aware of it than tonight.

With the satin coverlet stowed safely out of the way, Jessy turned back the top sheet and slipped between the covers. Meanwhile Ty turned off the light switch, leaving only the bedside table lamp to illuminate the room.

"One of the first things I want you to do," he said as he crawled into the wide bed, "is to get rid of this king-size monstrosity. I'm tired of having to search for you when I climb into bed."

"Is that right?" Jessy scooted closer and rolled onto her side to face him, always careful of his shoulder.

She reached up to caress a fingertip over the black brush of his mustache with its first few strands of gray showing. Jessy had never been one to avoid issues. It was her nature to confront them. All this talk about redoing the master suite was an oblique reference to Tara. The woman was on both their minds, and it was time they faced it.

"She still wants you, Ty," Jessy murmured and studied him with knowing eyes.

He caught hold of her caressing fingers and pressed them to his lips, then held them against his chest. "Anything that's out of reach, Tara has always regarded as a personal challenge. And I'm taken. Remember?"

It was never her memory that Jessy questioned, but she played along with him and pretended to give his question heavy thought. "It gets a little faulty at times. Maybe you need to refresh it."

"With pleasure." Ty cupped a hand to the back of her head and drew her lips to his mouth.

Drawn against his hard-muscled length, the heat of his body flooded over her, warming the bareness of her long legs. She wound herself closer, responding to the hungry demand of his kiss, understanding it. Like him, she had a desperate need to blot out the past. And this was the way to do it—together, in the darkness.

She pulled away long enough to switch off the lamp and peel off the long T-shirt, then she came back to him, all slim-hipped and naked, her stomach swollen with child as were her once-flat breasts.

In the skies far to the south, the corporate jet continued to wing its way into the night, on course for Fort

Worth. In the lushly appointed cabin, E.J. Dyson sat huddled with his chief financial officer, poring over a set of quarterly reports.

Free at last from the necessity of making conversation, Tara slipped off her high heels and settled back in the plushly cushioned seat, delicately curling her legs beneath her. Briefly her glance strayed to her father, noting his drawn and haggard look. She made a mental note to urge him to slow down, then turned her face toward the porthole window by her seat and gazed into the blackness beyond the panes.

Finally there was time to let her thoughts dwell on that fateful meeting with Ty. A meeting that had been full of such horrible irony.

Tara had never wanted the divorce. Never. At the back of her mind, she had always planned, one day, to win him back, convinced that it would require only a reasonable passage of time in order for her to achieve that goal.

A near sob caught in her throat. Dear God, she had waited too long. She balled a hand into a fist, long nails digging into her palm.

But the truth was—she never truly realized how very much she loved Ty until that shattering moment when she learned he had been shot. It all had become crystal-clear to her in that instant.

For a time, Tara had reveled in the role of the gay, Texas divorcee. But not a single man she met had ever measured up even close to Ty. A discovery she had made too late.

The bitterness of that disappointment didn't last, giving way almost immediately to an overwhelming rage at the knowledge that Jessy was going to have Ty's child. Even worse, she was going to have twins.

Ty would never walk away from the mother of his

children. That stupid code he lived by wouldn't allow him to do it.

Not for the first time, Tara cursed herself for not giving Ty a child. She had always known he wanted one, but she had been too worried about the damage it would do to her figure. Now she had lost him forever.

Every ounce of her body screamed that it wasn't fair.

Suddenly her life stretched before her as miserable and empty as the sky behind the plane's window.

How could Ty do this to her? Surely he knew how much she loved him. Then came the cold, killing realization that he knew and didn't care. As disgustingly trite as it sounded, he had dumped her for another woman. Tara couldn't let him get away with that, not without making him pay. Dearly.

Chapter Three

～

The bawl of cow and calf traveled across the rolling grass plains mixed in with shouts from ranchhands and the clang and rattle of iron chutes and headgate. High in the vast blue sky, the sun looked on, indifferent to the noisy activity below.

It was preg-check time on the Triple C, a time when every cow was palpated to verify whether she was pregnant or not. It was one of many thankless tasks on the ranch that was completely bereft of glamour. At the same time it was necessary to the operation's ultimate financial success. No rancher could afford to winter over a cow that remained barren more than two years, or a bull that couldn't service all his cows. Nor could a rancher afford to wait until the following spring to learn the outcome.

Astride a dun-colored buckskin, Jessy slapped a coiled rope against her leg and herded the last cow out of the holding pen into a long narrow chute that led to the head gate. A cowboy on the ground swung the pen gate shut, trapping the cow in the chute. Outside the pen, a calf bawled a lusty protest over the temporary separation from its mother. The cow answered with an angry bellow of her own.

Ignoring both, Jessy reined her horse away from the scene, her work done for the time being. In past years, she would have been taking her turn on the ground, down there in the thick of the action. But there was too much risk of getting kicked by a range-wild cow. The decision wasn't prompted by any fear of personal injury to herself, but rather by a concern for the safety of her unborn twins.

As she walked her horse to the main gate, Jessy was joined by the second rider who had worked the penned cattle with her. "That's the last of this bunch," Dick Ballard announced, more as a conversation opener than a passing-on of information.

The sandy-haired cowboy liked to talk to anyone about anything. Tall and strong he might be, but not silent. There was nothing braggy in his voice. It had a lazy, conversational pitch to it, and a distinctly cowboy cadence that was warm and friendly.

It was rather like his face, which was otherwise ordinary in its features. Over the years, his sand-colored hair had thinned until he was almost bald on top, but few people noticed that, and not because he wore a hat most of the time. It was because of his eyes, Ballard's most compelling feature. They were kind eyes, the dark blue color of new denim, always with a sparkle of dry humor lurking somewhere in their depths.

Jessy caught a glimpse of it when she started to reply to his idle remark, but Ballard held up a hand, checking her words.

"Don't say it. I already know. We've got three more bunches to go."

The line of her mouth softened into a near smile. "This is a cow calf operation," she reminded him.

"That's why I like my job."

As the pair approached the pen's gate, it was apparent to both that Jessy was in a better position to maneuver her horse around to open it. And it never occurred to Ballard to do the gentlemanly thing and alter the circumstances. Long before Jessy had married Ty Calder, she had worked as a cowhand. No deference had ever been shown to her, and none was expected. Drawing a man's wage meant doing a man's work, regardless of the gender.

Jessy unlatched the gate, swung it open and walked her horse through, then gave the gate a push for Ballard to catch. He caught it, gave it another push, and trotted his horse through.

"I worked one long winter at a feedlot," Ballard remarked. "The wages were high, plus a full range of benefits. But when spring thaw hit, the mud was so deep in that lot it was halfway up to a horse's belly. It was nothin' to wear out three horses doing one morning's work. It's the kind of job that's probably good for a guy with a wife and family, but I couldn't call it cowboyin'."

"Isn't it about time you got married, Ballard?" Jessy let the dun-colored gelding come to a stop by the pen's fence rails.

"Me? Get married?" He drew his head back in feigned surprise and flashed her a wry grin. "That's not likely to happen."

"Why not? I heard you've been seeing Debby Simpson." Jessy had spent too many years of her life razzing cowboys about their love lives, or lack thereof, to quit now just because she was the boss's wife.

"I've two-stepped around the dance floor with her a

couple of Saturday nights," Ballard acknowledged. "But marriage just isn't likely to be in the cards for me."

"Don't tell me you're going to turn into a confirmed bachelor like old Nate Moore was," Jessy retorted in an absently teasing fashion as her glance strayed to the activity at the headgate.

Old Doc Rivers, the paunch-heavy veterinarian, had completed his examination of the cow. Stepping back, he motioned to one of the hands to release the animal from the stanchion-like gate then turned to wash the fecal matter from the OB glove that sleeved his hand and arm.

"I don't know about the confirmed part." Ballard, too, glanced at the vet. "But it's true, I am a bachelor. Don't misunderstand, though. I don't have anything against marriage myself."

"Then what's the problem?"

"My horse does," he replied with a straight face, and only the smallest hint of a laughing gleam in his eyes.

Jessy just gave him a look and shook her head. Although Ballard wasn't among the descendants of families long associated with the Triple C, she had known him for years, certainly enough time to be comfortable with him, and with his attempts at humor.

Years ago, they had gone out together a few times. But Jessy had never regarded it as dating, although others had. In her mind, Ballard had simply stopped by her cabin a few times to shoot the breeze and have some coffee. On a couple of other occasions, he had given her a ride into Sally's on a Saturday night. There definitely had never been anything remotely romantic about their relationship.

As the last cow was prodded into the headgate, Ballard observed, "Looks like I'll have time for a smoke." He reached inside the breast pocket of his yoked-front shirt, pulled out a thin packet, and extracted an even thinner square of paper from it. After returning the folder to its pocket, he reached in the other and came out with a flat tin of loose tobacco.

Jessy's eyes rounded in amazement as he proceeded to tap a line of tobacco into the crease of the paper square. "When did you start rolling your own cigarettes?"

"About a month ago." None too deftly, Ballard slipped the tobacco can back in his pocket and began rolling the paper around the tobacco, losing a good bit of it.

"I knew you were tight with a dollar," Jessy declared. "But I never realized you were so cheap that you wouldn't buy ready-mades."

"It's isn't the money." He licked the edge of the paper in an attempt to seal the roll, then began digging in his pocket for a lighter. "I'm trying to quit."

"So you're rolling your own?" Jessy wasn't impressed with his logic.

"Well, you've gotta admit—a fella has to want a cigarette really bad before he'll go through all this rigmarole." With a snap of his thumb, the lighter flared to life. Ballard held the flame to the tip of the cigarette. The paper end blazed briefly.

Jessy grinned. "One of these times you're going to burn your nose."

"There's that problem, too," he agreed and puffed experimentally then pulled in a deep drag. "Ty looked me up the other day. Did he tell you?"

"He mentioned it."

"Did he pass on what I told him?"

"About what?"

"About all the money the Triple C is leaving on the table when you sell registered stock." Range-wise to the fire hazards of such dry conditions, he kept a hand cupped around the cigarette and deposited its ash in his shirt pocket.

Ty hadn't said anything at all about that. But knowing how little stock Ty put in anything Ballard said, Jessy wasn't surprised by the omission. Just the same, she kept her gaze fixed on the headgate and remained silent, fully aware that Ballard would fill the void.

He did. "Whenever the Triple C has registered cattle to sell, they get sold through livestock auctions that are restricted to registered animals. Granted they bring high dollar, for the most part. But they could bring more. You see," he went on, warming to his subject, "if there's one thing I've learned knocking around the country during the winter months, it's that people like to brag about the things they own, especially that breed of gentlemen ranchers with more money than brains—at least when it comes to ranching. And as much as one of these guys likes to brag about what a fine bull or pen of cows he just bought, he likes to brag even more about who he bought them from. It's like these collectors who go in debt over their heads just so they can buy a car once owned by Elvis."

"Our cattle are always sold as Triple C–bred stock at the auctions," Jessy reminded him.

"The buyers are told that," Ballard agreed. "But being told something doesn't make nearly the impression as buying that stock at a production sale held right here on the Triple C."

Stunned by his suggestion, Jessy turned in her saddle to stare at him. "You're not serious?"

"I'm dead serious." He repeatedly licked his fingers to pinch out the fire in his cigarette before tucking the crumbling butt into his jean pocket. "You'd have to do a lot of advertising and make a big event out of it, but if you did, these bigwigs would fly in from all parts of the country with their checkbooks open."

"You're crazy, Ballard." Now she understood why Ty hadn't mentioned his wild scheme to her.

"Crazy smart," he replied with unshaken confidence.

She made a snorting sound of disagreement and turned her head away, facing the front again.

For a long run of seconds, the silence was thick. "I'm right about this, Jessy," he stated quietly.

"I'm sure you think you are."

"You've got the same problem Ty has—and nearly every single man, woman, and child on the Triple C."

"I suppose I might as well ask what that problem is, because I know you're going to tell me anyway," she stated, letting her impatience with him show.

"First, answer me one question," Ballard challenged.

"What's that?"

"How many times have you been off the Triple C? And I don't mean going into Blue Moon."

"I've been to Miles City a couple of times," Jessy replied, feeling oddly defensive.

"If you add them all up, I'll bet you can count all the trips on one hand."

Unable to deny it, she went on the offensive. "What's your point."

"Simple. In ranching circles, every time the conversation gets around to big ranches in the country, Triple C's name always comes up. But nobody knows much about it. So any talk is always full of rumors and speculations."

"So?" Jessy prompted, not following him.

"It's created an aura of mystery about the ranch, made the Triple C into kind of a legend. And no one is sure what is myth and what is reality."

"Why would they even care?"

"Because it's big. Over the years, Old Man Calder hasn't invited more than a dozen people to come here. And none of them were people who mattered. But the few who have been here—when they drop the name 'Calder' in a conversation, they have everybody's attention."

Jessy didn't say anything. She was too busy trying to absorb all this new information. She had always known the Calder name carried considerable weight in this part of Montana. But in the rest of the country, too?

"Is this true, Ballard?" she asked, dead serious.

"It's true. But don't take my word for it. Ask Ty. Have him tell you what it's like when he attends regional meetings of the livestock associations. He's bound to have noticed the stares and whispers when he enters a room, the deference that's shown him. If he showed up in Texas, it would be the same."

"I see." At least, she was beginning to see.

"Your registered cattle are among the best in the land, Jessy. As for your strain of cutting horses, I've never forked my leg over better in all my years of competition. And I've ridden champions. Ranching is a precarious business nowadays. To be successful, a rancher's gotta make money any way he can. For years, Chase has done things the old way. I'm not saying that's totally wrong," Ballard added quickly. "But if there's gonna be a Triple C in the years to come, you and Ty might want to take a harder look at the things that are done now, in the New West."

"Like this production sale you suggested," she murmured.

"That, and all the marketing and publicity that go with it."

Jessy didn't have the first clue how to do any of that.

Give her a sick cow and she could doctor it; a broken fence and she could mend it; a rank horse and she could ride; a pair of babies and she could raise and care for them. But production sales, marketing, publicity, those were completely out of her realm of knowledge. Did Ty know?

"You need to take the Triple C name and make it one people shout, not whisper about," Ballard concluded.

"That's easier said than done," Jessy replied, speaking more to herself than to the sandy-haired cowboy.

"Maybe. But there'll be money in it. Big money."

Turning, she looked him squarely in the eyes. "Why are you telling us all this?"

His mouth widened in a long grin as he sat slouched in the saddle, both hands resting on the saddle horn. "You mean—what's in it for me?" Ballard looked off into the distance, his gaze making a sweep of the surrounding plains. "I was seventeen the first time I came here to day work. And I've been here on and off ever since. More on than off. This place gets into a man's system. The bigness of it, and the rawness. I don't care where you go, there's no other place like it. But"—he brought his glance back to Jessy—"to answer your question, I guess I'm telling you this because for years I've seen the potential here and watched it go untapped. Do you know how frustrating that can be? It can eat a man up. The other day, when Ty asked me about that bull, it was like uncorkin' a champagne bottle. It all just came bubblin' out. I suppose I'm repeatin' it all to you for the simple reason that, when a man knows he has a good idea, he wants everybody else to get on their horses and ride with him. So far, all I've seen out of you and Ty is skepticism. What I want is for him to say—you're right, Ballard; we're goin' for it. I'd get a lot of satisfaction out of that, Jessy."

She believed him. She didn't know a single cowboy who didn't welcome a pat on the back for a job well done. Dick Ballard was no exception.

"We do appreciate the information." She kept her response simple, without commitment.

He nodded. "That's what I wanted to hear."

"Hey, Ballard!" somebody yelled from the chute area. "Come give us a hand."

He lifted the reins to his horse, started to swing his mount to the side, then checked it. "By the way, you might have Ty check out a rumor I heard."

"What's that?"

"I was talkin' with Guy Phelps on the phone the other night. He wants me to ride his cutting horse in a big competition comin' up in August. According to him, Parker sold a half interest in that bull for close to a quarter million."

Without waiting for Jessy to reply, he kneed his horse forward, pushing it into a slow trot. She stared at his back, her thoughts reeling at the number.

For the rest of the day she couldn't get the conversation off her mind. It was late in the afternoon by the time work was wrapped up for the day and Jessy returned to the Triple C headquarters.

From force of habit, she stayed at the barns long enough to unload her horse from the trailer, see that it was rubbed down and fed, and her saddle and gear stowed in the stack room. Only when that was finished did she set out for the house.

But there was no hurry in her stride. Everywhere she looked, Jessy noticed things she had taken for granted her entire life—the neatness of the sprawling ranchyard, all the buildings in good repair, the huge, century-old barn with its massive timbers and rustic look and the summer-gold sea of grass that rolled away from it, its

expanse broken only by the towering, green cottonwoods that lined the banks of the river to the south.

Ballard's remarks had given Jessy a fresh perspective
on everything, but especially on The Homestead. It was
with these new eyes that she gazed at the imposing two-
story structure, built atop a flat knoll of land that elevated
it above the rest of the headquarters. A wide porch ran
the length of its south-facing front, with towering white
pillars rising at intervals from its edge. The grand scale of
it should have looked out of place, but anything smaller
wouldn't have suited the site. Jessy understood for the
first time that The Homestead was a statement of ownership, a claim of dominion over this vast sweep of land.

When she paused at the bottom of the porch steps,
one of the babies moved inside her. She laid a reassur-
ing hand on her stomach, suddenly awed by the
thought that The Homestead was only a small part of all
that would one day belong to their children.

As usual, the conversation at the evening dinner table
centered around the day's activity, the tasks accomplished, and those yet to be finished. But Ty was quick to
notice Jessy's lack of participation in the discussion that
was normally three-sided. He glanced across the table at
her down-turned head, her tawny hair still showing
some of the damp gleam from her earlier shower.

"You're unusually quiet tonight, Jessy," Ty remarked,
then frowned in concern when he observed the way she
was pushing the food around on her plate, a direct contrast to her customarily ravenous appetite. "Are you
feeling okay?"

"I feel fine." Jessy gave him one of her calm-eyed
looks that told him absolutely nothing. She speared a
piece of beef with her fork, then said in a voice that was

a tad too offhand, "By the way, I was talking with Dick Ballard today. He heard a rumor about that registered bull we sold Parker, one that he thinks you should check out. Supposedly Parker sold a half interest in the bull for close to a quarter-million dollars."

Chase reared back his head and scoffed his disbelief, "What fool would pay that kind of money for a half interest in a bull?"

Ty didn't turn a hair. "Apparently there are a number of fools out there. That isn't a rumor. It's the truth." He intercepted Jessy's questioning glance and explained, "I was making some calls today and heard that same rumor from more than one source. I did some checking and managed to verify it."

"Ballard is right then." Jessy held his glance, leaving Ty in little doubt that Ballard had spoken at length to her about his idea.

"It's possible." Ty nodded.

With eyes narrowed in suspicion, Chase looked at first one, then the other. "Right about what?" he challenged. "Why do I have this feeling that something has been discussed that I don't know about?"

"I planned on talking to you about it after dinner tonight," Ty admitted. "When I spoke to Ballard the other day, he made some suggestions about ways to increase the ranch's gross revenue. And its profits." Ty briefly explained Ballard's proposal to hold auctions of their registered livestock at the ranch, and watched his father's expression darken with distaste.

"I've been to a couple of those fancy shindigs they call sales. And you're saying you want to hold one here, on the Triple C?"

"Initially that was my reaction."

"And now?" The very quietness of Chase's voice gave it the weight of challenge.

"I don't like the idea any better than you do. But I think it's one we should investigate further, put some facts and figures together, and see if there would be a substantial return," Ty reasoned. "When we sold that bull to Parker, I was more than satisfied with the price he paid. But a quarter of a million dollars for an animal that was inferior to the ones we kept"—he shook his head—"that isn't something I can easily dismiss."

"That happens every time a man sells anything," Chase insisted, but none too convincingly for either of them. "He always wonders if he could have gotten more money."

"I know. But we're already operating on an extremely narrow profit margin, and that's in good years. You string together a few bad years in a row, and we're in trouble."

Chase grunted a nonanswer, sliced off another bite of roast beef, then asked, "Exactly what is your proposal?"

"To do some more checking, find out what it would entail in both manpower and facilities, put some numbers to it, and see if it's something we should seriously consider."

"What do you think about all this, Jessy?" Chase pinned her with a look.

She met the hard bore of his gaze without flinching. "I think it's a wise move."

He considered her answer quietly for moment then nodded with reluctance. "Probably. But I still don't like the idea of a bunch of strangers descending on us, even for a day." He sighed and shot a glance at Ty. "If your mother was alive, she'd know how to keep them all organized and happy."

So would Tara, Jessy realized.

Chapter Four

～

Snowflakes, fat and lazy, drifted toward the ground, making a white landscape out of the Triple C headquarters and the surrounding plains. The outside temperature was a good ten degrees below the freezing mark, but there was no wind to swirl the flakes or blow the fallen snow into drifts.

On this snowy Sunday morning in December, all was quiet on the ranch. Smoke curled from one of The Homestead's brick chimneys, the gray of it quickly lost against the backdrop of an equally gray sky, thickly speckled with snow.

The steady hum of an approaching vehicle penetrated the snowfall's hushed silence. Soon the dark Suburban became visible through the white screen of flakes as it traveled along the ranch's forty-mile-long driveway to the Triple C headquarters.

With tires crunching over the heavy wet snow, the vehicle rolled to a stop in front of The Homestead. The wipers ceased their rhythmic sweep of the windshield and the engine died. The passenger doors opened, both front and back.

Five-year-old Quint Echohawk hopped out of one side, his slender body made plump by the heavy parka and snow pants he wore, but on his head, he wore his favorite cowboy hat. With barely disguised impatience, he waited for the others to join him.

After stepping out of the front passenger side into the snow, Cathleen Calder Echohawk, affectionately known by everyone on the Triple C as Cat, handed her son the smaller of the two wrapped gifts she had in her arms.

"Will you carry this one, Quint?"

"Okay." Taking it, he tucked the present under his arm.

On the driver's side, Logan Echohawk held the rear door open and offered an assisting hand to Sally Brogan as she climbed out of the back seat. Like Cat, she also carried two presents, but hers were on the large and cumbersome side.

"Let me carry those for you?" Logan relieved Sally of them.

"Mom." Quint looked at Cat with earnest eyes, the same shade of gray as his father's. "Can I hold one of the babies? I'd be extra careful."

"I know you would, but you'll have to ask Aunt Jessy."

"Couldn't I ask Uncle Ty instead? I think he'd let me."

"Oh, you do, do you?" Cat struggled to hide a smile.

Logan paused beside her. "Have we got everything out of the truck?" he asked. "What about the camera?"

"It's in my pocket." She patted the bulge it made.

Together the four of them trooped up the steps and paused by the front door to stomp the snow from their boots. Cat didn't bother to caution her young son to be quiet in case the babies were sleeping. It wasn't in her son's nature to be loud and rambunctious.

"We're here," Cat announced unnecessarily when Logan closed the front door behind them.

"I'm in here," Ty's voice came from the living room that opened off the large entry hall.

Before all four managed to shed their heavy outer garments, hang them on the utilitarian coat rack, and deposit their wet snow boots in the large box placed by the front door specifically for that purpose, an angry wail shattered the stillness, originating from the living room as well.

Obeying, by now, her well-honed mother's instincts, Cat moved quickly toward the sound. Sally Brogan followed right behind her. There sat Ty on the large leather sofa, one whimpering, blanket-wrapped infant nestled in the crook of his arm. The second, squawling baby was strapped in an infant seat on the cushion beside him.

With a none-too-deft left hand, Ty attempted to slip a pacifier into the open mouth of the crying baby. But one suckle and the baby spit it out with an even louder wail.

"Where's Jessy?" Cat wasted little time in coming to the rescue of both her brother and the baby.

"In the kitchen warming their bottles." His voice had a frazzled edge to it, a tone most new fathers would recognize. Then it took on a dry quality. "Meet your new niece and nephew."

"Come to Aunty Cat." With the strap unfastened, Cat lifted the angry, red-faced infant from the carrier. Instead of being soothed and comforted by the contact, the baby unleashed an even louder wail of rage. "My, but we have a temper."

"You can say that again." Ty willingly surrendered

the other baby into Sally's reaching arms. "She has made it plain from the first day that when she wants something, she wants it now."

"It doesn't work that way, sweetheart," Cat murmured and cupped a hand over the back of the baby's head, pressing a kiss on the downy soft cap of hair, the palest shade of gold.

Quint tugged at her pant leg. In response, Cat sank onto the sofa's leather cushion to give him a closer look at the baby. "Meet your cousin Laura, Quint."

"Why's she crying?" he wanted to know.

"Because she's hungry."

Quint thought about that a minute, then stated, "She's awfully loud."

"She certainly is," Sally Brogan agreed. "But not this little guy." Gently she steered the baby's flailing fist closer to its mouth, allowing him to gnaw on it between hungry whimpers. "Just look at all the hair you've got." She stroked a finger over his thick shock of hair, as dark as his sister's was fair. "What did you name him again?"

"Chase Benteen Calder the Third," Ty replied. "And the demanding one is Laura Marie Calder."

"Chase and Laura," Sally repeated in approval as Jessy entered the living room, carrying the bottles of warmed formula.

Despite the warm light of motherhood in her eyes, Jessy had the telltale weary and harried look of a new mother. She offered only token resistance when the two women insisted on feeding the pair. She sat down next to Ty and watched, not quite able to completely relax.

Sally glanced up from the nursing baby in her arms and looked around. "Where's Chase?"

"He's in the kitchen, adding the finishing touches to dinner," Jessy answered, then added with a hint of guilt, "He keeps saying that he doesn't mind, that it reminds him of his bachelor days when he did a lot of his own cooking."

Cat sent Jessy a questioning glance. "Where's Audrey?" Audrey Simpson had taken over much of the housekeeping and cooking duties from Ruth Haskell years ago.

"Cat, I'm sorry," Ty said with quick regret. "In all the confusion of bringing the twins home, I forgot to let you know that Bob Simpson was rushed to the hospital in Miles City yesterday morning. He's suffered a stroke."

Cat breathed in sharply then murmured, "How bad is it?"

"Severe. He can't talk, and the doctors are still trying to determine the extent of his paralysis."

"Poor Audrey," Cat murmured in sympathy.

"Let's hope it isn't true that bad news comes in threes." Logan stood by the large stone fireplace, where a cheery fire blazed.

"Why?" Chase joined the group in the living room.

"The word reached Blue Moon yesterday that E.J. Dyson had passed away. He had a massive heart attack and died within seconds."

His announcement was met by a heavy silence. It was Cat who finally broke it. "I can't help thinking what a terrible blow this has to be to Tara. You know how extremely close she was to her father, Ty."

"I know." It had been a source of contention during his marriage to Tara. But this did not seem like the time to recall that. "I suppose it would be appropriate to send flowers."

"I don't know why not," Cat retorted, flashing her father a look that dared him to dispute it. "The funeral services will be held on Wednesday. Weather permitting, I plan to fly to Fort Worth on Tuesday and attend the services on behalf of the family."

Ty doubted that his father liked the idea any better than he did. But it was useless to argue with Cat when she had her mind set on something. Her decision didn't really surprise Ty. Right or wrong, Cat had always thought a lot of Tara. More than that, she wasn't asking permission from either of them.

"I imagine Tara would appreciate your being there," Ty remarked instead. Although, knowing Tara, he wasn't sure whether she would care or not. But it was important to Cat to make this gesture.

"I think she will." There was almost a defensive tilt to her head as if Cat knew what he was thinking.

For several long seconds, no one said anything. Then Sally spoke into the silence, "Not all the news has been bad. I have some good news."

Jessy was quick to pick up on her statement, eager to turn the conversation away from the Dysons. "What's that?"

"I accepted an offer for the restaurant on Friday."

No one was more stunned than Chase. "You did what? From whom?"

"The buyers are a retired couple, Harry and Agnes Weldon. They'll take possession on the first." After she had related the essential bits of information to the group, Sally's glance finally strayed to Chase, a hint of uncertainty for the first time clouding the glow of pleasure that had been in her eyes.

"What are you going to do after you sell it?" Jessy held her breath, half hoping.

"I don't know," Sally admitted. "But I'll have to think of something soon, won't I?"

Jessy didn't hesitate. Their need was too great. "What are the chances that we could talk you into coming to work for us? It would be an answer to our prayers with Audrey gone and no idea when she can come back—

assuming that Bob gets well enough so that she can return to work at all."

"Work here?" Sally's face lit up for a second. Then she hesitated, glancing at Chase. "Are you sure?" As usual, his expression provided little insight into the privacy of his thoughts.

The line of his mouth softened into something close to a smile. "I can't think of a better candidate for the position. And I've eaten enough of your cooking over the years to know you're a better cook than I am. As far as I'm concerned, the job is yours if you want it."

"Want it? There's nowhere else I'd rather be." Tears shone in her eyes, and she released a short laugh to cover them. "After the restaurant, can you imagine how easy it will seem here cooking for one family, keeping house and helping Jessy look after these two little treasures." Sally glanced down at the baby boy hungrily sucking on his bottle. "Whether Jessy wants to admit it or not, she's going to need help with you two for a while."

"Oh, I admit it," Jessy readily agreed. "It's taken only one day for me to realize that—especially when it comes to this little gal." She ran a caressing finger over the pale hair of the baby in Cat's arm.

"With that hair of hers, it's obvious she is going to take after you, Jessy." It seemed fitting to Sally that little Laura would favor her mother.

"And it's just as obvious," Chase inserted with a nod toward the baby Sally held, "that this little trey-spot is a Calder."

"The dark hair definitely marks him as a Calder," Sally acknowledged. "Just the same, I'm glad one of the twins is a girl. The outfits they have for little girls these days are absolutely precious."

"If little Laura takes after her mother, *precious* will

not be one of the adjectives used to describe her." Ty cast an affectionate smile at his wife. "Strong and beautiful, maybe. But definitely not precious."

His comment drew amused looks from everyone, including Jessy. But the intruding ring of the telephone prevented anyone from responding. Chase was closest to the phone.

"I'll get it," he said and picked up the living room extension. "Triple C." A fraction of a second later, he shot a glance at Ty, all expression vanishing. "Yes, he's here." After another brief pause, he said, "Just a minute." He extended the receiver in Ty's direction. "It's for you. It's Tara."

Without a word, Ty rose from the sofa and walked over to take the phone from his father. The instant he identified himself, Tara's emotion-choked voice rushed through the line to him.

"Ty. Thank God, you're there. Have you heard about Daddy?" Her voice quivered with the effort to hold back a sob.

"Just a few minutes ago. Cat is already making arrangements to fly down for the funeral."

"You're coming, too, aren't you?" There was a desperation to her question that bordered on hysteria. "Ty, you must. Please." Her voice broke on a sob. "You don't know what it's like here. They're hovering around like vultures. I don't have anybody I can trust. Not a single one, Ty. I thought it would be enough just to hear your voice, but it isn't. I need to see you. I need to know someone is here for me."

The emotion in her voice, the needy words were like a snare, trapping him into something he didn't want—just like in the old days. "Tara," he began in resistance.

"Ty, you have to come," Tara rushed in a trembling voice that ripped at him. "If I ever meant anything to you at all, you'll do this. I need you." She broke down and began to weep in delicate, but wrenching sobs. In between each one, he could hear her little murmurs of "Please, please, please." It aroused all of his protective instincts.

The Tara he knew had never pleaded for anything in her life. Schemed and manipulated, yes. Sweet-talked and cajoled, yes. But she didn't beg.

Still Ty hesitated a moment longer before he finally said, "I'll see what I can arrange, Tara." His statement was met by barely coherent sobs of gratitude. He said his goodbyes and hung up.

Even before he turned to the group, Jessy felt a cold chill of foreboding run down her spine. She mentally braced herself for what was to come.

"She wants me to come to the funeral." It was more or less a general announcement, but Jessy knew it was her reaction he was seeking.

"You're going, of course." She said it matter-of-factly, without betraying the sick feeling in her stomach.

His mouth slanted in a crooked smile that was so full of warmth it was like a caress. "I knew you would understand."

"Of course." Jessy suspected that she understood better than he did. Even though his marriage to Tara had ended years ago, he still felt a lingering sense of responsibility toward her—a husband's responsibility, if not to Tara, then to his dream of Tara. And it was his dream image of Tara that was the most dangerous thing.

Ty shifted his attention to Chase. "Ballard gave me a list of places with on-premise sale barns. A couple of them are in Texas. I planned on checking out a few of them after the holidays, but I might as well look them over while I'm down there for the funeral. Before we can decide whether we want to go the private auction

route, we'll need to know the type of facility it would require, plus the cost of construction."

Chase concurred.

On the day of the funeral, one of Texas's infamous
blue northers blew in, shrouding the sky with heavy
gray clouds. The outside temperature plummeted to near
the freezing mark.

But it was warm inside the hushed church. Almost
too warm. Ty sat next to Cat, his topcoat draped across
his lap and his dress black Stetson resting atop it. The
place was full to capacity with mourners, many notables
among them as befitted someone with the status and
wealth of E.J. Dyson.

Baskets of elaborate floral arrangements crowded the
sanctuary, their cloying fragrance permeating the already stifling air. When the minister at last asked the
gathering to bow their heads in prayer, drawing the service to a close, Ty breathed out in relief, even though it
brought nearer the moment he dreaded.

Having flown into Fort Worth only that morning, he
had yet to catch more than a glimpse of Tara before the
memorial service had begun. There was a part of him
that still wasn't sure why he was there, or what he would
say to her when they did meet. But he already felt the
awkwardness of it.

He stood in silence while the pallbearers brought the
ornate pewter-gray casket up the main aisle. Tara followed
it, leaning heavily on the arm of an older gentleman.
Dramatic in black, she wore an elegant Chanel suit, un-
adorned with any trimmings. On her head was a small and
simple black hat with a half-veil attached, creating a sheer
shadow over the upper half of her face. Her only concession to jewelry was the black opal ring on her finger.

As Tara came up the aisle, she kept her gaze fixed on a point somewhere ahead of her, glancing neither to the right nor the left. There was a woodenness to her movements that was completely unnatural, and a pallor to her grief-numbed face that couldn't be faked.

"Oh, Ty," Cat murmured when she saw Tara. "Look at her. Have you ever seen so much pain?" she asked in a voice husky with empathy.

"I know," he murmured in return.

"I remember the way I felt at Mother's funeral." Cat paused and brushed away a tear that slipped off her lashes. "It hurt so very much."

In reply, Ty curved an arm around her and rubbed a hand over her shoulder, remembering his own pain that day. In this, he had no difficulty empathizing with the loss Tara felt.

Together, he and Cat joined the long receiving line as the mourners filed by to extend their sympathies. To each, Tara responded with a faint nod that was almost robot-like, her gaze barely focusing on any of them.

Then it was their turn. Cat stepped up, Ty at her side. The first glimmer of recognition registered in Tara's dark eyes. "Cat." The word was almost a sob as Tara reached out with needing hands. "Where's—" A slight turn of her head and she saw him.

"Tara," Ty began, but Tara's knees had already buckled as she sank in a dead faint.

Ty caught Tara before she fell and scooped her into his arms amid a rush of concerned gasps and alarmed murmurs. As others pressed in to offer aid, one of the funeral directors intervened and quickly ushered Ty to an out-of-the-way anteroom, complete with a small cushioned sofa.

With Cat at his heels, Ty crossed to the sofa and laid Tara on it while Cat hurriedly pushed a pair of throw pillows behind her, propping Tara in a reclining position. After closing the door, the funeral director joined them, taking a vial of ammonia from his pocket and uncapping it. He waved it briefly under Tara's nose.

There was a protesting movement of her head as she surfaced groggily. "She'll be fine," the director announced. He was about to add more when he was interrupted by a sharp knock at the door.

After a disoriented second, Tara focused her eyes, black with grief, on Ty. "You came." Her cry was almost a whimper as she reached out both arms to him. "Oh, God, hold me, Ty. Hold me."

With that one simple gesture, she eliminated all need for words. Sitting on the edge of a cushion, Ty gathered her close. Tara wound both arms around his neck, buried her face in his suit jacket, and wept brokenly. "I needed you so much. So very, very much."

A corner of her hat snagged on his jacket, knocking the hat askew. Ty slipped off the small hat with its attached veil, passed it to Cat, then stroked a smoothing hand over Tara's silken black hair.

"It's all right," he murmured in comfort. "I'm here now."

A second man appeared at Ty's elbow, impeccably dressed in a dark suit and tie, a pair of steel-rimmed glasses precisely matching the sprinkling of gray in his neatly trimmed hair. "I'm Dr. Davis Parker," he identified himself, his fingers already reaching to seek the pulse in Tara's wrist. "I've been attending Tara since her father's death."

"No," Tara moaned in protest and pulled her arm away from his searching fingers, then pressed even more tightly against Ty. "Make them go away, Ty. Please."

"She's distraught." The doctor took a small, brown prescription bottle from his pocket and glanced at the hovering funeral director. "Could we have a glass of water?"

"I have one right here." He handed a foam cup to the doctor.

"Tara, take one of these." The doctor shook out a pill and offered it to her. "It will make you feel better."

She shook her head then lifted her tear-wet face to Ty. "Make him leave me alone. Make them all leave me alone," she insisted in a sobbing voice. "I don't want all these people around me anymore. Make them go."

"But, Mrs. Calder," the funeral director interposed in his most soothing voice, "we still have the graveside services. You know your father would want—"

"My father is dead!" Tara practically screamed the words. "He won't care whether I'm there or not. How could he? He's dead." She abruptly began to laugh and sob uncontrollably at the same time.

"She's hysterical," the doctor announced grimly. "I think it would be best if we took her home, where I can safely sedate her."

"Is there a side exit?" Ty directed the question at the funeral director.

"There is." The man nodded. "I'll arrange for a car to be brought around at once."

"Do that," Ty said, then attempted to make Tara understand. "We're going to take you home. Okay?"

But instead of being comforted, his statement seemed to throw her into a frenzy. "Don't leave me, Ty. Don't leave me. Don't leave me." The words came in panicked sobs that clutched at him as frantically as her hands.

"We aren't going anywhere, Tara," Cat assured her. "We'll stay with you as long as you want."

Ty stiffened in silent opposition to his sister's unqualified promise. As broken and pitiful as Tara was at this moment, he was still very much aware of the familiar shape and warmth of the woman pressed so tightly against him. The heady, signature scent of Tara's perfume swirled around him, evoking memories of the fire and passion they had once shared.

But for the time being, Ty said nothing to contradict Cat's claim. That discussion could wait until later, when Tara was home and sedated. He concentrated instead on comforting the weeping woman in his arms.

The funeral director returned within minutes, accompanied by two assistants. With Ty carrying Tara and the others forming a phalanx around her, they whisked her out a side entrance to a waiting stretch limousine.

The minute Ty attempted to deposit Tara on the rear passenger seat, her clutching hands tightened their grip in panic. "Don't leave me, Ty. Don't leave me," she whimpered in a sobbing, little-girl voice.

"I'm not," he assured her. "We're just getting in the car so we can go home."

With reluctance, Tara relinquished her hold on him long enough for Ty to climb into the limo, but she was back in his arms the instant he was seated. The doctor held the door open for Cat while she scrambled into the rear seat next to them.

"I'll meet you at the house," the doctor told them and closed the door, slapping the roof of the limo twice, signaling the chauffeur to move out.

In the unnatural silence of the limousine, they glided along the streets, skirting the silver-skinned towers of downtown Fort Worth. Even the brick-topped Camp Bowie Boulevard was reduced to a nonintrusive purr.

Turning off the boulevard, they wound their way into the exclusive River Crest area, long favored by the Forth Worth elite. The chauffeur traveled a road that snaked along the hills that rose above the Trinity River, and eventually pulled up to a pair of iron gates. After the smallest of pauses, the gates swung open, admitting them to the private grounds of the Dyson residence.

After following the driveway's looping curve, the limo rolled to a silent stop in front of the Dysons' twenty-thousand-square-feet, Italianate mansion. Before the engine was switched off, a handful of servants spilled from the house, clearly anticipating their arrival.

With Tara cradled in his arms like a baby, Ty climbed out of the vehicle and found himself face to face with the ever-efficient head of the household staff, a balding man with the improbable name of Brownsmith. Of indeterminate age, the man no doubt looked fifty when he was twenty, and would still look like fifty at the age of eighty. He disdained the term "butler", preferring the title of "houseman" to the Dysons.

His recognition of Ty was instant. "Mr. Calder. I regret that we should meet again under such tragic circumstances." Despite his constant attempt to adopt the clipped, precise speech of his English counterparts, his voice had never lost its distinctive Texas drawl. To eliminate any need for a response from Ty, Brownsmith added quickly, as he pivoted with a gesturing sweep of his hand, "If you'll bring Miss Tara this way."

With the houseman in the lead, Ty carried Tara into the house, across a marbled foyer, styled to resemble an interior courtyard, up a palatial grand staircase, and along a wide corridor to a suite of rooms. All the while Brownsmith directed a flurry of scurrying servants.

Two maids waited to guide Ty through the sitting room to the bedroom, decorated in a daring but deft mix of scarlet and gold, softened with delicate touches of pink.

Again Tara protested the separation when Ty attempted to lay her on the bed. "No. Don't go."

"I'm not going anywhere. But you can't get in bed with your shoes on," he chided, which apparently made sense to Tara because she sank onto the satin coverlet, lying quietly while he slipped off her black pumps. A maid was there to take them from him before he could drop them on the floor.

"Dr. Parker should be here directly. He had to stop at his clinic to pick up some medication for Miss Tara," the houseman explained, then lifted his head sharply, catching some sound that escaped Ty's hearing. He stepped to the window, parting the sheers to look out. "Here he is now. I'll bring him right up." He moved away from the window, issuing orders to the maids as he went. "Close the draperies, and see that Mr. Calder has a chair by the bed so that he can sit with Miss Tara." On his way into the sitting room, Brownsmith met Cat in the connecting doorway. He immediately intercepted her. "Forgive me but these are Miss Tara's private quarters."

Turning, Ty saw Cat. "That's my sister, Brownsmith." The houseman recovered quickly. "Miss Cathleen," he said, making use of his instant recall to address her by her full given name. "You have grown into a lovely young woman. Forgive me for failing to recognize you."

"Of course," Cat replied as he waved her into the room, then disappeared himself into the sitting room. "How could he remember me when I barely remember him?"

Ty nodded in agreement. "You couldn't have met more than once or twice." Then Tara was reaching for him, on the verge of panic again.

Even after the doctor administered the sedative, Tara clung to him, locking his hand in a death grip and refusing to let go. With the doctor's departure, the maids withdrew, leaving Ty and Cat alone in the darkened room with Tara. They spoke little and then in hushed voices.

Late in the afternoon, it started to rain. Ty sat by the bed and listened to the sound of the wind-whipped rain pelting the windowpanes. It was a lonely sound, made more so by the dim light and the thick silence.

It was along about early evening when Brownsmith

returned to the room and informed them that a light supper was waiting for them in the sitting room.

Cat shook her head when Ty suggested she eat first. "She seems to be sleeping soundly. I'll sit with her. It's time you had a break."

Ty didn't argue with that. Instead, he untangled his hand from Tara's fingers and walked quietly into the sitting room. A tall lamp cast a pool of light over the table set for two by the window. He cast one glance at the table then crossed to the telephone extension on a gilded table next to an easy chair, upholstered in a scarlet and pink plaid silk. He picked up the receiver and dialed the ranch. Jessy answered on the second ring. In the background, he could hear a baby crying.

"Sounds like I called at a bad time."

"It's just Laura, wanting her diaper changed. I take it you're back at the hotel. How was the funeral?"

Ty hesitated. "Actually I'm at Tara's."

"Oh." Pain cut through her, sharp and swift, caused as much by the small pause as by his reply. Jessy felt the old flare of anger and resentment, but kept it out of her voice. "How is she?"

"She collapsed at the church. The doctor gave her a sedative after we brought her back to the house. Cat's sitting with her now."

There wasn't any comment Jessy could make that wouldn't sound trite or false. So she said instead, "Then you haven't had time to make any calls to set up appointments to look over the sale facilities."

"No. Not yet. If I get back to the hotel early enough tonight, I'll call and see what I can arrange."

Which told Jessy that he didn't plan to leave Tara's anytime soon. Maybe it was simple jealousy she felt; Jessy wasn't sure, but she didn't trust Tara, not completely. And she never would.

PART TWO

That grass, it's a-feelin' the footsteps
Of those who walked it before.
One took the land
and one raised his hand.
A Calder just don't know
who to trust anymore.

Chapter Five

Morning brought an end to the rain, but the clouds and the wind stayed, making it another gloomy and blustery day. It had been close to midnight when the limo dropped Ty and Cat at their hotel. Ty hadn't slept well; he seldom did in a strange bed.

After an early breakfast with Cat, he returned to his room to make the necessary phone calls while she went off to do some shopping. It was a slow process, making the calls and waiting for his to be returned. Each time the phone rang, he expected to hear Tara on the other end. But it never was.

Ty found it difficult not to remember the sight of Tara lying alone in that bed, looking small and lost — and so very vulnerable. The Tara he knew had never been vulnerable. Not even for one second.

Abruptly he tore off the notepad sheet listing the places, the contact names, and the directions to them, swung away from the silent telephone, grabbed up his hat and sheepskin-lined jacket, and headed for the door, stuffing the list in his jacket pocket.

Before he reached it, someone rapped on the door. Assuming it was the maid coming to clean the room, Ty opened it. Tara stood in the hall, her hands buried in the pockets of a fur-lined raincoat. She wore little makeup, a touch of mascara, a blush of lipstick, but no more than that. It had the effect of heightening the pallor of her skin and enhancing that aura of vulnerability. But it was the lack of vitality that struck him hardest.

"I didn't dream you," Tara murmured. "You did come."

"Yes." Ty wanted to ask what she was doing there, what she wanted from him. But she seemed too fragile to respond to such a direct question without shattering.

"Brownsmith told me that you sat by my bed until nearly midnight. Thank you."

"You're welcome."

Her glance drifted down to the hat and coat he carried. The sight of them seemed to momentarily fluster her. "Are you going somewhere?" The question held a note of panic, reinforcing the impression of fragility.

"As a matter of fact, I was," Ty admitted. "Why?"

"Because . . ." Tara hesitated then appeared to gather herself. "I didn't go to the cemetery yesterday. I wanted to visit Daddy's grave today, but I was hoping you would take me." She lifted her head, her dark eyes vocal in their appeal. "Please. I don't want to be alone."

It was such a small request, one that wouldn't take more than an hour or two of his time. To refuse seemed somehow vindictive and callous.

His lack of an immediate response prompted Tara to add, with a downcast look, "You probably have an appointment." Head down, she started to turn away.

"It won't hurt anything if I'm a little late." Ty stepped into the hall, closing the door behind him.

"Thank you." Her soft voice was husky with gratitude.

A brisk wind stirred through the damp leaves, raking the willing ones into small piles at the base of the gravestones. It was a cold and damp day, made all the more bleak by the low, gray clouds.

Ty kept a steadying hand around Tara as they made their way over the uneven ground, past the orderly rows of ancient markers. With one hand, she clutched the up-turned fur collar tight around her neck, completing the frame of her cameo-perfect features. In the other hand, she carried a single Texas-yellow rose.

Their destination was just ahead, Dyson's final resting place marked by a rectangular mound of freshly turned earth, a sharp contrast to the winter-brown grasses. When they reached the site, Ty removed his hat out of respect, conscious of the wind ruffling his hair, as it was doing to Tara's.

They stood silently beside the new grave for a long run of seconds. For all of Dyson's Texas-flash while living, his granite headstone was an unusually modest one, containing no more than his name, date of birth, and a blank space for the date of his death to be engraved.

Stepping forward, Tara bent down and placed the yellow rose atop the dirt. The wind immediately blew at it, but it caught against a large clod and stayed in place.

Rising, Tara brushed back a strand of hair the wind had whipped across her face. "Daddy left written instructions that we were to move heaven and earth, if necessary, to see that he was buried here. He said he wanted to lie among real Texans, not a bunch of newcomers. Silly, isn't it?" she mused.

"He was proud of his Texas roots."

"I know." With a turn of her head, she looked up at Ty. Just for a minute there was that knowing gleam of the old Tara in her eyes. "Whereas the Calders rarely mention theirs at all."

It was the kind of subtly flirtatious look that invited a smile. Ty responded with a slow one. "I guess we've been in Montana too long."

Tara watched the smiling movement of his mouth, finding something sexy in the laziness of it that still had the power to snatch at her breath. There was a time when she would have tilted her head at just the right angle, inviting more than his smile. But she was much too wise to try that ploy this time. Instead Tara hooked an arm around his and let her gaze wander over the old cemetery.

"Do you remember the last time you brought me here, Ty? You wanted to show me where your great-grandfather was buried. We were both still in college." At a leisurely pace, she began to stroll in the direction of the car, drawing Ty with her, arm in arm.

"That was a long time ago."

"You proposed to me that day," Tara reminded him, giving him one of her patented sideways glances that was both coy and mischievous.

"For either the third or fourth time. I did a lot of proposing back then, as I recall."

There was an opening there, but Tara let it pass. "We were so young back then. Or at least I was. You were too serious to ever really be young."

"I suppose."

She deliberately let the silence lengthen a little. "It's sad, isn't it?"

"What?" Ty's glance touched her with mild interest.

"That you have to lose someone close to you, some-one you loved very much, before you realize that money, status, the opinions of others—none of that matters. Only the people in your life are important. All my life I've been so ambitious—" Tara stopped and darted him a wry look. "But you know that better than anybody. Now—now, I realize that I spent all that time chasing the wrong things. And that is very, very sad." She knew there was nothing Ty could say to that, so she didn't give him the chance to respond. "Sorry. As always, I'm so wrapped up in myself and my troubles that I haven't even asked how you are."

"I'm fine. Busy as usual." It was exactly the kind of noncommittal response Tara expected from him.

"And Jessy?" It was so hard to keep her lip from curling in dislike.

"She and the twins are fine."

"She's had the babies, then." The news was like a lead weight in her stomach.

"Last week," Ty replied, with a hint of pride in his voice. "A boy *and* a girl."

"A boy and a girl." Tara didn't have to feign her surprise. Therefore, she let it work for her. "Then, you have been doubly blessed."

"We think so."

The pronoun grated at her with its reference to Jessy. "What are their names?" She tried to sound interested.

"Laura Marie and Chase Benteen Calder III."

So the name continues, Tara thought, tasting bitterness. She had never gotten along with her former father-in-law despite numerous attempts to gain his favor. In his inimitable way, Chase Calder had made it clear he tolerated her only because his son had chosen her to be his wife.

"That's quite a mouthful for a little baby," was the comment she made.

"Dad has taken to calling him Trey, and the nickname's caught on."

Tara leaned into his shoulder as they walked. "You sound very happy, Ty. I'm glad for you."

When he glanced down, Tara observed the doubt flicker in his eyes, questioning the sincerity of her words. She looked away, irritated that, in some ways, he knew her so well.

A gust of wind buffeted both of them. Taking advantage of its cold blast, she shuddered. "It's positively freezing. I don't suppose you would have time to buy a girl a cup of coffee, would you?"

"I think it could be arranged."

The café Ty chose was in the Stockyards District, not far from the cemetery. Personally Tara would have picked a trendier spot than this over-the-top cowboy-themed café that catered mainly to the tourists. But the abundance of empty tables suited her purposes, creating a privacy and intimacy that she might not have attained in other places where she would have been more readily recognized and their conversation possibly interrupted.

With her usual skill, Tara made sure that *she* became the subject under discussion. She was well aware that Ty pitied her. If pity was the only emotion she aroused in him, then she was determined to use it.

"I was there when Daddy died. Did you know?"

"No." His expression softened with deepening sympathy.

"He was gone so quick, there wasn't anything anyone could do. The heart attack was massive and sudden. He collapsed and I screamed. In those few seconds it took to rush to him, it was over and he was dead. I keep tell-

ing myself that I'm glad he didn't suffer long, but—"
Tara broke off the rest of the sentence, punctuating it
with a vague shrug and a teary-eyed smile.

"At least you were with him," Ty offered.

"Yes." She nodded. "These last few months, Daddy
looked so tired. I tried to get him to slow down, but he
wouldn't listen. It's clear now that he knew he wasn't
well. Possibly he even knew that he didn't have much
longer. Maybe that's why he pushed himself so hard
lately. He wanted to get his affairs in order. Isn't that a
horrible phrase—'get his affairs in order'? I despise it,"
Tara declared.

"I'm sure he did it for you."

"I know. And the lawyers tell me that he succeeded
admirably. As far as the business side goes, I have mini-
mum responsibilities, and absolutely no financial wor-
ries, personally. My time and money are my own now.
Unfortunately I'm not sure what to do with either of
them. Life looks so empty right now."

"That's to be expected," Ty assured her. "But later
on, you'll find plenty of things to do, places to go, parties to give."

Tara wondered if he truly believed she was that frivolous. Had he forgotten that she had never entertained
anyone without a purpose? Not even now.

"Logic tells me you're right. But at the moment, the
future looks horribly bleak—and much too depressing
to talk about anymore. Tell me about the ranch. What's
going on there? Has your father acquired title to that
Wolf Meadow land yet?"

"We're working on it."

"Dealing with the government is never easy. Even
though he was very good at it, Daddy hated it. He said it
was always such a hassle. Just about the time you had a
deal struck, there would be an election and a big shuf-

fling of people. Suddenly, there you were with a brand new person in charge and you had to start almost from the beginning."

"We've run into our share of that," Ty admitted, but didn't elaborate. Tara recalled a time when he would have discussed his problems in detail with her. But he was being as close-mouthed as his father about them now.

"The environmental lobby is very strong right now, too. That has to be an obstacle as well."

"They have definitely been among the opposition."

After a moment's pause, Tara chose not to pursue the subject. "It's good to talk about things like this—for me, anyway. It gets my mind off things," she said, determined not to give him the impression she was probing for information. "At the hotel, you mentioned you had someplace you needed to be. As I recall, you only flew to Texas when you were in the market for a bull or some brood mares. So, which is it this time?"

Ty smiled, revealing that he was comfortable with this subject. "Actually, it's neither."

"Really?" Tara lifted the coffee mug to her lips, peering curiously over the rim at him.

"We're considering holding private auctions for our registered livestock. Since I was here in Texas, I thought I would scout out the kinds of facilities other ranchers use for theirs."

Eyes widening, Tara lowered the mug, her interest piqued. "Some of those private sales are incredibly lavish affairs, private jets flying in from all over the country. They are almost as much social events as they are buying sprees." She hesitated, deliberately. "I don't know how to say this, Ty, but—this doesn't sound like the kind of thing that would meet with your father's approval."

His mouth slanted in a crooked smile. "He isn't all

that keen on the idea. But if the preliminary figures we've run are only half right, the profit margin could still be staggering, more than enough to warrant being temporarily inconvenienced."

"When is your first sale scheduled? I would love to come."

"That's at least a year or two away. We still need to determine the type of facility that's required, design and build it, plus have plenty of advance time to promote the sale."

"It sounds exciting." Tara itched to get in the middle of it all. Maybe she could. She took a sip of her coffee and thought about that.

"We really aren't far enough along to have a timetable. Personally, I think we'll be lucky if we have plans drawn for the building by fall. More than likely, it will be next winter. It's more important to build it right, than to build it in a hurry."

Tara injected all the right questions in all the right places to keep Ty talking about the project, gleaning every kernel of information and filing it away for future use. Where Ty was concerned, no information was too trivial.

It wouldn't be easy to insinuate herself into his life again. But Tara never doubted for a moment that she would ultimately succeed. If not one way, then another. Possibly, both. That prospect made her smile.

A summer wind blew through the pickup's opened windows, its air laden with the scent of ripening grasses. Jessy turned her face to it, breathing in the smells. The land rolled away from the dirt road, big, wide, and empty. There was nothing to be seen but earth and sky for miles upon miles upon miles.

Behind the wheel, Ty slid his glance in her direction. "Penny for your thoughts?"

"What makes you think they aren't worth any more than that?" Jessy challenged lightly.

"Because, if I had to guess, I'd say that you were thinking about the twins."

Jessy released a heavy sigh of admission. "Sally will have her hands full, trying to take care of those two."

"She has Dad to help her. They'll manage."

"I know, but Laura has become such an old fuss-budget lately. You know how she pitches a fit if she gets the least little bit of dirt on her. Heaven forbid if you accidentally miss her mouth with the spoon and smear baby food on her face. And ever since Trey learned to crawl, he shoots out of sight the instant you turn your back."

"He just likes to explore," Ty said in his son's defense, then conceded, "He is quick as lightning though."

"Imagine what it will be like when he starts walking." As fast as their son disappeared now, that thought was enough to make Jessy shudder.

"What about Laura?" Ty countered. "Can you imagine Miss Priss toddling around the ranchyard? I'm still surprised she didn't scream her head off when Dad took her for a horseback ride."

"She actually liked it, didn't she?" Jessy took comfort from that. "She smiled and laughed—and even patted the horse. Up to then, I was beginning to wonder if she was really my daughter."

"I wouldn't worry about that."

"I won't, but the thought has crossed my mind a time or two." Jessy relaxed against the seatback, smiling at the memories. But it wasn't long before her uneasiness returned. "I still think it would be a good idea if we get home early. Just in case."

"Not a chance." Ty slowed the pickup as they approached an intersecting ranch road. "We aren't going home until the cows do."

"But—"

"No buts. It's our anniversary, and we are going to do it up right. Okay?"

She looked at him for a long second, all of her instincts protesting the plan. Then everything smoothed out inside. "Okay," Jessy agreed.

"What? No more arguments?" Ty eyed her skeptically.

"No more arguments," she promised. "I just remembered something my mother told me when the twins were about a month old."

"And what was that?"

"She said there were times to be a mother and times to be a wife. And I just realized this is one of those times to be a wife."

"Wise woman." Ty swung the pickup, making a right turn onto the intersecting road.

Jessy sat up, noting the change of direction. "What's this? Are you taking a scenic route to town?"

"Something like that." A smile tugged at a corner of his mouth, arousing her suspicions.

"Exactly where are we going, Ty Calder?"

"It's a surprise."

And one he was very pleased about, she could tell.

Within minutes, Jessy guessed their destination. "You're taking me to the old Stanton cabin." She gazed at the log structure's low roofline, visible among the cottonwood trees that grew along the nearby riverbank. Years ago, she had lived in it when Ty was first married to Tara.

"Now if I was doing this right, you would be riding behind my saddle, just like you were the first time when you invited me in for coffee."

"You remember." She was moved by that.

"Did you think I wouldn't?" Ty slowed the pickup as they approached the narrow track to the cabin. "This is where we fell in love."

"It's where *you* fell in love, maybe," Jessy corrected. "For me, it was the calving sheds. I was about ten years old and you were sixteen."

"That long ago." Ty frowned in surprise. "You never told me that."

"You never asked," she replied with a fetching smugness.

The cabin's driveway was little more than twin tire tracks with grass growing between them. Just as Jessy noticed the vehicle already parked beside the cabin, Cat came out the door.

Jessy cast an accusing glance at Ty. "What is this? A family conspiracy?"

"Something like that," he admitted and parked the pickup next to Cat's truck.

When they climbed out of the pickup, Cat greeted them with a hurried, "Sorry, I thought I would be gone before you got here. I left you a note inside," she said, backing toward her own vehicle. "Your dinner is in the oven. It should be done in about"—she checked her watch—"twenty-five minutes. If Logan should call looking for me, tell him I'm going to run by the Shamrock and look in on Uncle Culley before I head home."

"He's not there," Ty stated.

That stopped Cat. "Who isn't?"

"O'Rourke." With a nod of his head, he directed her attention to a spot beyond the trees. On the other side of the riverbank, partially obscured by the trunks of the cottonwood trees, a horse and rider watched them.

"I should have known Uncle Culley would follow me." Cat's voice carried a trace of sadness. "Funny, isn't it? I can't convince him to live with us. But he's always close by, somewhere in the shadows."

"He's in no shape to be skulking around like a coyote." It was a habit of O'Rourke's that Ty had never particularly liked, conscious that the man was obsessively devoted to his sister.

"Tell him that." Cat's smile was full of skepticism over the likelihood her uncle would listen.

"How is he?" Jessy asked with sincere concern.

Cat sighed. "He hardly sleeps at all and doesn't eat right. I guess you could say he's back to normal." She lifted her shoulders in a what-can-you-do shrug and moved again toward her truck. "Enjoy yourselves. And remember." Cat pointed to Ty. "You owe me one."

He waved in acknowledgment then spread his hand over the small of Jessy's back. "Shall we?" He nodded toward the cabin.

Her gaze wandered over the old building, memories flooding back as they moved toward it. "Hasn't this been sitting empty for a while?"

"Nearly two years," Ty replied. "Long enough that it took two full days to get it cleaned up and everything in running order again." He opened the door, then stepped back to let her enter first.

The cabin was small, just three rooms, with white plastered walls and chintz curtains at the windows. The simple fireplace, the old sofa, everything looked almost the same as when she'd lived in it except for the old kitchen table.

A gleaming white tablecloth, the best china and crystal from The Homestead, a pair of silver candlesticks, and a colorful bouquet of flowers had transformed it into an elegant table set for two. Jessy stared at it, tears welling in her eyes.

"Happy Anniversary," Ty murmured, then steered

her to the table and stepped forward to light the candles. "A few years back, right here in this house, you told me something that I have never forgotten. You said, even though you could ride like a man and work like a man, that didn't mean you didn't like flowers and candy."

It was then that Jessy noticed the small, beribboned box of expensive chocolates, placed next to one of the settings. Completely lost for words and too choked with emotion to utter them anyway, Jessy could only look at him.

"Cat thought there should be a bottle of Dom Perignon on ice, but I explained that coffee was our drink," Ty said. "She didn't think it was a very romantic choice."

Eyes swimming with tears, Jessy stood there for a long second, more touched by this simple gift than words could express. But she had never been good with words. By nature, she was a woman of action.

Her feet didn't feel as if they touched the ground as she crossed the space and into his arms. His mouth came down, claiming hers in a kiss, filled with that slow, deep-burning warmth that had always been between them. It was the kind that steadied rather than shook, the kind that strengthened rather than weakened, that brought boldness rather than hesitancy. That was the magic of it, and the power.

He lifted his mouth a fraction of an inch, to murmur against her lips, "Dinner won't be ready for another twenty minutes."

His breath washed over her in hot, moist waves, and the brush of his mustache was whisper-soft against her skin. In answer, Jessy slid her hands around his neck, clasping them there as she echoed the phrase she had once used on a long-ago night, "Carry me."

Ty smiled in remembrance. Bending, he scooped

her into his arms and carried her that short distance into the bedroom. The slanting rays of the afternoon sun spilled through the window, falling across the bed's down-turned covers and the saucy silk-and-lace night-gown lying atop it. Over in the corner stood an overnight bag.

"Something tells me we're spending the night here," Jessy remarked when she saw it.

"You are very quick," Ty mocked as he let her feet slip to the floor.

"I try to be." Jessy turned away to face the bed. "You have planned everything extremely well except for this." She picked up the silky nightgown and tossed it on the floor. "That's where it belongs."

As Jessy reached back to unzip her dress, Ty was there, moving her hands out of the way. "Let me."

With a single downward glide of his hand, the material parted. His hands came up to slip the garment off her shoulders while he nibbled his way along the leanly muscled squareness of them, arousing evocative little shivers to dance over her skin.

They undressed with the familiarity of husbands and wives, intent on reexploring old delights. The urgency was always there, just below the surface, but it didn't push them. They made love with slow pleasure, letting passion build at its own unhurried pace to the inevitable climax.

Later they dined and drank their coffee by the flickering blaze of the fire Ty built in the fireplace after the sun sank below the horizon and the air had cooled. It was a lazy evening, reminiscing about old times and planning new ones, just the two of them alone, the way it had begun for them.

It was an easy intimacy they shared, both by the fire and in the subsequent darkness of the bedroom.

Neither missed the giddiness of new love; they had found something better, something with strength and staying power. As usual, they slept tangled together, each warmed by the body heat of the other.

A bird trilled its morning call outside the cabin window, but its song was drowned out by the strident ring of the telephone. Groggily Ty rolled over and squinted a look at the light beyond the bedroom window, then fumbled around until his groping fingers located the telephone on the bedside table. He picked up the receiver, cutting short the second loud ring. Beside him, Jessy had snapped awake with a mother's instant alertness at the first sharp ring. It took her a second to remember where she was. By then Ty had answered the phone.

"Yeah. What's the problem?" He tried, but he couldn't keep all of the sleep out of his voice.

"That depends on your definition of a problem."

At the sound of his father's voice coming over the line, Ty came fully awake. Jessy caught the muffled sound of it and levered up on an elbow, dragging the covers up over her breasts.

"The twins? Are they all right?"

Without an answer, Ty could only shake his head. "Is something wrong, Dad?"

"In a manner of speaking, yes. But tell Jessy not to worry. The twins are fine. Sally is just about to give Laura her morning bath, and Trey is here in the den with me. I'm calling because Tara phoned last night."

"Tara." Ty frowned and pushed into a sitting position. "What did she want?"

"She wanted to know if we had finalized our building

plans for the new sale barn yet. How did she know about that?"

"I think I mentioned it in passing while I was in Fort Worth for the funeral." But it was little more than a vague memory.

"I figured it was probably something like that. Anyway, she wants us to put any plans we've made on hold until she talks to you. I didn't bother to pass her message on last night. There didn't seem to be any need to spoil your evening. But—here's the bad news—she's flying in this morning."

"She's what?" His fingers tightened their grip on the receiver, shock and disbelief racing through him.

"You heard me," Chase replied flatly. "And she's bringing an architect with her. Her plane should land at our strip between ten and eleven. I thought I'd better let you know that."

There was a click, and the line went dead. Ty replaced the receiver on its cradle and swept back the covers, swinging his legs out of bed.

"That was Dad," he said needlessly, his sideways glance bouncing off Jessy.

"I gathered," was her dry response. "What was that about Tara?"

"She's flying in this morning, with an architect. They should be landing around ten or eleven."

Happy Anniversary, Jessy thought, and followed Ty's lead, climbing out of bed to get dressed.

Chapter Six

～

On its final approach, the private jet angled for the runway, a long gray line of concrete cutting a path through the sea of summer-yellow grass. In the plane's cabin, Tara faced the double-paned window, idling looking out while her mind hummed, determined to make sure there was no argument she had overlooked.

"I thought we were going to land at the ranch."

Roused from her thoughts, Tara glanced across the aisle at the young, athletically built architect seated across from her. "That is the ranch below us," she informed him, smiling at the surprise that flickered over his clean-cut, college-boy features.

"All of those buildings?" Noah Richardson, a preservationist at heart and the current wunderkind of the architectural world, peered out his side window, eager for a closer look.

"I told you the Triple C was different from other

ranches you've seen. There are few like it in the world, I suspect."

"It looks like a small town," he marveled.

"And just as self-sufficient as one. At least, where the necessities are concerned," Tara qualified.

As the plane continued its descent, the outbuildings disappeared from view. Only The Homestead remained in sight. Tara could almost pinpoint the exact moment when Noah Richardson switched his attention to the high plains mansion.

Losing interest in her traveling companion, Tara let her gaze wander to her own window, catching a brief glimpse of two men waiting by the hangar as the plane sped past, beginning its rapid deceleration. Brief, though it may have been, it was enough for Tara to recognize both Ty and his father. Unworried, she settled back in her seat.

By the hangar, Chase watched the sleek plane taxiing toward them, the line of his mouth thinning in annoyance. "An architect," he grunted, not for the first time, then shot a glance at his son. "I know Tara and her extravagant ideas, and I'm telling you right now we are not building some grandiose monstrosity just to sell a few cattle in it."

"You won't get any argument from me."

Chase nodded in approval.

Engines whining, the streamlined aircraft swung abreast of them and braked to a stop. One of the ranch hands trotted out from the hangar and positioned the chocks behind the plane's tires. In a succession of minutes, the engine's high-pitched whine faded into silence, the cabin door was cracked, and a copilot in a white shirt and tie latched the door open. With the push of a button, he lowered the flight of steps, skipped down them, and turned to offer assistance to his passengers.

Tara stepped into the doorway and paused on the top step, her darkly vivacious looks accented by the matching powder blue top and slacks she wore. A chiffon scarf of the same shade was loosely knotted at her throat. Her searching gaze finally landed on Ty. A warm smile broke across her face as she lifted a hand in greeting, then descended the steps with a lithe grace.

Without a backward glance, she moved across the tarmac toward them. But Chase's attention focused on the young man at the head of the steps, clad in blue jeans, a tan shirt with thin, white stripes, and a navy tie.

"If that's the architect she brought," he muttered under his breath to Ty, "he looks like he's straight out of college."

But Ty had no opportunity to reply as Tara reached them, her dark eyes sparkling and alive to him. Gone were all traces of grief's dullness and pallor. She was once again a ripely beautiful woman, certain of herself and her allure.

"Ty." She spoke his name in simple greeting, then turned to his father. "I'm so glad you're here, Chase. Forgive me for forcing myself on you. I know I should apologize for sticking my nose into something that is absolutely none of my business. But I'm so excited about my idea that I just had to tell you and Ty about it in person. I know you both are going to love it."

"We'll see," Chase replied, deliberately cool.

Undeterred, she half turned to include the young man just joining them. "Ty, Chase, I want you to meet Noah Richardson. Don't be fooled by his looks," she warned. "His stunning renovations of abandoned factories and a variety of historic buildings have made him the talk of the entire Southwest. There is absolutely no one better qualified than Noah for the job I have in mind."

Ty waited until Tara had finished the introductions to ask, "Just what is this job you have in mind?"

She paused for effect. "The barn."

"I assumed this was probably about the new sale barn we're planning to build. We already have an architect working on drawings for one," Ty replied.

"Not a new barn, Ty," she corrected, a knowing gleam in her eyes. "I'm talking about that old, timbered monstrosity you already have."

Caught completely off guard by her answer, Ty exchanged a quick glance with his father then asked for a clarification, "You're talking about remodeling the old barn into a sale facility?"

"It makes sense, doesn't it?" she reasoned, confident of his agreement. "After all, why build a new facility that can be used for little else when you can remodel an existing structure to serve a dual purpose?"

"Assuming it can be done," Chase inserted.

"Of course. That's why I brought Noah. So he can look it over and see if it's possible."

Noah finally spoke for himself. "If it's the same building I saw from the air, it certainly looked big enough. But size isn't the only determining factor. I really need to spend some time in it."

"Well? What do you think?" Tara looked at Ty with bright-eyed expectancy.

"I think it's worth checking out." There was way too much logic in the suggestion for Ty to argue with it. He didn't ask, but he took his father's silence on the matter as an agreement.

Without further discussion, the four of them climbed into the four-door Suburban parked near the hangar. Ty slid behind the wheel while Tara took the front passenger seat. Leaving the private airstrip, Ty drove along the narrow road that led southwest to the ranch head-quarters.

He parked close to the barn and walked over to open its massive double doors. After an initial groan of protest, they slid apart to reveal the shadowed gloom of the barn's cavernous interior and its wide alleyway.

The young architect walked directly into it, his head on a swivel as he began a visual inspection. He paused near one of the stout, upright supports and ran a hand over its uneven surface.

"These timbers are hand-hewn." He turned back toward Chase. "How old is this barn?"

"Well over a hundred years," he replied.

The architect leaned a shoulder against it, giving the rustic column a testing shove, then stepped back, murmuring, "Solid as a rock."

"Can't you just picture it, Ty?" Tara edged closer to him, gesturing at the interior. "All this old wood varnished and gleaming, washed with indirect light. It's the perfect setting, utterly rustic and Western, steeped in history and tradition. The sheer ambiance of it will be a draw in itself."

A fuzzy image flickered in his mind's eye, indistinct, yet enough to stir him. "It would be different than any sale barn I saw," he conceded.

"That's an understatement," Tara said with a laugh. "Most of them are little more than huge metal sheds. They have no charm, no character at all. *This* will be a sensation that will have everybody buzzing. Anyone who fails to attend your first auction will definitely not miss the next one." Tara slipped an arm around him as naturally as if they were still married. "If there's one thing I learned from Daddy, it's that success in business requires more than an excellent product. Equally important is the image of the product that you project to the public. In other words, it's how you wrap it."

"It's all about marketing," Ty agreed.

"Am I forgiven for barging in, then?" Tara had a way of looking up at him from below her lashes that aroused a man's senses.

Ty became aware of the warmth of her body pressed along his length and rounded imprint of her breast against his arm. The pull of the past was strong, reminding him of a time when loving her had been a habit. And one that seemed much too easy to resume.

Gently but firmly, he untangled himself from her encircling arm, putting a little distance between them. "There's nothing to forgive. It remains to be seen whether this barn can be converted into an auction facility."

After spending the better part of an hour poking in corners, clambering up the crude ladder to the hayloft and surveying the outer perimeter, the young architect's verdict was favorable.

"So far," he told Chase and Ty, "I haven't found a single thing that would lead me to believe it can't be done. It's a grand old barn." There was genuine fondness in the sweeping glance he gave it. "It'll be a real challenge. I'll have to do some research to get a clear picture of the specific needs you'll have before I can start any design work." He paused a beat and focused a questioning look on Chase. "I don't suppose you have any as-built blueprints of the barn."

"Not hardly."

"That's what I figured." He dragged in a deep breath and let it sigh out. "I'll need to create one. Which means I'll have to measure every inch of it. Usually I have a couple of assistants to help with something like this."

"I'm sure it can be arranged to have a couple of ranch hands help you," Tara inserted then added, "assuming, that is, that you want Noah to go forward?"

In theory, Ty much preferred remodeling the existing barn than building a new structure. But he had learned during their marriage just how expensive Tara's tastes could be, and the steep fees that were charged by the professionals she hired.

"Before we give Mr. Richardson the go-ahead, we'll need to sit down with him and discuss exactly what this design work will cost."

"Of course," Tara demurred.

"That's fine with me, too. It's just"—the architect hesitated—"you do realize that getting all the measurements on this old barn will be considerably more than a two or three hour job."

Only Tara expressed surprise at his statement.

"Really?"

"Oh, it'll easily take a full day. And"—he glanced at the gold Rolex on his wrist—"half of this one is already gone."

"I am so sorry." Tara turned to Ty and Chase with a look of earnest apology. "I'm afraid I'll have to impose on you further. The company house in Blue Moon is occupied, and there simply isn't any other place we can stay—unless we can spend the night here."

Irritation flickered through Ty. Tara knew as well as he did that a visitor was never turned away from their door. It was one of the unwritten codes.

"Not a problem," Chase replied. "We have plenty of room at The Homestead. We'll arrange for your luggage to be brought from the plane."

"I do appreciate this, Chase," Tara smiled, "especially because it gives me a chance to see the twins."

* * *

In The Homestead's old kitchen, Jessy sat close to the highchair and scooped up another small spoonful of cereal to feed her son. Trey immediately grabbed for it, interested not in the spoon, but in getting his fingers in the cereal. There was more cereal smeared over his face, hands, and hair, not to mention the high chair, than had made its way into his mouth.

She caught at his grabbing hand and held it out of the way while she carried the spoon to his mouth. Straining, he turned his face away from it, babbling a protest.

Jessy drew the spoon back. "You do realize that your sister has already gotten her bottle, don't you, Trey?" She made another attempt to feed him, but it was no more successful than the first. "Not hungry, huh." Setting the baby spoon and small cereal bowl on the table, she picked up a wet washcloth and wiped his face and hands, then lifted him out of the high chair. "What you really need is another bath, little boy," she chided and tickled his tummy. He squirmed in her arms, gurgling with laughter.

"Hellooo!" The seeking call came from the entry hall.

"I'm in the kitchen," Jessy yelled back, and shifted Trey onto a hip while she set about wiping up the worst of the cereal from the high chair before it hardened into concrete.

The big house echoed with the approaching jangle of spurs and the heavy *clump* of booted feet on the hardwood floors. Jessy looked up from her work when they reached the kitchen doorway. Dick Ballard stood in the opening, a simple canvas duffel bag hanging from a shoulder strap and two, huge expensive suitcases weighing down his hands. Jessy knew immediately that the suitcases were Tara's. From that, it was easy to surmise that Tara was spending the night.

"I was told to bring these suitcases from the plane," Ballard began, then stopped and frowned. "What's she doing here anyway?"

It was a direct question he wouldn't have put to either Ty or Chase. Jessy may have married into the Calder family, but in the eyes of the ranch hands and their families, she was still one of them. They felt comfortable saying things to her that they would never dream of uttering in front of Ty or Chase.

Jessy's glance flicked to the two suitcases bearing the Gucci label. "At a guess, I'd say she's spending the night."

"Are you okay with that?" The gentle concern in Ballard's voice was almost her undoing.

Turning away from the probe of his kind blue eyes, Jessy retrieved the bottle from its warming pan on the stove. "Why shouldn't I be?" she countered in a deliberately careless tone. "She isn't married to Ty anymore."

"But she had him wrapped around her finger for a long time. And something tells me she's pulling the strings again."

It smacked of it to Jessy, too, but she didn't say so. The ranch grapevine would be buzzing with the news of Tara's arrival. She wasn't about to add any grist to the rumor mill.

"I was on my way upstairs to give Trey his bottle. Follow me and I'll show you where to put the luggage." As she crossed the kitchen, Ballard pivoted out of the doorway to let her pass, then followed her down the hall to the living room. "Why has it taken so long to bring the bags to the house? The plane landed over an hour ago," Jessy remarked, her own curiosity getting the better of her.

"You got me," Ballard said from his trailing position. "I was at the corrals working with one of the young horses when the big boss," which was the affectionate title the ranch hands had given Chase to differentiate between father and son, "told me to get the bags from the plane and take them to The Homestead."

"Where are they now?" Jessy wondered aloud.

"When I left them, they were still at the old barn. They showed up there shortly after the plane landed, and they've been there ever since," Ballard replied. "She's got some young kid with her. He's been crawling all over that barn like a termite inspector."

The old barn. Jessy slowed her steps, trying to make sense of that, as they entered the living room. She had expected that Ty would be showing Tara the two sites they had chosen as potential locations for the new sale facility.

"That must be the architect you're talking about," she guessed. "She told Chase she was bringing one with her."

"An architect? You mean for the new sale barn? Wait a minute." Ballard stopped abruptly, spurs rattling with the suddenness of it. Jessy swung around in time to see the light dawning in his expression. "They're thinking about using the old barn for it. What a helluva an idea!"

Jessy had her own moment of dawning shock as images flashed in her mind of the old barn at Christmas time, aglow with twinkling lights hung from the rafters. From there, it was no trouble at all to imagine a parade of registered cattle across a raised platform, similar to the one used for the annual Christmas pageant put on by the children of the ranch families. She felt a lick of excitement over the idea.

But she had no time to dwell on it as the front door opened and Tara swept in, followed closely by Ty, Chase, and a third young man. A tension, born of a raw dislike for the woman who had been Ty's wife, curled its way through Jessy.

She knew her manners, however, and moved forward to greet the new arrivals. "Welcome back to The Homestead, Tara."

"Jessy," Tara began in greeting, then broke it off, releasing a little gasp of delight at the sight of the baby in Jessy's arms. "You have one of the twins!" With quickened steps, she rushed to Jessy's side. "Aren't you the sweet one," she cooed and tickled Trey under the chin. The happy-natured boy traitorously smiled and flailed his arms with glee. "Which one is this?" she asked Jessy.

"Chase Benteen the Third."

"Little Trey. I should have known," Tara cooed some more and continued chucking Trey under his chin.

But the easy use of the nickname was like a slap in the face to Jessy. When Ty had returned from Dyson's funeral, he had given Jessy the impression that Tara had been overwhelmed with grief over her father's death, certainly much too distraught for there to be much conversation. But the two had clearly talked a great deal more than Ty had let on.

"Oh, Ty," Tara gushed, throwing a look over her shoulder. "He looks just like you. The same dark hair and dark eyes." She turned back to the baby and murmured in a sickening baby-talk voice, "And just like your papa, you'll break a lot of girls' hearts when you grow up, won't you, little Trey?"

With difficulty, Jessy held her silence, certain that Tara's gushing over the baby was strictly for Ty's benefit. Ty joined them, smiling indulgently when his young son squealed in pleasure at the sight of him.

Ty's glance flicked to Ballard with its customary coolness then back to Jessy. "I imagine Ballard told you that

Tara and Mr. Richardson will be spending the night here." He nodded in the direction of the younger man in the group then formally introduced him to Jessy.

After the usual pleasantries were exchanged, Jessy motioned toward the staircase that ascended from the living room to the second floor. "I was just on my way upstairs to show Ballard where to put your luggage. If you'd like, you can come with me, and I'll show you which rooms you'll have. I'm sure you would welcome the opportunity to freshen up after your long flight." The latter she directed to Tara.

"I would, yes," Tara agreed quickly, then glanced at the architect. "Noah?"

He shook his head. "I prefer to get down to business."

"In that case," Ty said, "we'll be in the den."

It was no more than a statement of general information, but Tara chose a different interpretation of it. "I'll join you later then." Without a break in rhythm, she swung away and moved toward the stairs. "Which room will I be in, Jessy? I'm sure I can find my way." The remark was a none-too-subtle reminder of her familiarity with The Homestead.

Jessy longed to strip off the gloves, but she refused to give Tara the satisfaction of knowing that she was getting to her. "I thought you could stay in Cat's old room. Unless you have some objection to that." She followed Tara to the stairs, irritated anew that Tara was the one leading the way.

"Cat's room will be fine," Tara assured her. "I always thought it had the best view of the ranch."

Spurs jangling, Ballard trailed after both of them, lugging the suitcases up the steps. When they reached the bedroom that had formerly been occupied by Cat, Tara directed Ballard on where she wanted each suitcase placed.

When he set the last one down, Tara inquired, "Which room will Noah have?"

"The first guestroom in the west hall," Jessy replied, and immediately provided Ballard with directions to it. After he exited the room, she turned to take her leave of Tara.

But she wasn't given the opportunity. "Everything is just the way I remember it," Tara declared. "The old place hasn't changed a bit."

"Not in the ways that count," Jessy agreed. "Now, if you'll excuse me, I need to give Trey his bottle. If there's anything else you need, please let me know."

On that parting note, Jessy walked out of the room, closing the door behind her. She continued down the hall to the master suite. Sally was just putting Laura in her crib when Jessy walked in.

Straightening, Sally lifted a shushing finger to her lips and whispered, "She's asleep."

Jessy nodded and crossed to the rocking chair. "By the way," she said, keeping her voice pitched low, "you should know there will be two more for dinner."

"No problem." Sally smiled. "I got out extra on the chance that Chase would invite them to lunch."

"They will be here for dinner as well as lunch." Cradling Trey in her arm, Jessy slipped the plastic nipple into his mouth, tipping the bottle. "They're spending the night."

Startled by the announcement, Sally didn't have the skill to hide it. "Tara is staying here?" A look of utter dismay claimed her expression. "Oh, Jessy, how awkward for you."

Jessy couldn't help thinking that Tara didn't appear to find the situation at all awkward. Which made her all the more determined to control her temper and maintain an outward aura of calm.

"Which room is she in?" Sally asked with sudden concern. "You didn't put her in your old room, did you?"

"No, she's in Cat's, and the architect is in the first guest room."

An absent frown knitted Sally's forehead. "I don't think there are extra towels in Cat's bathroom. I'd better get some." She hurried from the room, leaving Jessy alone with the twins and her thoughts.

Leaning close to the dressing table's mirror, Tara inspected her reflection. The face in the mirror was as smooth as ivory without a hint of a wrinkle, thanks to the artistic skill of Tara's plastic surgeon. His fee had been exorbitant, but the result was worth every dollar he charged.

There was satisfaction in knowing that Jessy and her sun-creased lines suffered in comparison. Tara drew back from the mirror and added a touch more gloss to her lips, then adjusted the folds of the chiffon scarf around her neck.

There was a light rap on the bedroom door. Thinking it was Jessy, Tara lingered at the mirror and gave her black hair a few fluffing pushes then walked over to the door.

But it was Sally Brogan who stood in the hall, a stack of towels in her arms. Tara recovered in a flash and stepped back, adopting a quick look of astonishment. "Sally." She breathed the woman's name then released a confused laugh. "I didn't expect to see you here. This is a surprise."

"I work here now."

Reaching out, Tara placed a warm hand on the woman's arm, her eyes misting over on command. "We're both hopeless, aren't we?"

"I beg your pardon." Sally frowned, puzzled by the comment.

"Even though they don't love us, we can't stop loving them. For us, it's enough to be under the same roof with them, isn't it?"

Clearly embarrassed, Sally turned away. "I . . . I don't know what you're talking about."

"I'm sorry," Tara murmured, instantly contrite. "I probably shouldn't have said anything. I think I must have known in my heart that you were secretly in love with Chase. Perhaps that's why, when I saw you here, I was so quick to recognize a kindred soul." She paused and made a show of gathering herself, brushing away the sheen of tears, and drawing in a long breath. "But you're right. It's better not to talk about it. It makes it just that much harder to conceal when we're around others."

Sally lifted her head, a marveling look in her eyes. "You do understand."

"Of course, I do," Tara said softly and embraced the woman, towels and all, in a warm hug, then retreated, managing to exhibit a trace of self-consciousness. "Gracious, look at us," she declared, thickening the drawl in her voice. "We had better stop this before I start crying." Half turning, Tara delicately pressed a finger to the corner of an eye as if blotting away a tear.

Sally hesitated. "I guess I'd best be putting these towels away."

"Sally." Tara reached out a hand in a stalling gesture when the woman started to turn away. "Sometimes it's—good to share your pain with another who is going through the same thing. It helps somehow. Thank you."

Tara read the hesitancy and doubt in the older woman's eyes. As clearly moved as she was by their exchange, Sally still didn't fully trust her.

Tara was confident that she would in time. After all, there was no truer adage than the old one about misery loving company. And Tara needed an ally in the Calder household, a conduit of its happenings. There was no better candidate for that than Sally Brogan.

This was not a time to press for undying friendship, however. This was the moment to step back and allow it to develop gradually over the next few months.

"Now you go put those towels away," Tara declared with an affectionate shooing motion. "It's time I went downstairs before Noah decides that I have completely deserted him."

By late the following afternoon, the Calders had struck a deal with the young architect, detailed measurements had been taken of the barn, and the pair had departed for Fort Worth with promises to be in touch soon.

Four short days later a UPS truck pulled up to The Homestead. The rear of the van was jammed with packages. The brown-uniformed driver hauled all but a very few of them into the house. Jessy stared in disbelief at the boxes stacked high in the large foyer, with only a small walk space left from the front door to the hall.

Each of them identified the sender as Tara.

On the box marked in big letters OPEN FIRST was an envelope with a note from Tara, addressed to both Ty and Jessy. In it, she expressed her gratitude for their hospitality and apologized for the late arrival of the baby gifts for the twins.

It took the better part of an hour for Jessy to open all the packages. When she had finished, she was overwhelmed by the multitude of gifts. In the toy category, there were elaborate mobiles, fancy rattles and teething rings, and a menagerie of stuffed animals, large and small. Each twin had a complete set of porcelain dishes, plus a full setting of silver baby utensils. In addition, there were clothes—twelve outfits apiece. In Laura's case, all of them consisted of dressy confections, full of ruffles and lace, complete with matching shoes, hair ribbons, and an assortment of other accessories. With one exception, Trey's clothes were variations of suits and ties, blazers and matching slacks, with an accompanying collection of little shirts, socks, and shoes. The exception was a cowboy outfit, complete with full regalia—boots with tiny spurs, jeans, a cowboy hat, a yoked-front shirt with pearl snaps, a cowhide vest, fringed leather chaps, and a buckskin jacket.

Hands on her hips, Jessy stared at the mound of gifts. "Would you look at all this?" she exclaimed to Sally, annoyance riddling her voice. "When and where does Tara expect the twins to wear all these fancy outfits? Do you realize there is not one practical item in the whole batch?"

"I know." Sally clicked her tongue in dismay then picked one of the frillier dresses, her expression melting. "But have you ever seen anything so precious? Laura will look like a little doll in this."

Jessy's opinion didn't change when she glanced at the dainty pink number. She had never been able to abide ruffles and lace herself. The thought of dressing her daughter in such an outfit was equally repugnant.

"This must have cost a fortune," Sally murmured.

Jessy harrumphed. "She can afford it. Her daddy left her the equivalent of probably seven or eight fortunes. For two cents, I would give most of this away, but I doubt there are enough babies in the whole county to wear all these clothes." Then her expression softened

with grudging fondness when her glance fell on the
cowboy outfit. Jessy fingered the cowhide vest and
fringed chaps. "I have to admit, though, Grandpa Calder
will get a real kick out of seeing Trey in this one."

"Wouldn't he, though."

For the life of her, Jessy couldn't imagine what kind
of thank-you card a person sent to someone who had
bought out an entire baby store. In the end she penned
a simple note.

Humming to herself, Sally dusted the walnut table
next to Chase's favorite chair, then set everything back
on it just the way Chase liked it. Before she stepped
away, the telephone rang. Automatically she picked up
the extension.

"Calder residence."

"May I speak to Ty, please?"

"I'm sorry, he isn't here right now. May I take a message
and have him call you back?" Sally searched around for
a pencil and paper.

"Is that you, Sally?"

"Yes."

"It's Tara." The tone of her voice turned decidedly
friendly.

"Hello. How are you?" Sally paused in her search for
the notepad.

"I'm fine. I was wondering—have the presents for the
twins arrived yet?"

"They were delivered three days ago. I believe Jessy
mailed you a card yesterday."

"I'll bet Ty was furious with me when he saw all the
gifts."

"He did think that you sent too many."

"Well, he was right. I went way over the top. But there

were so many things, too precious for words, that I couldn't stop with just two or three items. You must know how it is, Sally," Tara declared in that confiding manner. "Being there every day, taking care of the twins, watching them grow—it's bound to feel like you are their grandmother. It does, doesn't it? Now, tell the truth."

"It's crazy, but I do," Sally admitted without any qualm.

"If you can be a grandmother to them, then I can be a doting aunt, lavishing gifts on them from afar and spoiling them outrageously. Like you, I will never have children of my own. The twins allow me to indulge in some of those deep maternal instincts all women have."

Later that evening, Tara made much the same argument to Ty, before getting to the main purpose of her phone call, which was to apprise him of the progress the architect had made. An as-built blueprint of the barn, identifying all the existing mechanicals, was scheduled to be finished during the following week. Noah was already at work on some design sketches and hoped to have preliminary drawings ready for their review in three or four weeks.

As it turned out, it was closer to five weeks. Again the architect Noah Richardson arrived at the Triple C aboard Tara's private jet, accompanied by its owner. Tara came along, as well, on the third and fourth trips.

The architect's fifth visit, with final drawings in hand, coincided with fall roundup, one of the ranch's busier times. In previous years, Jessy would have been in the thick of the gather. But a pair of cranky, teething twins had kept her sidelined at The Homestead.

Being housebound while all the activity was going on elsewhere combined with the stress of being confined with two irritable babies had given Jessy a bad case of cabin fever, complete with frayed nerves. When Old Joe

Gibbs walked into The Homestead, toting that all-too-familiar Gucci luggage set under his arms, the sight of them cracked across her like a whip, shredding what little control she had of her temper.

Turning on her heel, Jessy charged into the kitchen, grabbed a set of truck keys off the board, and snapped at Sally, "Our company just arrived. You'll have to deal with them. If the twins start crying again, let them."

Startled by the sharpness in Jessy's voice, Sally was slow to react. "But—where are you going?"

But the back door had already slammed shut behind Jessy.

"Jessy?" Joe Gibbs's questioning voice came from the front of the house. "Hey, Jessy, where am I supposed to put these bags?"

Pushed into action by the call, Sally hurriedly wiped her hands on a towel and left the blueberry torte on the counter, unfinished, to hurry to the entry hall.

The minute the old ranch hand saw Sally, a gray eyebrow shot up. "What happened to Jessy? I swear, the very second she laid eyes on me, she took out of here like she'd been scalded."

Tara's timely entrance spared Sally from answering Joe's question as she turned to greet the arriving guests. Through the opened front door came the sound of spinning tires and flying gravel.

Drawn by the noise, Tara stepped back into the doorway. "Good heavens, who is that?"

"Jessy." Sally attempted to sound matter-of-fact.

Tara's interest went up another notch. "Where is she going in such a hurry?"

"I'm not sure," Sally admitted, showing her uncertainty. "I imagine she went to let Ty know you're here. We're in the middle of roundup, you know."

"Yes, Ty mentioned it on the phone the other night.

In fact, I had my pilot fly over the gather so Noah could have a bird's-eye view of a genuine roundup. But from the air, you can't get a true sense of the noise, dust, and confusion of the real thing. I'm hoping we will have time to slip away for an afternoon so he can see it all up close."

"I'm sure he'll enjoy it," Sally agreed even as her glance slid in the direction of the speeding pickup, a detail Tara noticed with her usual perceptiveness. The woman was clearly bothered by Jessy's sudden and hasty departure. Tara's curiosity over it was aroused as well.

Spurred by a nameless fury, Jessy drove at a reckless pace, mindless of the dust cloud billowing behind her. She was halfway to the Broken Butte area before she remembered they had finished the gather there and moved to Wolf Meadow. Slamming on the brakes, she fishtailed to a stop, threw the truck into reverse, turned around in the middle of the road, and took off again in the opposite direction.

By the time she reached the Wolf Meadow section, her anger had cooled to a slow burn. Leaving the ranch road, she followed twin tracks of flattened grass, left by the motorized cookshack and horse trailers, to the gathering point. Avoiding the branding area, she headed for the cookshack. As she neared the picket line, Jessy spotted a weary horse and rider coming toward her and rolled down the window.

"Hey, stranger," Ballard greeted her with a tuckered smile. "It's been a while since we've seen you out and about."

Jessy didn't waste time with pleasantries. "Where's Ty?"

Ballard reined in his horse, surprise flickering in his

expression. "You should have passed him on the way here. He left about twenty—maybe thirty minutes ago, right after he saw the plane fly over." If anything, the kindness in his eyes took on an even gentler quality. "She's back, isn't she?"

His remark ignited a fresh spark of anger. Clamping her mouth shut, Jessy spun the steering wheel in a circle and jammed her foot on the accelerator to jolt back across the uneven grassland to the road.

Ballard watched her, recognizing the show of temper for what it was. Jessy had her back up. That didn't happen often, and he had never known it to occur without cause.

It didn't take much guessing to lay a finger on where the trouble was, although he was hesitant to put the blame on Tara. She was a she-cat, all right, one who clearly had designs on sinking her claws back into Ty. Everyone on the Triple C saw it. Ballard didn't fault Tara for that; it would be like trying to blame a polecat for stinking.

But Ty—that was another matter. Ballard had never put much truck in him. Ty was a Calder by birth, born out of wedlock in California. He was fifteen years old before he ever set foot on the Triple C to claim his birthright. It had taken time, but Ty had eventually adapted to his new home and a new way of life. But Ty hadn't lost all his California ways. That was clear to Ballard as well, certain that it had to be California thinking that would prompt a man to welcome an ex-wife into his home.

With a small, disgusted movement of his head, Ballard reined his horse away from the sight of the departing pickup and walked it to the picket line.

*   *   *

The aroma of baking ham, drenched with honey, wafted in the air when Jessy swept into the kitchen. The oven door stood open with Sally bent over the roaster pan, basting the ham with its sweetened juices. She straightened, with a glance over her shoulder, when Jessy walked in.

"You're back," she began.

"Where's Ty?"

"I think I heard him go upstairs to clean up before dinner."

By the time Sally finished, Jessy had crossed the room and entered the hall, heading for the staircase. Long and lithe, she went up the steps two at a time, pushed by an inner demand for a confrontation that had been too long in coming.

In her side vision, Jessy noted the door to Cat's old room was open a crack, but she paid no attention to it. She was too intent on her goal.

As she pushed through the doorway into the master bedroom, Ty came out of the bath area, a towel hooked around his middle and another one slung around his muscled shoulders. His dark hair gleamed wet from the shower, and beads of moisture glistened on his tanned skin.

"Where have you been?" he asked idly. "Joe Gibbs said you peeled out of here like a cat with its tail on fire."

Jessy paused long enough to close the door then came straight to the point. "Answer me one thing, Ty Calder. What is she doing here again?"

He stopped short, a frown gathering on his forehead. "Who? Tara?"

"Of course, Tara," she exploded. "Who else would I be talking about?"

"How the hell should I know?" Ty declared in exasperation. "I don't even know why we're talking about her."

"Did you know she was coming?" Hands on her hips, Jessy faced him squarely, alert to any subtle shift in his expression.

"No."

"Then, I repeat—what is she doing here again?"

His eyes narrowed, and the set of his jaw hardened, showing a wearing of patience. "According to Tara," he stated slowly and concisely, "she brought a list of publicists and caterers that she wants to go over with me."

"And this required a personal visit?" Jessy challenged. "She couldn't have sent you the list, then discussed it with you over the phone?"

"I wouldn't know. That's something you'll have to take up with Tara."

As much as she wanted to find fault with his answer, it was just the sort of flimsy excuse Tara would use. Which only annoyed Jessy all the more.

She half turned, her hands sliding off her hips in a frustrated need for movement. "Caterers," she muttered in disgust. "As if we need a list from her."

"And just how many professional caterers can *you* name?" Ty flared, his own temper now aroused. "Or did you even realize that we would need one for a function like this? Maybe you thought this was like some local auction where you contacted the women's auxiliary from a local church and had them run the concession stand."

"I knew a professional would be required." But it hadn't really sunk home until that moment. "But it's a little early to be worrying about which one when we don't even have a place built to hold the auction."

"With a function of this scope and size, you can't plan too far ahead." He glared at her for a half-second then shook his head with a kind of disgust. "You don't have the first clue about this type of event. You should be thanking Tara for her assistance instead of resenting it."

"Maybe I would if I knew just why she was so eager to offer it."

His head came up, his gaze fixing itself on her once again. "Good god, Jessy, you aren't jealous, are you? In case you've forgotten, I'm not married to her anymore."

"I know it, and you know it, but it seems to have totally slipped her mind."

"The divorce was final nearly eight years ago. Isn't it time we all put the past behind us?" he argued. "Or would you rather that we were bitter enemies?"

"I would feel safer if you were." Jessy turned thoughtful. "I don't know what her game is, but she won't win."

Out in the hallway, Tara straightened away from the hall door to the master bedroom, her lips curving in a knowing smile. "Oh, won't I?" she murmured in response to Jessy's last remark. "But it won't be the way you think."

Still, there were troubled waters that needed to be smoothed. It was something that needed to be handled sooner rather than later.

Her opportunity came yet that evening. As always, they gathered after dinner in the den, long the heart of the Triple C. The room was dominated by a cavernous stone fireplace, crowned with the wide-sweeping horns of a longhorn steer mounted above the mantelpiece.

Chase Calder occupied his customary place, the chair behind the big desk. On the wall, just beyond his shoulder, hung a framed map, yellowed with age, its lines hand-drawn, delineating the wide-reaching boundaries of the Triple C.

Ty was by the fireplace, a shoulder leaning against the wooden mantel, his stance loose and relaxed as he idly sipped at a glass of bourbon and water. Reclining on the age-softened leather couch, Tara held her wineglass by its stem and swirled the fine port it held. Dressed in a black cashmere sweater and matching slacks, she wore her hair down in a softly rumpled style. In addition to the black opal ring that never left her finger, her only other concession to jewelry was a strand of baroque pearls interspersed with long onyx beads. She fingered them absently as her gaze strayed to the map on the wall, only half interested in Noah's discourse on the merits of some new coolant system.

"It costs more, but it should save you money in the long run. I have some brochures on it upstairs. I'll go get them," the architect said, rising from the wing-back chair in front of the desk. "That way you can look them over and let me know in a few days if you want to go that route."

As he exited the den, Jessy walked in, a twin on each hip. "We just finished our baths. I thought we would come in and say good night before we headed off to bed."

Young, dark-haired Trey spotted his father by the fireplace and immediately stretched out his arms, babbling excitedly, "Da da da da."

Leaving his drink glass on the mantel, Ty walked over to take the wiggling toddler from Jessy's arm. Rising, Tara slipped her wineglass onto the coffee table and glided across the room to claim the tow-haired girl.

"Aren't you the precious one." Tara lifted the child into her arms with an effortless ease. "Look at all those beautiful golden curls."

But little Laura had eyes only for one thing—the

pearls around Tara's neck. Her fingers fastened around them with greedy quickness.

"Laura, no." But Jessy's protest came too late.

Tara laughed. "It's all right," she insisted and cooed to the child, "It's a smart girl who knows her jewelry."

"Maybe, but she's teething." Jessy stepped forward to rescue the necklace from her daughter, but not before Laura managed to get them in her mouth. "I better take her," Jessy said after she managed to extricate the necklace from her daughter's grasp. When Laura was safely in her arms again, she apologized, "I'm sorry. I should have warned you."

"No harm done," Tara assured her. "Besides, just think—when she grows up, she can brag that she cut her teeth on pearls."

Unimpressed, Jessy smiled a nonanswer. "Come on, Trey." She reached for her son. "Time for bed."

"Wait." Tara held up a detaining hand. "Before you go, I just want to thank you—all of you"—she included Chase in her sweeping glance—"for letting me help in the planning for all this."

Jessy couldn't recall being given a choice, but she refrained from saying so.

"It's meant more to me than you can possibly know," she went on. "After Daddy died, I was completely lost. I didn't know what to do with myself. My life seemed totally without purpose. If it wasn't for that chance remark Ty made when he came for the funeral—" Pausing, Tara gave him a misty-eyed look that Jessy didn't believe for one minute. "But he did, thankfully. Because I needed the work—the challenge of a project like this." She paused again to shift her focus to Jessy. "Heaven knows, it's been an awkward situation at times, considering I am the ex–Mrs. Calder, but I will always be grateful that you have been magnanimous enough to look past that. We do all want the same thing—for this auction to be a huge success."

And Tara was going to be there, claiming her share of the glory for it—if not all of the glory—while Jessy stood on the sidelines, completely eclipsed by her husband's first wife. Tara clearly had a need to show how inferior Jessy was. It was obviously an ego thing, childish and silly, something to be ignored. Except, it was also a matter of pride. Jessy had never bowed her head to any man; she wasn't about to bow it to a woman—and never to Tara.

Chapter Seven

〰️

A blustery wind came out of the north, a nip in its breath that signaled the approach of winter. In the open plains, there were no trees to break it, only the occasional cutbank or coulee. But there were none in sight at the spot of the Wolf Meadow gather.

The wind rolled, unchecked, across the herd of red-coated Herefords, held closely bunched by a circle of riders. Bawling their discontent, the cattle milled in confusion, the thick grass underfoot muffling the thuddings of their hooves. The sound underscored the rolling snorts of horses, the creaking saddle leather, the jangle of spurs, and the chomp of bridle bits.

From his vantage point on a crest of the plain, Ty looked on while a pair of riders walked their horses into the herd, quietly working in tandem to single out a cow that had been deemed too old to be productive.

Fall roundup was the time when the herd was culled of the old, the infirm, and the inferior stock, as well as the occasional steer that had escaped the spring gather.

After the cull was finished, the herd was reevaluated to determine whether the numbers needed to be further reduced.

In a good year, the range could winter over only a certain number of cattle. During a bad year, that number was reduced, sometimes sharply. And the year's scant rainfall qualified it as one that had been considerably less than good.

Ty's thoughts weren't on that, however. At the moment, his attention was focused on the long, slender rider working the cut, her honey-gold hair hanging down her back in a single braid. Jessy sat deep and easy in the saddle, balanced and ready for any dip or spin her cat-quick horse made as it worked to separate the cow from the herd and frustrate its every attempt to rejoin it.

Suddenly an animal on the outer circle made a break from the herd and bolted for the open grassland beyond it. Immediately a pair of flanking riders gave chase.

Ty felt the light pressure of a small, gloved hand on his arm. "Ty look," Tara said, her voice low and musical. "It's Noah." She nodded to one of the riders giving chase, his arms flapping like a chicken as he raced his horse after it. "He's having the time of his life."

"Let's hope he doesn't go airborne with all that wing flapping," Ty remarked dryly.

Tara's amused laugh had a low and throaty sound, innately sensual. "His horsemanship does leave something to be desired. But you have to admit, he has been positively enthralled by all this."

"City boys usually are. Give him a few more hours, and he'll discover that there is a lot more sweat and grime than glamour."

"You used to be a city boy."

His mouth quirked in that hard, familiar way Tara remembered. "Not anymore."

"No, not anymore." She ran her glance over the chiseled strength of his features. "This is your element. I realized that the first time I saw you here at the ranch. That was during roundup, too. Remember?"

"I remember." He nodded. "But that time it was spring roundup."

"With mud everywhere," Tara recalled. "I couldn't put a foot down without sinking up to my ankles in it. At least this time it's dry."

"Too dry." His glance made an assessing sweep of the sky, but there wasn't a cloud in sight.

Tara glanced up as well, but not for long. The sky was huge, blue, and empty, like all the rest of this land. Suffocatingly so, in her opinion, but she didn't voice that.

"I know you need rain, but I confess, I greatly appreciate the sunshine this morning."

"I imagine you do." His mouth crooked in an absent smile.

The continued briefness of his answers was irritating, indicating, as they did, that she had only half of his attention. The rest was centered on those damned cattle.

Tara let the silence stretch between them for a while, and chose her next subject with care. "This area," she began on a curious note, "isn't this part of the land that you're seeking to gain title to?"

His dark gaze pinned her, sharp and probing. "How did you know that?"

Tara smiled that enigmatic smile he knew so well. "Surely you haven't forgotten, Ty, that I lived on this ranch for a while, too."

He relented a little. "You never seemed that interested in the ranch."

"I was always interested, Ty. Too often, though, that interest ran at cross-purposes with yours—or your father's."

There was too much truth in that for Ty to deny—not that he wanted to rehash it all again. Yet he hadn't expected that kind of an admission from Tara.

He made a slow reassessment of her, but it was hard to see more than her dark, vibrant beauty with its porcelain skin and soft curves. Even in Western garb of black jeans, a cable knit sweater of winter white under a white woolly vest, and a flat-crowned cowboy hat, Tara managed to look the picture of stylish elegance, completely untouched by the dust and the noise and the confusion before her.

"This is the land, isn't it," she repeated, but this time it wasn't so much a question as a statement.

"It is," he confirmed.

"Have you made any progress in obtaining title?"

"We're working on it."

The curve of her lips lengthened. "When a Calder gives you an answer like that, it usually means you are no closer than you were before." She slanted him a mocking look. "I speak from experience."

"Truthfully, I couldn't say one way or the other," Ty replied smoothly. "Dad's been handling that end of it. I've been too busy with roundup and the plans for the new facility to check on the status of things."

"Actually I expected Chase to bring us out here this morning. He isn't as active as he used to be." Tara hesitated, a flicker of concern clouding her eyes. "Or am I wrong about that?"

"He's been bothered a bit more by arthritis lately," Ty admitted. "It goes back to the injuries he suffered in the plane crash. The doctors warned him that he would be troubled by it when he got older. Nowadays, he can't spend much time in the saddle without a lot of pain."

"He must hate that."

"Almost as much as he hates doing paperwork."

"Then he's left most of the actual running of the ranch to you."

"We've divvied up the responsibility. Or," one corner of his mouth lifted in a dry smile, "to put it in your lingo, he's the chairman of the board and I'm the president."

"You make a fine president, but I always knew you would." Tara saw the shutters close, turning his features expressionless. "Don't go getting all aloof on me," she chided with playful mockery. "What I said is absolutely true. Maybe we aren't man and wife anymore, but we made a good team. We still do. This time it just happens to be a business relationship. It's not without precedent for a Calder, you know."

A brow arched in a puzzled question. "What do you mean?"

"Don't you remember that story Ruth Stanton used to tell about Lady Crawford, wife to the Earl of Dunshill, and the unique business relationship that existed between her and the first Chase Benteen Calder, your great-grandfather?"

He nodded. "I remember some of it."

"I was always fascinated by the thought of a woman of that time period arranging government beef contracts. And lucrative ones at that, according to Ruth. Such things require skill and considerable influence."

"I suppose." But it wasn't a subject that interested Ty.

Tara turned in the saddle, her expression brightening with the flash of another memory. "You know, I had almost forgotten about that old tintype I found when

Cat and I were rummaging around in one of the old trunks in the attic. It was a photo of your great-great-grandmother. And I was struck by her resemblance to pictures I had seen of Lady Crawford. It made me wonder if they were the same woman." The possibility appealed to her again. "You really should give some thought to checking it out."

"Why?" It seemed a waste of time and energy to Ty.

Tara released another patented throaty laugh. "Darling, the press loves nothing better than delicious little skeletons in family closets. Everybody here knows that your great-great-grandmother ran off with another man when the first Chase Benteen Calder was a little boy. As scandals go, that is a tame one. But if she eventually married into the British aristocracy, that—my dear Ty—is the juicy tidbit people love to buzz about. Even if it isn't true, you should hint at it. It will only add to the Calder legend and mystique. And that will bring people to your auction. The right people."

"We'll see," was Ty's only comment.

"You don't like the idea. I can tell," Tara murmured. "But I'm right."

"You probably are." He redirected his attention back to the gather, spotting Jessy as she returned from escorting the aged cow to the culled herd, held in a grass basin on the other side of the lower hill. A second later, his eye was caught by another rider on foot, leading a limping horse toward the picket line. Ty was quick to recognize the lanky rider as Dick Ballard. Jessy had spotted Ballard as well, and reined her horse toward him.

As Jessy pulled up beside him, Ballard pushed his hat to the back of his head and started jawing as usual. Jessy smiled at something Ballard said. Ty watched the easy interplay between the two, his own expression darkening.

"Who's that with Jessy?" Tara asked.

"Dick Ballard. He's worked on and off for the Triple C for years."

Jessy took her foot out of the near stirrup, offering Ballard a lift to the picket line. He grabbed hold of the saddle horn and swung up behind her.

"Ballard," Tara murmured thoughtfully. "I've heard that name before. Isn't he the one who first suggested the idea for this auction?"

"Yes. When he isn't working for us, he often rides cutting horses in competition for other owners or trainers. I understand that a time or two he helped out at some of these big auctions."

"Has he seen the design for yours?"

"No."

"Can he read blueprints?"

"I don't know. Why?"

"I was thinking that if he could, it might be wise to let him take a look at them. It's possible he might see something the rest of us have missed." Even as she spoke, Tara was distracted by the obvious camaraderie that existed between Jessy and this man Ballard. "Jessy seems very friendly with him."

"Like I said," Ty replied, "he's worked for the Triple C on and off for years."

"Yes, you have always had a tight-knit group," Tara recalled. It was all part of the Old West code of loyalty to the brand, something she had always found quite stifling. Yet for all the smoothness of Ty's response, Tara detected something tight-lipped about it. It made her wonder. "Don't you like Ballard?"

Ty shrugged his indifference toward the man. "He tends to talk a lot. Sometimes it can get on the nerves."

A talker. Tara filed away that tidbit of information, aware that it might prove useful in the future.

Ballard rode easy behind the saddle, swaying with the horse's slow, walking rhythm, one hand resting on a dusty thigh, the other holding the reins to his lame horse. Of necessity, their pace was slow.

"It's good to see you back on a horse, working with the rest of us," he remarked to Jessy.

"It feels good. I've missed it," she admitted freely. "But the twins need me at home right now."

"I've never met a woman yet who didn't need a break from her kids now and then."

"That's what my mother said when she walked into The Homestead this morning."

"Something tells me Grandma just wanted a chance to spoil them."

"Probably," Jessy agreed. "What happened to your horse?"

"I'm not sure. Either he put his foot down wrong or stepped in a hole and strained something. It doesn't look too serious. Rest and some liniment, and he'll be good as new in a few days."

"I was wondering something," Jessy began, not entirely sure what to ask or how to ask it. "How can I find out when and where there will be another big livestock auction like the kind we plan to have?"

"It shouldn't be hard. I can make some calls and find out if you want."

"I would appreciate it if you would."

"Consider it done." He paused then asked. "Why? What have you got in mind?"

"I was thinking it was time we went to one and saw for ourselves what they are all about."

"Already worried about what you're gonna wear, are you?" Ballard grinned, certain that Ty's fashion plate of an ex-wife was the cause of that.

Startled, Jessy jerked her head around, slicing a look

at the man behind her. "Clothes? Why on earth would I care about such a thing?"

The response was so typical of Jessy that Ballard laughed out loud. "You're right. I should have known better. I can't say I have seen you in a dress more than a handful of times, let alone in fancy duds."

"My reason for wanting to attend one of these auctions is simply to see the way it's set up, how it's run, the way it's organized. I want to get a head start on some of that so ours will run smoothly." Jessy sounded half-angry, as if she resented his assumption that she would be concerned about something as frivolous as clothes.

"Heck, Jessy. You hire ninety percent of that," Ballard explained. "As far as the sale itself goes, the auction firm sets all that up. The same with whatever company's handling the food. Your PR people will meet and greet your buyers, and keep them happy. I've heard each company gives you options on doing things this way or that."

"But knowing which option is the best one, that's the problem." Jessy reined in a few yards from the picket line.

"I guess you need to ask a lot of questions and use common sense." Reaching around her, Ballard gripped the saddle horn and slid off the side. Her horse swung its rump away from him, shifting its position so that Jessy faced the man on the ground. "I'd ask what brought about all these questions, but I think I already know the answer. What excuse did she have for coming this time?"

His question told Jessy just how rampant the speculation had been about Tara's frequent visits, confirming what she had long suspected.

"She brought a list of public relation firms and recommendations for caterers that she wanted to go over with us." To stave off some of the gossip, Jessy added, "Actually she's been very helpful."

"I'll just bet she has." His drawled response was thick with skepticism. "It seems to me that what you should be concentrating on next is getting an advertising agency. Your PR people will have suggestions on that, but you need to be deciding on an ad campaign. Unless you get lucky, laying one of them out can take time."

"Thanks." Jessy appreciated the information, especially because it hadn't come from Tara. She gathered the reins to leave, then checked her horse's movement, nagged by his initial comment. "Buyers really dress up for these auctions, do they?"

"Whooey! I hope to shout they do, especially the wives. Of course, the clothes can run the gamut. Depending on the time of year, you can see everything from furs to jeans with holes in 'em. For the most part, though, the women drag out every piece of turquoise and silver jewelry they own, and dude themselves up in gaudy Western outfits that could put to shame anything Dale Evans and Roy Rogers ever wore. Some of the auctions even have what they call a private showing the night before. But it's just another name for a cocktail party, full of a lot of satin and diamond glitter."

"We aren't planning anything like that." At least Jessy didn't think they were.

"Yeah, I can't see the Old Man agreeing to anything like that," Ballard replied, then measured her with a glance. "Just the same, I know you're not gonna want'a hear this, but people will be taking a close look at what the wife of a Calder is wearing. I just thought I ought'a warn you about that."

"Thanks, but I can't be anything but what I am." With a turn of the reins and a squeeze of the knees, Jessy turned her horse from Ballard and lifted it into a lope back toward the herd.

* * *

When noontime rolled around, Ty offered to drive Tara, Jessy, and Noah Richardson back to The Homestead for lunch. It was, after all, to have been only a morning excursion. But the architect had yet to have his fill of the cowboy experience and suggested that they eat with the crew before returning to headquarters.

He seemed disappointed to discover they weren't having beef and beans with skillet bread. But he found a place among the cowhands and dug with gusto into his plate of braised brisket, scalloped potatoes, and green beans.

A dusty wind swirled around the motorized cookshack, seasoning the food with some of nature's grit. This was definitely not Tara's idea of dining al fresco. Rising from the campstool that had been provided for her, she carried her nearly full plate over to the wreck pan.

"Let me take that for you, ma'am," a male voice drawled.

"Thank you." Handing it over, she absently flicked a glance at the cowboy then let it stay when she recognized the sandy-haired rider she had noticed earlier with Jessy.

"Why, you barely pecked at this," Ballard observed as he dumped the remains in a plastic trash bag. "The great outdoors usually whets up most people's appetite. But I guess that's how you keep that slim figure of yours."

"I'll take that as a compliment." Tara smiled. "You're Dick Ballard, aren't you?"

He made a mock bow of admission, giving his dusty hat a little tip. "Now I'm the one who's flattered that you remembered me, Miss Tara."

Realizing that he assumed she recognized him from her days when she was married to Ty, Tara didn't bother to correct him. "Ty mentioned that you were the one to first suggest the idea of an auction."

"It just seemed like a logical thing for the Triple C to be doin'." He noticed she still held the tin coffee cup. "Want me to freshen your coffee for you? I was just about to pour myself another cup."

"Please." She surrendered the cup to him.

Waiting while he filled both cups, Tara used the opportunity to make a closer study of the lanky cowboy. He was nice-looking in an innocuous sort of way. His eyes were unquestionably his best feature, blue and thickly fringed with a soft, gentle quality about them.

"Milk or sugar in your coffee?" He glanced over his shoulder.

"Milk, please."

"I figured as much." He picked up the milk jug set out for that purpose, poured some in, then passed the cup to her, handle first. "This range coffee can be almost as strong as espresso."

There was a delicate arch to her eyebrow at his comment. "I didn't expect a Triple C cowboy to know about espresso."

"The truth is out, I guess." He took a sip of his own undiluted coffee, eyeing her over the cup's tin rim. "I'm not what you would call a true Triple C hand. Like you, I'm something of an outsider." He used the cup to gesture toward the other riders in camp, busy chowing down. "That's what they call somebody who hasn't been born and raised here."

"But when I saw you earlier with Jessy, the two of you seemed very friendly."

"I'm just the friendly sort," Ballard replied, but Tara was certain she detected a sudden leap of wariness in his eyes. Briefly they sharpened their focus before he let a slow grin sweep across his face. "Besides, even though I'm technically an outsider, I've known Jess since heck was a pup."

"Then you must have known her when she worked as an ordinary ranch hand."

"That's right," he acknowledged, then said, "The architect mentioned that work should be starting in the next week or so. That was a good idea you had, revampin' the old barn into an auction facility."

Her smile lengthened knowingly. "That was a deft change of subject, Mr. Ballard. I didn't realized that I was making you uncomfortable by talking about Jessy."

There was a definite cooling in his eyes. "It strikes me, that if a lady noticed that, she would have had the good manners not to point it out."

For a split second, her temper flared at the veiled insult, however gently worded, but Tara quickly controlled it. "The gloves are off, are they?" she murmured somewhat mockingly.

"That's up to you."

"Is it?" she countered, hurriedly reassessing her opinion of the cowboy.

"Look. I don't know what your game is, but something tells me you're here to make trouble. What kind of trouble, I don't know."

"I'm afraid you're completely wrong," Tara replied smoothly. "I'm only here to help in whatever way I can. Having come up with the idea to convert the barn into a sale facility, I'm eager to see it come to pass."

"If you say so." Ballard took another drink of his coffee.

"You don't believe me, do you?" She could see it in his face.

"Let's just say that I've never known a skunk to change its stripes yet."

"I must say you don't have a very high opinion of me." Tara regarded that as a challenge, something to be overcome.

"I guess I'm just rememberin' all the trouble you caused in the past, and I don't want to see Jessy gettin' hurt again."

"We're back to Jessy, are we? You seem to be very fond of her."

"I'd like to think that she looks on me as a friend, somebody she can depend on, but don't be thinkin' you can use that," Ballard warned. "Jessy only has eyes for Ty. I've known that for a long time. So you aren't going to be able to use me to cause trouble between them, if that's your thought."

"How long have you been in love with her?"

"Ma'am, I think this conversation is over." His glance slid past her. "Ty and Jessy are headed this way. It looks like they're ready to leave for headquarters."

"I wouldn't rush," Tara said when he started to turn away. "It will only look suspicious." Confident that Ballard would remain, she half turned to greet the approaching pair. "There you two are. I was just having the most interesting conversation with Mr. Ballard here."

"Really." With an unusual aloofness, Ty briefly nodded an acknowledgment of the cowboy's presence. "I imagine he was telling you about his latest suggestion that Jessy just passed on to me."

"Which one is that?" Tara asked to cover her ignorance.

"About getting an ad agency on board right away."

The wisdom of the suggestion struck Tara first, then surprise that it should come from an ordinary cowboy. But she was careful not to let it show.

"I know. I'm surprised I didn't think of it," she admitted lightly, then turned to Ballard, her conviction growing that he was far from ordinary. "You are remarkably savvy about such things, Mr. Ballard."

"It comes from experience I guess—that, and a natural curiosity. Over the years I've been around a good many of these big auction events, and I just naturally nosed around to find what all went on behind the scenes to put one of these things together." With that, Ballard dumped the remaining coffee from his cup and tossed it into the wreck pan. "I'd better be gettin' back to work." He touched his hat to Jessy and Tara, and moved off.

Tara watched him a moment. "Who would have thought you would have someone so knowledgeable right in your own backyard? It might be wise to involve him more in the auction, Ty. His input could prove to be valuable."

"Jessy just suggested the same thing," Ty informed her.

"Then there are already two votes for Mr. Ballard," Tara declared. "You might as well make it unanimous, Ty. Heaven knows, there will be hundreds of details to be handled. And with the ranch to run, you already have enough on your plate. You will need to delegate responsibility to someone. Maybe that will prove to be Mr. Ballard."

"Maybe." But the prospect didn't appeal to Ty. He just couldn't seem to shake his dislike of the man.

Chapter Eight

〜

On a lamblike morning in late March, Ty stood with his father outside the old timbered barn, his sheepskin jacket hanging open. After a long and brutally cold winter with the temperature and wind chill hovering near the zero mark for days on end, the last patches of snow had finally melted, exposing the brown stalks of dormant grass. With the thermometer already registering above the forty-degree mark, the morning felt downright balmy.

The rough winter had created any number of construction delays in the remodeling of the old barn. Even now there was considerable work to be done on the inside, but the exterior was all but finished. Ty studied the single-story addition that had been added to the side, noting the way it seamlessly blended with the original structure.

"It's hard to tell where the old ends and the new begins, isn't it?" he remarked to his father.

Chase nodded in agreement. "And to think we planned

to bulldoze that old shed at South Fork this spring," he mused. "It was a good thing Ballard went scavenging around the ranch to see what he could find after those lumber bids came in so high. We had some labor costs salvaging that shed, but we still came out dollars ahead."

As reluctant as Ty was to admit it, Ballard had proved his worth on more than one occasion, both in the preliminary planning for the auction and in the construction of the facility. "Ballard never struck me as having so much business sense."

"We never hired him to do more than rope and ride and mend fence. That makes it hard to judge whether a man is capable of more than that," Chase replied. "Speaking of fences, did you see the quotes we got for new steel fence posts?"

"I saw them. They were a helluva lot higher than I expected."

Chase grunted an agreement. "With the up-front cash we have to spend for this auction, we will have to make do with the fencing we have until next year."

"Or late fall, after the sale." A date in early September had been set for the livestock auction. "With any luck, we'll recoup a big chunk of the money we have invested."

"With the high hay costs we had this winter, we'll need it." Chase shifted his position, conscious of the immediate and sharp protest of his joints. "Ballard has things well in hand here. We might as well head back to the house."

Turning toward the pickup parked nearby, Ty sent a glance toward The Homestead. "Tara said last night that she wanted to fly back to Fort Worth early this morning. She should be just about ready to leave."

Together they crossed to the pickup. Any other time

Ty would have walked from The Homestead to the old barn, but as a concession to his father's stiffened joints, Ty had driven instead. It was a short drive up the slope to the big house that crowned the rise.

Parking in front of it, Ty climbed out the driver's side and caught the sound of a vehicle approaching from the east. The morning sun was in his eyes, and he lifted a hand to block the glare of it. The minute he spotted the light bar mounted atop the sports utility van, he guessed at the identity of its occupant even before he saw the county sheriff insignia on the side.

"It looks like Logan. I wonder what he wants."

"We'll soon find out," Chase dryly stated the obvious.

The white van pulled up alongside the pickup. The engine rumbled to a stop and Logan stepped out of the driver's side, wearing a down-filled leather jacket over the tan of his uniform. He adjusted the set of his hat, the sunlight briefly gleaming on the blue-black ends of his hair.

"Ty. Chase." He nodded to both of them and approached the steps where they waited. "I didn't expect to catch both of you home."

Something in Logan's tone of voice and the way he held himself aloof had Chase lifting his head, sharply alert. "Why do I have the feeling this isn't a social call?"

Logan dipped his head, then raised it again, a pair of dark sunglasses shielding his eyes from view. "You're right. It isn't."

"What's wrong?" Ty asked in quick demand. "Cat and Quint are all right, aren't they?"

"They're fine," Logan assured them. "No, I'm here on another matter. I started to call, then decided to come out myself. I have some news that I understand you aren't going to like, Chase."

"What's that?"

"Buck Haskell was released from prison this week."

Of all the things Logan might have said, that was the last one Chase expected to hear. Shock and surprise ripped through him, opening up the past and making fury and outrage as fresh as yesterday.

Chase's voice trembled with the force of it. "I was supposed to be notified before he was released."

"There must have been an oversight somewhere," was Logan's only explanation. "One of the deputies saw Haskell in Blue Moon yesterday. I overheard him telling someone else. When your name was mentioned, I asked some questions. Otherwise I wouldn't have known it was your late wife he attempted to kill."

"I never expected this day to come." Chase looked away, feeling older and, somehow, less in control.

The front door to The Homestead opened, and Tara emerged, her booted feet *tap-tap-tapping* across the porch's wood flooring as she walked swiftly to the steps.

"There you are, Ty. I was beginning to think I wouldn't have time to tell you goodbye before we left." She glided down the steps to his side, an ermine jacket slung about her shoulders, the white fur contrasting with the shining darkness of her hair. "Why, Logan, I didn't know you were here. Did Cat come with you?"

"No, she's at home," Logan replied.

"What a shame. I would have loved to see her, even for a few minutes." Belatedly Tara became conscious of the heavy tension in the air. Her glance made a quick and probing sweep of the trio. "My, but you are a solemn group. Is something wrong?"

"Nothing," Ty lied, trapped by his own memories of that long-ago day when he had climbed in the saddle, his head still pounding from the blow Buck had delivered to it. He could still hear his mother's voice, shouting at him to ride for help. He remembered the fear and indecision he had felt gripping him once again.

"Here comes somebody else." Tara's remark drew the attention of all three men to the pickup traveling up the lane. "This is your morning for company, Ty."

"It seems like it," he agreed and watched the vehicle as it made a swing toward The Homestead. With a growing uneasiness, he spared a glance at his father. "I don't recognize the pickup. Do you?"

"No." But like Ty, Chase watched it, every muscle in his body tightening up.

The pickup slowly rolled to a stop fifteen feet from them. For a long moment, its sole occupant remained behind the wheel while the truck's rapidly cooling engine made its noises in the morning stillness. No one said a word when Buck Haskell stepped out of the vehicle.

Chase had eyes only for the man who had once been as close as a brother to him. Age had changed Buck. His short-cropped hair had retained its curl, but its once blond color was now snow-white. His blue eyes had an old and hard look to them, minus their cocky sparkle. Gone was the big grin that once came so easily to Buck, and his skin had a prison pallor to it instead of a burned-deep range tan. There seemed to be more muscle and heft to his wiry frame than before, and his clothes were plainer than the ones he had once favored.

But his voice, when he spoke, was exactly the same. "I didn't figure you'd be surprised to see me, but I wasn't expecting this kind of reception."

"You aren't welcome here." Chase's words were hard and flat, intolerant of any argument.

"I know that," Buck acknowledged, unconcerned. "I also know that you'd be well within your rights to have your son-in-law here arrest me for trespassing. But I'll ask you not to do that."

"Why?" Chase challenged.

"Don't worry." Buck's mouth curved with a ghost of its former grin. "You already gave me a second chance once. I'm not here to ask for another."

"What do you want?"

"I served my time, Chase. Every single day of it. I'm a free man now, and there's nothing you can do about it. I've rented me a place in town, and I've come here to visit my mother's grave and fetch my father."

"That is Vern's decision to make. Not yours," Chase stated curtly. "He has a place on the Triple C as long as he wants it. He knows that."

"He don't want your charity any more than I do. But don't take my word for it. Come along and ask him yourself," Buck challenged with some of his former cockiness.

"Don't think I won't," Chase retorted. "He's an old man, Buck. We can take better care of him than you."

Buck shook his head. "You can *tend* to him better, maybe, but you won't *care* about him more than I will. He's my father, the only family I got left. Now that I'm out, his place is with me," he stated. "He wrote that he was staying with Walt and Ruby Atkins. Is he still there?"

"He is."

"Then that's where I'm going." Buck swung around and jerked open the pickup door, then paused to fire another look at Chase. "Are you coming along or not?"

"I'm coming," Chase answered grimly. "I'm not about to let you bulldoze an old man into leaving here." He shot a quick look at Ty. "I'll handle this. You go ahead and take Tara to her plane."

Logan spoke up. "Why don't you ride with me, Chase? I'll tag along just to keep things peaceable."

"Suit yourself." Changing directions, Chase headed for the patrol vehicle. He didn't expect any trouble from Buck, convinced that the man knew Chase would grab any excuse to throw him behind bars again.

Through it all, Tara had been a silent but interested observer. She gazed after the departing vehicles, trying to piece together the tidbits of information she had gleaned from the exchange, but there were too many blank spots.

"Who was that, Ty?" she asked curiously.

"Buck Haskell."

At that instant it all came together. "Ruth's son," she murmured with the certainty of knowledge.

"Yes." Ty's answer was short. Just as abruptly, he said, "Are you ready? What about your luggage?"

"It's already been taken to the plane. I'm ready if you are."

Out of habit, Ty took Tara's arm and escorted her to the truck, opening the door and giving her a hand into the cab, but he was preoccupied, his thoughts on his father and Buck Haskell.

The Atkinses lived in one of the houses the ranch provided for its married hands. Buck was waiting by the front stoop when Logan and Chase arrived at the house.

"I figured you'd want to be the one to do the knocking," Buck said by way of explanation when they joined him.

Making no response, Chase walked past him and rapped lightly on the front door. After a brief interval, Ruby Atkins opened the door, a stout woman in her early forties. She stepped back in surprise when she saw Chase,

"Mr. Calder, I didn't expect it to be you at the door." Her glance darted past him, touching on Buck and lingering an instant on Logan. "If you're looking for Walt, he's at the calving shed."

"No. We're here to see Vern," Chase stated.

"Oh." She blinked in surprise and backed out of the doorway. "Please come in. He's in his room as usual. He seems to prefer it there." She held the door open while the three men filed through, then hurried ahead of them to lead the way. "His room is right through here. Honestly, given a choice, I think Vern would stay in there all the time. But I have insisted that he join us for our meals. The minute he's finished, though, right back in the room he goes." Ruby paused outside a closed door and knocked twice. "It's me, Vern," she said and walked in.

Shriveled and old, Vern Haskell sat in a cane-backed rocking chair in the corner, his gaunt face turned toward the bedroom's only window. A space heater glowed a few feet away, raising the room's temperature to an almost suffocating eighty degrees. Yet he was bundled in a turtleneck and heavy flannel shirt with an orange and brown afghan draped over his bony legs.

Without pause, Ruby crossed directly to his chair and bent close. "Vern." She spoke in a deliberately loud voice. "Mr. Calder is here to see you."

The announcement roused him, bringing his head around to stare with vacant, cataract-clouded eyes toward the doorway. Chase moved forward as Ruby swung away from the rocker, pausing long enough to bend down and switch off the heater.

"You'll have to speak up," she warned Chase when she passed him. "He has gotten very hard of hearing."

Chase nodded and continued on to the corner. "Vern, it's Chase Calder."

The old man craned his neck back to look up at him. "What do you want?" he demanded in a crotchety tone, then waved a skeletal hand at the others. "And who's that with you? You're figurin' on cartin' me off to a nursin' home, aren't you?"

"No. I brought you a visitor," Chase began.

"Tell 'im to go away. There ain't nobody I want to see."

"You'll want to talk to this one," Chase stated and turned to motion Buck forward, but he was already on his way.

Bending, he crouched directly in front of the rocker. "Hey, Pop, it's me, Buck."

The old man rocked forward and peered intently at the white-haired man before him. "Is that really you, boy?" he demanded with wary doubt.

"It's me, Pop. White hair and all," Buck replied with a flash of his old grin. "I told you I'd come as soon as I got out."

A kind of wonder stole through the old man's expression. Reaching out, he clasped Buck's face with both hands. "It is you," he breathed the words, then released a sound that fell somewhere between a laugh and a sob. With tears shining in his eyes, he let go of Buck's face and excitedly fumbled around in his shirt pocket before he finally succeeded in pulling out a slip of folded paper. He showed it to Buck. "You wrote you would come. I've been carrying your letter with me ever since. I was afraid to hope." His voice had a quaver to it. "I just knew that sunavabitchin' Calder would find some way to keep you there. But—you're really here."

"I'm really here," Buck repeated in emphasis. "I'm a free man, Pop. I did my time and there is nothing anybody can do to send me back there."

"You're free." Tears ran down the hollows of Vern's cheeks. "If only your mother could have lived to see this."

"I know." Buck nodded then patted the old man on the knee. "Look, Pop, I rented a small little house in town, the old Kromke place. Do you remember it?"

"Yeah, I know the place."

"It isn't much, but it's big enough for the two of us. I want you to come live with me."

In answer, Vern began to frantically grope around the chair arms looking first one way then the other. "Where the hell did that damned woman hide my cane this time?"

Straightening, Buck retrieved the cane that had been hooked on the windowsill. "Here it is, Pop." He pressed it into the man's hand.

Immediately, Vern struggled to rise from the rocker, using the cane for leverage and support. "Give me a hand, will you?" he said with impatience.

As Buck assisted him to his feet, Chase spoke up. "You don't have to live with him, Vern. You are more than welcome to stay right here."

"And just why the hell would I want to do that?" Vern challenged with vehemence. "This ain't my home, and the Atkinses ain't any kin of mine. Why would I want to stay in a place where I've gotta eat when they say, and I'm not allowed to smoke or drink? She won't even let me have a chew now and again."

Made self-conscious by the criticism, Ruby defended herself, "But you can't see well enough to spit into the cup, Vern. You had tobacco juice all over the place."

Vern either didn't hear her protest or didn't care. Leaning on the cane, he took a shuffling step toward the closet. "I'll just get my clothes and we'll get out of here." He took another step then stopped to glare at Ruby. "Don't just stand there, woman. Go get me something to put my clothes in."

Hesitating, she glanced at Chase. He nodded. "If Vern wants to leave with Buck, that's his choice."

Vern's belongings were few. In less than twenty minutes, all of them were stowed in the back of Buck's used truck. Buck was the only one to thank Ruby for looking after his father. Vern never offered so much as a good-bye to any of them.

From the northeast came the rumbling roar of a plane taking off, its engines at full power. The noise of it masked the sound of Buck's pickup when it pulled away from the house. Chase lingered long enough to express his own gratitude to Ruby for the care she had given Vern, then rode back to The Homestead with Logan.

"That went smoothly," Logan remarked.

"I didn't expect any trouble," Chase replied grimly. "Buck is smarter than that. If you can, keep an eye on him."

"I will."

Ty stood by the desk in the den, sifting through the stack of morning mail, when Chase walked in. He looked up, running a searching glance over his father's face.

"How did it go?"

"Vern left with him." That closed the subject as far as Chase was concerned.

"Maybe that's best," Ty said as Chase walked around the desk and sat down in the big chair. "Logan left, did he?"

Chase nodded. "I invited him in for coffee, but he said he had a mountain of paperwork waiting for him. Anything in the mail?"

"Bills mostly." Ty resumed sorting through it, then paused when he came across an envelope bearing the return address of the federal government. "Here's one from the BLM." He idly passed it to his father. "I asked Sally to bring us some coffee."

"Good. I could use some." Chase tore open the flap and pulled the letter out of its envelope as approaching footsteps echoed from the outer hallway.

It was Jessy, not Sally, who walked into the den, carrying a tray with an insulated coffee carafe and three cups. "Who wants coffee?" she said brightly and set the tray on the occasional table between the two wing-backed leather chairs in front of the desk.

Ty glanced at the three cups. "Are you joining us?"

"Actually the third cup was for Logan, but—since he's not here—I thought I would have a cup with you." Jessy proceeded to fill all three cups.

"What the hell!" The near roar of outrage from Chase whipped Ty's attention back to him.

"What's wrong?"

Chase looked up from the letter in his hand, eyes blazing. "They revoked our grazing permit. We have three days to remove all our livestock. Here. Read it for yourself." He shoved the letter to Ty and picked up the phone, angrily punching in a series of numbers.

The coffee forgotten, Jessy was at Ty's side in an instant, needing to see the words for herself. There they were, plain and blunt and final.

"They can't do this," Jessy murmured.

"The government can do anything it damn well pleases," Ty replied, the anger in his voice tightly leashed.

"But—why?" Jessy frowned in confusion. "Why would they do it after all these years?"

Behind the desk, Chase spoke into the phone, his voice hard and clipped. "Get me Justin Farnsworth." After a small pause, he erupted, "I don't give a damn if he's in a meeting. You tell him Chase Calder is on the line. I need to talk to him, and I need to talk to him now!"

Distracted by the contents of the letter, none of them heard the front door open or the approaching thud of booted feet. Not until Ballard walked into the den did they become aware of his presence in the house.

"There you are, Ty," he said. "I'm glad I caught you before you headed to the calving sheds. You never told me what you decided about using a concrete stain on the floor. If you're—"

"Later," Ty abruptly cut across his words. "I'm tied up right now. Before I leave, I'll swing by the barn and go over it with you."

Darting one quick glance at Chase's grim face with the phone to his ear, Ballard immediately picked up on the room's charged atmosphere and nodded, backing toward the door. "I'll talk to you then."

"Wait. There was a phone call for you early this morning," Jessy remembered and retrieved the message slip from the desk. Taking it to him, she explained, "It's from the supplier of the light fixtures that were back-ordered."

"Justin. It's Chase Calder here," Chase said behind her, finally making the connection with the lawyer.

Jessy smoothly steered Ballard out of the den. "The supplier promised that the shipment would go out yet this week. We should have it by the first of next week at the latest."

"We better." Ballard glanced briefly at the message before tucking it in his shirt pocket. "Until they get here, the electrician is pretty much at a standstill."

"I know." Jessy kept walking, escorting him to the front door.

Ballard lagged a bit and threw a glance over his shoulder when he caught the sound of Chase Calder's raised voice. "It sounds like somebody is on the receiving end of a chewin' out from the Old Man. It takes a helluva lot to make him blow, which tells me there's some big trouble somewhere."

Jessy felt the curious probe of his gaze and knew Ballard had an ear tuned to the one-sided telephone conversation coming from the den. She had little doubt that he had gleaned enough from it to make an accurate guess. And with the order contained on the letter, to remove any and all livestock within three days, its contents would soon become common knowledge of necessity.

"We lost the grazing lease on Wolf Meadow," Jessy admitted. "We have three days to remove all our cattle."

"Three days," Ballard repeated, then whistled softly. "There's something like ten thousand acres in that chunk, isn't there?"

"That's right."

"That'll take some doin' to comb that much country in only three days," Ballard mused aloud. "A lot of it will have to be done from the air."

"More than likely," Jessy agreed.

Even if Chase was eventually successful in getting the order rescinded and the grazing permit reinstated, it was highly unlikely he could accomplish it within the three-day deadline. And a failure to remove their livestock within that time frame would result in the imposition of stiff fines for every day they failed to comply with the order. Payment of the fines would be demanded, regardless of the final outcome. She stood by the front door, the full ramifications of the letter sinking in.

"Say," Ballard began, his forehead creasing in a thoughtful frown. "Isn't that the same piece of land Dy-Corp had its hands on a few years ago?"

"Yes, but Dyson relinquished all rights to it a long time ago."

"Maybe he did, but now that he's dead, that's not to say that whoever heads up his company now didn't decide to grab control of it again. And there was a time when they wanted the coal under it pretty bad."

His suggestion stunned Jessy into a protest. "They wouldn't."

"Why?" Ballard countered with a scoffing tone. "Because of what happened the last time? Corporations don't have a conscience, not where money and profits are concerned. And there's a lot of both to be made from all the coal under that ground."

Jessy stiffened, horror stricken by the thought of that rich grassland being ripped open by bulldozers to expose the coal beneath it, destroying its productiveness forever, leaving it scarred and ugly.

"Good god, Jessy, you're white as a sheet." Ballard gripped her shoulders as if expecting her to crumble any second.

Lowering her head, she gave it a small shake to dismiss his concern while she struggled to throw off the sick fear that gripped her. "I'm all right."

He bent his head, trying to get a look at her face. "You don't look all right."

"They can't be allowed to get their hands on that land," Jessy said with the force of conviction.

"Hey." He crooked a finger under her chin and lifted it, his mouth curved in a coaxing smile. "I never said they would succeed. We both know the Old Man would fight that to his last breath."

"Take your hands off my wife." Ty's ominously low voice sliced between them like a knife.

Ballard stepped back in surprise, his hands automatically falling away from her when Jessy turned to stare at Ty. She was stunned by the look of icy rage in his expression.

"Ty, it's not what you're thinking," she began.

But he didn't allow her to finish. "If it was, Ballard would never set foot again on the Triple C," he stated and shifted his gaze to Ballard. "You have work to do. Go get it done."

For a long, cool second, Ballard held his gaze. "You're makin' a mistake, Calder," he said easily. "But I reckon you'll find that out for yourself."

Stepping past Jessy, he went out the door, pulling it

closed behind him. She waited until she heard the *clump* of his boots on the front steps, then let her own temper fly.

"Don't you ever do that again, Ty Calder!"

Ty came right back with equal heat. "If you think for one minute that I am going to stand by and watch while that Romeo puts his hands all over my wife, you can think again!"

"You don't own me." Jessy's voice vibrated with anger. "I am your wife, not one of your possessions. I am the only one who has the right to say who touches me, and who doesn't! You better remember that."

"And you better remember that I run this ranch and the people who work on it," Ty fired right back. "I decide what behavior is acceptable and what isn't. Ballard was out of line."

"You are the only one who is out of line here."

When she started past him, Ty caught her arm. "Dammit, Jessy—"

"Let go of me." The demand was calmly voiced, but as determined as the look Jessy gave him.

Male pride wouldn't allow him to release her. Instead, Ty turned Jessy toward him, catching hold of her arm. "What are we arguing about anyway?" he demanded in exasperation.

"This isn't an argument. It's a fight. And you started it."

"Dammit, Jessy, I don't want to quarrel with you. I had enough of that with Tara."

But that was the wrong thing to say. New sparks snapped in Jessy's eyes. "Don't you ever compare me with Tara."

"You couldn't be less like her if you tried," Ty replied. "But understand this, Jessy—I can't and I won't apologize for what I said to Ballard. You think I was too harsh.

Maybe I was." That was the only concession he was prepared to make. "But we have enough problems right now. This isn't the time for there to be trouble between us."

"I suppose you expect me to simply overlook it."

His gaze narrowed at the heat that remained in her voice. "I don't expect anything." Ty could see there was no reasoning with her when she had her back up. He left her standing there and walked to the front door.

Irritated that he had left with nothing finished between them, Jessy demanded, "Just where are you going?"

He paused in the doorway and turned back, his tall broad-shouldered frame filling the opening, his expression hard and unrelenting. "I don't have time to stand around and thrash this out with you. In case you forgot, we have cattle to move and not much time to do it in. It will take every hand I can spare from the calving sheds and then some. That includes you. So you better give your mother a call and see if she can help Sally look after the twins for the next few days."

His statement left no room for protest, which perversely angered Jessy all the more. Pivoting on her heel, she stalked to the telephone in the living room as Ty closed the door behind him.

Neither mentioned the incident again. But it simmered between them, unspoken and unresolved.

Chapter Nine

~~~

The area known as Wolf Meadow had a large stretch of broken country, crowned with flat tablelands and riven with wide coulees. In every direction it sprawled, vast and primitive, in endlessly stretching miles of more of the same.

A red-and-white Cessna aircraft swooped low to the ground, flushing a pair of cows with calves from their hiding place. Spooked by the low-flying plane, they bolted into the open, tails high. The minute they saw the waiting riders, they swerved.

Closest to them, Jessy reined her tired horse after them, spurring it into a gallop. She chased them for nearly a quarter of a mile before she succeeded in turning them. Once the little group was headed toward the bunch that had already been gathered, her weary horse slowed to a rough trot that jarred every bone in her body.

It had been over two years since Jessy had spent this

many hours in the saddle. She was out of shape; every stiff and sore muscle in her body attested to it.

To her relief, the sun hung low in the western sky, its rays already painting the undersides of the scattered clouds with a fuchsia brush. Soon it would be too dark to continue the search for more cattle. There was just enough daylight to get this bunch to the holding pens that were better than a mile distant.

When she reached the small herd, Jessy took up her former flanking position and called to the other two riders, "Let's take these home."

High overhead, the Cessna flew by and wagged its wings in a signal that it was heading to the landing strip. Jessy watched it with a trace of envy, knowing it would reach the headquarters long before she would. As beat as she was, the end of the day couldn't come soon enough.

When they topped the last rise and finally saw the portable holding pens near the fence line, the setting sun bathed the entire scene in a golden light, giving it the look of an old tintype. But Jessy was too tired to admire the picture it made.

As soon as they had driven their cattle into the first pen, Jessy peeled away to head for the picket line. Her legs felt a little rubbery when she dismounted. She blocked it out and loosened the cinch on her saddle, then rubbed down her horse.

Convinced that a jolt of range coffee would revive her, she headed for the cookshack. As she neared it, seven-year-old Quint came running up, displaying a great deal more energy than Jessy possessed.

"Hi, Aunt Jessy. I saw you ride in," he told her, his gray eyes shining with excitement. "I've been helping with the roundup."

"You have?"

"Yup. Grandpa said I did a good job, too."

"Is he here?" Jessy scanned the handful of riders gathered around the cookshack. She spotted Cat by the coffeepot, but there was no sign of Chase.

"He's over by the pens." Quint flung an arm in their direction. "They're getting ready to load some more cattle."

As if on cue, Jessy heard the rumble of a diesel engine, the *whoosh* of air brakes, and the grind of shifting gears as a semi maneuvered its slatted stock trailer up to the loading chute. But her attention was on the cup of coffee Cat extended toward her.

"You look like you could use this," Cat said.

"It shows, does it?" Jessy wasted no time taking a quick sip of the strong brew.

"Not really," Cat replied. "But I figured you had to be as tired as I am."

"I'm so tired I'm dragging." Which was something Jessy would never have admitted to a man.

"A good long soak in the tub is what we both need. You can tell that brother of mine he owes me a massage and a manicure for drafting me into this."

"I'll tell him," Jessy promised.

"Whoops, there's Logan." Looking past her, Cat waved at the patrol vehicle that had pulled up along the roadside. "Come on, Quint. Your dad is here. It's time to go home."

"I'll see you tomorrow," Jessy said.

Cat grimaced wryly. "Let's don't think about tomorrow until it gets here."

"I'll drink to that." Jessy lifted her tin cup in a mock toast and called a goodbye to Quint when he raced off to meet his father.

Convinced that her muscles would stiffen into stone if she didn't keep moving, Jessy made her way to the pens and joined Chase by the loading chute. Cup in hand, she propped a foot on the lower rail.

"How's it going?" she asked.

Chase acknowledged her presence with a sideways glance, then brought his attention back to the work at hand as the first cow reluctantly clattered up the chute and balked at the entrance to the trailer. "Better than I expected."

"We only have one day left. Are we going to make it?"

"With luck, we should."

Crowded from behind, the first cow was forced into the trailer. The others followed, lowing in protest. "Where are you taking this bunch?"

"Back to headquarters for the time being," Chase replied. "South Branch was able to handle only another fifty head. Broken Butte is already at capacity. Trumbo is checking the Lone Tree range to see if it can handle any more cattle. If we're lucky, we can scatter another twenty or thirty head around the ranch, but that's about it. The majority we'll have to hold at headquarters until we find out whether we'll get the grazing permit reinstated."

"What are the lawyers saying?"

"They claim to be as surprised as we are by all this, and insist they didn't see it coming." The grimness in his voice didn't entirely mask its underlying note of anger.

"Have you heard anything more from them?"

Chase leaned on the top rail, his big hands folded together. "Farnsworth called this morning. So far, all their inquiries have been met with a wall of silence. They haven't found anybody who will admit to knowing anything about the government's decision."

"Then we still don't know why it was done," Jessy murmured thoughtfully.

"I don't give a good goddamn why it was done." The low-voiced words fairly exploded from him. "I just want the rights to this land back. We can't hold all these cattle at headquarters forever. If we don't get the land back soon, we won't have any choice but to sell them." His hands clenched tightly together, knuckles showing white. "Dammit, we need this land, Jessy. We get more hay out of these coulees than we get from all the rest of the ranch combined. Even more than the hay, we need the water from it. I can't remember a single time when any of its wells went dry, not even during the worst droughts. Losing this land cripples our entire operation."

For the first time, Jessy felt a clutch of fear. "Ballard thinks Dy-Corp might be behind this." Which was something she hadn't mentioned until that moment.

"That possibility already crossed my mind." When the last cow was prodded into the trailer, Chase pushed off the rail and hollered to one of the hands, "All right, close it up and take 'em home. I'll meet you there." To Jessy, he said, "Ty is still out there somewhere. You might as well ride home with me."

Aching from head to foot, Jessy walked into The Homestead and headed straight for the stairs. The house seemed unnaturally silent. She was halfway up the steps when she met Sally on her way down. At that instant, Jessy knew why it seemed so quiet.

"Where are the twins?"

"Your mother, bless her heart, decided they should spend the night with her. She knew you would be late getting home, and tired as well."

"She was right on both counts."

"Did Chase and Ty come with you?" Sally glanced downstairs expectantly.

"Chase is down at the corrals getting the cattle unloaded. Ty was still at Wolf Meadow when we left." Grabbing hold of the smooth banister, Jessy started hauling herself up the steps again. "You better not plan on dinner for at least another hour. I'm going to go climb in the tub. If I'm not down in an hour, you'd better check to make sure I didn't fall asleep and drown."

Entering the master bedroom, Jessy swept off her hat, hooked it on a corner of a chair back, paused long enough to unbuckle her spurs, then crossed directly to the master bath. She filled the tub with water, hot as she could stand, stripped to the skin, piled her hair atop her head, and climbed into the tub.

A groan of pure pleasure slipped from her throat as the water's heat flowed over and around her. Eyes closed, she stretched out full length and let it work its magic on her sore muscles. For the time being Jessy was content simply to soak and enjoy. There was time enough later to think about scrubbing away the day's grime.

Distantly she heard a door open somewhere, but the sound didn't really register. Nothing did but the relaxing warmth of the bath.

Something, perhaps the sensation of being watched, prompted Jessy to open her eyes and send a heavy-lidded look at the bedroom door.

Ty stood motionless in the doorway, lines of tiredness etched across his strong-boned features, his expression unreadable. His hat was off, and his dark hair showed the rake of combing fingers. But it was the darkness of his eyes that held her attention, their depths impenetrable as their gaze made a slow survey of her nude length, easily visible beneath the clear bath water.

Made oddly uncomfortable by the look, Jessy sat up, breaking eye contact as she reached for the loofah sponge and bar of soap and began the task of lathering herself down.

"The shower is all yours." Her sideways glance bounced

off his face, but not before she saw his mouth quirk at that familiar angle. Only this time there was a coldness to it.

It matched the hard edge in his voice when he spoke. "Don't worry. I have no intention of dragging you out of the tub and throwing you on the bed." He pushed out of the doorway, long impatient strides carrying him across the bathroom to the shower area. His hands jerked his shirttail loose and made fast work of the buttoned front as he went. "The thought crossed my mind, but you made damned sure it didn't take root."

Startled by the accusation, Jessy whirled in the tub, the sudden movement sloshing the water against the sides. "What?"

"The shower is all yours," Ty mimicked in sarcasm and shrugged out of his shirt, wadded it into a ball, and threw it toward the hamper. "That's a surefire way to get the message across that you're not interested in any lovemaking." He sat down on the velvet-cushioned vanity bench, a holdover from Tara's days, and began tugging off his boots, dropping them to the floor. "I ought to know. Tara was an expert at it."

Infuriated, Jessy demanded, "Stop comparing me with her!" All interest in the relaxing bath was gone. She rose to her feet and climbed out of the tub, snatching an oversized bath towel off its bar and wrapping it around her.

"It must be something you women learn at birth," Ty grumbled and tossed his socks after his shirt, then stood to unbuckle his belt.

"That is ridiculous." As far as Jessy was concerned, this entire conversation was ridiculous. And she wanted no more of it. Mindless of the water still dripping from her, she started for the bedroom.

"Leaving, are you?" Ty's mouth twisted with grim

amusement. "That's another female trick. When the conversation takes a turn you don't like, you just walk out."

She spun back to face him. "You are clearly aching for a fight. Keep it up and you'll get one."

That had the ring of a threat. A Calder had never backed down from a fight, and Ty wasn't about to be the first. In two strides, he crossed the space between them and caught her up. Jessy immediately pushed against his chest in hard resistance. Angered by it, Ty ground his mouth across hers, the clipped ends of his mustache scraping her skin. She fought him, but she was no match for his strength. They both knew it.

There was no letup in his demand. He wanted her with a kind of desperation even he didn't understand. He molded her closer and felt her indecision, the wanting and not wanting of his kiss.

When she ceased her struggles, he rolled his mouth from hers and lifted his head to view her up-turned face. In her eyes were the first stirrings of desire, but they were still mixed with the heat of anger.

A dozen protests lay unspoken in her throat, each of them sounding too much like what Tara would have said. That galled Jessy even more.

"Sometimes I hate you, Ty Calder." She pushed the words through her teeth.

A sudden softness warmed his eyes. "You told me that once before," Ty remembered. "At the old Stanton cabin."

That time their angry fight had ended in fierce lovemaking. She recalled it, too. He could see it in her eyes, feel it in the lessening of tension in her body. When he lowered his mouth to hers a second time, she kissed him back with a driving hunger that matched his own.

Ty scooped her up, towel and all, and carried her into the bedroom. Unceremoniously he dropped her on the bed. The loosely tucked towel fell open, revealing every inch of her slim length, still glistening with dampness. With a swiftness that belied his earlier fatigue, he stripped off his jeans and shorts, and sank a knee onto the bed, lowering himself onto it.

Her hands were already reaching for him, avid in their need to reassert a closeness. Ty needed no urging. His hands slid over her, finding and cupping her small but highly sensitive breasts. He swallowed the sound of pleasure that came from her throat and nibbled his way along the long curve of her neck. She smelled of soap and all things earthy and strong. It swirled around him, primitive and potent.

Over the years, he had learned all the places that drove her wild. He explored them again, resisting the urgent press of her hands before finally stretching her arms above her head and slipping into her.

There was nothing between them. It was skin to skin, flesh to flesh, and need to need. This coupling between man and wife was old as time and new as tomorrow, full of heat and building pressure as they each strained for release, their bodies bucking in harmony when it came.

Jessy lay tucked along Ty's side, her head pillowed on a shoulder, one leg draped over his muscled thigh. A liquid contentment flowed through her, leaving her feeling all limp and satisfied. She idly slid her fingers into his wiry chest hair, conscious of the slowing *thud* of his heart.

"I'm glad you threw me on the bed," she murmured.

"Enjoyed it, did you?" His voice emanated from someplace deep inside. She felt the vibrations of it beneath her hand.

Jessy lifted her head and turned to look at him, resting the point of her chin on his shoulder. "Something tells me you made very sure I would." A small, pleased smile touched her lips that he would care that much.

Ty shifted slightly to study to her face, noting the after-effect of their lovemaking visible in her kiss-swollen lips, the lack of tension in her face muscles and the sated look in her heavy-lidded eyes. He took great male satisfaction in knowing he had put them there, not some other man.

It was a simple leap from that thought to the next. "Ballard could never make you feel like that."

In that split second, all the good feelings were gone. Jessy rolled away and slipped off the opposite side of the bed.

"For your information, he will never have the chance," she replied in a hard, flat voice then stalked to the tall bureau and began jerking open drawers.

Ty's reaction was instant and firmly grim. "You're damned right he won't." He levered up on an elbow.

"As if you have any say in it," Jessy muttered, irritated, not for the first time, by such a possessive male attitude. "What is it going to take to get it through that thick head of yours that Ballard is simply a friend." Jessy snatched up a set of underclothes and began tugging them on. "I have known him almost as long as I've known you."

"Calders don't have friends." Ty sat up. "If you need proof, ask my father about Buck Haskell."

"And just what category do you put Tara in?" In bra and panties, Jessy pulled a pair of jeans and a sweater out of the closet.

"It is strictly business between us," Ty snapped the retort.

"No doubt that's the reason she calls you 'darling' all the time," Jessy mocked.

"Dammit, you know that is just Tara's way."

"And maybe it's just Ballard's way to be kind and considerate." She pulled on her jeans one leg at a time and tugged them over her slim hips.

"Ballard is a woman chaser. That's why he hangs around you every chance he gets."

With both arms in the sweater sleeves, Jessy paused before pulling it over her head. "In all honesty, I can't call Tara a man chaser. But by your definition, she's a Ty chaser. She hangs around you all the time."

Ty stood up and snatched the oversized towel off the bed and wrapped it around his middle. "I told you, it's business with Tara. We're not talking about her anyway."

"And my dealings with Ballard are business." Jessy yanked the sweater down around her waist. "But you choose to forget that. And let's definitely not bring Tara in this. If we did, you might have to admit that a double standard is being applied here."

"The circumstances are different, and you know it. I don't trust Ballard."

"Then that makes us even," Jessy retorted. "Because I don't trust Tara."

"Tara has her faults. At times, she can be thoughtless, self-centered, and spoiled, but she isn't mean-spirited or vindictive."

"Which shows how much you know about women. I would sooner trust a cornered rattler than Tara. At least a rattler will give you some warning before it strikes." Jessy shoved a foot into a boot and stomped it into position. "With Ballard, the worst he'll do is make a pass. And if he does, I guarantee you he'll be walking around hunched over and spraddle-legged for a week." As soon as the second boot was on, she headed for the door. "You still need that shower. You'd better go take one. I'm going downstairs and give Sally a hand with dinner."

Grim-lipped, Ty stared after her. "Meek" had never been an adjective that described Jessy. But "stubborn" was proving to be very accurate. She was a fool to think Ballard was harmless. No man was harmless. And no woman, for that matter.

Yet Ty couldn't help thinking that there was one name they hadn't discussed—Buck Haskell. Ty had a nagging feeling that Buck wasn't about to fade into the background. They would be hearing from him again.

Dust swirled about the stock pens at the Triple C headquarters, kicked up by milling cattle, bawling in confusion. Their noise was underscored by the clatter of cloven hooves as animals were prodded up the wooden chute and into the slat-sided stock trailer. The curses and shouts from those on the ground and on horseback added to the racket.

In the midst of it all, a photographer and his assistant darted about, seeking the right angle and lighting for the shots they wanted, and further spooking the range-wild cattle in the process. Watching it all from his perch on the top rail, Ty kept his mouth shut with difficulty. For two cents, he would yank them out of the pen, shove them in their car, and tell them to get the hell down the road.

A pair of small white hands gripped the rail next to his leg. He glanced down as Tara pulled herself up to lean against the top rail, her arm brushing against his leg.

"How is the photo shoot going?" She scanned the pen to locate the photographers.

"Don't ask," Ty replied as the photographer knelt in the middle of the stock pen, his camera aimed at a horse and rider working hard to turn a bunch of cattle toward the chute. The same cattle the photographer had just scattered. "These cattle should have been loaded and gone an hour ago."

"It will be worth it," Tara stated confidently. "A feature article with photographs—that's free publicity."

"That's why I haven't kicked them out of here yet. But they'll be damned lucky if they don't get roped and hog-tied by one of the ranch hands."

"As soon as they get the shots they want of this, they will be all finished."

"It can't come soon enough."

"Oh, I almost forgot. Chase wants you at the house. He's closeted in the den with those lawyers."

Ty frowned in surprise. "They're here?"

Tara nodded. "Their plane landed a few minutes ago."

"Keep an eye on those two. If you can hurry them along, do it," he said and vaulted to the ground.

He signaled to Art Trumbo that he was in charge, then struck out for The Homestead. The brim of his hat shielded his eyes from the morning sun, sitting midway up in the sky. For the first of April, the temperature was unseasonably mild. But Ty was too preoccupied to notice, his thoughts already centering on the coming meeting with the lawyers.

Any hope that they might have arrived with good news died the minute he entered the den and saw the professional masks they wore, serious and businesslike, projecting an aura of competence. He shook hands all around and endured the jovial backslap from the blustery Justin Farnsworth, dressed as always more like a cattleman in cowboy boots and a flashy bolo tie. But his interest was piqued by the presence of Ed Talbot in the group, a former police detective and crack investigator.

Convinced the lawyers had arrived with some news, Ty walked over to the side table and poured himself a cup of coffee. Farnsworth resumed his seat in the wing-backed chair facing the desk.

"Chase was just telling me that you are shipping the cattle off to market," Farnsworth remarked, settling back in the chair and assuming an attitude of ease. "That is probably best."

Cup in hand, Ty hooked a leg over a corner of the desk and leaned on it. "What have you found out about the land?"

The investigator studied the steer horns mounted above the mantel, saying nothing and looking for all the world like an accountant. It was Farnsworth who answered Ty's question.

"It's just as we suspected. The environmentalists appear to be behind this one. I don't have to tell you how strong their lobby has become these last few years." He waved a hand in Chase's direction. "Save the trees. Save the whales. Save the snail darter. They are always hot to save something."

"And now they want to save my land, is that what you're telling me?" Chase rocked back in the big swivel chair, his hard gaze fixed on the lawyer.

With a politician's deftness, Farnsworth neither confirmed nor denied it. "You heard the hue and cry they raised about the damage done by cattle grazing in the national forest lands. It doesn't seem to matter to them that a hundred years ago herds of buffalo, numbering in the millions, used to roam the same land. Or that the herds of wild horses that they are so determined to see run free do more damage than cattle. And horses aren't even a species indigenous to this continent. But that is neither here nor there," he admitted. "Now, they have turned their attention to grass. Native grass, like the kind growing on your land. They have decided it needs to be protected, too."

"From whom? Certainly not from us. Calders have taken care of this land for well over a century now. Do you see that map on the wall behind me?" Chase jerked a thumb toward it. "There is native grass still growing on all of it."

"I'm sure there is." Farnsworth nodded his head. "Are you saying the government plans to set aside that land as a nature preserve?" Ty asked, trying to cut through the rhetoric.

"Something of that sort seems to be afoot," the lawyer confirmed.

"That is the stupidest thing I ever heard." Chase's voice was thick with disgust. "Nature never intended grass to grow untouched. It was meant to be cut by grazing animals, cropped close to stimulate more growth. The damage comes from overgrazing."

"I quite agree with you. And I don't know of a single rancher who wouldn't."

"How can we stop this?" Ty asked.

"That's what we are trying to figure out. You see, there appears to be a slight problem." Farnsworth slid a brief glance at the investigator.

"What's the problem?" Ty directed his question to Talbot.

At a nod from Farnsworth, Talbot replied, "It seems the government no longer holds title to the land."

Chapter Ten

〜

Stunned, Ty came to his feet as Chase shot forward in his chair. "Seemed?" Chase pounced on the word. "Either they own it or they don't. Which way is it?"

"They don't," Talbot confirmed with obvious regret.

"Who does?" Ty watched the man with narrowed eyes.

"It's Dy-Corp, isn't it?" Chase guessed, then glared at the lawyer. "Environmentalists, my eye. It's not the grass. It's the coal they're after. I warned you to watch out for them."

"I know you did." Farnsworth's glance fell under the weight of Chase's hard look. "But we can't say for certain that Dy-Corp is behind this. You explain, Talbot."

Once again the investigator was the cynosure of all eyes. "I can tell you that title to the land is held by a Delaware corporation called Montana, Inc. Its sole stockholder is another corporation. Its name is unimportant since it is also owned by another company. So far, I have followed the ownership trail through five corporations. The last one is an offshore company by the name of

Arateel. And I haven't been able to bribe, steal, or strong-arm a single piece of information from anyone." He paused and cast a considering glance over both Ty and Chase. "It has been like trying to find your way through an elaborate maze. Someone has gone to a lot of trouble to conceal his identity."

"It has to be Dy-Corp," Chase concluded grimly.

"It could be," Talbot conceded. "But why? What would be the point? I can't tell you that Dy-Corp isn't at the bottom of this, but my gut says they aren't."

Ty studied the man, convinced his opinion was based on more than just instinct. "Who do you suspect is behind this? And why is Farnsworth so certain it's an environmental group?"

"To answer that, let me tell you what we do know," Talbot began. "One of the companies in the corporate trail appears to be a philanthropic organization with a past history of purchasing other property for preservation purposes. According to a secretary for one of the more influential environmental lobbyists in Washington, a representative from that particular company met with her boss. After the representative left, her boss asked for a detailed map of Montana and told her to gather all the information they had on virgin prairies. A few days later, a hefty check arrived in the mail. That set in motion a bunch of high-level meetings. Shortly after that, you received official notice of the government's decision not to renew your grazing permit." His mouth twisted in a smile without humor. "This is one of those cases where, if it looks like a rat, walks like a rat, and smells like a rat, it has to be a rat. Can I prove the connection? No. But I can see it as clearly as I see my own hand."

Farnsworth shifted in his chair, the movement drawing focus to him. "In my mind, the information Ed uncovered explains how and why your particular acreage was singled out. I grant you other ranchers have recently had difficulties obtaining permits for land they have grazed their stock on for years. Invariably, however, it has been in areas already set aside as national forest land or something similar. Your land has never been given any such designation."

"But it isn't my land anymore, is it?" Chase leaned back in his chair, his gaze hard with challenge.

"Regrettably no." Farnsworth dipped his head in acknowledgment.

"And you can't tell me who owns it other than some corporation called—" Unable to come up with the name, Chase looked to Talbot.

The investigator supplied it. "Arateel."

"Whoever the hell that is," Chase grumbled in disgust.

"In our opinion, Chase," the lawyer began, both elbows propped on their respective armrests, his fingers steepled in front of him, "given the connection to the environmentalists, it seems highly likely that the new owner or owners intend to leave the land untouched. What else can they do?" He opened his hands, palms up. "The property is completely landlocked by yours. Assuming you are correct and Dy-Corp is somehow behind this, what good would the land be to them? I don't care how rich the coal deposit might be. They have no way to get their machinery in or the coal out. And you are under no legal obligation to grant access to it."

"That is all well and good, but it doesn't change the fact that we don't own the land," Ty stated and glanced to the window as a diesel truck, stock trailer in tow, rolled toward the lane, the muffled rumble of its cranking motor penetrating into the house. "Do you see that semi out there? It's loaded with three-, four-, and five-year-old cows, each capable of producing a calf every spring for the next ten years and more. Do you have any idea how much money that represents in lost revenue? We need that land. We need its water and its hay as well as its grass. Without it, we will probably have to cut back our operation even more."

"It has been a critical loss, I know, even for a ranch this size," the lawyer began.

"That's a major understatement, Farnsworth," Chase declared.

"Of course. But as crippling as this loss may be right now, I believe it can ultimately work to your benefit." Farnsworth leaned forward, determined to put a positive spin on the situation. "You know the hell we have been through these last few years trying to deal with the government. Now the property is in private hands. As soon as we can identify the new owner, we can begin negotiations—preferably for the purchase of it, or at the very least, a lease."

"How long will that take?" Ty wanted to know.

"It is difficult to say. Talbot has three of his associates working on it right now. We may not get the answer tomorrow or next week, but hopefully it will come soon. Isn't that right, Ed?"

"Nothing stays a secret forever," Talbot replied. "Sooner or later we will ask the right person or grease the right palm, and we will learn who is behind the corporation. Once we have a name, tracking that individual down will be a snap."

The minute Talbot finished, Farnsworth spoke up again. "Obviously, we would have preferred to come here armed with that information. But when it became apparent that it wasn't likely to be forthcoming in the next few days, we realized that we needed to apprise you about the turn of events. Given the unexpectedness of them, we felt we should tell you in person rather than over the telephone, even though we couldn't fill in all the blanks."

Talbot raised his cup. "Is there any coffee left?" His question signaled an end to any further information. The conversation reverted to a rehash of facts and supposition, and exploration of their options.

Tara sailed into the house, the denim collar of her silver-studded jacket turned up about her neck. As she passed the door to the den, she caught the hum of male voices coming from within. Her mouth curved in a feline smile of satisfaction. She continued without pause through the living room, heading toward the sound of banging pots.

The smile was still in place when she walked into the kitchen and paused at the sight of the twins. Armed with a wooden spoon, Trey pounded on an aluminum pot with relish while Laura scowled furiously at him. Jessy was at the sink, washing up some baking dishes, and Sally was bent over the oven's open door, where the aroma of freshly baked cookies emanated.

"Who is making all this racket?" Tara chided in a playful voice.

Laura let out a squeal of delight and made a beeline straight for her, toddling as fast as her young legs could carry her. "Tatie, Tatie, Tatie," she cried, which was the closest she could come to saying Tara's name, and stretched her arms out to Tara.

Laughing, Tara scooped her up. "How's my favorite little girl?"

Laura flashed her a big smile and immediately transferred her attention to the shiny silver studs that adorned Tara's jacket. After a short pause, Trey resumed his drumming practice.

Still holding Laura, Tara crossed to the sink. "How on earth do you two hear yourselves think?" she asked, raising her voice to make herself heard above the banging.

An absent smile played across Jessy's mouth. "You learn to tune it out." She rinsed a mixing bowl under the tap water and set it on the rack to drain. "Have the photographers left?"

"They are loading the last of their equipment now. Do you mind if I borrow one of your vehicles? I have a couple of errands I need to run in town, and the ranch-hands talked so much about Blue Moon that the photographer wants to see it. I told them they could follow me into town."

"Sure. The keys to the Blazer are on the hook by the back door." Jessy nodded toward them, her hands once more immersed in dishwater.

"Thanks." Tara set Laura on the floor. Immediately the toddler scrunched her face and opened her mouth to hiccough out the first sob. Tara patted her blond curls. "Don't worry, sweetie. I'll be back in a couple hours," she told her, then turned to Sally. "I'll grab a bite in town, so don't bother to set a place for me at lunch. Is there anything you need from Fedderson's while I'm there?"

Sally frowned thoughtfully, then shook her head. "I can't think of anything," she said then reconsidered. "Although you might see if they have any fresh strawberries. Shortcake for dessert tonight would be a nice change."

"Will two quarts be enough?" Tara plucked the set of keys off its hook.

"Plenty," Sally assured her.

With a wave, Tara went out the back door. Young Trey didn't bother to look up as Laura wailed a protest and toddled to the back door.

A steady stream of dump trucks, loaded with coal, rolled past the mine office. A fine black dust sooted the building's windows and metal siding. More of it darkened the vehicles parked in the lot next to it. Buck Haskell parked his truck in a slot marked for visitors. He wasn't sure that he exactly qualified as a visitor, but it was the closest to the front door.

Conscious of the nervous churning in his stomach, Buck climbed out of the pickup, tucked his shirttail a little deeper inside his jeans, and made the long walk to the door. As he opened it, another truck rumbled past, kicking up a fresh swirl of road dust and soot.

The receptionist looked up when he entered. Like nearly everybody in Blue Moon, she was a stranger to him. But that didn't ease his tension any.

"May I help you?"

Buck opened his mouth to answer, but his throat locked up. After all the years he had spent in prison, it angered him that a mere slip of a woman could scare him into silence.

Buck tried again. "I'm here to see a Mr. . . . uh—" For a split second, he blanked on the name. Then it came to him. "Mr. Daigle."

"And this is in regard to what?"

"A job interview." His palms felt sweaty. Buck buried them in the pockets of his tan windbreaker.

"And you want to see Mr. Daigle?" She eyed him in surprise.

He faltered a second then insisted gruffly, "That's the name he gave me when he called for me to come in."

Clearly skeptical, she picked up the phone. "Let me check," she said, then paused, her fingers above the buttons. "And your name is?"

"Haskell. Buck Haskell."

"Just a moment." She punched in a number, waited, then slid a look at Buck and said into the mouthpiece, "There is a Mr. Haskell here. He says he has an appointment with you." She shot Buck another look and nodded. "Of course. I'll send him right in. He's expecting you," she said to Buck as she hung up the phone. "Down that hall, the second door on your right."

Nodding his thanks, Buck moved away from the desk and started down the hall. As he approached the door, he felt his throat tightening up again and swallowed nervously.

The door opened before he reached it. A burly man in shirtsleeves and a tie stepped out, his mouth curved in a polite smile of inquiry. "Mr. Haskell?"

"Yes, sir." Buck halted, automatically squaring his shoulders in reaction to the authority the man exuded.

"We have been expecting you." The man stepped to the side and motioned for Buck to precede him into the room.

He hesitated a split second, then moved past the man and through the doorway. It was one of those grand offices with lots of gleaming wood, bookshelves, and an oversized desk with a pair of facing chairs. But it was the petite, dark-haired woman, dressed in a flashy denim outfit, who claimed his attention. She stood by the window, her back to the door.

She made a slow, regal turn to face him. The beauty of her face was not one that a man of any age would forget. Even as it made its impact on him, Buck remembered exactly where he had seen her before. It stiffened him. At the same time, the anxiety he had felt toward the coming interview vanished completely.

Her glance bounced off Buck and centered on the man behind him. "That will be all, Daigle. Thank you."

Swiveling at the hips, Buck looked back as the burly mine manager made a slight bow and withdrew from the office, closing the door behind him. When Buck turned around, she had moved away from the window to approach him. Every step of the way, he was conscious of the measuring inspection of her eyes on him.

"We haven't been formally introduced, Mr. Haskell." There was a musical quality to her voice, with just a touch of Texas in it. "I am Tara Calder."

She extended a hand to him. It took Buck a full second to react to it. "Sorry. I'm not used to shaking hands with people. We didn't do much of it in prison." A fact he wanted out and on the table from the start, without apology or explanation. Buck smiled, thinking of how hard it would have been for him to say that to the plant manager.

Her hand gripped his only briefly. Her skin felt as soft as a baby's to him. He caught a whiff of perfume and knew it was probably the expensive kind.

"Please, have a seat, Mr. Haskell." She gestured to the chairs with a graceful sweep of her arm.

He looked at the chairs, but didn't move, his hands tucked back in the pockets of his windbreaker. "I was told to come here for a job interview."

"That's what this is," she assured him, then paused, a sudden knowing gleam lighting her dark eyes. "Perhaps I should have explained—I was Ty's first wife. For reasons of my own, I chose to keep the Calder name after we broke up."

Buck nodded in remembrance. "My father wrote a while back that Ty had gotten a divorce. I never thought I would see the day when a Calder would get a divorce. A Calder believes when you give your word, you keep it, come heaven or hell." This time he was the one to measure her with a look. "You two seemed friendly enough when I saw you together a month ago at headquarters."

"Ty and I have an unusual relationship that suits us both. Do sit down, Mr. Haskell." She took a seat in one of the chairs, moving with the fluid grace of a model. Women with her beauty and poise, Buck had only seen in films. He had never met one face to face. She glanced up at him, that knowing look in her eyes somehow mocking him. "You are interested in going to work, aren't you?"

"I'm interested." He lowered himself into the other chair and ran his gaze around the office. "Your daddy used to own this before he died, didn't he?"

"Among other things."

"I expect you're in charge now."

"Not really." She sat back in the chair, openly studying him. "I went over your application. I knew sooner or later you would come here seeking employment, but quite frankly, I was surprised to learn you had applied for the custodian job."

"At my age, fresh out of prison, jobs of any kind are hard to come by. It's not like I can pick and choose what I want to do."

"Then you should be pleased to learn that I have a position that should suit you perfectly." Her manner was one of absolute confidence that he would accept it.

But Buck was too canny, and too wary. There was something here that didn't smell right. "I get the feeling that the job you're offering me isn't here with Dy-Corp."

"I was told you were intelligent. I'm glad to see that's true." She smiled, and there was something catlike about it, a little too smooth and a little too secretive. It reinforced the feeling that there was a lot more behind this than she had told him thus far. "As a matter of fact, you will be working directly for me."

"Maybe I'm just naturally suspicious," Buck said. "But I can't help wondering what kind of job a woman like you would have in mind for an ex-convict."

"Nothing illegal, if that's what you are thinking."

"It crossed my mind," he admitted. "I've got my father living with me now. And if I got into any kind of trouble that would send me back to prison, Calder isn't about to let him come back to the Triple C to live out whatever time he has left."

"I understand your concern. Having recently lost my own father, I find it very admirable. But to be quite frank, Mr. Haskell, if you go back to prison, it will be for something you did of your own volition, not at any direction from me."

Buck nodded, taking her statement at face value for the time being. "All right, but you still haven't told me what kind of work you want me to do?"

"You would be a caretaker of sorts," she replied smoothly. "I have recently acquired some property in the area. Obviously I won't be living on it all the time, so I will need someone to look after it for me. You see, the work won't be strenuous at all, and should provide you ample time to see to your father's daily needs."

"Now, that's interesting." He thoughtfully dipped his chin and gazed at the intricate pattern of the Oriental rug on the floor, disconnected bits of information beginning to click together in his mind. "There's been some talk that Calder had to yank all his cattle off the Wolf Meadow range. Title to that ten thousand acres has been a problem to him. He's been fighting with the government over it for years. Now he just lost the grazing rights to it." Smiling, Buck cocked his head and regarded her with amusement. "That wouldn't be because you just bought it, would it?"

"I never said that, Mr. Haskell." But the gleam of approval and amusement in her eyes was all the confirmation Buck needed.

"You aren't as friendly with the Calders as you lead people to believe, are you? Why else would you be wanting to hire me?" It was a rhetorical question. He had his answers about her motives; she was out for revenge. "Do you know how mad Calder is going to be when he finds out?" Buck wondered. "That land is almost sacred to him."

Unmoved, she replied, "I'll make them like it. You'll see."

"And what am I? The final tweak of the man's nose?" He grinned crookedly.

"Does that bother you?"

"Nope." He buried his hands deeper in his jacket pockets, and laughed under his breath. "But it sure as hell will bother Chase."

"And that pleases you, doesn't it?"

"I didn't say that, ma'am." The wide smile remained etched on his face.

"The words weren't necessary. We both know you hold a grudge against Chase Calder for sending you to prison, not once, but twice."

Still smiling, he gazed once again at the rug. "That was a long time ago."

"Not so long ago that you have forgotten, though." She pushed out of her chair and crossed to the side of the desk, turned a sheet of paper toward her, and scanned its contents. "At your first trial on robbery and assault charges, it was essentially Chase's testimony that convicted you. With that on your record, when you were found guilty of attempted murder, the judge threw the book at you. Calder made sure of it."

"Like I said, that was a long time ago." But his smile didn't reach his eyes.

"And you were much too greedy," she declared. "I think you should know, Mr. Haskell, that I have run a very thorough check on you. There is very little about you that I don't already know—your likes and dislikes, the books you checked out of the prison library, the educational courses you took, which prisoners you associated with, and which ones you didn't. In your day, you were one of the best in the saddle, a top hand with rope, an expert on cattle, and a competent boss of the men beneath you. Currently I can itemize the contents of the house you are renting, and tell you to the penny how much money you bring in each month. I know where you applied for a job and where you didn't. I must admit I was surprised it took you so long to make an application here."

"You decided to hire me the day you saw me at the ranch, didn't you?"

"That's when it first occurred to me." She came around to the front of the desk and casually braced herself against it. "But you will learn that I never act rashly."

"How long did it take to get that report back on me?" He nodded toward the papers she had consulted. "One week? Two?"

"A little less than two weeks."

"So how come it took you so long to offer me the job?"

"Really, Mr. Haskell," she said in a chiding voice. "I could hardly come knocking on your door. Blue Moon is a very small town. Nothing happens in it that isn't common knowledge by the end of the day. And if I had called you on the phone, you might have listened to my offer, and you might have hung up the minute you heard my name. That wasn't a risk I wanted to take. No, it's better this way. The mine is the only large employer in the area. Anyone would expect you to apply for work here."

Buck read between the lines. "In other words, I'm not supposed to tell anyone that I'm working for you."

"Not yet. Not until I'm ready to take possession. At that point, secrecy will no longer be necessary. Will you take the job? I promise you the salary will be more than adequate to meet your needs."

"Oh, I'm taking it all right, ma'am," Buck drawled in answer. "To be honest, I'd pay for the chance to see Calder's face when he finds you've got title to that land. You just tell me when I start, and I'll be there, all spit and polished and ready to gloat."

"Not for a while yet. I'll let you know. In the meantime," she reached behind her and picked up a slim, square handbag, unfastened its flap, and removed a slender stack of crisp new bills from inside it, "here is your first month's salary in advance."

"You're paying me in cash?" He took it from her and automatically counted it.

"For the time being, I don't want anybody making a connection between us. A check you would have to cash somewhere. And as I said, this is a small town."

"What about the people here?"

"As E.J. Dyson's daughter, I command the loyalty here. This is my ground. Besides, Daigle is the only one who knows I'm meeting with you. And he won't breathe a word of it for fear of losing his job." She straightened from the desk and extended a hand again.

"It's good to have you on board, Mr. Haskell," she said, sending a clear signal that their meeting was concluded.

Slipping the bills into his inside jacket pocket, Buck stood up and shook her hand, sealing their bargain. "It will be interesting, ma'am. It surely will be that."

The first stars gleamed in the evening sky. Scattered across the sprawling headquarters, towering yard lights cast pools of amber light onto the ground beneath them, simultaneously bringing light to the darkness and deepening its shadows.

But Ty noticed none of it as he leaned his shoulder against a pillar and bent his head to light a cigar. He puffed on it until the tip glowed, then shook out the match, pinched the burnt sulfur end until it felt cool, then tossed it away.

Behind him the front door opened, briefly throwing interior light onto the veranda. Then it closed and light footsteps approached. He recognized the gliding tread of them as Tara's and didn't turn.

"I didn't know you were out here, Ty," she declared as she joined him, then smiled when she saw the cigar in his mouth. "Smoking a cigar, I see. Do you remember how much I hated the smell of one? Now, I actually like it. It must come from living in a house without a man around. Smoking cigars is such a masculine thing." She turned her face to the night air. "Isn't it unusually warm for April?"

"Yes," he replied through the cigar, accepting her presence and the underlying sexual tension that always accompanied it. Being with her was a habit he had picked up again over the last year.

"I thought so. Oh, Ty, look at that full moon," she rushed. "Isn't it spectacular? It looks like a big fat pumpkin sitting on the lip of the horizon."

He glanced at the moonrise. "It is beautiful," he agreed, but there was a perfunctory tone to his reply.

Catching it, Tara studied him curiously. "Is something wrong, Ty? You were so preoccupied at dinner tonight. And now?" She left the phrase unfinished, making a question of it.

He felt the probe of her gaze and avoided it by examining the buildup of ash on the glowing tip of his cigar. "Just tired. It's been a long day."

She released the breath she had been holding. "That's a relief. For a minute, I thought the attorneys may have brought you bad news today. And I couldn't imagine them flying in unless they had some positive information." Fortunately she left him no opening to respond. "It has been a long day, but it's been a good one, too. The photographer was absolutely certain that he captured some stunning images on film, both of the ranch itself and the life on it. I know it's been inconvenient having them underfoot for the last three days, but a picture spread will make a much greater impact than an article alone."

"I'll take your word for it." The subtle fragrance of her perfume wrapped itself around him, sensuous and alluring, like its wearer.

"Good, because it's true," Tara declared and again perused the nightscape before them. "The photographer could hardly wait to get back and start developing all the rolls of film he shot. To give you an idea of just how excited he was, he wants to come back when the trees have leafed out and the land has greened up."

"God, no," Ty snapped emphatically.

Tara laughed, low in her throat. He felt the caress of it. "I knew that's how you would react. I promise, I didn't encourage him to return."

"Good."

"This auction is going to be a huge success. I can just feel it." She hugged her arms about her middle, a self-satisfied look on her face.

"It better, with all we have invested in it, both in money and hard work."

"It will." There was a confident curve to her lips. "Do you know what is so ironic, Ty?" Her gaze slanted up to him, partially screened by the thick sweep of her dark lashes. It was an evocative look, full of tantalizing promise.

"What?" His glance drifted of its own accord to her lips, glistening in the moonlight.

"When we were married, ninety percent of all our arguments were about business. Now look at how well we work together. Looking back, I can see the fault was mine. I'll bet you thought I would never admit that," she teased.

Oddly enough, her confession took the sting out of their past. Ty smiled back. "Quite honestly, I didn't."

"I guess it was only natural for me to believe that my father's way was the only way," Tara mused. "After all, he spent his life exploiting natural gas, oil, and coal reserves. I was raised in that world, Ty. But the ranch was totally alien to me. I didn't seem to fit in anywhere. There was nothing I could contribute—no way I could help. And I am simply not the type of woman who is content with home and hearth. I need the mental stimulation that business provides. When Daddy wanted to mine the coal on the Triple C, I pushed for it. This was a business I knew. For the first time I could be useful. You will never know how important that was to me back then," she explained, emphasizing it with a quick glance his way. "That's why I sided against you all those years ago—and destroyed our marriage in the process."

"I never realized any of this." Ty stared, moved by her explanation. It was his first glimpse into their married life from her side of it. He suddenly understood the cause for all the restlessness and dissatisfaction she had exhibited back then.

"Why should you?" Tara shrugged, a beautifully rueful smile playing across her lips. "I spent two years on an analyst's couch before I guessed at any of it. Most of the time I acted like a spoiled, petulant brat. In a way, that is exactly what I was. Instead of sitting around feeling sorry for myself or flying off to some party or function where I felt important and my views mattered, I should have used that energy to learn the ranch business. I could have asked you to teach me. I knew about these private livestock auctions back then. Maybe if I had tried to learn more about ranching, I would have said something about them to you. But I was too busy trying to force you to become part of my world to take the time to become a part of yours." Her eyes darkened with honest and profound regret. It stirred through his emotions, awakening them.

"I wish I had known. I wish I had guessed." His husky voice echoed the regret in her eyes.

"I have wished that a million times. Even though I never meant to do it, I drove you away. But, Ty," she took a step closer, her expression earnest and imploring, a look of utter longing in her eyes, "it was never because I didn't trust you or believe in you. I truly loved you. That's what is so horribly sad about this. That's why it still hurts." Tara whispered the last in a tremulous voice as tears brimmed in her eyes.

"I know." Ty felt the same pain over this new insight into the past. It linked them closer than before.

"Do you? Do you really?" She looked at him, breathless with hope.

"Yes." He gathered her close to him, seeking the comfort to be found in physical contact, something they both needed. Tara slid her arms around him and rested her head on his chest. It was an embrace without demand, full of warmth and closeness.

"Sometimes, Ty," Tara murmured, "I can't help wondering about what might have been if things had worked out differently."

For the first time, Ty did, too. And it confused him. Suddenly nothing was black and white anymore. He felt again the same tear of loyalties between his feelings for Tara and Jessy that he had experienced back when he was still married to Tara.

"We can't turn back the clock." Ty said it as much for himself as for Tara.

She sighed and pulled fractionally away, allowing a wedge of space to come between them, her hands gliding to rest on his hips as she tipped her head back. "No, we can't, can we? Too many other people are involved now. It's too late for us," she admitted, raising a hand and resting it lightly along his cheek, a fondness in its touch. "But I can't help wishing that wasn't so."

She stretched upward, her lips moving onto his in a

tenderly warm kiss of sweet longing. Ty responded in perfect accord, gripped by a sense of madness and loss.

Some distance off to his right, there was a scuff of a boot on the graveled drive, followed by the tumbling roll of stones. The sounds signaled the approach of someone to the house. Breaking off the kiss, Ty lifted his head.

Tara stepped apart from him, but without haste or guilt. Innocent as the kiss had been, Ty felt unease over it.

"If I plan on leaving in the morning, I need to get my things packed." Tara spoke clearly in a tone that carried without an increase in volume. "Enjoy your cigar, Ty."

But it had gone out long ago. When she crossed to the front door, Ty dug another match from his pocket, watching the hatted figure moving out of the shadows toward the steps. Ty struck the match and held the flame beneath the cigar tip, his gaze on the man not yet close enough to identify. Smoke puffed from the corners of his mouth. He shook out the match, everything inside him hardening when he saw Ballard step into the light.

"What are you doing out and about this evening, Ballard?" Ty demanded, all the time wondering how much Ballard had seen and angered by the sense of guilt the question produced.

"I've been going over the construction billings with Matt Sullivan," he said, identifying by name the Triple C's bookkeeper. "We have a problem with the lighting supplier."

"What kind of problem?"

Ballard climbed the steps and came to a stop in front of Ty. His expression was too bland to tell Ty anything. He detected a certain coolness in Ballard's attitude, but that had been there ever since Ty jumped him for touching Jessy.

"He's refusing to sign a lien waiver. He keeps insisting that we owe him for some equipment that was never delivered. Matt sent him copies of the bills of lading on all the deliveries from his firm, but he claims the equipment was shipped and we owe him for it." Ballard paused, then added, "I thought I'd better go over it with you so you can decide how you want to handle it."

Ty glanced at the sheaf of papers in Ballard's hand, then back to the man's face. "There is nothing I can do about it tonight. You should have waited until morning and saved yourself the walk."

"You're forgetting that I won't be here in the morning. I'm driving in to Miles City tonight so I can pick up that load of antiques Tara bought to add to the barn's *decor."* He underscored the word with sardonic emphasis. But there was little Ty could read into that. Tara never had been exactly popular with the ranch hands. "I won't make it back until tomorrow afternoon. By then, who knows where you'll be."

"You're right. I had forgotten," Ty admitted and turned toward the front door. "Come on inside and we'll go over it."

At no time during their meeting was there anything in Ballard's manner to indicate that he had observed the embrace. Ty was left to wonder whether he had or not. It only increased his sense of unease.

Chapter Eleven

〜

Saturdays always brought a change in atmosphere at the Triple C, tingeing the air with an underlying crackle of excitement. Routines were altered. There was a slight spring in the step of those still on duty, and a hustle and bustle in the others, eager to get the odd tasks done so they could head into Blue Moon for a night on the town.

Standing at the top of the veranda steps, Chase felt the familiar pull of it and remembered the day when he had been as eager as the next cowboy to whoop it up after a hard, long week in the saddle. These last years since Maggie died, Saturdays hadn't been different than any other days for him. He just couldn't summon the old enthusiasm for a night out.

There was a time when he would have gone to town a couple times a week to check on Sally. Since she'd sold the restaurant and moved to the Triple C, he didn't have a reason to go anymore. A dry smile tugged at a corner of his mouth as it occurred to him that he was the only one who felt the way.

Chase swung away from the view of the ranch head-quarters and went back inside. "Sally!" he boomed her name. "Sally!"

"I'm in the kitchen." Her shouted answer rang above the squeals and giggles of the twins.

"She is always in the kitchen," Chase muttered to himself and set out in its direction at a hobble, his arthritis acting up again.

When he walked into the kitchen, young Trey was struggling to climb out of the playpen while little Laura sat contentedly in the middle of it, playing with one of their toys. Jessy was busy sweeping the floor. Sally turned from the countertop, a white-speckled roaster pan in her hands.

"What did you need, Chase?" Sally questioned with mild interest.

Ignoring the question, he frowned and asked, "What's that in your hands?"

"A roast for tonight's dinner. Why?"

"Let me have that." He limped over to take it from her. Sally immediately hurried to the oven to open the door for him, but Chase walked over to the refrigerator instead.

"What are you doing, Chase?" Sally stared at him with a dumbfounded look.

"What does it look like I'm doing?" he retorted and opened the refrigerator door. "I'm putting this away. I'm taking you out to dinner tonight. It is time you ate somebody's cooking other than your own." The look of pleasure that leaped into her face made Chase wish he had thought of doing this before. "You want to go out, don't you?" he challenged, a smile taking all the gruff-ness out of his voice.

"Of course, I do." The corners of her mouth deepened in a smile that chided him for suggesting otherwise. "But I still have to put that roast in the oven so Ty and Jessy will have something to eat tonight."

"If they want a roast for dinner, they can fix it themselves." Chase immediately set about making space for the long roaster pan in the oven. "For all you know, they just might decide to eat in town, too."

"Which shows how much you know," Sally retorted. "Jessy's parents are playing cards with the Trumbos tonight. There's no one to baby-sit the twins."

"And what is stopping them from bringing the twins along?" Chase countered. "It's time they were taking them out and getting them around strangers. They need to learn how to behave in public sometime. Why couldn't they start tonight?"

"Chase Calder, you know how raucous that place is on Saturday night. It will be packed with people, the jukebox blaring—"

Before Sally could complete her list, Chase interrupted, "You never know. All the commotion might keep them entertained. Isn't that right, Jessy?"

Up to then, Jessy had stayed out of their conversation, preferring to be a fly on the wall while the two of them squabbled like an old married couple. Now Chase had drawn her into it.

"They are old enough now that they probably would enjoy it," she agreed. "Trey would certainly be intrigued by all the action, and Laura would be fascinated by the music and dancing. But I don't think we'll go. You two deserve an evening without the twins underfoot."

Startled by the inference that this was a date of sorts, Sally darted an anxious look at Chase. She had known him too long to believe there was anything romantic behind his invitation. And she was reluctant to have him think she might.

"That's nonsense, Jessy," she rushed in protest. "We wouldn't mind in the least. Would we, Chase?"

"I wouldn't have suggested it if I did. We will make it a family night out," he concluded.

"That sounds fun." The more Jessy thought about it, the more it appealed to her. Lately she and Ty had been bickering a lot. A night out, away from the ranch, might be good for both of them.

The restaurant and bar, formerly owned by Sally, had been repainted a dark brown that was already dulled by a coat of dust. Newly mounted atop its porch roof was a huge neon sign that spelled out the letters HARRY'S HIDE-AWAY in fluorescent green.

The summer sun had yet to set in the evening sky, but already the parking lot was full when they arrived. Stopping in the driveway, Ty let the others out, then headed across the highway to park at Fedderson's combination gas station, grocery store, and post office.

Pausing near the base of the entrance steps, Chase surveyed the long, green-glowing sign and snorted his disgust. "Harry's Hideaway. It doesn't look to me like a place to hide. I'll bet you can see the glow of that sign in Miles City."

Laura had a different opinion as she stared up at the bright letters. She pointed a finger at them and jabbered excitedly to Jessy, her expression all alight.

"Laura seems to like it," Jessy remarked with a smile.

Chase slanted a sideways glance at his granddaughter and muttered, "Sometimes I wonder about that child's taste."

Jessy had only to recall how fascinated Laura was with Tara to agree with him. "My mom says she's at that age where she's fascinated by anything bright and shiny."

"That sign is definitely on the gawdy side of that," Chase declared and glanced at the young boy hooked in his arm. "Don't you agree, Trey?"

But Trey's entire attention was focused on the building's entrance and the steady hum of voices and muffled blare of music that emanated from it.

"Come on. Let's go in." Chase signaled for the women to precede him.

"As crowded as it is, we may be in for a long wait to get a table," Sally murmured worriedly.

"We'd better not. I called ahead to reserve one," Chase stated.

A cacophony of noise greeted them when they walked inside. Interspersed with the steady chatter of voices were hoots of laughter, and the clink and clatter of dishes and drinks. A honky-tonk song played on the jukebox, its volume cranked as high as it would go. From the bar side came the *crack* of a cue ball and the rumble of billiard balls rattling across the pool table's slate surface.

The establishment's new owner and namesake, Harry Weldon, pumped Chase's hand in greeting. He was a barrel-chested man with an apron tied around his middle and sweat running down his flushed face.

"It's crazy in here tonight, but it's always like that on Saturday nights now. You can't stir 'em with a stick," he said with considerable pride, nearly shouting to make himself heard above the noise. "Your table will be ready in two seconds."

The two seconds were closer to two minutes. By the time Harry Weldon returned, Ty had joined them and taken a squirming Trey from Chase's arms. The toddler's head was on a swivel, straining to see everything at once.

"I got ya' a table fixed up over here in the corner."

Plastic-coated menus in hand, Harry started in that direction, parting a path through the crowd and glancing over his shoulder. "Sorry it took so long. I had to get another keg from the back."

A soft shoulder bumped into Ty from behind. "Whoops, sorry," a female voice said. Ty looked back and saw a familiar face among the throng of strangers. It belonged to a Trumbo girl, Emily, the youngest. She recognized him at the same moment. "Ty. I didn't expect to run into you here, literally. I'm afraid I wasn't looking where I was going. I was too busy giving Dick a hard time."

His glance flicked to the man behind her and encountered Ballard's cool blue eyes. Ty knew it was logical that Ballard would be here tonight. It was the only watering hole for miles, making it the natural gathering point for both sexes on a Saturday night. But the realization came as an afterthought.

Emily Trumbo didn't appear to notice the sudden temperature drop as she continued talking. "Tell him what you told me, Dick," she urged, then jumped in when he didn't immediately respond. "He claims he saw a helicopter flying over the ranch on his way into town. I have never seen a helicopter except in the movies. And he says there was one flying over the Triple C. Can you believe it?"

Eyes narrowing at the possible significance of the sighting, Ty pinned his gaze on Ballard. "What kind of helicopter? Military or private?"

"It was too far away to tell. It could have been either."

"Where was it when you spotted it?" Ty had to raise his voice to make himself heard above the din.

"Northeast of the road," Ballard all but shouted his answer.

"Near Wolf Meadow?"

"That general area," Ballard confirmed.

"Which way was it headed?"

"On an easterly course."

"Toward Blue Moon?"

"Maybe." Then Ballard asked the question that was on Ty's mind. "Does Dy-Corp have a helicopter here?"

"I don't know." But he knew it wouldn't be hard to find out.

"Do you really think Dy-Corp has a helicopter?" Excited by the thought, Emily turned to Ballard. "I know a guy who works there. Maybe he could get me a ride on it. Wouldn't that be something?"

"Really something," Ballard assured her, then turned her back around. "We're headed for the dance floor, remember."

"Right." But as she moved past Ty, she was already craning her head trying to see above the crowd. "I wonder if Rick's here tonight."

By the time Ty worked his way through the crowd to the corner table, the others were already seated. After he had Trey buckled in the high chair, Ty relayed the information about the helicopter.

"Even if it wasn't military, it still might have been a government helicopter, state or federal," Sally suggested in an attempt to chase away the cloud that suddenly hung over their table.

"It's possible," Chase conceded. "But logic tells me differently. I can only think of one person with reason to fly over that section of the ranch, and that would be the new owner of it. They were bound to show up sooner or later. And I certainly didn't expect them to drive up to The Homestead and introduce themselves."

"You keep saying 'they,'" Jessy inserted. "You are convinced it's Dy-Corp, aren't you?"

"Let's put it this way," Chase replied. "Dy-Corp knows

we aren't going to let them cross our land to get to the Wolf Meadow range. Their only access to it is by air. And nobody else in the area is likely to have a helicopter other than the government or military."

"I know they want the coal on that land, but what good is it to them?" That was the part Jessy had trouble understanding. "They can't get their mining equipment in, or the coal out."

"They have something up their sleeves. You can bet on it." Chase opened the plastic-covered menu and squinted at the small type.

Ty spoke up. "I'll pass the word tomorrow for everybody to keep a lookout for any more helicopters in the area. Maybe next time we'll get lucky and get an aircraft identification number—assuming there is a next time. Meanwhile we need to find out whether Dy-Corp owns a helicopter."

"Or leases one," Chase added, then frowned and looked up. "Aren't there any barbeque ribs on this menu?"

"Right there." Sally pointed to them, relieved by the change of subject.

"That's what I'll have." He folded the menu shut and pushed it onto the table. "Although I doubt they will be as tasty and tender as the ones you make."

It was the warm look he gave her more than the praise for her cooking that had Sally glowing like a schoolgirl. But Jessy had little time to dwell on it as Trey let out a gleeful shriek and struggled to get out of the high chair. She reached to push him back in his seat just as the cause of excitement ran up to the chair.

"Hi, Trey. I didn't know you were going to be here tonight," Quint declared.

Cat and Logan were only a few steps behind him. Chase leaned back in his chair, his surprise quickly giving way to pleasure at the sight of his daughter and her family.

"Look who's here," he declared and immediately began issuing orders. "Pull that table over here and join us. We might as well make this a night out for the whole family."

After the initial confusion of moving tables and chairs, shifting positions, and everyone sitting down, Ty wasted no time mentioning the helicopter to Logan and their suspicion that it belonged to Dy-Corp.

"Unless it flew in today, Dy-Corp doesn't have a helicopter based here in Blue Moon," Logan stated. "But that doesn't mean they couldn't have chartered one from the copter service in Miles City. I'll ask around and see what I can find out. Unofficially, of course."

"I would appreciate that," Chase acknowledged.

"No more ranch talk," Cat decreed then grinned. "At least not the business end." Green eyes twinkling, she glanced at Jessy. "I planned to call you later tonight. I'm flying to Dallas next weekend and I thought you might like to come with me."

"Dallas?" Jessy wasn't sure which surprised her more— that Cat was going to Dallas or that she wanted her to go along.

"What's in Dallas?" Chase frowned at his daughter.

Logan inserted dryly, "Out of two closets full of clothes, she can't find a thing to wear."

"That's not true. I have plenty of clothes. I just don't have a knock-'em-out-of-their-boots outfit to wear to the auction," Cat explained to all then redirected her attention to Jessy. "I know you plan on buying something new for it. I thought we could shop together. It's a lot more fun that way."

"Yes, but—I was just going to pick something up in

Miles City." The idea of flying all the way to Dallas to shop struck Jessy as totally unnecessary.

"Believe me, Jess, you aren't going to find what you need in Miles City," Cat advised as the waitress arrived, balancing a tray loaded with water glasses. "Initially I considered going to Denver since it's closer, but I'm much more familiar with the shops in Dallas and Fort Worth."

"As much as I hate to admit it"—Ty paused to hold Trey's hand when he made a grab for one of the glasses— "my sister is right. You won't find high fashion in Miles City. For that, you'll have to shop somewhere else."

"I suppose," Jessy conceded, but inside she was screaming at the very idea. All this talk about projecting the proper image and creating the right impression went against the grain and smacked of phoniness. As far as Jessy was concerned, she was who and what she was and everyone else was welcome to take it or leave it.

Besides, "high fashion" was a term she equated with Tara, not herself. Never herself.

"Then you will come with me?" Cat pressed for a more definite answer.

"Of course she'll go," Chase answered for her, then added, "A couple days away from the ranch and the twins will do you good."

It wasn't in Jessy's nature to be anything less than candid. "I can't imagine anything more painful than going from store to store trying on clothes. And I'm telling you right now, I am not wearing a dress or putting on makeup for this affair. It's an auction, for heaven's sake."

Smiling, Ty eyed his wife with a mixture of amusement and appreciation then glanced at Cat. "You have your work cut out for you on this trip, sis."

"I'm not one bit worried." She spoke with confidence.

"They are making some fabulous Western clothes these days. We'll find the perfect outfit. Wait and see."

Slapping her order pad on the tray and clicking her ballpoint pen, the waitress broke into their conversation, "Anybody ready to order?"

She went around the long table, writing down each one's food and drink order until she came to Chase. "You aren't going to like those ribs, Mr. Calder." The pen remained poised above the pad. "They are dry and tough. Why don't you have a steak instead?"

"Make it well done."

"I'll see that the cook burns it," she promised with an emphatic nod. Once all their orders were taken, she closed the book and slipped it inside her roomy apron pocket. "I'll be right back with your drinks. The food's another story. It's crazy in that kitchen," she warned, already moving away from the table.

Quint patted Logan's arm in an attention-getting gesture. "Dad, is it all right if I go watch them play pool?"

Logan glanced at his wristwatch. "It shouldn't be too rowdy over there yet. You can go, but only for a little while."

"Thanks." Quint flashed him a rare smile and scooted off his chair, intent on reaching the bar's billiard area as fast as possible.

The minute he darted away from the table, Trey screamed in protest and worked furiously to get out of the highchair and follow his older cousin. After initial attempts to distract him with soda crackers and his toy truck failed, Jessy gave up and lifted him out of his high chair. But his angry yowls made it clear that he wasn't interested in sitting on her lap; he wanted to go after Quint.

Rising from his chair, Ty reached for the squirming toddler. "I'll take him," he said to Jessy and swung the little boy onto his hip. "Come on, little guy. Let's go find Quint."

As abruptly as the fit-throwing started, it stopped. Trey pointed a finger in the direction Quint had gone and jabbered in excitement, none of it intelligible except for the word "Kint," which was the closest the toddler could come to saying Quint's name.

Ty worked his way through the crowded restaurant area toward the bar where the occasional *crack* of a billiard ball could be heard above the din of loud-talking voices and even louder music from the jukebox. All the way, Trey twisted and turned, straining to catch the first glimpse of his cousin.

But the first person to catch Ty's eye when he entered the bar area was Buck Haskell. He was perched atop a stool in front of the long bar, a mug of beer in front of him and an empty long neck beside it. He was sporting a new black Stetson and a pair of fancy-stitched cowboy boots to go along with crisp new jeans and a pearl-snapped Western shirt. His skin had lost its prison pallor and taken on the hue of a tan, which made his curly hair seem all the whiter. In short, he looked like what he was, in a sense, an old cowhand dressed for a Saturday night on the town.

His eyes had a knowing glint when he met Ty's look and raised his beer mug, acknowledging Ty's presence. It wasn't in Ty to simply ignore the man. A Calder faced his enemies; he didn't walk away from them.

" 'Lo, Buck." He injected a coolness in his voice. "Looks like you're doing well."

"As a matter of fact, I am," Buck declared, his mouth curving in a canny smile. "That your boy?"

"It is."

"He looks like a Calder," Buck observed. "Heard you named him after your pa."

"That's right."

"I guess that means there will be a Chase Benteen Calder running the Triple C for a good many years to come."

The last thing Ty wanted to talk about with Buck Haskell was his young son. "I see you bought some new duds."

"I didn't have much choice." Buck continued to smile. "They don't let you take those prison uniforms with you when they turn you loose."

"But a hat and a pair of boots like that don't come cheap. You must be working somewhere."

"Not yet. But I've got me a job lined up. Looks like I'll be startin' soon."

"Where?"

"That's for me to know and you to find out," Buck replied and took a swig of beer.

"Don't worry. We will." Ty spotted Quint standing quietly by the wall, watching the pool game in progress.

As he started to move toward the boy, Buck said, "I'd tell you to give my regards to your pa, but I don't think he cares to hear from me. You'll be seein' me, though. You can count on that."

Ty had the uneasy feeling the man spoke the truth. But he didn't have time to dwell on it as Trey suddenly spied Quint. He kicked at Ty with his legs as if to hurry him along.

The restaurant and bar had filled up. Some of the families with younger children were leaving while the local cowboys and mine workers filed into the café in twos and threes. Most of them knew Ty by sight if not by name. They hailed him with greetings. He acknowledged them with a wave or a lift of his head.

Ty sidestepped a cue stick, drawn back by its shooter, and jostled a towheaded boy of eighteen, his freckled face sunburned except for a white band across the top of his forehead.

"Sorry, Taylor." Ty apologized to the son from a family that ranched some land that adjoined the south boundary of the Triple C. There was a passel of kids in the family, and Ty never could keep their names straight.

"It's okay." The lanky boy shifted, giving Ty a glimpse of the girl with him.

"Hey, Emily." Ty was surprised to see her in Taylor's company. "I thought you were here with Ballard."

"No. I just danced with him. That's all," she replied, then leaned closer, cupping a hand next to her mouth to whisper in a secretive manner. "Rick says Dy-Corp doesn't have a helicopter. He says they don't need one."

"Really." Ty straightened, absorbing the information. "He works at the mine."

"Yeah. It's a job," she said, as if in defense of his choice.

Ty nodded absently in understanding, and filed the information away.

As he worked his way through the crowded bar to reach Quint, Ty skirted a group of onlookers that had gathered by the pool table to watch the game in progress. Ty was quick to notice that Dick Ballard was among them, one hand hooked on the opposite shoulder of the shapely brunette beside him. The woman was no one Ty recognized, but she definitely wasn't Emily Trumbo.

Leaning closer, Ballard whispered something in the woman's ear then bent his head to catch her answer. He responded with a quick smile that might appear sexy to a woman, but to Ty, it had the distinctive wheedling quality of a man on the make. It reinforced his opinion that Ballard was little more than Casanova in cowboy boots. Why Jessy thought of him as a friend Ty would never understand, which made him all the more irritated by the man.

At the table, the cue ball ricocheted off the black eight ball and sent it spinning into a side pocket. Amid the accompanying cheers of victory, there were a few hoots of derision and an exchange of money.

The balls were already being racked up to start a new game by the time Ty reached Quint's side. The gray-eyed boy scooted to one side, making room for Ty to stand next to him along the wall.

"I didn't know you were coming, too," Quint said.

"Trey wanted to see what was going on." Ty noticed how quickly Quint's attention reverted to the table when it appeared another game was about to start. "Like pool, do you?"

Quint responded with an emphatic nod. "When I get bigger, my dad's going to teach me how to play."

"That's good."

A heavyset cowboy bent over the table, sighted down his cue stick, drew it back, and sent it shooting forward. Trey's eyes widened at the explosive *crack* and *clatter* of the break. He stared in wonder at the brightly colored balls careening off each other in every direction.

He pointed to them, then looked at Ty. "Baw."

"That's right. Those are balls, but they aren't the kind little boys can play with."

"Only big boys, Trey," Quint chimed in.

For a time Trey was fascinated by all the noise and action at the pool table. But his own restless nature made it impossible for anything to hold his interest for long. Within minutes he wanted down. The instant his feet touched the floor, he made a dash for the pool table and the cache of balls that had fallen into the pockets.

"Sorry, guy." Ty scooped him back up.

As usual, Trey simply looked around for another distraction and settled for the rhythmic gyrations of the people on the dance floor. Several more minutes passed before Ty noticed that Ballard and the brunette were no longer among the spectators at the pool table. Too soon the fast music ended and a slow song took its place, too slow to interest Trey.

Idly Ty ran his glance around the area. There was no sign of Ballard in the immediate vicinity, but he did catch sight of Logan working his way toward the bar area.

He touched Quint's shoulder. "Here comes your dad. It must be time for us to head back to the table."

"Okay." With a barely perceptible sigh of resignation, Quint dragged his gaze from the pool table and moved away from the wall.

Ty shifted Trey to his left hip and followed behind Quint. Near the bar, they hooked up with Logan. The jam of people made for slow going as Logan led the way with Quint sandwiched between the two men.

Their route took them by the small dance floor. Just ahead on Ty's right a burly mineworker slapped one of his compatriots on his shoulder and pivoted blindly right into Ty's path. Ty stepped quickly to the side to avoid running into the man and bumped one of the couples on the dance floor.

"Sorry," he began then found himself staring into Ballard's face. A quick glance revealed that his partner wasn't the shapely brunette Ty had seen him with earlier, or Emily Trumbo. This one was a bleached blonde. Ty shot Ballard a look of disgust. "Why can't you be satisfied with just one woman?"

Ballard's eyes narrowed briefly. Then a faintly taunting smile curved his mouth. "At least I'm not married like you."

In the fraction of an instant that it took the words to register, Ty realized that Ballard had seen that innocent kiss between himself and Tara—seen it and put his own construction on it.

Furious, Ty let his fist fly, slamming it against Ballard's jaw. The force of the impact jarred his whole arm and knocked Ballard sideways into other dancers, where he stumbled, lost his balance, and fell.

One minute Ty was staring at Ballard, propped on one elbow, trying to shake off the effects of the blow; and in the next, Logan blocked his view, stepping between them.

"That's enough!" He shot Ty a look of sharp warning.

It wasn't necessary. That momentary fury was gone. Ty loosened the muscles in his shoulders and opened his fist, spreading his fingers wide, all the while conscious of the aura of stillness and expectancy that surrounded him. He felt the stares and heard the low hum of murmuring voices as Ballard got to his feet, rubbing his jaw.

"I'll give you that one, Calder," he said in a low but audible voice.

"Are you all right?" Logan asked him.

"Except for a sore jaw, I'm just jim dandy, Sheriff," Ballard assured him with a return of his slow smile. "But I'm sure going to watch closer for flying objects. Now, if you'll excuse me, I've got a dance to finish."

Turning from both of them back to the blonde, Ballard effectively signaled an end to the moment. Immediately the milling and talking began in an eager exchange of information.

Logan glanced sideways at Ty, his gaze curious and measuring. "What was that about?"

"That's my business." Brother-in-law or not, Ty wasn't about to explain.

"I'll accept that." Logan continued to study him. "Just make sure that it doesn't eventually become my business."

Among the many things Logan had learned about the Calders since moving to Montana, he knew they demanded loyalty from those who worked for them, and they gave it in return. He hadn't heard the words the two men exchanged, but he had seen enough to know that something Ballard said provoked Ty's swing. And Ty wasn't a man to rile easily, or likely to punch one of his employees. So why had he? Logan hated questions without quick answers.

Chapter Twelve

～

The high and wide Montana sky was a startling blue, lit by a bright morning sun. A twin-engine Beechcraft bearing the Triple C insignia on its door sped down the runway. Buckled in the passenger seat across the aisle from Cat, Jessy gazed out the window at the rolling grassland whipping by.

Unlike Cat, she couldn't summon any enthusiasm for this shopping trip to Dallas. Logic told her it was necessary, but as far as she was concerned, it was one of life's unpleasantries that had to be endured.

With the engines roaring at full power, the plane's nose lifted. A moment later the craft was airborne, the land falling away beneath it. Somewhere around eight hundred feet it began a banking turn to the south.

"I've been thinking," Cat said.

"About what?" Jessy asked when Cat failed to continue.

"We will actually need two outfits. One for the auction, and another for the open house the day before."

"What open house?" Jessy stiffened. "No one said anything to me about having one at The Homestead."

"I don't mean it literally. But a lot of the buyers will want to come the day before the auction to look over the sale stock and decide which they want to bid on. People will probably be coming and going most of the day. In that sense, it will be a bit less informal, but we still need to dress appropriately."

There was that word again, Jessy thought with an inward sign, but she managed to joke, "I guess jeans and a shirt wouldn't be appropriate."

Cat laughed, as Jessy knew she would. "Don't you wish."

"Don't I, though," Jessy agreed with a rueful smile and automatically glanced out the plane's window again. This bird's-eye view of the land on which she was born was one she never tired of seeing. And she had cowboyed for too many years not to instinctively watch for the unusual.

Intent on the ground, she almost missed the aircraft sweeping across the eastern sky. But its movement caught her eye. Leaning closer to the porthole, she took a second look then hurriedly unbuckled her belt and scrambled out of her seat.

"What's wrong?" Cat frowned.

Jessy didn't bother to answer as she made her way up the aisle to the cockpit. "Jack." She tapped the pilot on the shoulder and pointed to his left. "Do you see that helicopter off your wing?"

He turned his head in that direction and nodded. "Got it."

"Try to raise somebody at the ranch and tell them a helicopter is flying on a course toward the Wolf Meadow range."

"Will do," he promised and glanced at his copilot.

"Get on the horn, Andy. Frank still might be in the hangar area." Over his shoulder, he said to Jessy, "If we can't get Frank, we'll patch a call into headquarters."

"Thanks," she said and turned away.

The minute she stepped into the cabin, Cat's eyes were on her, a mixture of curiosity and concern in her expression. "What's wrong?"

"I spotted a helicopter that might be headed for Wolf Meadow," Jessy explained, returning to her seat. "Jack's going to make sure Ty knows about it."

A grimly determined look stole over Cat's features at the news. "Maybe at last we'll find out who bought the land."

"I don't have a good feeling about this." She hadn't from the moment they learned the government was not renewing their lease.

"We'll get it back," Cat stated. "Whatever it takes, we'll get it back. After all, what good is it to anybody? We have it completely landlocked. Their only access to it is by air."

"Maybe whoever bought it wants to turn it into a nature preserve." That seemed to be the general consensus of the attorneys.

"Do you believe that?" Cat eyed her closely.

Jessy shook her head. "No." But she couldn't put her finger on why she felt so certain about that.

"Neither do I." Cat replied then sighed rather grimly. "With any luck, we'll learn the identity of the new owner before the day's out."

But something told Jessy that any satisfaction to be gained from solving the mystery of the new owner's identity wouldn't last long.

Up front, the copilot climbed out of the right seat and stepped into the cabin doorway while the plane continued to climb to its assigned altitude. "Thought you would want to know we passed on the word about the helicopter. Ty is going to check it out."

"Thanks," Cat said and glanced at Jessy. "It won't be long now."

"We received word that there might be some clear-air turbulence up ahead. Better make sure you keep your seat belts fastened," the copilot added in warning.

As far as Jessy was concerned, she didn't need to be warned of impending trouble. She sensed it.

There were few curves in the dirt ranch road as it followed the undulations of the rolling plains. With his foot pressed hard on the pickup's accelerator, Ty drove as fast as he dared.

He ducked his head low to scan the sky ahead of him, making sure the chopper was still in sight. Fighting through the glare of the rising sun, he caught a glimpse of it still some distance ahead of him but lower than before. It was descending. A quick check of its angle confirmed Ty's suspicions—its landing point would be well north of the road on the Wolf Meadow range.

But exactly where, he couldn't tell. The helicopter was too far away yet. Which made it all the more important for him to keep it in sight as long as possible.

As the helicopter swooped lower, the land's natural rise and fall soon made it difficult for Ty to keep the craft in view. Then it disappeared completely. Cursing his luck, Ty tried to gauge how far north of the road it had been at his last sighting of it. Close to a mile was his best guess. Next he attempted to triangulate where a line from that point would intersect the road. It wasn't an easy task without landmarks to guide him.

As he approached the imaginary junction, Ty spotted a fence gate just ahead. Slowing the pickup, he pulled into it, stopped, hopped out of the cab, and dragged open the gate. Back in the truck, he removed the binoculars from their leather carrying case and laid them on the seat beside him then switched the pickup into four-wheel drive and took off.

Speed was no longer important; only finding the helicopter was. At the crest of each rise, Ty pulled up and made a one-hundred-and-eighty-degree sweep of the country before him with the binoculars. It was a rough and broken land, dotted with low mesas and gouged with wide coulees.

When that scan turned up nothing, he traveled on to the next vantage point and glassed the area again. Still nothing. On his third stop, he spotted the chopper on the ground approximately a half-mile northeast of him. It had landed a short distance away from windmill eleven near the base of Antelope Butte.

With its location pinpointed, Ty drove in an easterly direction until he reached the dim trail, used by Triple C hands to service the windmill. After he turned onto it, it was a more-or-less straight shot to the site.

Within minutes the butte face loomed before him, but Ty's gaze was centered on the two men standing near the helicopter. Leaving the overgrown trail, he aimed the pickup toward the two men, taking his measure of them. The taller of the two, in shirt sleeves and aviator glasses, Ty quickly dismissed as the chopper pilot and centered his attention on the second man, dressed in jeans, a leather jacket, and a black cowboy hat.

Observing Ty's approach, he said something to the pilot and split away from him, moving forward to meet the truck. At a point of his choosing, the man stopped, dipped his head down, and waited for Ty to stop.

With a grim kind of eagerness for the coming meeting, Ty switched off the engine and climbed out of the pickup. Rounding the hood of the truck, he walked toward the hatted figure, mildly annoyed that the man had yet to look up.

When Ty was only steps from him, the man slowly raised his head, giving Ty his first good look at his face.

Recognition splintered through Ty like an electric shock. It was Buck Haskell.

"I expected either you or your pa to show up," Buck stated with a smile. "I'm kinda' sorry it's you."

"What are you doing here?" Ty demanded and shot a quick look at the second man by the chopper.

"My job." Buck's smile deepened, but his eyes had a watchful look to them. "I told you last week I'd be starting any day."

"So you did." Behind him, the windmill groaned a protest as a stiff wind tugged at its tied-down blades. Ty ignored it.

"You do realize you're on private property," Buck reminded him. "Technically you're trespassing."

Unconcerned, Ty smiled. "Technically, maybe. And maybe I'm just doing the neighborly thing by coming to meet the new owner." He nodded in the direction of the man by the helicopter. "Is that him?"

"Nope. That's the pilot."

"So where's your boss?" Ty challenged.

"Over there." With a sideways bob of his head, Buck directed Ty's attention toward the butte.

Making a half-turn toward it, Ty stared in surprise at the couple seemingly intent on studying the stretch of land at the base of the bluff some distance from the windmill. For a moment he was stunned that he had failed to notice them before now, then realized that he had been too intent on the helicopter to look far beyond it. Coupled with the fact that both the man and the woman wore tan-colored clothes, his oversight was understandable. The man was hatless, exposing a head of iron-gray hair. But the woman wore a beige scarf that fluttered in the wind. With their backs to him, there was little more that Ty could discern about either of them.

"I'll go introduce myself," Ty said to Buck.

"I think I'll come along." Buck's smile had an amused quality that Ty didn't like.

"Suit yourself," Ty replied and struck out across the grass toward the couple, indifferent to whether the older Buck could keep up with the pace Ty set.

Buck remained only a half a stride behind, saying nothing, his smile never faltering. When they were less than twenty feet from the couple, Buck called ahead, "Sorry to interrupt, but you've got a visitor."

As one, the man and woman turned and Ty had his first glimpse of Tara's raven hair and jet-black eyes. Ty stopped dead in his tracks, a fury surging through him.

"You bought this land," he thundered the accusation.

Contrition swept her expression. "Ty, I'm sorry. I tried a hundred times to tell you—"

Without waiting to hear more, Ty pivoted on his heel and headed back toward his truck, anger vibrating through every muscle.

"Ty, please." Tara ran after him. "Let me explain."

"I'm not interested in your explanations." He pushed the words through his teeth, his voice low and curt.

"It's not what you think," she insisted and moved into his path, forcing him to stop. "Just listen to me for one minute please. Then if you still want to leave, I won't stop you."

He studied her with cold eyes, his attitude hardened by her act of betrayal. "I suppose you're going to tell me that you don't own the land."

"Technically, I don't, but in fact I do, since I am the

sole shareholder of the corporation that holds the title to it."

"Then there is nothing more you can say that I care to hear."

When he started to move by her, Tara reached out to stop him. "You don't understand," she protested, her eyes dark with entreaty. "The whole thing began as nothing more than a lark. Your father has tried for years to get title to this land without success. It became a challenge of sorts. I wanted to see if I could do it."

"Then you must be feeling very proud of yourself about now." Ty looked at her with nothing but contempt in his eyes.

"How can I when it has made you so angry." Her own expression was full of pain, but Ty was unmoved by it. "Don't you see—I always knew you were going about things the wrong way. The days when the government sold land to individuals is gone. It's no longer interested in divesting itself of property, regardless of the price that might be offered for it."

"You didn't seem to have any difficulty buying it," Ty reminded her.

"I didn't buy it, at least not with cash. I traded for it."

In spite of himself, her answer snagged his interest. "You traded?"

"It wasn't exactly an even swap either, considering the exorbitant sum I had to pay for the other tract of land adjacent to one of the national parks. But I knew there were certain officials in positions of authority who wanted to see it come under government control. From there, it wasn't difficult to get them to agree to an exchange."

"Very clever. But then you have always been clever." There was nothing in his tone of voice that made it a compliment.

"But not clever enough to keep you." The look of abject regret Tara gave him failed to tunnel through his defenses as it had done little more than a week ago.

"Fortunately." Ty had no pity for her.

She dropped her glance. "I had that coming."

He wasn't about to refute that. "How much do you want, Tara?"

Her head came up, her dark eyes wide with confusion. "For what?"

"For Wolf Meadow, of course."

"I . . ." Tara faltered and looked away, running her gaze through the broken land. "I'm not sure I want to sell it."

His eyes narrowed with a new wariness. "Exactly what do you plan to do with it then?"

The wind whipped a corner of her silk scarf onto her face. Reaching up, Tara pushed it off her cheek and turned imploring eyes on him. "I know you aren't going to believe this. It's hard for me to believe it when I remember how much I hated this empty country with its suffocating sky. But this past year I have come to realize how much I miss it."

"Are you saying that you plan to live here?" Ty demanded.

"I do," Tara admitted, then added in appeal, "Is that so terribly wrong?"

"Not on this land, you aren't," Ty stated, flat and hard.

For the first time there was a snap of anger in her dark eyes. "You don't really have any control over that, do you?"

It didn't sit well that she was absolutely right. There was very little he could do to stop her. He looked away, his glance briefly landing on Buck Haskell, standing a short distance away but within earshot.

"What's your game, Tara?" His stony gaze sliced back to her.

"Please don't take that attitude, Ty," she murmured in hurt protest. "Not everything I do is a game."

"That has been my experience." It was not in him to relent.

"You can't have forgotten how well we worked together this past year. Not so quickly. We are good for each other," Tara insisted in an attempt to appeal to his reason. "Don't ruin our relationship because of this."

"You ruined it yourself when you went behind my back and bought this land."

"Why does that make you so angry?" Tara demanded in frustration. "Why aren't you congratulating me for finally getting clear title to it from the government? Does it bother you so much that I succeeded where you and your father failed? This is all about that stiff-necked Calder pride, isn't it?"

"No, it's about you and the way you kept your acquisition of it such a deep dark secret. Even though you knew I would eventually find out, you still didn't have the guts to come tell me. You let me show up here instead."

"I didn't know how to tell you. Can't you understand that?" Tara said.

"I might buy that from anyone else, but not from you."

"Don't you see—when I started out, I didn't say anything in case I wasn't successful. By not saying anything in the beginning, it made it harder to tell you later. And it became even more complicated when I realized I wanted to make my home here. I never guessed I would come to feel that way, but I do. Is that so wrong?"

"I don't give a damn whether you live in Montana or Marrakesh, just as long as it isn't on this land." His gaze sharpened on her. "But you are bound to know that so why are you doing it?"

Her lips curved in a smile of beguilement. "Isn't it obvious? I want to be near you." Tara stepped closer and slid her hands onto his shirtfront, spreading them across his chest. "Even if we aren't married anymore, that doesn't mean we still can't be close."

Grim-eyed, Ty grabbed her wrists and shoved her away from him. "Goodbye, Tara." He strode toward the ranch pickup.

"Not goodbye, Ty," she called after him. "We'll see each other again. If you have any hope of getting this land now, you will have to deal directly with me. I'll be flying back to Fort Worth this afternoon. Talk it over with your father then give me a call in the next day or two and we will arrange a time when the three of us can sit down and talk."

Offering no response, Ty climbed into the pickup and slammed the door. An instant later the engine roared to life. After a reversing turn, the truck charged down the dim track toward the south fence line.

Buck waited a beat then sauntered over to Tara, his side glance inspecting the smooth satisfaction in her expression. "Reckon he'll call?"

"He doesn't have a choice," Tara replied with certainty.

With a push of his thumb, Buck tipped the brim of his hat back. "I guess you haven't learned a Calder always has a choice."

"Not this time." There wasn't even the smallest trace of doubt in her voice.

Buck wasn't so sure of that, but he didn't say so as the wind carried to him the distinctive *chop-chop* of a helicopter's rotating blades. Looking up, he spotted the big workhorse chopper lumbering out of the eastern sky, a piece of machinery suspended beneath it.

"Here comes the backhoe," he told Tara then cautioned, "You might want to move back a ways. The dust is gonna be flyin'."

"That's fine. The architect and I need to decide on a final building site anyway." Taking his suggestion, Tara moved away to rejoin the other man, studiously pacing off a section of ground, oblivious to everything else.

A thick and heavy silence hung over the den, weighted by the news Ty had brought back with him. Chase sat behind the desk, grimly contemplating its many ramifications. Ty stood at the window, one hand braced against its frame, a thumb of the other hooked in his back pocket while he stared blindly at the sprawl of ranch buildings beyond its glass. A high and angry tension ridged the muscles along his jaw and darkened his eyes to blackened pinpoints of suppressed rage.

The big leather chair creaked as Chase rocked forward. "It won't be long before the range telegraph gets wind of this and flashes it to every corner of the ranch. We won't be able to ignore it."

Ty slammed his hand against the window frame, the sharp hard sound of it shattering the room's stillness like a clap of thunder. "She wants something. What the hell is it?"

"We won't know that until we meet with her," Chase stated.

"I hate playing into her hand." Ty swung from the window, no longer able to contain the simmering energy inside.

"At least we know the stakes are Wolf Meadow." Chase settled back in his chair, turning thoughtful again.

"And she isn't bluffing about building a house on it or that chopper wouldn't be flying in a backhoe."

"So it would seem," Chase murmured in absent agreement. "But what is she doing with Buck Haskell on the payroll?"

"I didn't ask. More than likely it's pure spite on her part." Too impatient to sit, Ty wandered over to the front of the desk.

"You do realize that Jessy will be calling the minute they land in Fort Worth to see what you found out," Chase said, then added, "I wouldn't tell her anything yet."

Ty's head came up, a questioning frown knitting his brows. "Why not? It won't come as any great surprise to her. Jessy has been convinced Tara was up to something for more than a year."

"I wasn't thinking about Jessy," Chase replied, a touch of grimness about his mouth. "It's Cat I'm worried about. She's always looked up to Tara. This will be a blow to her. Why ruin her shopping trip if it can be avoided."

"You don't know Jessy." A dry smile tugged at one corner of Ty's mouth. "She isn't going to buy the idea that I didn't learn anything."

"Admit that you did, but explain that it looks like you won't be able to tell her the new owner's name until they get home tomorrow. Which will be the truth, as far as it goes. You can explain later about Cat. She'll understand."

Knowing his wife, Ty couldn't argue with that logic.

Late on Sunday afternoon the twin-engine Beechcraft taxied toward the hangar apron where the welcoming committee of Ty, Logan, and Quint waited for it. Upon reaching its tie-down area, the pilot slew the craft around and cut its engines.

Frank came out of the hangar shed at a waddling

trot, toting the wheel chocks. Grunting with the effort, he jammed a set around each wheel, then scrambled around to slap a hand on the cabin door. As soon as it swung open, he latched it back and pulled the steps down.

When Cat came into view, Quint broke from his father's side and ran to meet her. "I'm glad you're home, Mom. We missed you a lot."

"I missed you, too." She crouched down to wrap him in a hug and smack a kiss on his cheek then straightened, tipping her head up in anticipation of Logan's welcoming kiss.

He didn't disappoint her as Jessy emerged from the plane. Her glance ran straight to Ty in an unspoken question. Ty didn't need to hear the words to know what she was asking—whether he had learned the identity of the new owner. He responded with a barely perceptible nod then moved forward to greet her.

"Welcome home." He dropped a light kiss on her lips.

"You have no idea how glad I am to be back," Jessy murmured.

"An ordeal, was it?" Ty smiled at this rare woman who was his wife.

"And then some," Jessy answered with a mock roll of her eyes.

"Did you two succeed in buying out the stores before you left?" Logan teased.

"We made a gallant effort at it," Cat responded in kind.

"Did you find a new jacket for me, Mom?" Quint asked, his gray eyes alight with hope.

"I certainly did."

"Where is it?" Quint wanted to know.

"Yes." Logan picked up the question. "Where is this

haul you made? I expected you two to be loaded down with packages."

"They're in the baggage compartment. Get your arms ready," Cat warned. "You have some heavy-duty carrying to do."

Frank opened the hatch to the luggage compartment, paused, and shot a wide-eyed look at Cat. "Good Lord, Miss Cat, you did buy out the stores there."

He hauled box after box out of the rear compartment—long boxes, tall boxes, fat boxes, shoeboxes, and hatboxes. Cat sorted through them as they came out, identifying what belonged to whom. When she had finished, all but two were in her own stack.

Ty stared from the two lonely boxes to Jessy in disbelief. "Is that all you bought?"

"Don't you wish." Cat laughed. "That is merely what your wife brought home with her. Jessy has the most incredible eye for what looks great on her."

The compliment was so unexpected that Ty couldn't keep from sliding a skeptical glance at his wife. Jessy had a kind of natural beauty that was simple and strong, but she had never been one to spend much time worrying about what to wear. He had counted on Cat's fashion sense to guide Jessy in purchasing the appropriate clothes for the auction.

"I'm serious." Cat caught the doubt that had flickered in his eyes. "On Saturday, I must have had her try on twenty different outfits that looked sensational on the hanger but didn't suit her at all. Finally, we were in this one shop and I had already selected two or three things for Jessy to try on when she walked over to a rack, pulled out a short jacket in a brick-red wool, and grabbed a pair of black jeans off the shelf and a high-crowned black hat with a concho band. Then she said to me, 'I'll try this on first.' When she walked out of the changing room, my chin hit the floor. Except for the blond hair, she looked exactly like one of those cowgirls in a Doreman Burns painting. It's a perfect outfit for the open house."

"What did you buy for the auction?" Ty asked, his curiosity aroused, taking more interest in the subject than he might have before this weekend's turn of events.

"A pair of suede jeans and a matching shirt." Even now, Jessy had lost interest in the subject.

"Sounds plain, doesn't it?" Cat said. "But Jessy is striking in it. I guarantee heads will turn. She found the set in the men's side of the store, tried it on, and the search was over. Of course it didn't fit properly. But fortunately it was the work of a local designer. Rather than do a lot of major alterations to the outfit, a new one is being made just for her. It should be here in a couple of months, complete with matching boots and hat. Believe me, she will be sensational in it."

"I believe you." There was satisfaction in the thought that Jessy would be the one making the fashion statement, something that had always been Tara's province.

"Enough about clothes." Jessy said with her usual bluntness. As far as she was concerned, the subject had been exhausted long ago. There were more important matters at hand. "Were you able to learn who the new owner is?"

"Actually I knew it when I talked to you yesterday, but Dad and I decided to wait until you were back to tell you," Ty admitted, watching as Jessy mentally braced herself. He slid a glance at his sister, aware that she would be the one shocked by the news. Logan shifted closer to Cat. "It's Tara."

"No." Cat stepped back from him, bumping into Logan, her green eyes round with denial and disbelief. "She wouldn't do that. You made a mistake."

"There is no mistake, Cat," Ty stated with a gentle firmness. "I talked with her myself."

"But . . . why? Why would she do it?" Cat looked at him with heart-touching bewilderment.

"Her reasons don't really matter," Ty replied. "She owns it and we have to deal with that."

It was on the tip of Jessy's tongue to throw it in Ty's face that she had warned him all along that Tara wasn't to be trusted. But she was wise enough to know that indulging in I-told-you-so was a waste of precious energies when they needed to concentrate their efforts on dealing with this new circumstance.

"What does she plan to do with it?" Jessy asked instead, every inch of her intent on his answer.

"She claims she wants to live on it." Ty was obviously not completely convinced of that. "But we'll have a better idea of her intentions after Friday."

"Why Friday?" Cat frowned.

"She's coming to dinner—at her suggestion," Ty added with dry emphasis. "Afterwards we will sit down and talk."

"She's after the coal, Ty." It was the only explanation that made sense to Jessy. "It was what her father wanted. Now she intends to fulfill his dream for it."

"If it is, she will play hell getting it out."

Chapter Thirteen

~

News of Tara's purchase of the Wolf Meadow range spread across the Triple C faster than a summer squall. By the middle of the week there wasn't a single individual who hadn't heard about it. Only the very young ones failed to understand its significance.

Mention of it was never made around anyone in the Calder household. But Jessy found it impossible not to be aware of the watchful glances directed her way each time she ventured out of The Homestead. They were all waiting to see what was going to be done about it, which increased the subtle tension that gripped all of them.

Patience had always been a forte of hers, but even Jessy found the waiting difficult. Keeping her mind occupied was the best antidote for it. And there was no better way to do that than astride a green-broke horse.

The three-year-old stud colt tugged at the bit, its muscles bunching with eagerness for a faster pace, but he maintained the sedate trot Jessy had set around the training pen. The colt was a flashy buckskin with a sharply white blaze down its face, jet-black mane, tail, and leg stockings, and its coat was that yellow-gold color associated with a palomino. His registered name was Lion's Paw, but Jessy had long ago dubbed him Dandy, short for Dandelion.

Halfway along the corral fence, Jessy signaled the colt to cut across it with a combination of leg cues, weight shift, and rein pressure. As always, the buckskin's response was lightning quick. One bit of inattention on her part and Jessy knew the colt had the ability to jump out from under her and leave her sitting in the air. That awareness was enough to keep her alert to every flex and shift of its muscle.

As if on cue, the colt broke stride, snorting in alarm as he rolled an eye at the cowboy climbing onto the opposite fence rail. Without difficulty, Jessy straightened the colt back up and brought him down to a walk. Only then did she let her attention stray long enough to identify Ballard with a quick glance his way.

"That's not fair, Jessy," Ballard protested. "He was wantin' an excuse to run and kick up his heels."

"And he would have done just that if I had given him a chance." Reaching forward, she stroked the buckskin's sleek neck.

"The twins must be takin' their afternoon nap," Ballard guessed.

"They fell asleep about twenty minutes ago," Jessy confirmed.

Ballard ran an admiring eye over the horse. "That colt is definitely something special."

"He should be. He is a double grandson to Cougar." She referred to the long-dead ranch stallion that had sired nearly all of the Triple C's top cow horses. "I can hardly wait until he is ready to work cattle."

"From what I've heard, if he's anything like his granddaddy, he'll be a natural." Ballard continued to study the three-year-old. "How's he comin' along?"

"Fast," Jessy admitted. "He's already getting bored with the routine of the training pen."

"In that case, give me a couple minutes to saddle up Jake and we'll take a ride down by the river and give the colt a chance to stretch its legs a little."

"Sounds good," Jessy agreed. "By the time you're ready, I should have most of the freshness worked out of him."

The dun gelding Ballard rode provided a steadying influence for the colt. Just the same Jessy had her hands full when she first rode the buckskin out of the pen. They were halfway to the river before he stopped his dancing and sidestepping and settled into a brisk walk.

With the gelding leading the way, they crossed the river at its shallow point, climbed the sloping bank, and headed into the grass expanse beyond it at an easy lope. The sun was warm on Jessy's face, and the south breeze had a hint of wildness in it.

A half-mile from the ranch headquarters, Ballard reined his horse down to a walk. Jessy followed suit, and the young colt raised no objections to the slower pace.

"He's settled down in fine shape," Ballard observed, noting the young horse's quietness.

"He has," Jessy agreed absently while her gaze took in the broad expanse of plains before them, rugged and rolling into forever.

For a long time, Ballard said nothing more. The stretch of silence was unlike him and Jessy was too used to his gab not to notice its absence.

Just about the time it started to become uncomfortable, he said, "You know the whole ranch is buzzing about Tara buying Wolf Meadow."

"Mom told me," Jessy admitted although she had guessed it long before that.

"Helicopters have been seen flying in and out of there a half-dozen times a day. Talk is she's buildin' something."

"I've heard that, too."

There was a pressed tightness about his mouth. "I knew the minute she showed up again that woman was going to bring trouble—just like before," he muttered thickly. "If Ty had a lick of sense, he would have shown her the door and given her a shove out of it. But not him. He let her become a fixture around here." He cocked his head at Jessy, a curious but sober glint in his eye. "Of course, the question is—what is he going to do about her now?"

"You'll know when everybody else does," Jessy retorted. "And don't be bad-mouthing Ty to me."

"You're married to him so you have to stand up for him, I understand that," Ballard said with an accepting nod of his head. "But you've gotta understand that I'm only saying what everybody else is."

"Maybe so, but I don't want to hear it."

Deliberately ignoring her, he continued, "Nobody would be sayin' much if it wasn't for the fact the old man is slippin'. There was a time if anybody crossed him, he would'a been on 'em like a lightning bolt. But he isn't the tough old bird he once was. And Ty is too soft to move against a woman. He finds it even harder to go against that one. She's always had some sort of spell over him. Leastwise, that's the talk," Ballard added, as if to assert it wasn't coming from him.

Angry, mostly because she knew that was likely what was being said, Jessy shot back, "Don't underestimate either of them. Spread that word."

She reined the buckskin around, pointing him back toward the Triple C headquarters, and urged him into a canter. Ballard brought his mount alongside, aware that she was setting a pace that discouraged further conversation.

That was fine with him. He had said what he had to say, though there was a good deal more he had left unsaid. He had his own suspicions about Tara's plans. To him, they were as obvious as a tree in the middle of a prairie.

Now that she had her hands on the perfect bait to guarantee success—Wolf Meadow, she would have Ty jumping through hoops to get it.

Promptly at six-thirty on Friday evening, a black Range Rover with Texas license plates pulled up to The Homestead. Ty waited at the top of the steps, his eyes narrowing in an effort to penetrate the windshield's tinted glass and identify the hatted figure behind the wheel.

Buck Haskell stepped out of the driver's side, dressed in jeans, a white shirt, and a Western-style blazer. There was a smug gleam in his eyes when he met Ty's gaze. Without a word, he came around the front of the Rover and opened the rear passenger door, extending an assisting hand to Tara.

With typical grace, she emerged from the vehicle, suitably attired for a business dinner in a tailored, but flattering, navy pinstriped suit and spectator pumps.

Ty stayed where he was, quietly watching while Buck escorted Tara to the front steps. Only when she was about to ascend did Ty speak.

"He isn't welcome inside."

Looking up, Tara replied smoothly, "He is with me."

"So I see. Just the same, he isn't coming inside," Ty stated with steely calm. "You can come in by yourself or stay out here with him. It's your choice."

Tara studied him for a considering moment, then murmured to Buck, "Wait here."

Dipping his head in mock obedience, he touched a finger to his hat and grinned. "With pleasure, ma'am. This way I don't have to worry about someone slippin' poison in my food."

"And our meal will be more enjoyable for the same reason." Ty swung away from the steps and crossed to the front door then held it open for Tara to precede him into the house.

Inside the foyer, she paused to smile up at him. "I truly didn't mean for our meeting to start off on the wrong foot."

"Don't worry. It didn't." He motioned toward the dining room. "Dinner is ready. I believe you know the way."

"No drinks in the den first?" Tara chided lightly.

"It didn't seem appropriate."

"Perhaps not," she agreed.

Jessy was busy buckling Trey into his highchair when Tara entered the dining room followed by Ty. Little Laura was her traitorous self, squealing with delight at the sight of Tara.

In an odd way, Jessy was equally glad to see Tara. Her presence signaled an end to a week's worth of waiting. That alone was something to celebrate.

"Hello, Tara." Jessy scooted Trey's highchair closer to the table. "Please have a seat. Sally is bringing the food in now."

"In that case, I will give her a hand." Tara slipped the strap of her shoulder bag over the corner of a chair back and moved toward the kitchen.

"That isn't necessary," Jessy began.

"Nonsense. It's the least I can do after the way I invited myself to dinner," Tara insisted and continued to the kitchen.

When Jessy stepped away from the highchair, Ty said, "Let her go."

"I wasn't going to stop her," Jessy replied. Just the same she was irked that the woman would act as if nothing had changed.

Chase shuffled into the dining room and halted, his glance shooting around the room before stopping on Ty.

"Where is Tara?"

"In the kitchen giving Sally a hand."

Chase harrumphed and started toward the chair at the head of the table. "That woman has nerve."

"She brought Buck with her." Ty pulled out his customary chair to the right of his father.

That stopped Chase again. "Where is he now?"

"Waiting outside."

Stepping to the window, Chase lifted aside the curtain and looked out. Just as abruptly, he crossed to the dining room extension and picked up the receiver. Squinting at the numbers, he punched out a series of them. "Jobe. It's Chase Calder. Get two men over to The Homestead on the double. Buck Haskell is out front. I want him watched the whole time he is here. And I want him to know that he's being watched." After a short pause, he responded to a question from the man. "If he wants to go to the cemetery and visit his mother's grave, that's fine. But nowhere else."

"He wouldn't be fool enough to try anything tonight," Ty said after Chase hung up.

"I agree." Untroubled, Chase crossed to his chair and sat down. "But why let him relax and get comfortable?"

Sally had her back to the connecting door when Tara walked into the kitchen. "Something smells delicious in here," Tara declared with airy brightness.

Startled, Sally turned around, a look of shock on her face at the sight of Tara. Immediately she pressed her lips together in a tight line of disapproval, all stiff and cool.

"What are you doing in here?"

"I came to give you a hand carrying things in." Tara crossed to the counter where a serving platter held a long roll of pastry-wrapped meat. Appreciatively she inhaled the steamy aromas emanating from it. "Beef Wellington. You always do it so well."

"I don't need any help, thank you very much." Sally was deliberately curt. "I prefer to do it myself."

"Sally," Tara murmured with a wounded look, "you aren't angry with me, too, are you?"

"After what you did, I am surprised that you would dare to show your face around here." Her movements were as crisp and quick as her voice as Sally retrieved serving spoons from the utensil drawer and stuffed them in the various dishes.

"Sally." Tara moved to the woman's side, placing both hands on her arm in silent supplication. "You, of all people, should understand why I did it."

Ignoring her plea, Sally declared, "Chase should have thrown you out. Why he ever agreed to this is beyond me."

"But, Sally—"

"Don't you but Sally me." She turned on her, the brightness of angry tears burning in her eyes. "I trusted you. I honestly thought—" She clamped her mouth shut on the rest of the sentence and pivoted away, shoulders rigid.

"Every word I told you was true," Tara assured her. "That's why I bought the land—so I could be near him."

"But to buy *that* land." Sally kept her back to Tara.

"How could you buy that piece? You know how much Chase has wanted it."

"Of course I know. But don't you see, now that I own it, it's practically the same as if he did. In a manner of speaking, it's in the family now."

Half turning, Sally searched Tara's face, her own expression wary yet hopeful. "Are you saying that you intend to deed it over to him?"

"Not right away, I can't," Tara replied. "They are both so upset with me now that they would never allow me to build a home on it. And I have already broken ground for it. Wait until you see it. It is going to be beautiful. Spacious, but not too large or imposing, just a cozy little retreat on the Montana plains."

"But later," Sally persisted, seeking a more definitive answer to her question, "you will turn it over to them?"

"Isn't that what I just said?" Tara said with a warm and easy smile. "It will obviously take some time before I can do anything, but it will all work out perfectly in the end. You'll see."

Sally wanted desperately to believe her, but it wasn't easy. When she had learned that Tara was the mysterious buyer, she had never felt so betrayed in all her life. Even worse, she felt she had betrayed Chase by befriending Tara, only to realize the woman had used her.

Tara pressed both hands on Sally's arm once more and looked at her with earnest and imploring eyes. "Please tell me I still have one friend in the Calder household."

After a moment's hesitation, Sally nodded. "You do."

But she wouldn't be nearly as trusting as she was before.

* * *

Although the atmosphere at the dinner table that evening was far from amiable, Tara seemed to be impervious to the heavy undercurrents. If anything, she seemed perfectly at ease with the situation.

Naturally the antics of the twins occupied much of the spotlight, both as a diversion and a safe topic for conversation. If Tara noticed that any responses tended to be coolly civil, she didn't let it show.

But Jessy felt the strain of having the enemy in their midst. It evoked a kind of quiet, simmering anger toward Tara. She knew exactly what the woman had achieved by being there: Tara was in a position of power and she had forced them to acknowledge it. And that was one more thing Jessy held against her.

It was with a trace of relief that Jessy rose at last to help Sally clear away the dessert dishes. "I will be right back with the coffee," Sally promised.

"We'll have ours in the den." Chase pushed his chair back from the table and glanced pointedly at Tara. "You do plan to join us, don't you?"

"Of course." Rising, Tara retrieved her oversized shoulder bag from the chair back and smiled lightly. "To be honest, I feel a bit like Daniel. Only I'm about to enter the den with two Calder lions."

Unable to suppress her resentment any longer, Jessy countered smoothly, "I'm sure you are very experienced at catfighting, Tara."

Jessy had the satisfaction of seeing a flicker of annoyance in the woman's eyes before Jessy departed for the kitchen, a stack of dessert plates in each hand. Sally was already there, busily arranging the coffee service on its tray.

She looked up when Jessy entered. "I'll help you with the twins just as soon as I take coffee in to Chase."

"For two cents, I would put poison in her cup." Jessy shoved the dirty plates onto the sink counter.

After a moment's hesitation, Sally suggested, in an attempt at offhandedness, "Maybe it won't be as bad as you think."

"I am not going to hold my breath."

As far as Jessy was concerned, Tara and trouble were synonymous. She had a history of bringing it, and the uneasy grumblings among the Triple C riders bothered Jessy.

Much of the ranch's success was predicated on a combination of strong leadership, loyalty, and a guardianship of the land. Every blade of grass had long been held to be precious. When Tara obtained legal title to those ten thousand acres that had been considered Calder property for years, she had rocked its foundation.

Everyone on the ranch was anxious for something to be done about it. But in typical Triple C fashion, there was the usual way to handle a problem—and there was the Calder way. And it was the Calder way they wanted to see, but the grumblings revealed a doubt that they would get it.

Truthfully Jessy was a little concerned as well. For the life of her, she couldn't think of any action Chase and Ty could take.

Sandwiched between the two men during the walk to the den, Tara covertly studied them. She was struck again by the strong resemblance between them, both possessing the same granite chin and brow, the same impenetrable darkness of wide, deeply set eyes, and the same high, hard cheekbones. In Chase, age had chiseled extra lines in his face, and there was a sagging of the skin beneath the jawline, but neither made him any less formidable.

Tonight both men wore the same mask of polite indifference. As yet, she had detected no break in it, no hint of temper or impatience. She smiled to herself, recalling how her father had often complained that the Calders were as impossible to read as the Saudis. It was true. Although in the past, Ty hadn't been as adept as his father. Therefore Tara watched him a little more closely. With few exceptions, she had always been able to manage him.

When they reached the den, Chase stepped aside, allowing her to precede him. But there was little about it that made her regard it as a gentleman's courtesy. Which made her wonder if he was reluctant to present his back to her, a possibility she found most interesting. For herself, she had no such qualms, entering the room ahead of both men.

"Have a seat." Chase motioned to the matching wing-backed chairs that faced the desk, and made his way to the big one behind it.

"Thank you." Slipping the handbag off her shoulder, Tara sat down in the first chair and tucked her purse in the small space next to it, wanting to keep it within easy reach.

She was a bit surprised when Ty folded his long frame into the other chair. In the past, he had usually ranged about the stone fireplace. She was quick to note the break in his pattern, although it was difficult to tell what it signaled.

Tara searched but found no trace of tension in Ty. He appeared to be loose and relaxed, almost as though he were the one in control. But Tara knew better.

Hampered by his arthritis, Chase was slow, as usual,

to get settled in the big leather chair. Tara didn't attempt any small talk to fill the moment. For the time being she was content with the silence. Once she began her pitch, she wanted no interruptions. And, like Ty and Chase, she was aware that Sally would arrive at any moment with the coffee.

Her glance strayed briefly to the framed map behind Chase, depicting the immense scope of the Triple C Ranch and its boundaries, its paper yellowed with age. Tara was smugly aware that she had snatched a great big chunk out of it.

Footsteps in the hall signaled Sally's approach. Tara took advantage of these last few seconds to mentally review her proposal, satisfying herself once again that there was no objection to it that she couldn't reason away logically.

It was with eagerness that Tara observed Sally's entrance into the den. She had anticipated this meeting for so long, and now it was almost here. It seemed to take interminable minutes for the coffee to be poured and the cups passed to each. At last Sally exited the room, leaving them alone.

Ignoring the steaming cup of coffee in front of him, Chase rocked back in his chair and folded his hands together. "Since this was your idea, why don't you begin?"

"Of course." Tara continued to balance her cup and saucer on her lap. "I hope both of you can appreciate how very, very awkward this is for me. In the last year, we have managed to reach a close friendship of sorts. It is something I value a great deal even though my recent purchase of Wolf Meadow might suggest otherwise to you."

"What's your point, Tara?" Ty's voice was full of dry disinterest as he raised his cup, eyeing her over its rim.

"It's simply to clarify that if I had it to do over again,

I would go about it differently, without all the secrecy that makes it seem like such a betrayal of your friendship."

Her voice and her expression held just the right note of sincerity, but Ty couldn't shake the feeling that it was nothing more than lines delivered by a skilled actress.

"We all have our regrets," he said. "It doesn't change anything."

"I know that," Tara agreed easily. "But I hope you will give me a chance to convince you that they are more than just words to me."

"How do you propose to accomplish that?" Chase laced his fingers together, a gesture that reinforced his challenging skepticism.

In answer, Tara set her cup and saucer on the desk, opened the large purse at her side, and extracted a slim folder. "With this, I hope." Fluidly, she rose and placed it in front of him.

Ty wasn't about to go for the bait. Like his father, he remained motionless. "What is it?" He wanted her to tell him.

Resuming her seat, Tara answered, "I took the liberty of having my attorney draft a lease for your review."

If anything, her explanation hardened something inside Ty. "I take it you have changed your mind about building a second home there."

"Actually I haven't. In the lease you will see that a fifty-acre tract, on which it will sit, has been excluded. Out of roughly ten thousand acres, that is no more than a postage stamp."

"The site is at windmill eleven, you said?" Chase arched a questioning glance at Ty.

"That's right," Ty replied then idly studied his hands. "The only water source in three miles, and some of the best hay ground in Wolf Meadow."

"Quite honestly I wasn't aware of that," Tara admitted. "But we can incorporate some kind of language that would allow you access to both. After all, this is just a first draft, and I am determined to find a way to make this work for both of us. It's the least I can do," Tara added, her whole demeanor soft and persuasive.

Chase grunted a nonanswer and rocked forward, pulling a pair of reading glasses from his pocket. After slipping them on, he flipped open the folder and perused the enclosed document.

"What are the terms?" Chase slid Tara a glance over the top of his glasses.

"I think you will find they are quite generous. Fortunately my income is such that I don't have to be concerned about a return on my investment. In fact, I have my tax lawyers working now on finding a way to deed the land over to you without creating a lot of tax complications for either of us."

As dangled carrots went, Ty gave Tara high marks for finding a particularly tempting one. But knowing her, he was certain there would be conditions attached to it. There always were, even if they weren't spelled out at the beginning.

"That's a very grand gesture," Ty remarked, aware that it was one without substance at the moment.

"On the surface I suppose it seems that way. But it isn't really. Since my father passed away, you are the closest thing I have to a family. And I will never forget the way you were there when I needed you," Tara declared in a subtle bid for more sympathy, her eyes glistening with unshed tears. "It meant more to me than you will ever know."

"It was nothing."

"Maybe not to you, but it was to me. That is how this whole thing got started—I wanted to do something for you. Considering that my father was more or less responsible for you losing title to Wolf Meadow in the first place, it seemed only right that I should try to get it back for you." Pausing, Tara allowed a small smile to play across her lips, one that was a little rueful and apologetic. "Then I became a little selfish and decided to keep a little piece of the Triple C for myself so I could live here, too. I knew that was something neither of you would normally permit."

"So you resorted to extortion to get it," Ty concluded.

"That's putting it a bit strongly, I think, considering that my intent is to restore your ownership of the property."

"Except for fifty acres of it," he countered dryly.

"I am certain that we can ultimately come to some sort of understanding whereby it is titled in your name with a proviso that I have a life estate to it. That's something our attorneys can work out."

"In the meantime you want"—Chase paused to locate the precise phrase in the document—" 'ten dollars and other valuable considerations' for a one-year lease."

"Obviously if a transfer of ownership can be accomplished sooner than that, we will." Tara's expression brimmed with confidence.

"By the way," Chase addressed his remark to Ty, "among the 'other valuable considerations,' she wants access to the fifty-acre tract as well as a utility easement."

"I am building a home there," Tara said, as if they needed to be reminded of it.

Leaning back in his chair, Chase removed the reading glasses and idly toyed with them. "There is something I've been wondering."

"What's that?" Tara asked, all bright and helpful.

"Your reason for hiring Buck Haskell to work for you."

He studied her with a look of detached interest yet he was alert for the smallest change.

Her smile was quick and careless, mildly chiding. "Who else could I find who knows every inch of the ranch as well as he does? I can understand why you would have reservations about him. But believe me, I checked him out thoroughly. I know it sounds terribly trite, but he is truly a changed man."

"Take it from me"—Chase tossed the reading glasses onto his desk—"he is as skilled at acting as you are."

She drew back fractionally, a wounded look in her eyes. "Please. This is not an act."

"Maybe not," Chase agreed without conceding the fact. "Just the same, you had best keep an eye on him. And whatever you do, don't let him slap you on the back without first checking to make sure his hand doesn't have a knife in it."

"I appreciate the advice, and I will follow it," Tara promised.

"I hope you do. As for this lease"—Chase touched the document before him—"I'm afraid we won't be able to sign it."

Undeterred, Tara smiled away his answer. "Obviously I didn't expect you to sign it tonight. I know you will need to review it with your lawyers. There are always minor changes that need to be made for one side or the other. I—"

"You don't understand," Ty interrupted. "We don't need to have our attorneys look at it because we can't accept it."

Startled, Tara divided her questioning look between the two of them. "Why ever not? What possible objection could you have to it?"

"We aren't in a position financially to take it on,"

Chase responded. "It isn't so much the ten dollars as it is the cost to stock it. We have already sold the cattle, and we don't have the spare capital to buy more. What resources we have available are committed to this auction. As tempting as your offer is, it simply wouldn't be prudent for us to accept it at this time."

"Why don't you give us a raincheck?" Ty suggested. "Then later, if the auction is as successful as we believe it will be, we can sit down with you again."

"Flabbergasted" was not an adjective that normally would be applied to Tara, but it described her reaction perfectly. "But signing the lease doesn't require any financial commitment on your part. It merely gives you control of the land. Surely you want that?"

"Wanting something and not being able to afford it are two very different things. But I doubt you have had much experience with that." Rising, Ty reached across the desk, slipped the lease back in its folder, and offered them to Tara. "I hope this hasn't inconvenienced you too much."

"Inconvenienced me? What about you?" Tara argued. "What about the winter hay you always got from Wolf Meadow? You will need it. And the water, too."

"We have already committed to buy our hay from an outside source. And without additional cattle, we don't need the water." Ty's smile was wry with regret. "If you had said something about this before, I could have saved you from going through all the trouble and expense of having a lease drawn up."

"I believe Buck is still outside waiting to drive you back to town," Chase inserted. "Ty, why don't you walk Tara to her car?"

Short of creating a scene, Tara realized she had no choice but to leave. As furious as she was over her plans being thwarted, she longed to indulge herself with a nasty scene. But both men had been much too cordial, too reasonable in their rejection, leaving her with no opening.

Keeping an iron control on her temper, Tara accepted the folder from Ty and rose to her feet then paused, determined to gain something positive from the evening. "At least tell me you aren't angry with me anymore? That you understand my reasons for doing this?"

"Naturally we understand. You explained things very well." Chase nodded in assurance. "And we always try to get along with our neighbors. Which is what you will be, right?"

"Right." Try as she might, Tara didn't know what to make of any of this. Both Ty and Chase were too calm, too congenial. It worried her. Did they know something she didn't?

PART THREE

The wind, it's blowin' dry through the grass.
Trouble's brewin' a-plenty.
You hear its hum,
But where will it come?
It's a question that's makin' a Calder worry.

Chapter Fourteen

Reclining in the driver's seat, Buck had his hat tipped forward to shield his eyes. The radio was tuned to a country music station, the volume low enough that he could still hear the murmured voices of the two cowboys lounging by the porch steps. He didn't recognize either man, but assumed they were more than likely the offspring of somebody he knew.

Neither cowboy had so much as nodded a hello to him when they walked up to The Homestead. Buck knew right away that Chase had given orders for them to watch him. It had crossed his mind to see if he couldn't engage them in some small talk just to pass the time, then decided not to give them anything to report, convinced that would bother Chase more.

A long rectangle of light spilled into his side vision, its presence signaling the opening of the front door. With a slight turn of his head, Buck glanced at the couple exiting The Homestead, quickly identifying Ty and Tara.

Giving his hat a push off his forehead, Buck sat up and popped the lever that brought the driver's seat back to its upright position. By the time he stepped out of the car, the two were coming down the steps. Quickening his steps, he had the passenger door open for Tara before she reached it.

All smiles, she turned to take her leave of Ty. "Please tell your father how grateful I am for his understanding. I meant it when I said you all are the same as family to me."

"I will tell him," Ty promised, smiling easily as he stepped back. "Have a good evening."

"You, too." With a farewell wave to him, Tara slid into the seat.

As Buck moved to shut the door, he got a good look at Ty's face. There was something just a little too pleased and a little too confident about his expression in Buck's way of thinking. He had a feeling that his employer had just found out what it was like to tangle with the Calders.

After he had climbed into the driver's seat, Buck flicked a quick glance at the rearview mirror, inspecting Tara's reflection in it. But he could tell little from her expression.

Buck waited until he was headed down the forty-mile-long lane to town before he asked, "How did it go?"

She met his reflected glance in the mirror, her gaze cool and sharp. "That is really none of your business."

Buck grinned. "That bad, huh?"

In a burst of angry frustration, Tara snapped, "If you must know, yes!"

"That's what I thought." He nodded in amusement.

"I don't understand," Tara murmured in irritation, an intensity and determination to her expression as she mentally searched for an explanation. "It was a sweet deal. Why didn't they accept it?"

"Just out of curiosity, ma'am, exactly what did you offer 'em?"

She shot him an annoyed look in the mirror then relented. "A year's lease to the property for ten dollars, excluding the fifty-acre building site, of course. It was all very straightforward, completely in their favor."

"Except for one thing, I'm guessin'."

"What?" Her gaze sharpened on him.

"I'll bet there was a clause in there somewhere that gave you access to the property. Right?"

"Naturally. I expected it to be an issue, but they didn't raise any objection to it. It was almost as if they had decided to turn down any offer I made before they even saw it," Tara mused, mostly to herself as she replayed the meeting in her mind. "And you think access alone killed the idea?"

"Deader than roadkill," Buck confirmed. "It's just my opinion ma'am, but as long as you have title to the Wolf Meadow range, the Calders won't give you access to diddly-squat."

"But why? What can they possibly gain from it? It won't stop me from building. I should think they would have already realized that. I have been flying men and equipment in for a week now. If necessary, I can continue to do it until the lodge is finished. It will likely double the construction costs, but I can easily afford it."

"While you're at it, you might as well figure on buying yourself a flock of those whirlybirds. Because you can bet those Calders plan on makin' getting' to or from that property as inconvenient as hell."

"I can deal with it," she stated firmly.

"Sure you can." Buck nodded in agreement, the

same amused smile edging the corners of his mouth. "But it's gonna get mighty old after a while. It wouldn't surprise me if the Calders aren't counting on that."

Clearly irritated by his obvious insight into the Calders, Tara challenged, "Do you have any suggestions, Mr. Haskell?"

"Not off the top of my head."

"If you should come up with anything, let me know." After delivering the sentence with a curt finality, she turned her gaze out the window to stare at the night-darkened grass sea beyond it.

"I'll do that," Buck replied. "Just one question, though."

"What's that?" Disinterested in any further conversation with him, Tara didn't bother to glance his way.

"If it should come to it, are you prepared to go to war with the Calders?"

For a long run of seconds, she remained silent. "Not yet," was her ultimate decision.

Buck drove another mile before curiosity got the better of him. "If you don't mind me asking, what are you going to do now?"

After a thoughtful pause, Tara replied, "Perhaps make a point." Buck could tell that she had a plan formulating in that brain of hers. "Step on it, will you? I have some calls I need to make."

"Yes, ma'am." Buck pushed the accelerator pedal a little closer to the floorboard and the vehicle surged forward, leaving a dust cloud behind it to linger in the night air.

The two cowboys, Jobe Garvey and Kyle Sullivan, followed Ty into the den. Chase waited behind the desk for their report on Buck's movements, nodding to them when they entered.

"What happened?" He glanced sharply from one to the other.

"Nothing really, sir." It was Jobe Garvey who answered. "When we showed up, he kinda acted like he had been expecting us. He hung around the Rover for a while then ambled off to the cemetery."

"You went with him?" Ty sought confirmation.

"Like a couple of puppy dogs," Kyle replied. "He spent some time at Ruth's grave then headed straight back here and climbed into the Rover. He never budged from it until she came out to leave."

"So he didn't say anything to you, ask you any questions," Chase said thoughtfully, not actually phrasing it as a question.

Garvey answered him just the same. "He never said one word."

"Good." Chase nodded in satisfaction and smiled. "Thanks for coming out tonight, boys. We appreciate it." As soon as the two men had left the den, he switched his attention to Ty. "Did Tara say anything outside?"

"Just the usual small talk." Ty settled back in his chair and draped a bent leg across his knee. "But you can bet she was confused and annoyed that we didn't accept the deal. She'll be back. Probably not for a few days, but she will be in touch."

"I'm sure she will," Chase agreed absently, a slight frown creasing his forehead. "There was one thing she said tonight that rang true. Outside of our own men, no one knows the Triple C better than Buck Haskell. He has ridden every hill and gully on this ranch—and can tell you every back trail and which one is the quickest or shortest way to anywhere." He swiveled the leather chair around to stare at the framed map. "And she has him planted damned near in the middle of it all."

Ty studied the map as well. "I still can't believe he would be fool enough to try anything."

"Maybe. Then again, maybe not." Chase swung his chair back around. "The smart thing is to play it safe and pass the word tomorrow for everyone to keep an eye out for any strange vehicles traveling over the ranch roads."

"Consider it done." Ty idly adjusted the hem of his jeans, smoothing its line over his boots.

But Chase wasn't finished. "Does O'Rourke still prowl around?"

"Not as much as he used to. Every now and then, you'll catch sight of him, usually if Cat's in the vicinity. Why?"

Chase reached for the telephone. "I think I'll have Cat ask O'Rourke to keep his eyes peeled for anything unusual or suspicious. He is one man who could teach you, me, and Buck a few things about moving from one end of this ranch to the other without being seen."

"Do you think that's wise?" Ty questioned the decision. "Buck used him once before. And O'Rourke has never had any love for either one of us. He only tolerates us for Cat's sake."

"Good point. Just the same, I think Cat can handle him and make sure nothing like that happens again." Chase slipped on his reading glasses again to punch his daughter's telephone number.

The next morning Ty spread the word for everyone to keep a lookout for any strange vehicle traveling within the Triple C boundaries. He also made a point of mentioning that Tara had offered to lease them the Wolf Meadow range—and they had refused.

Each time the reaction was the same. After a moment or two of stunned disbelief came the smile and the wry shake of the head. The message was clear to all—the Calders would not be dancing to whatever tune Tara chose to call, as many had feared. Just how Chase and Ty intended to get the land back, no one knew. But they were confident that the Calders would find a way—their way.

Within days after the word went out, the telephone at The Homestead was ringing off the wall—not with reports of unknown vehicles being sighted, but with complaints over the marked increase of air traffic over the ranch's north and east quadrants.

Shortly after lunch on Thursday, longtime ranchhand Jasper Karlsen stomped into the dining room, each heavy step punctuated by the harsh *chank* of his spurs. He walked straight to Chase's chair, the angry scowl on his face was as black as a thundercloud.

He didn't waste time coming to the point, exploding, "Dammit, Chase, you've gotta do somethin' about those damned choppers! They're flying in and out of Wolf Meadow in swarms now. The cattle over on Long Creek pasture are flighty as hell from bein' spooked all the time. In the last couple days they must have dropped nearly a hundred pounds just from runnin' when those damned choppers fly over."

Ty spoke up. "I have already left a message for Tara to call me right away. When she does, hopefully I'll be able to convince her to have the pilots fly at a higher altitude."

"In the event he doesn't succeed," Chase inserted, "I already have Stumpy checking to see if he can handle any more cattle at South Branch in case we have to move them."

"If you do, you'll play hell roundin' them up," Jasper warned. "About the time you get 'em bunched together, the helicopters fly over and scatter them to hell an' gone. What the hell is she doin' over there anyway?"

"Ferrying in equipment and supplies for the house she's building, I guess." That was Ty's supposition.

"More'n likely she's flying in her own damned army," Jasper retorted, then sprang to his own defense. "You think I'm exaggeratin', but if you were out there with me, you'd swear, too, that the military must be holdin' war maneuvers."

"Until we get this handled, just do the best you can," Chase advised.

The cowboy snorted in disgust. "I might as well piss up a rope. At least I'd stand a chance of accomplishin' that," he grumbled and stalked out of the room.

He passed Cat on her way in, grunting a response when she greeted him. "What's wrong with Jasper?" she asked curiously. "He looked as grouchy as an old bear."

"He's having trouble over at Long Creek with the helicopters spooking the cattle," Ty explained as the twins clamored for Cat's attention.

"Uncle Culley mentioned last night that he had seen a bunch of them flying toward Blue Moon." Cat paused by the highchairs to give each child a hug and a kiss on the cheek. "Hi, sweeties."

Jessy frowned. "I don't understand why she needs so many."

"Presumably, to haul all the construction workers she has hired." Cat picked up the insulated coffee carafe and gave it a shake, checking for the telltale slosh of liquid within. There was none. "Do you have more coffee made, Sally? I could use a cup."

"There's some in the kitchen." The woman rose from her chair, gathering a few plates to carry with her. "I'll get it."

"Thanks." Cat pulled out an empty chair next to Jessy and sat down. "According to Logan, she is bringing in workers by the droves. I guess it's absolute chaos in Blue Moon—even worse than when Dy-Corp opened its mining operation. Every time I think about her buying that land away from us, I get so mad I could personally strangle her."

Jessy glimpsed some of that anger in Cat's eyes. Truthfully she felt the same. Unfortunately it didn't solve anything.

"Isn't there some way we can stop her from building on it, Dad?" There was a hint of desperation mixed in with the frustration in Cat's voice.

"As long as she has the necessary permits, which she does, she can do anything she likes. We can only step in if she attempts to cross our land to get to it," Chase stated what they all already knew.

When the telephone rang, Ty excused himself from the table to answer it and crossed to the dining room extension. "Triple C Ranch, Ty speaking."

"Ty. It's Tara. You left an urgent message for me to call you. I—"

"Yes, I did." He cut across her words, wasting no time with preliminaries. "It's about your helicopters. They are flying so low over our range, they're spooking our cattle."

"Ty, I'm sorry. I had no idea," Tara rushed in apology. "I'll put a stop to it at once."

"I'd appreciate it if you would."

"As you pointed out, we are neighbors." Her voice softened, all conciliatory. "If I had given it a moment's thought, I would never have allowed it to happen in the first place, but it never crossed my mind that I would need to warn the pilots about flying too low. By the way," Tara continued without a break, "would it be convenient if I came by the ranch tomorrow morning? I took the liberty of picking up the sale catalogs from the printers and thought I would drop them off."

"What time?"

"Between ten-thirty and eleven. Would that suit you?"

"I'll be here."

"Good. I'll see you tomorrow then," she said and rang off.

Chase glanced at him expectantly. "Tara?"

"Yes." Ty turned from the phone. "She said she would take care of the problem with the helicopters right away."

"Let's hope she does," Chase grunted.

"She will," Ty said.

"How can you be so sure of that?" Cat challenged, voicing Jessy's very thought.

"Because I don't think she wants to do anything more to cross us, at least not intentionally." Ty resumed his seat at the table. "And all those helicopters indicate to me that she isn't going to make an attempt to cross our land—and probably won't for a good long while."

"Just the same, I asked Uncle Culley to keep an eye out for anything out of the ordinary," Cat stated. "He promised he would."

Stars dusted the night sky, glittering brightly amid the darkness. Culley O'Rourke knew them all. They had been his companions on many an evening ride; they were as familiar to him as the gelding he rode. It was that familiarity with all things of the night that made him quick to notice the faint glow in the distance.

He reined his horse to study it. As dry as the land

was, fire was Culley's first thought. He tested the wind but detected no trace of smoke in it. The glow was steady, without the wane and leap of moving flames.

"That's no fire," he murmured to his horse. "Let's go take a look-see."

The decision was born out of his own curiosity reinforced by the remembered request from Cat to keep an eye out for anything unusual.

In no hurry, Culley swung the gelding's head toward the distant glow and urged it forward at an easy shuffling trot. Culley and sleep had never been frequent companions. As he had gotten older, it seemed he needed less and less of it. A couple three catnaps a day seemed to do him just fine.

These night rambles had become a habit with him. Culley liked having the sky above him and a wide stretch of land on each side. Nothing made him restless quicker than being confined within four walls, shut away from the wild smell of the wind.

Over the years Culley had learned the slow and the fast way to just about anywhere on the Triple C. Tonight he chose the easy way, seeing no need to tire either himself or his mount.

It didn't take him long to figure out the glow was coming from somewhere on the Wolf Meadow range. He couldn't help smiling at the recollection that Tara had bought that land out from under Calder's nose. He knew Cat had been mighty upset over it, but Culley figured Calder had been due for a comeuppance. Because of Cat, he didn't take as much pleasure in it as he once might have. But he definitely didn't lose any sleep over it.

The closer he got to the light, the bigger and brighter it became. It reminded him of the glow from a city, reaching out to dim all but the brightest stars. As near as he could tell, it was coming from the area of that old windmill not far from Antelope Butte. If he remembered right, Cat had said something about Tara planning to build a house out here. But that still didn't solve the puzzle of the light.

Less than a mile from its source, Culley reined his horse to a walk. The rolling terrain still blocked his view, but he began to pick up the low rumble of machinery.

Following a fold in the plains, he worked his way around to approach the site from the far side of the bluff. The noise was louder now, the light reaching out to deepen the shadows around him. Turning cautious, Culley pulled his horse up behind a low rise and dismounted, dropping the reins to ground-tie the gelding. On silent feet, he moved toward the rise.

"Well, well, well," a familiar voice drawled on his right. "If it ain't Culley O'Rourke himself."

Culley froze on the spot. With a fractional turn of his head, he swept his gaze over the shadows, searching for the owner of that voice he couldn't quite place. There was a whisper of movement, the grass against a leather boot. Culley zeroed in on the sound just as a figure separated itself from the darkness. The reflected glow from the other side of the rise touched the face of an old man. The features weren't quite the same, but Culley was quick to recognize that grin. It could only belong to one man—Buck Haskell.

Even after identifying him, Culley didn't venture a reply. He remained motionless, fully alert and fully aware of the rifle casually cradled in Buck's arm.

"You know you're trespassin', Culley," Buck remarked idly and strolled into the open.

"What're ya' gonna do about it?" Culley watched him with care.

"I guess it depends on whether you came to make mischief or not."

"I saw the glow."

Nodding, Buck glanced toward the light. "It's kinda hard to miss."

"You can see it for miles." Culley didn't take his eyes off Buck. "What's makin' it?"

"Giant floodlights," Buck replied easily. "Come on. We'll take a look."

Veering to the side, Buck started up the low rise. Culley let Buck take the lead then followed, keeping a little distance to one side of him.

Culley didn't bother to climb all the way to the top, just far enough to have an unobstructed view of the other side. A half-dozen huge floodlights, mounted atop towering poles, surrounded a work site. The blinding brilliance of them made the entire area bright as daylight. Culley stared at the men and machinery in constant but unhurried motion. Accustomed as he was to the softness of night sounds, the racket of revving engines and droning generators was loud to his ears, even at this distance.

"Quite a sight, isn't it?" Buck remarked.

"How come they're workin' so late?" That's what puzzled Culley.

"The duchess decided she wants the house done by fall, so she put the construction on a fast track. Work goes on twenty-four hours a day. And not just here either," he added. "Instead of ferryin' all the lumber here by chopper, crews in Blue Moon are buildin' the framework there so it can be flown out in sections and set in place. In a couple weeks, they figure to be puttin' the finishin' touches on the outside and goin' full bore on the inside."

Culley frowned. "The duchess?"

Buck smiled crookedly. "That's what I call Tara. She's definitely the queen bee around here."

"I heard you were workin' for her."

"To tell you the truth, O'Rourke, I've never had an easier job or better pay."

Culley continued to scan the area before him, not content until he finally spotted the windmill's black skeleton silhouetted against the night just beyond the reach of the lights. His curiosity satisfied, he turned and headed down the slope toward his horse.

"You aren't leavin' already, are you?" Buck chided.

"Already seen what I came for." In Culley's thinking, there was no more reason to stay.

"I guess you gotta rush off and report this to Calder." Buck's voice sounded closer, an indication he had trailed him down the slope.

"No need. He'll find out soon enough on his own."

"I reckon he will. Don't you know he'll be mad when he does. He figured to slow her down by not letting her cross Calder land. But it just kicked the duchess into high gear." After a slight break, Buck said, "Still hate him, do you?"

"I let him be, and Calder lets me be," Culley replied without emotion.

"That's what happens when a body gets older, I guess. But I noticed age hasn't stopped you from ghostin' around this country at night. I've been sittin' out here for two nights, waitin' for you to show up. The ground was gettin' a little hard for these old bones of mine. Say, I still have some coffee left in my thermos over here. Want a cup?"

"No thanks." Culley gathered up the trailing reins to his horse.

"You never were very sociable," Buck recalled.

"And you were never my friend." Culley stepped to the saddle, a hand on the horn.

"That's true," Buck agreed. "All we ever shared was a mutual hatred for Calder."

"Maybe." Culley shot him a hard, accusing glance. "But I ain't forgetting you once tried to kill my sister."

"You and I both know it was the boy I was after. Maggie got in the way. But I didn't hurt her," Buck reminded him, then shrugged. "That was all a long time ago. And I did my time for it." He watched as Culley hauled himself into the saddle, not as effortlessly as he once had. "We're both older now, O'Rourke. And a little wiser."

The saddle creaked as Culley settled himself into the seat. "Leave me be, Buck."

"There's trouble brewin'." Buck's voice had the ring of a warning.

Culley responded with a curt nod of agreement. "I can smell it in the wind."

Buck grinned. "You and I are alike that way."

"I'm giving you fair warning, Buck." He stared him in the eye. "Stay away from the girl."

"I saw her in town a week or so ago. She's the spittin' image of Maggie, isn't she?"

"You hurt a hair on her head, and I swear I'll kill you with my bare hands."

Buck knew the difference between a threat and a promise. In O'Rourke's case, the statement belonged in the latter category.

"Whatever's coming, I don't think she'll be part of it." Buck based that purely on a gut feeling.

"See that she isn't." He backed his horse deeper into the shadows behind him before reining it into a half-circle and slipping into the night.

Buck stared after him, his head cocked at a listening angle to catch the faint scuff of iron shoes on the hard ground. But there were few sounds to betray the exact route of O'Rourke's retreat from the area. Smiling, Buck realized the night horse Culley rode was almost as soft-footed as its rider.

On the other side of the rise, a piece of heavy machinery revved its diesel motor a couple times, then roared forward, belching black smoke from its exhaust. Distracted by the sudden increase in the noise level, Buck glanced toward the work site, but he made no move toward it. He preferred the relative quiet of the high plains over the racket of the construction site, the smell of greening grass over diesel fumes, the feel of a fresh wind on his face over the grit of churned-up dust. In that he was like O'Rourke.

His gaze drifted over the ranchland, land he had been born and raised on. Despite all the years he had spent away from it, locked in a prison cell, this Calder land was still in his blood. Standing here, in the middle of it, Buck felt as if he had finally come home.

Under a high sun, Tara stood at the rear of the Range Rover and watched while two ranch hands unloaded the boxes from the back of the vehicle. When the last box was carried away, Ty closed the door.

"That should do it," he said with finality and glanced her way. "Thanks for dropping off the catalogs."

"No problem at all," Tara assured him. "I know I could have easily had the printer ship them to you, but it didn't make sense when I was going to be so close. This way you don't have to worry about them getting lost en route."

"I guess not." He could feel her gaze on him, bright with interest, probing to gauge his mood.

"To be honest, I was half afraid you might not want me to ever set foot on the ranch again, despite all your talk about us being neighbors."

"Really?" Ty knew she was angling for something, but he didn't know what. It made him wary.

"Did your people let you know that I stopped the helicopters from flying so low on their way to the construction site?"

"As a matter of fact, I spoke to Jasper shortly before you arrived. He said everything was relatively quiet so far," Ty admitted.

"And it will be from now on. You have my word on that," Tara promised and turned slightly, raising a hand to shield her eyes from the sun's glare as she glanced toward the old barn. "Have they finished the work on the barn yet?"

"Almost."

She tilted her head in his direction, a persuasively hopeful gleam in her dark eyes. "Would it be terribly much to ask if I might have a tour of it? Since the idea to remodel it was mine to begin with, it feels like the project is my baby. I can't help wanting to know how it's coming along."

Ty weighed her request, trying to guess at her ulterior motive for it. But he couldn't come up with any obvious one, other than a desire to wiggle back into his good graces. And that wasn't likely to happen.

"I have enough time to give you a quick tour of it," he consented.

"Great." Tara set off toward it, clearly anticipating him to fall in step with her. "It's hard not to be a part of this, involved on a daily basis planning all the details for the auction, especially after living with it constantly for over a year. I can't help feeling shut out."

"I would have thought you would be too busy with your own project these days to give much thought to the auction," Ty said in a dry but pointed reference to the construction in progress at Wolf Meadow.

Her smile was quick and warm. "Not so busy that I don't have time to think about this." Then her smile took on a rueful quality. "I know you don't believe me, but I really do miss working with you on this."

Ty wasn't about to let the conversation become personal. "How is the house coming along?"

"Quickly." If she was irritated by his change of subject, Tara didn't let it show. "I have crews working on it night and day. If you have time one of these days, why don't you come over and I'll show you around. And I promise—I won't object in the slightest if you cross my land to get to the site," she teased.

His sole acknowledgment of the latter remark was a slight smile. "It's a bit busy around here right now. But I'll see what I can arrange in the next few days."

"I hope you can come. I would like to show you the plans. It truly suits its environs, all rustic and open, very earthy and warm. I'm excited about it, as if you hadn't guessed that already." Tara was at her vivacious and vibrant best, aglow with enthusiasm for the subject. "Do you realize that this will be the first home that I designed, built, and decorated myself? Everything will be just the way I want it, not someone else. It's a good feeling to put your stamp on something. I know at my home in Fort Worth, I can see Daddy's mark in every room. Which is probably why I am reluctant to change anything there. Sometimes the past shouldn't be abolished."

"Perhaps not." Ty stepped ahead of her to open the barn's Dutch door.

Light bathed much of the barn's cavernous interior, most of it coming from indirect sources mounted among the rafters of massive rough hewn timbers. Tara stepped inside onto the alleyway's new floor, made from salvaged street brick laid in a herringbone pattern. One of the workers had cranked up the volume on the radio, filling the silence with a honky-tonk song.

Tara gazed about her with a mixture of pride and satisfaction. "This is clearly the exception, Ty. On occasions, you can take the past and improve on it. The lighting is the only obvious modern item in the whole place. It's stunning. You must be pleased with it."

"I am."

In a far corner of the barn, a telephone rang, its bell amplified to be heard outside. After a second, ear-harsh ring, someone turned down the radio.

"It was impressive the last time I saw it," Tara recalled. "But you have added so many finishing touches since then that it somehow increases the impact. This is a look others will try to duplicate. Wait and see."

Ballard stepped from behind one of the partitions at the far end of the alleyway. "Stumpy's on the phone, Ty. He wants to talk to you."

"Sorry. It's important," Ty said in a brief aside to Tara and moved away, too quickly to catch the flicker of annoyance in her expression. Ballard saw it, though. "While I'm on the phone, show Tara the holding pens, Ballard."

Ballard acknowledged the order with a nod and ambled in her direction, unaffected by the pleasant smile she beamed his way.

"Ty pawned me off on you, didn't he?" Tara guessed. "It really isn't necessary. I don't mind waiting until he's through, and I'm sure you have work to do."

"He said to show you the holding pens, and that's what I aim to do," Ballard replied, deflecting her suggestion with an easy smile that didn't quite match the amused glint in his eyes. "He seems to think you want to see them."

"But I do." The assurance came quickly, reinforced by a turn in their direction.

"Really? I could've sworn your purpose here was to do some fence mending," he drawled.

"Isn't that simple range courtesy?" Tara countered. "When there's a break in the fence, you try to repair it."

"At least you're not denyin' that you set out to get back in Ty's good graces again."

"I have the impression you don't approve. To tell you the truth, I'm not surprised. I am certain nearly everyone on the Triple C regards me as an enemy since I bought Wolf Meadow property. But it was never my intent to keep the property," Tara replied, most persuasively.

"I believe you," Ballard stated, taking her by surprise. "In fact, I think you bought it strictly for insurance."

"I don't know what you mean." She frowned in bewilderment even as her gaze sharpened on him.

"You're out to get Ty back—one way or the other. That's why you're danglin' Wolf Meadow in front of him. I wonder how long it will take him to realize that the only way he'll ever get his hands on it is if he takes you as part of the package. That's your plan, isn't it?" Ballard challenged lightly. "To make him choose between you and Jessy."

Her look was cool and unflinching. "You seem to have forgotten he made that choice a long time ago."

Ballard's eyebrows arched up, his eyes widening in sudden revelation. "You're gettin' back at him for that— by takin' the one thing that means more to a Calder than anything else. The land. He'll never get his hands on it, not even if he leaves Jessy and marries you, will he?"

"What utter nonsense," Tara laughed in derision. "You surely don't believe I'm that devious."

He ignored her response, his thoughts running ahead. "It'll work. Not right away maybe, but over time, it will work, especially if you keep on being all friendly-like and helpful. Eventually he'll talk himself into believin' it's you he wants and that his decision's got nothin' to do with Wolf Meadow."

"You have a very vivid imagination, Mr. Ballard," Tara chided.

"What are you gonna do about Jessy and the kids?" He mulled the question over in his mind, not seeing the answer. "You're gonna have a bit of a problem gettin' them out of the picture."

"Why are you telling me all this?" Tara demanded, her dark eyes ablaze with indignation. "Why don't you go to Ty with all your ludicrous accusations?"

"Simple. He wouldn't believe me, not for long. You'd see to that." Everyone else might underestimate her ability, but Ballard didn't.

He couldn't prove a single thing. At best, he could plant some doubt, delay the inevitable. But he couldn't think of any way that might change the outcome.

Her eyes widened in a look of sudden alarm. "You're insane," she whispered and moved quickly away from him, her shoes *click-click-clicking* over the brick as she walked hurriedly toward the opposite end of the barn. She saw Ty and almost ran the last few steps to his side. "You're back. That didn't take long."

His frowning glance skipped over her, darting to the cowboy still standing in the middle of the alleyway. "Did Ballard show you the pens?"

"You surely don't think he wouldn't. You practically made it a direct order." Tara slipped a hand under his arm, but he detected something in her voice that was a little too bright, a little too dismissive of the question.

"Is something wrong?"

"Wrong? Why on earth would you ask that?" Wearing a fixed smile of unconcern, she tried and failed to meet his eyes.

"You seem upset. Did Ballard say something out of line?"

"It wasn't anything he said. It was the way he looked at me. He frightened me a little." She gave a faint but expressive shudder.

"He puts the make on anything in a skirt. Sometimes he comes close to going too far."

Tara darted another glance at Ballard. "I wish you'd let him go, Ty."

"As I recall, you are the one who suggested that we take advantage of his experience and put him in charge of handling a lot of the details for the auction."

"I know I did. It seemed a good idea at the time, but I am living here now. I can easily handle them for you."

The offer raised all sorts of red flags. "Under the circumstances, Tara, I don't think that's a good idea." Ty was cool in his rejection of it.

Tara made an attractive little moue of mock chagrin. "I forgot. To just about everyone on the Triple C, I'm persona non grata. But not with you, I hope."

"Our neighbors are always welcome here."

The word was like a shield Ty threw up to ward off any suggestion their relationship was more personal than that. His constant use of it was enough to set Tara's teeth on edge.

"I'm glad to hear that," she lied with ease. "Just the same, though, there are plenty of other people qualified to handle all the auction details. Let me find one for you."

"Thanks, but the auction's not that far away. I would just as soon not change horses when I'm nearly to the other side of the stream."

Although far from pleased with his decision, Tara gave in with as much good grace as she could muster. "You're the boss. But if you should change your mind, let me know."

"It's not likely."

"In the meantime, Ty, please don't mention to Ballard that I complained about his behavior to me. I'm sure everyone here already hates me for buying Wolf Meadow. They will think I'm just trying to stir up more trouble. And I'm not. I'm trying to do the opposite and make everything right again."

"I understand," Ty said with a nod.

"Does that mean you won't jump all over him after I leave?" Tara slanted him a teasing look.

"He deserves it."

"Maybe he does, but it will just create more hard feelings. It will be enough if you keep your eye on him."

"If that's the way you want it," Ty conceded.

"It is." Tara smiled, satisfied that Ty would keep his word.

Chapter Fifteen

﹏

Tara's visit was the first of several during the next two weeks. Her excuses were as varied as the time of day she called, running the gamut from the auction to dropping off a wading pool for the twins.

Regardless of the reasons she used, her frequent presence didn't set well with the ranch hands, especially the older ones, who had weathered many a stormy time. Neither did Ty's failure to show any objection to her visits. It had them looking sideways at him whenever Tara was around. And sometimes when she wasn't.

As usual, Jessy was aware of it although nothing was ever overtly said to her. The ranch hands conveyed their feelings through seemingly innocuous remarks uttered in a voice dry with disapproval. In their eyes Tara was a traitor and they didn't want her in the midst. It ground at them that Ty was allowing it. Yet if pressed, they admitted that Tara's stated purposes for each of her visits allowed little room for objections.

Like this morning, when Tara had arrived at the Triple

C headquarters around nine-thirty, with Buck Haskell behind the wheel and a horse trailer in tow. The purpose of her visit was simple: she was in the market for a pair of riding horses. And as Tara had been quick to point out, it was common knowledge that the Triple C had the best-trained mounts around.

Tara had spent the last two hours inspecting each of the dozen geldings available for sale, discussing the merits of each of them with Ty and occasionally seeking Buck Haskell's opinion. Out of the twelve, she picked four that she asked to ride before making her final selection.

Standing outside the corral fence, Jessy had one arm wrapped firmly around Trey's middle while he sat on the top rail, clapping his hands at the sight of the dappled-gray gelding cantering around the pen. For him, the big lure was horses, not the woman riding one. Every time he set foot outside The Homestead, Trey had only one destination in mind—the corrals.

The same couldn't be said for the towheaded Laura as she straddled Jessy's left hip, a fistful of wildflowers in her hand. She liked horses well enough, but her true fascination was with Tara. It was something Jessy couldn't begin to understand or explain; she could only hope that Laura would outgrow it.

At almost eighteen months old, Laura was becoming the watcher of the two, and Trey was the doer. Trey was content to sit on the rail only as long as something was happening in the pen. The minute the action stopped, so would his interest.

Taking advantage of his momentary absorption, Jessy let her attention stray to the horse and rider. She made an assessing study of the big gray they called Iron Mike and found little to fault about him.

Jobe Garvey stood a few yards away, close enough

that Jessy overheard when he muttered to Kyle Sullivan, "Bet you anything she picks the gray."

"It's a good horse," Kyle replied.

"They're all good usin' horses, but she's wantin' somethin' with flash. The gray and the stockinged chestnut are the only ones in this bunch that's got any."

He made a sound of disgust in his throat, turned his head to the side, and spat. "I don't know why she's makin' such a big project out of this. It ain't like she's gonna work cattle with 'em. She wants 'em strictly for pleasure ridin'. Did ya' hear what she said to Ty when she first got here?"

"No."

"She said, 'Oh Ty, darlin',' " Jobe drawled in mimicry, giving his voice a high, girlish pitch. "That big open country just cries for me to get on a horse and ride across it." His voice resumed its gravelly register, and Jessy averted her face to hide the smile she couldn't suppress.

"It was enough to make ya' sick," Jobe declared. "Why, I remember when nothin' around here was good enough for her."

"Maybe she's changed," Kyle suggested.

"In a pig's eye she has." Jobe straightened away from the fence, alert to the fact Tara had just reined in next to Ty. She swung a leg out of the saddle.

Trey immediately began to fidget. Jessy lifted him off the fence and set him on the ground, quickly catching hold of his hand before he could take off.

"Hey, Jobe," she called to the man. "As soon as Tara picks the horses she wants, would you throw a saddle on one of the others so I can give these two a ride?"

"Not a problem," he replied.

Just as Jobe predicted, Tara chose the gray and the chestnut. While Buck supervised the loading of the two horses, Ty and Tara headed for The Homestead to take care of the necessary paperwork.

Laura was not at all happy about being left behind. Before she could lapse into a full-blown protest, the dun gelding that Jobe had saddled for Jessy nuzzled the flowers in Laura's hand. She giggled at the velvety soft brush of its nose, temporarily forgetting about Tara.

Trey, on the other hand, was in his height of glory, perched atop the saddle, both hands wrapped around the horn while Jessy led the horse around the corral. When it was Laura's turn to ride, Jessy made sure that Trey thought he had charge of the lead rope.

Keeping both twins entertained required her undivided attention. Jessy was unaware of Tara's return until she heard the rumble and rattle of the truck and horse trailer pulling away from the barn. She spotted Ty heading toward the ranch commissary. She assumed he was going to meet with Bud Ramsey, who managed the store for them. Ty had mentioned at breakfast that he needed to get together with him that morning, but Tara's arrival had necessitated a postponement.

A check of her watch indicated she had roughly an hour before lunch. Once again she hefted a skinny Trey onto the saddle.

"Okay, buster, two more turns around the corral then we have to call it quits so I can get you two cleaned up before lunch."

Unconcerned, Trey grinned from ear to ear, satisfied to be back on the horse.

"Something tells me you aren't gonna get any argument from him until you try to take him off," Ballard remarked as he swung himself onto the corral's top rail. "Looks like he'll be quite the horseman when he grows up."

"It does, doesn't it?" Jessy agreed with more than a little pride at the thought.

"Jobe tells me she bought a couple horses." Ballard didn't bother to identify Tara by name. On the Triple C, any use of the feminine pronoun invariably referred to Tara.

"That's right." Jessy continued walking the horse around the pen.

"I wonder how she's gonna get them to Wolf Meadow," Ballard mused absently.

"Probably the same way as always, she'll fly in."

"If it was me, I would pull up to one of the gates, offload the horses, throw a saddle on one, and lead the other through the gate."

"Who knows? Maybe she will."

"Did Ty have anybody to follow to see that she doesn't?"

"I don't know. You'll have to ask him." With the second and last circuit of the corral finished, Jessy led the horse to the gate.

Ballard hopped off the fence. "I'll open that for you. You've got your hands full."

He swung the gate wide, giving her plenty of room to pass. After the horse passed through, he dragged it shut and double-checked the latch.

"If you want, I'll be happy to unsaddle him and turn him out," Ballard offered.

"Thanks, but I can manage."

"Not easily, I'll wager." His smile had a wry slant to it, his eyes glinting with amusement. "Not when you've got to deal with these two at the same time."

"I never said it would be a breeze." Jessy smiled back. "But I want Trey to learn he is responsible for the care of his own horse, not somebody else. And it is never too early to start teaching that."

"You've got a point," Ballard conceded. "I don't know of anyone who's been able to say that a Calder doesn't pull his own weight."

"And they aren't going to start with Trey and Laura. Not if I have anything to say about it."

"You can bet if they were her kids, she'd have somebody waitin' on 'em hand and foot. They probably wouldn't do anything for themselves, let alone saddle or unsaddle a horse." He strolled along beside her and appreciatively sniffed the wilting flowers in Laura's hand when she held them out to him. "According to Gabe, he overheard Ty agreeing to go over to her place Friday morning right before she left. I suppose you know about that."

"I know Ty's been talking about going. Why wonder what she's doing when he can go look for himself." Jessy knew that was what Ballard was really asking, not whether she was aware of Ty's plans.

"You know, if Ty would share some of that, it might make everybody rest a little easier in their minds." Ballard frowned thoughtfully as he studied the hard-packed ground before them. "Take the way he's so friendly with her, for instance. It bothers 'em."

"Maybe because they don't know Tara as well as Ty does. Ty is convinced that she will eventually get tired of living here. Just like before, there won't be enough to see or do, no parties, no bright lights. When that happens, Tara will sell. But if we treat her like an enemy now, she is liable to sell to an outsider just to spite us."

"It makes sense." Ballard nodded his head in agreement.

"Ty knows what he's doing," Jessy stated, privately wishing that she shared Ty's confidence. On one point she certainly didn't disagree with Ty: Tara was more than capable of selling to someone other than a Calder, purely out of spite. At the same time, Jessy didn't trust the woman. Not on inch.

But Ty never made it to Wolf Meadow on Friday. As he was about to leave for there, word came of an accident to one of the men on the windmill crew. A misstep on a ladder had resulted in a twenty-foot fall.

Ty left it to Jessy to contact Tara and inform her that he wouldn't be coming that morning. She dialed the mobile number Tara had given them. But someone other than Tara answered. Jessy waited while Tara was summoned to the phone.

"Tara, it's Jessy. Ty asked me to call and let you know he won't be able to make it this morning. There's been an accident here at the ranch."

"Ty isn't hurt, is he?" There was real alarm in Tara's voice.

"No. One of the men on the windmill crew took a bad fall. Beyond an obvious broken leg, we aren't sure of the extent of his injuries. The last I heard he was still unconscious. Ty is on his way to pick up Amy Trumbo and take her to the scene," Jessy explained, referring to the ranch nurse.

"Where did it happen?" Tara's tone became brisk and businesslike, without any emotional edge.

"At windmill twenty-nine, down at South Branch."

"I can have one of my helicopters there in twenty minutes. We can airlift him directly to the hospital."

"Right now we have an ambulance on the way. Once the extent of his injuries can be determined, it might be necessary to fly him out. If it is, I'll call you back. But either way, thanks for offering."

"I just want to help any way I can," Tara replied. "I do remember that's the way it's done out here. Everybody pulls together in a crisis."

"That's right," Jessy agreed and hung up, wondering if the offer was prompted by genuine concern for the man's welfare or to project the right image.

Fortunately the helicopter wasn't needed. Beyond the broken leg and a concussion, the injured worker had only some severe bruising. By Monday, he was released from the hospital and sent home on crutches.

The fall, however, seemed to ignite a whole string of minor catastrophes over the next two weeks, everything from a grass fire along the road to Blue Moon that burned nearly a hundred acres to the sudden death of a prized broodmare that had the vet shaking his head in bewilderment.

Although none of these things was out of the ordinary, cowboys tended to be a superstitious lot. Some began to blame the bad luck the Triple C was experiencing on Tara's return, recalling the tragedies and near tragedies that had plagued the ranch when she was married to Ty. There were those of the certain opinion that more of the same was on the way. The loss of Wolf Meadow was just the start of the trouble to come. It made for a gloomy and sometimes churlish atmosphere.

Armed with a dust rag and a feather duster, Sally Brogan entered the den. As usual, Chase sat behind the desk, frowning over some papers in front of him, his reading glasses perched on the end of his nose.

Hearing her footsteps, he looked up, glaring at her over the rim of his glasses. "What do you want?"

"Nothing. Just doing a little dusting." She gave the dark-feathered duster a pointed shake and skipped her glance around the room, pursing her lips at the sight of the opened window that guaranteed a steady infiltration of dust. "Goodness knows, this room needs it."

"Can't you see I'm trying to get some work done?" Chase snapped.

His sharpness momentarily startled her, but Sally was quick to dismiss it. "My, you are irritable today."

"Who wouldn't be with all this damned paperwork to go through?" He jerked his glasses off and tapped the papers with them in emphasis then continued to gesture with them. "Not to mention that pile of forms waiting. And you decide the room needs to be cleaned. Well, clean it and be damned." He pushed stiffly out of the chair despite the protest of his achy joints.

Stunned by the explosion, Sally stared. She wasn't a woman given to losing her temper, but that didn't mean she didn't have one. The hair on her head might be white, but it was red when she was born.

She unleashed a portion of its fiery nature on him. "Just because you're in a bad mood, Chase Calder, don't you be taking it out on me! I won't stand for it."

The outburst was so out of character, it momentarily brought him up short. After a long second, Chase dragged in a deep breath and let it out.

"Sorry." His gaze darkened with regret even as the line of his mouth tightened in grimness. "I don't know why I'm so restless and edgy. Maybe it's from being cooped up behind that desk always dealing with a bunch of paperwork. There's a whole damned ranch out there." With an impatient sweep of his hand, he gestured toward the window. "And I don't know what's going on in half of it unless somebody puts it on a piece of paper. I feel so damned out of touch. It's like I have lost control of it somehow."

"It's this Tara thing, isn't it?" Sally guessed, a hint of worry creeping into her expression.

Chase sighed, the sound troubled and heavy, and resumed his seat in the big leather chair. "I wish I knew what she was up to."

"Maybe it's no more complicated than needing to feel that she belongs somewhere."

"Maybe." But he didn't believe that. "The first time I met her, I could see she was a hungry girl, always wanting something. And now she's a hungry woman. I can't shake the feeling that she's got a taste for something other than a home in the middle of the Triple C. It wasn't enough to satisfy her before. It isn't logical to think it would be now."

"But what would it be?" That's what puzzled Sally.

"I don't know, but I'll bet we won't have to wait long to find out. She is not only hungry by nature, she is impatient. The day is coming when she will tip her hand, and it won't be far off."

Through the opened window came the dull *clump* of booted feet climbing the front steps and crossing the porch's wooden floor. Chase listened to the familiar tread of them.

"Sounds like Ty," he said even as the front door opened.

Almost guiltily, Sally turned and began to busily run the soft furniture cloth over the side table. Observing it, Chase smiled faintly but said nothing.

Ty poked his head into the den, one hand on the doorjamb.

"Any idea where I can find Jessy?"

Sally answered, "She went upstairs about a half hour ago to put the twins down for their afternoon nap."

Chase glanced at the mantle clock and frowned. "Are you already back from Tara's?"

"Just getting ready to leave," Ty replied. "First I thought I would see if Jessy—"

"If Jessy would what?" Jessy challenged lightly, coming up behind him.

"There you are." His gaze moved warmly over her face. "You just saved me from going all the way upstairs."

"I'm glad, too. With my luck, the twins would have woken up when they heard you, and it would take forever to get them back to sleep," Jessy replied, then asked, "Why did you need to see me?"

"I'm headed over to see Tara's new house and thought you might like to ride along."

Jessy didn't immediately answer and looked instead at Sally. "Would you mind keeping an ear tuned for the twins?"

"I don't mind in the least," Sally assured her.

"Thanks. As tired as they were, they should sleep for a good two hours. Hopefully we'll be back around then." Jessy sought confirmation from Ty.

"Sooner, with any luck," Ty added, then directed his attention to Chase. "Before I forget, I sent Ballard into town this morning to pick up some things. Keep an eye out for him. If he gets back before I do, make sure he gets together with Sullivan about some possible double billing problems."

"Will do." The corners of Chase's mouth made a grim turn downward at the mere mention of anything connected with paperwork.

Minutes later Ty and Jessy were traveling along the ranch road, leaving a cloud of dust pluming behind them. A steady breeze danced through the grassland on either side of them, setting the stalks to swaying.

Ty skimmed Jessy's profile, taking note of the quiet strength and easy contentment in her features. "I wasn't sure you would want to come along."

Her smile was slow and easy. "I'm as curious as you

are about what she's doing there. Besides"—amusement glinted in her eyes—"if I'm around, she isn't apt to make a play for you."

"I wouldn't count on that." Out of habit, Ty loosely gripped both hands on the top of the steering wheel. "I decided a long time ago that Tara learned to flirt with every man she sees when she was still in the cradle. Maybe it's a Texas thing."

"When you were in college, were all the girls in Fort Worth like her?" Jessy asked curiously.

"Now that you mention it, they weren't," he admitted. "They had their moments. But I suppose all women do."

Except for Jessy, he thought to himself. She was too straightforward, too blunt spoken to ever attempt to practice such feminine tricks. She was a rare woman and he knew it.

Ahead, the dirt road leveled out. Automatically Ty increased the truck's speed to take advantage of the long, smooth stretch of surface.

Suddenly the wheel jerked under his hands. Simultaneously he heard the distinctive sound of a tire blowing and the pickup began a slight sideways skid. Before Ty could straighten the truck out, another tire blew.

In the next second, he had no control as a rear wheel slipped off the shoulder.

"Look out!" Ty shouted to Jessy when he felt the truck tip in the beginnings of a roll.

He heard her yell his name. Then they were going over, seemingly in slow motion, each second stretching into something longer. The adrenaline rush of fear seemed to mute the *thud* and *crunch* of the rollover. About the time Ty managed to avoid being hurled one way, he was slammed another.

After an eternity of seconds, the pickup rocked to a

stop on its side. Dust swirled in a thick cloud beyond the fractured windshield, engulfing them in a tan fog. Ty found himself sitting sideways on the seat partially wedged between the steering wheel and the door, trapped by the weight of Jessy's body crumpled against him.

His hands moved on to her, his left rib area shrieking a protest. "Jessy," he said, but there was no response to either his voice or his touch. A quiver of fear ran through him.

With great care, Ty shifted her sideways to give himself a little maneuvering room. That's when he saw the blood streaming from a wound to the side of her head.

Intent on stopping the bleeding, he tugged off his shirt. The close quarters had him bumping arms and elbows against the steering wheel and dashboard while he grunted from the pain the movement ignited along his ribs.

He wadded up the shirt and used it to apply pressure to Jessy's wound. A quick check verified her pulse was strong and her breathing was steady.

Satisfied that he had done all he could do, Ty turned his attention to finding a way out of the wrecked truck. The passenger side door was crumpled inward. He made one try at opening it, but it was jammed. That only left the front windshield, which was already a mosaic of splintered glass.

Searching, Ty found an old rag stuffed beneath the seat. He laid it over Jessy's face and neck then shifted himself around and began kicking out the windshield, sending pieces of glass flying in a tinkling shower.

With the afternoon sun warm on his back, Culley O'Rourke skirted his horse southward, avoiding Antelope Butte. After the passage of two weeks, he was curious about the progress that had been made at the construction site. At the same time he was wary of running into Buck Haskell again.

It was that wariness that had prompted Culley to take a circuitous approach to the site, dipping far southward and coming at it from a direction Buck wouldn't expect. And Culley knew all of the land's concealing folds.

When the wind carried to him the sharp report of a pair of rifle shots, spaced seconds apart, Culley didn't think much about them. It wasn't uncommon for a Triple C rider to shoot at any coyote he might spot.

But the distant thumps and thuds, crunches and clatter that followed the shots weren't common. Culley reined in his horse, convinced he had just heard a smashup on the road about a mile due south of him. He thought about it a moment or two then decided to take a look.

Pointing his horse's nose in the general direction of the road, Culley lifted it into an easy, ground-eating lope. A quarter mile from the road, he crested a swell in the plains and spotted a wrecked pickup farther up the road to the east.

It looked like it had rolled and ended up lying on the driver's side. The passenger side was all crumpled in, but not so badly that he couldn't make out the familiar Triple C insignia on it. About the same moment, Culley noticed a bare-chested man in jeans and boots moving about the hood. He was a tall, big-shouldered man with dark hair and a mustache. It didn't take two seconds for Culley to recognize Ty Calder, even at this distance.

Culley pulled his horse up, grimly acknowledging in his mind that it was the luck of a Calder to walk away from a wreck like that. Then he smiled faintly, thinking of the long walk to headquarters the Calder son had ahead of him. The chance of another vehicle happening along the stretch of ranch road was remote. Culley knew he could offer Ty a lift, but carrying double would tucker out his horse and make Culley late getting back to the Shamrock. Cat usually showed up there around seven with his supper.

Just as he had reached the decision to let Calder fend for himself, Ty spotted him and waved his arm, motioning for Culley to come. Culley picked up something urgent in Calder's body language. About then Ty bent over the windshield, and the thought crossed Culley's mind that there might be someone else still inside. He spurred his horse toward the wreck.

When he was yards from the fence line opposite the overturned truck, Ty yelled, "Jessy's inside. She's unconscious. I need a hand getting her out. It looks like the fuel tank ruptured. There is gasoline all over here."

Short of the fence, Culley pulled up and swung out of the saddle, dropping the reins. "Is it safe to move her?" He slipped between parallel strands of barbwire.

"It sure as hell isn't safe to leave her there."

Working together, with Ty inside the truck cab and Culley outside, they got Jessy out. Ty carried her to the other side of the road and carefully laid her on the grass. Culley stood back from her, still remembering the warm feel of her slim body and the red smears of blood on her face. Ty bent over her, blocking Culley's view.

"Ride to the ranch for help." Ty barked the order over his shoulder.

Crossing to the fence, Culley ducked between the wires again and scooped up the reins to his horse. He hauled himself into the saddle and reined the horse around before he buried his right foot in the stirrup.

But he wasn't headed for the ranch. As white as Jessy

was, Culley was convinced she was going to die without immediate help, maybe even with it. And the ranch was too far. He had never given much thought to Jessy one way or the other until now. But he found he couldn't hold it against her that she had married a Calder.

He spurred his horse toward the construction site.

Chapter Sixteen

~

Intersecting the overgrown track that led to windmill eleven, Culley swung his horse onto it and asked for more speed with a whip of the reins. The tiring horse gamely gave him another burst.

When he rounded the bend, the view of the work site opened up for him. The progress that had been made in two weeks' time was startling. Where before there were only concrete footings, a house stood. It was a big and sprawling affair that hugged the ground. Workers swarmed around its exterior walls, busy facing its lower sections with stone. From somewhere came the buzzing whine of a skill saw, mixing with the rhythmic pound of hammers and the drone of a powerful generator.

Culley pulled back on the reins, checking his mount's headlong pace when he reached the fringe of the site. Heads turned at the unexpected sight of a horse and rider. Culley scanned the faces, searching for Haskell among them. There was no sign of him, but he did see

Tara, standing with two men, both in hard hats, one in
work clothes and the other in a white shirt and tie.

Reluctant as he was to have any contact with her, Culley
knew who was in charge. He angled his horse forward.
The instant she recognized him, her expression darkened in a look of utter loathing.

"What are you doing here, O'Rourke?" Tara demanded
when he slid his horse to a stop only yards from her.
"This is private property and you are trespassing."

"There was an accident on the road." His horse skit-
tered sideways beneath him, tossing its head and throwing off flecks of foam from its lathered sides. "You need
to call the ranch an' tell 'em to get some help here
quick. She's in a bad way."

"Who is?" The question was quick and sharp.

"Jessy."

Something flickered in her eyes that Culley couldn't
quite identify. "Where is Ty?"

"He's with her."

"Where?"

"On the road a good half-mile west."

Having obtained the necessary information, Tara
lost any further interest in him. She turned to the man
in work clothes. "Call the Triple C *now*." She put sharp
emphasis on the word then swept her glance over the
work site. "Where's Buck?"

"I don't remember seeing him in the last hour. Shall
I—"

"Never mind," she interrupted curtly. "I'll drive myself."

"Take the blue truck," the man said. "It has a first aid
kit behind the seat. You might want it."

Splitting away, Tara walked swiftly toward a navy blue
pickup while the man trotted over to a different one. A

few seconds later Culley saw him holding a telephone receiver to his ear.

Satisfied that help was on the way, Culley reined his lathered horse around and left the construction area at an easy walk. With nothing better to do and no place he had to be anytime soon, he ambled toward the accident site. It wasn't that he was nosy; Cully just liked to know what went on.

By the time he reached a vantage point a quarter mile from the site, his horse had cooled off from its hard gallop and two Triple C ranch pickups were parked behind Tara's truck on the shoulder of the dirt road. Culley stepped out of the saddle and left his horse to graze. Taking a position on the shady side of a grassy knoll, he studied the scene below him.

There were three people huddled around the prone woman; one of them was the nurse Amy Trumbo. It wasn't long before he noticed Jessy's leg move. Then Amy was pushing Jessy's hand away from her head, a sure indication that she had regained consciousness.

Long before the ranch's pumper truck came into view, Culley spotted the dust cloud it raised. It slowed before it reached the accident site, but it still left a low dust fog in its wake as it continued past the figures on the roadside and pulled up near the wrecked pickup. Culley figured the pumper had been called to neutralize all the gasoline that saturated the ground, aware it was a fire just waiting to happen.

Soon the wail of a siren signaled the arrival of the ambulance. The longer Culley watched the unfolding events, the more certain he became that he didn't need to be in a hurry to get back to the Shamrock. Cat wouldn't be coming by with his dinner tonight. Just as soon as she heard about the accident, he knew she would head straight for The Homestead. That was the custom here; when trouble came, people banded together.

The idea of hanging around until the last dog had gone home suited Culley. There was something about the wreck that kept nagging at him. He couldn't put his finger on exactly what it was, but if he could poke around the truck after everybody left, it might come to him. Shifting into a more comfortable position, he settled down to wait.

The ranch hands manning the pumper truck were the last to leave. Culley waited until the vehicle was out of sight, then got to his feet and rounded up his grazing horse. Back in the saddle, he rode along the fence line until he came to the gate then backtracked along the road to the crash site.

The wrecked pickup had been righted. Now it stood drunkenly on the side of the shallow ditch, listing badly from the two blown tires. Culley walked his horse around, making two complete revolutions while he tried to figure out what it was that didn't strike him right.

Chase stood at the den's front window, his thoughts far from the sunset that flamed the sky. The instant he saw the blue pickup pull into the ranchyard, he turned from the window.

"Ty's back," he called, alerting the others.

When he stepped out the front door to meet him, Cat was right behind him. Giving Tara no more than a cursory glance, he ran an inspecting eye over his son, noting the stiff way Ty held himself to keep the pain in his ribs at bay. Chase also noticed the softness of relief in Ty's dark eyes.

The sight of it made it easier for him to ask, "How is Jessy?"

"Other than a concussion, they don't think she suffered any internal injuries, but they are keeping her at the hospital overnight for observation."

"I'll bet Jessy didn't like that," Cat guessed, smiling with the same relief they all felt.

"As a matter of fact, she was hurting too much to raise much of an objection," Ty replied.

"So is Ty, but he doesn't want anyone to know that." Tara had both hands on him in an attempt to assist him up the steps. "Not only is he bruised and battered, but he has two fractured ribs."

Ty dismissed her concern. "They gave me something at the hospital that has pretty well dulled the pain. How are the twins?"

"Sally and I just gave them their baths," Cat explained. "She's putting them to bed now."

Reaching the veranda, Ty started across it with slow, measured strides. His glance ran upward toward the second story. "I should go up and see them."

"You need to go inside and sit down," Tara insisted.

"First, I have to call Jessy's folks," Ty stated.

"No need for that," Chase told him. "They are inside. I told them to come over and wait with us. I think they would like a firsthand account of what happened. When you called from the hospital, you were sketchy with the details, not that they were very important at the time."

There wasn't much to tell, but Ty understood that others had a need to hear events replayed, that it somehow lessened the fear for them. At the same time, though, he had lived it, and there had been too much time both at the hospital and on the way home to replay it all in his mind. As reluctant as he was to go over it again, he went inside.

Minutes after Ty walked in the door, the telephone started ringing and more people dropped in. As usual, the ranch grapevine had been quick to spread the news of his return. It said as much for the high regard they held for Jessy as it did that she was married to a Calder.

Cat was in the kitchen, busy arranging an assortment of cold sandwiches on a serving platter when Dick Ballard stepped inside the back door. He swept off his hat and held it in front of him, turning it round and round by the brim.

"I thought I would find Sally here," he said in vague apology. "I wanted to find out how Jessy is."

She could see the worry in his gentle eyes. It touched her. "Jessy's going to be fine," Cat assured him. "The doctors think she suffered nothing worse than a concussion. They're simply keeping her overnight as a precaution."

"Somebody said her head was split open and she was bleedin' all over the place."

"I know. It must have been a nasty gash." Cat went back to her task, piling on the sandwiches. "Ty said it took twelve stitches to close it. But head wounds bleed a lot, even small ones."

"That's true enough. One time when I was steer wrestlin', a horn clipped my forehead. It wasn't deep at all, but I bled like a stuck hog," he recalled with some of his usual garrulity.

He seemed about to say more when Tara walked into the kitchen. Cat was surprised by the coolness that sprang into his eyes.

With a wave of his hat in Cat's direction, he turned to leave. "Thanks for the update," he said and went out the door, pushing his hat back onto his head as he left.

"What did he want?" Tara walked straight to the coffee maker and poured more coffee into the insulated carafe she carried.

"Just checking on Jessy like everybody else," Cat replied.

"I should have guessed," Tara admitted with a self deprecating smile. "Everybody is worried about Jessy—and with cause. It makes me shudder when I think how much worse it could have been, considering that neither of them was wearing a seat belt. They are lucky they weren't killed."

Her remark sent a cold chill through Cat. "Don't say that," she murmured in protest.

"It's frightening, isn't it?" Tara's voice had a thoughtful and sobering pitch to it. "I hate to think how many times I don't bother to buckle up when I get into a car simply because I'm not going very far. I never think about the possibility that in that four or five miles, a tire could blow."

"We all will from now on."

Cat paused while her pride warred with her conscience. But her conscience won. "By the way, I want to thank you for all you did today. I am grateful for the way you helped both Ty and Jessy."

"Thanks, but it really isn't necessary. I'm just glad everything turned out all right."

"And I'm glad you feel that way." Pride surfaced. "Because I don't want you to think that this in any way makes up for the fact that you bought the Wolf Meadow land. I don't think I will ever be able to forgive you for doing that. It was the cruelest thing you could do."

"But don't you see, Cat? In a manner of speaking, it's still in the family," Tara reasoned, her expression warm with assurance.

"No, it isn't." Cat was firm in her statement. "Families don't do that to one of their own."

Tara was about to argue the point when Culley O'Rourke slipped silently through the back door into the kitchen. He halted abruptly, his glance shooting in surprise to Tara, a clear indication he had been unaware of her presence.

"Culley, I'm so glad to see you," Tara all but gushed the greeting. "I wanted to apologize for being so unforgivably rude to you this afternoon. It was completely inexcusable and I'm sorry. Even though Jessy's injuries didn't turn out to be life-threatening, I'm still glad you came to my construction site instead of riding all the way to the ranch for help."

Culley listened to her little speech without comment, then turned to Cat. "Jessy is okay, then?"

"She'll be fine. They're keeping her in the hospital tonight merely as a precaution."

"That's good." He reached behind him for the doorknob.

"Oh, no you don't, Culley O'Rourke. You aren't leaving yet," Tara admonished with uncharacteristic friendliness toward the man. "If I know you, you haven't had a thing to eat. And here we are with more food than we know what to do with. You come over here and sit down at the table. Cat and I will fix you something to eat."

"No need for that." Even as he shook his head in a show of indifference, his glance ran to the platter of sandwiches.

Mildly annoyed that the invitation should have come from Tara, Cat stepped in to take over. "There most certainly is a need. It will make up for the supper I didn't get around to bringing you." She took him by the arm and led him to the table while directing a pointed glance over her shoulder at Tara. "You better take that coffee into the living room. I know Stumpy definitely wanted another cup."

Unable to object, Tara left the kitchen with the insulated coffee carafe in hand. Culley took a seat at the table while Cat brought him a plate and some silverware then set about retrieving various cold salads from the refrigerator.

"You don't like her much anymore, do you?" Culley observed, quick to pick up on Cat's mood.

She didn't have to ask whom he meant. "I am still mad at her for buying that land. I guess I will always hold that against her no matter what."

"She's got Haskell working for her." The remark had an offhand ring to it, like the idle voicing of a thought.

"I know. Dad hates that. Coffee to drink?"

"That's fine."

Cat paused in the act of filling a cup for him to frown curiously in his direction. "Why did you bring up Buck Haskell's name?"

"No reason. I just remembered it, that's all." After sitting all this time without making a move toward the food before him, Culley scooped some potato salad onto his plate and checked the contents of the other bowls.

"I know you better than that, Uncle Culley." Cat brought his cup to the table and set it on the table next to him. "You never say anything for no reason."

Culley attempted to shrug off the question. "It just seems odd that she'd want a jailbird workin' for her."

Cat had never thought about it in quite that way before. But she never had a chance to explore the possibilities as Quint ran into the kitchen, trailed by Logan.

"Hi, Mom. Hi, Uncle Culley. Got the chores done." Quint lost interest in both of them the instant he noticed the food on the table. "Can I have something to eat, Mom? I'm hungry."

"Of course. Grab a chair," she said, ruffling his coal-black hair.

"Me, too, Mom?" Logan mimicked their son, his gray eyes aglow with that special light he reserved just for her.

"You, too." Smiling, Cat tipped her head up to receive the light but warm kiss he dropped on her lips.

Within minutes both father and son were heaping food on their plates while Cat filled their drink orders, coffee for Logan and milk for Quint. Beyond a nod of acknowledgment, Logan didn't attempt to engage Culley in conversation. Culley wasn't the kind of man given to talking, although he seemed to have grown comfortable with both Logan and Quint.

After Quint had devoured half his sandwich, the edge was off his hunger. He turned his attention to the day's events. "Boy, Uncle Ty really smashed up his truck, didn't he?"

"You saw it?" Cat's glance ran from Quint to Logan.

Logan nodded in confirmation. "We drove by it on the way here."

"Did you see anything that didn't strike you right?" Culley pinned Logan with a close-watching gaze.

The question stirred Logan's professional instincts. "Nothing other than the fact that it's unusual to blow two tires on the same side. Why?" Culley had a reason for asking, and Logan wanted to know it.

"Just curious." Culley forked another bite of potato salad into his mouth. "I noticed the pickup's gun rack was empty. Guess one of the guys on the pump truck took the rifle out, though I don't remember seeing it."

"Could be," Logan agreed, unable to recall any mention of Culley returning to the accident site. Which likely meant the old man had watched from a distance. It was the sort of thing he was known for doing, observing without becoming involved.

"Did Ty mention anything about seein' coyotes?"

Culley continued to concentrate his attention on the food on his plate.

"Not to me." Like Culley, Logan pretended to take no great interest in this discussion. He wasn't sure where it was leading, but he strongly suspected it would end up being his business.

For several seconds, Culley held his silence then dropped his little bomb. "I was just wonderin' about the shots I heard."

"Shots?" The conversation now had Cat's attention. "What on earth are you talking about, Uncle Culley?"

Before he could explain, Ty walked into the kitchen. His gaze went straight to the old man. "Hello, Culley. Tara said you were out here. I didn't want you to leave before I had a chance to thank you for going for help today."

He extended a hand in gratitude. Culley reluctantly shook it, mumbled an unintelligible acknowledgment, and picked up his silverware.

"When you topped that rise, I was never so glad to see anybody in all my life," Ty told him.

"I imagine you were," Logan remarked then pursued the subject Culley had raised a moment ago. "Culley was just mentioning that he heard a couple shots."

"Really? When?" Ty asked, only mildly interested in the answer.

"About the same time I heard the crash." Culley kept his head down as if absorbed by the meal before him.

"You probably heard the blowouts," Ty concluded.

"Could be."

But Logan wasn't fooled by Culley's apparent concession, chalking it up to the man's natural reticence around the male side of the Calder clan. "But you don't think it was, do you, Culley." Although phrased as a question, Logan made a statement of it.

Culley fired him a quick look, his black eyes hard with certainty. "I know gunshots when I hear 'em." He lowered his head again and pushed the food around on his plate. "I figured somebody was shootin' at coyotes. But there wasn't nobody else around, an' there wasn't a rifle in the pickup."

"You think somebody shot out the tires." Logan lifted his glance to Ty to observe his reaction.

"Seems like a mighty big coincidence that one thing happens right after another." Culley didn't commit himself to more than that.

"What do you think?" Logan put the question to Ty, noticing the way Ty was already mulling over this new take on the crash.

"I'm not sure. But those tires should have been in good shape," Ty replied, his own suspicions beginning to grow.

Cat looked at all three of them, a hint of alarm darkening her eyes. "But who would do such a thing?"

"I wonder where Haskell was," Ty murmured thoughtfully.

"He wasn't at the construction site when I rode in. I know 'cause I looked for him," Culley stated in a flat voice that didn't have to point fingers.

"I'll take a look around tomorrow morning," Logan said then cautioned Ty, "Make sure your boys don't haul that pickup away before I get there. Considering the number of people milling around there, I'm not likely to find much, but—just in case."

"I'll see to it," Ty stated and left the kitchen.

No more mention of it was made by anyone that evening. Cat pushed it as far from her thoughts as she could, but it lurked there in the back of her mind along with the danger it might portend.

*   *   *

The midday sun beat down on the grass plains, blazing out of a sky bereft of clouds. A dry wind blew out of the north, sucking up the little moisture it found and leaving a gauzy haze of dust in its wake.

On any other day Ty's thoughts would have been on the tinder-dry conditions that gripped the ranch. But with Jessy riding in the truck beside him, still with a hint of underlying pallor and her seatbelt tightly buckled, Ty's mind was on other things.

He scanned her with a sideways glance, concern darkening his eyes. "Are you sure you don't mind if we swing by the crash site?"

Jessy looked at him with wise eyes. "I am not going to get all female on you and freak out at the sight of the truck if that is worrying you. I have been bucked off too many horses in my life. The accident left me with a dandy headache and some bad memories, but nothing worse than that."

"If it was an accident," Ty inserted, no longer certain that it was.

"That's one more reason I want to know what Logan found rather than hear about it secondhand later."

There was no trace of anxiety in her voice. Its absence drew his gaze to the strong, pure lines of her face. Sun wrinkles fanned from the corners of her eyes and the rounded ridges of her cheekbones stood out clearly. Her wide lips lay comfortably together, without a hint of strain or tension. He was struck again by what a remarkable woman she was.

"You have always been one to face any trouble head on," Ty recalled.

"It's better to see it coming than have it sneak behind you," Jessy stated calmly and closed her eyes to steal some rest.

She didn't open them again until they were nearly to

the crash site. "It's just ahead," Ty said when he noticed her looking around, trying to orient herself. "We can't be sure that Logan will still be there."

"I know."

A half-mile from the site, Ty spotted a vehicle parked on the shoulder, a telltale light bar mounted on its roof. Logan was by the wrecked pickup in the ditch when Ty pulled level with it. Ignoring the ever-present dust swirl, Ty rolled down the driver's window.

Logan walked over to the truck, his glance sliding past Ty to seek out Jessy. "Hello, Jessy. How are you feeling?"

"Better than I did last night," she replied. "More importantly, though, did you find anything?"

"Not one single thing." His mouth curved in a smile that was grim. "I don't think there is any doubt, though, that your tires were shot out. But I don't have one scrap of evidence to prove it."

"What do you mean?" Ty studied him with narrowed eyes.

"I think someone was very busy here last night. A part of both tires has been hacked out. If I had to guess, I would say it was the area where the bullet holes were. If he had to jack the truck up to do it, he didn't leave any clear impressions behind. Which means either the ground was too hard or he placed something under the jack to prevent leaving an impression. The ground around here is too trampled to tell anything for sure."

If Logan said it was so, Ty believed him. The man knew his business. But it raised another thought. Turning his head, Ty scanned the land that rolled away from the road to the north.

"He must have been out there somewhere," Ty stated.

"Had to be," Logan agreed. "I've combed a good section of it. Either he didn't have to wait very long before you came along, or the wind already straightened any grass he flattened. If he was thorough enough to cut out the bullet holes in the tires, I'll bet he picked up the shell casings."

"Yes. It sounds like he's a careful man." And Ty could think of only one man who was likely to know all the tricks—Buck Haskell. Anything Buck didn't know before he went to prison, he probably learned after he got there.

Logan gave the door an idle pat and straightened from the cab. "I'm going to look around some more. You never know. I might get lucky and find something he missed. In the meantime, I would be extra careful, Ty."

"I will." Like Logan, Ty believed his assailant would try again. "Have you found out where Haskell was?"

"Officially I have no cause to question him." Logan told him. "No evidence, no eyewitness. Nothing but a maybe-that-might-have-happened. So there isn't much I can do."

Maybe there was nothing he could do, but there was plenty Ty could do.

Chapter Seventeen

T he accident site was behind them, obscured by the churned-up dust cloud. Jessy studied Ty's strong-jawed profile, noting the taut ridges of tension.

"You are going to question Buck yourself, aren't you?" she guessed.

Patience had never come natural to him. It was something Ty had learned, but he had never been able to sit comfortably in its saddle.

"As soon as I get you home and settled." He tried to gentle his voice, but Jessy caught the undertone of hard decision. There would be no dissuading him from it.

In truth Jessy hadn't expected him to do anything else. Buck would never admit to anything. And without any proof the shooting had actually occurred, there was little Ty could do except put Buck on notice. Buck would know exactly what that meant. And it might be enough to make him think twice before trying anything again. It was a confrontation that had to take place.

"I have a feeling you won't have to worry about getting me settled," Jessy told him. "Between Sally and my mother, one of them will be fluttering around, coddling me like an invalid."

True to her prediction, Jessy had barely set foot on The Homestead's front porch when the two women scurried out of the house to surround her. Her mother took one look at the gauze bandage over Jessy's wound and bemoaned the loss of hair that had been snipped away, then brightly assured Jessy it would grow back.

Glancing over their heads, she looked at Ty. "Didn't I tell you? You might as well go before they shoo you out of the way." She observed his momentary indecision. "It needs to be done, Ty."

The simple phrase smoothed everything out inside him. Jessy was not a woman who needed her hand held, certainly not when there was a job to be done. Tara, on the other hand, would have been grievously hurt if he had left so soon after bringing her home from the hospital, but not Jessy. He took pride in that.

"Get some rest," he said and headed back to the truck.

Rest was all she had done for the last twelve hours. Jessy had no intention of climbing into another bed until nightfall. When she learned that Cat had taken the twins to give Jessy some peace and quiet on her first day home, she knew she was in for the full invalid treatment. Over the protestations of both women, Jessy insisted on sitting on the porch for a while.

"I feel like I've been cooped up inside for a week, constantly being poked and prodded, someone always hovering about to check my pulse or take my blood pressure. I just want to sit outside by myself and enjoy some fresh air. Believe me, it will be much more restful than lying in any bed," Jessy insisted.

Her mother wisely saw that Jessy had her heels dug

in. There would be no talking her out of this. Reluctantly she gave in to Jessy's wishes.

Ensconced in one of the high-backed rockers on the front porch, Jessy basked in the warmth of the sun. A glass and a pitcher of ice water sat on the table beside her, along with a bell to ring. A small neck roll pillow offered support for her throbbing head and another pillow cushioned her lower back. All that was missing was an afghan over her legs, Jessy thought with a faint smile.

Out of the corner of her eye, she noticed the dining room curtain move and knew it was either her mother or Sally checking on her. She closed her eyes and savored the familiar scents and sounds of the ranch, a little surprised that she was content simply to sit and do nothing. She blamed it on the hard blow to her head that she had taken, which turned her thoughts to the accident that hadn't been an accident at all and the confrontation between Ty and Buck Haskell that had either taken place already or was about to occur.

Catching the telltale crunch of gravel, Jessy opened her eyes to see Ballard making his way toward the front steps. He spotted her as well.

"Good morning."

"Good morning," she echoed his greeting.

"Seeing you sitting out here sure does make it a good morning," Ballard declared, mounting the steps. "I was just comin' to see how you were feelin', but I sure didn't expect to find you out here on the porch."

"Just getting some air," she told him.

"That's the best way I know to get that hospital smell out of your nose." He walked over and stretched out in the companion to her rocking chair, his gaze making a thorough examination of her. "You had us all good and worried, Jessy. How are you feeling?"

"Now you sound like a nurse," she countered lightly, a little weary of answering the same old question.

"I guess I do." The wry slant of his mouth gave his smile a rueful quality. He focused his attention on the bandaged area along the side of her temple, reaching into her scalp. "I'll bet your head feels like there's a bunch of carpenters inside poundin' away."

"They said I would have headaches for a while." Reaching up, she absently felt the gauze. The wound itself was sore to the touch.

"When's the bandage come off?" he asked.

"Tomorrow, as long it's not draining anymore."

"I'll bet you'll be glad to get rid of it. I never could stand having one on," Ballard declared then let his focus drift away from her. "Ty sure didn't hang around long after he brought you home."

"He had some business to take care of."

"I'm hearing talk that maybe it wasn't an accident. That maybe someone deliberately shot out those tires. It's just a rumor, mind you, but I was wondering if there was any truth in it." He looked to her for an answer.

"It looks that way," Jessy confirmed.

An unusual grimness hardened his features. "That's what I figured. It was just too much of a coincidence for both of those tires to blow. And I'm bettin' I know who's behind it, too. And Ty takin' off like that, headin' east, I'd say he's plannin' on havin' a little talk with her."

"Her?" Jessy repeated, taken aback by the feminine pronoun. "You don't seriously think Tara did the shooting?" The idea was ludicrous.

"No, but I'll give you odds she gave the order," he stated.

"Tara." The possibility that Tara had anything at all to do with this had never crossed her mind. It struck

Jessy as preposterous. "But why? What reason would she have?"

Ballard didn't even hesitate over the answer.

"To get rid of you so she can have Ty all to herself. It's what she's been wantin' ever since she showed up—only she's got tired of waitin' for him to come around. So she figured on hurryin' things up a bit by tryin' to get you out of the picture."

"But Ty was in the truck, too," Jessy argued. "Why would she risk having him hurt, possibly killed?"

"I've puzzled over that, too," Ballard admitted. "I figure that was Buck's doing. He probably liked the idea of taking out a Calder along with you. Don't you know he felt the sharp edge of her tongue afterwards."

Jessy struggled to wrap her mind around the conspiracy Ballard was painting. She had never liked or trusted Tara, but she still found it difficult to suspect her of this.

"Tara is good at scheming and manipulating, but I don't think she is capable of what you're suggesting," she stated.

"You don't, huh?" There was a kind of pity in the look Ballard gave her. "Then explain to me why she hired Haskell?"

"She said it was because he knew the Wolf Meadow range so well." It was an explanation that had always seemed weak to Jessy.

"I won't argue with that," Ballard replied. "In fact, he probably knows all the ideal spots for an ambush. And he's also the first one you'd suspect if there was any violence around here. After all, everybody knows how much he hates the Calders. Right?"

Reluctantly Jessy agreed as the pieces began to fit together. "Right."

"Let's suppose Haskell gets caught and points a fin-

ger at Tara. Who's gonna believe him? Oh, there might
be a few who do. But it won't matter 'cause she'll have
covered her tracks with him eight ways to Sunday. It'll
just be his word that she was part of it. With the high-
powered lawyers she can hire, the word of an ex-con is
never gonna convict her. Yes sir," Ballard concluded
with a decisive nod. "She's planned it all very carefully.
Buck's the only wild card. I'm guessin' she's findin' him
a little hard to control."

"Have you told anyone else what you suspect?"

"What good would it do? Suspicion is all I got. And
I'm not exactly popular with Ty these days," he reminded
her. "He wouldn't believe it about her anyway. She's got
him fooled. She always has."

"Not always," she corrected. "Or he would still be
married to her."

"And she will be again if she can get rid of you. She's
got him all set up for it. There Ty would be, a widower
with two kids to raise, and she's fussed over them from
the start. For some extra added insurance, she bought
Wolf Meadow. Hell, if you weren't around, Ty would
marry her just to get his hands on that land," he declared. "It would be one of those old-time business merg-
ers masqueradin' as a marriage."

Jessy wasn't so sure about that. Ty was first and fore-
most a Calder. Even though a Calder wasn't above making a loveless marriage, Ty would fight shy of making
the same mistake twice.

"Maybe," she said. "Then again, maybe not."

"Look, I'm not tellin' you all this to put Ty down,
though it might sound that way." He leaned toward her,
conveying an urgency. "I guess I'm sayin' all this to warn
you. If I'm right, there'll be another attempt on your
life. Maybe not right away. Maybe she'll let things cool

down for a while just to lull you into lettin' down your guard. But you need to keep your eyes and ears open."

"Don't worry. I will."

"There's no point in tellin' me not to worry, 'cause I will. I'd tell you to stick close to The Homestead, except I keep rememberin' those kidnappers busted right into the house. Still, if you stay around here, I can keep an eye on you. But most of all, don't go off anywhere by yourself. Who knows, maybe I'm all wet and nothin' will come of any of this."

"Let's hope so," Jessy agreed, aware that Ballard had nothing but his suspicions.

A pickup swung into the ranchyard and approached The Homestead. Jessy was quick to recognize Chase behind the wheel. Ballard did as well and rose from the chair without any show of haste.

"Be careful, Jessy." He looked serious and worried. "I don't want anything to happen to you."

"Thanks." She was touched by the concern he showed for her safety. She had yet to decide whether she felt it was warranted.

"Afternoon, Chase." Ballard nodded to him as they passed on the steps.

Chase responded with an absent nod, his attention zeroing in on Jessy, making a swift assessment. "You are looking better than I expected."

"I feel better, too."

He crossed to her chair, his glance leaving her to scan the ranchyard. "Is Ty around?"

"No." Jessy told him about their conversation with Logan, the conclusions Ty had drawn, and the lack of evidence to support it. "Ty went to Wolf Meadow to confront Buck."

Chase's expression was as hard as chiseled granite, his

eyes narrowing in a cold anger. But he made no comment beyond a slow nod of satisfaction. An attempt had been made against a Calder, but it was not going unanswered.

"What did Ballard want?" Chase asked, his glance only now traveling after the man.

"He thinks Tara might be involved in this," Jessy replied with her usual candor.

"I considered that possibility," Chase stated, but he didn't offer his opinion on it. He turned toward the door. "Are you coming in?"

"Not for a while."

"I'll be in the den if you need me," he said in parting and crossed to the door, his attention turning inward.

Chase regretted that he wasn't with Ty. It was a regret that wasn't based on any doubt that Ty could handle it. But he knew Haskell, and Ty didn't.

More importantly, Buck would know Chase never bluffed. Chase did what he said he would do, and be damned with the law.

The fan blades of windmill eleven stood against the sky, motionless and forgotten amid the hustle of activity nearby. Another time Ty would have taken time to study the low-slung dwelling that sprawled near the base of the butte. But at that moment, he had no interest in it.

Scanning the construction site, he spotted an office trailer parked off to the side, and drove straight to it. A score or more of men moved about the site but Buck Haskell wasn't among them.

Parking the pickup near the trailer steps, he switched off the ignition and climbed out of the cab. As he approached the trailer, its door opened and Tara stepped out.

"Ty." Her greeting echoed the surprise and pleasure

that claimed her expression. "I heard the truck and couldn't imagine who had driven out here. I thought you would be on your way home from the hospital with Jessy." Tara paused, a look of quick concern leaping into her eyes. "They did release her, didn't they?"

"Yes, she's home," Ty confirmed, half-impatiently.

"Thank goodness." Tara pressed a hand to her throat in an exaggerated gesture of relief then let it fall away. "You had me worried for a minute."

"Sorry," Ty began.

But she had already closed the distance between them and possessively claimed his arm, sliding him one of her patented provocative glances. "I can't believe I'm actually going to be able to give you a tour of my beautiful home, considering all the times you have postponed it."

"And I'll have to do it again." He firmly removed her hand from his arm. "This isn't a social call."

She drew back. A storminess briefly darkened her eyes since her wishes had been thwarted again. But Tara detected something in his expression, a kind of cold fury held tightly in check. She instantly sought its cause.

"What is it, Ty? What's wrong?"

"Where's Haskell?"

"Buck," Tara repeated, his question taking her by surprise. "He's around here somewhere. Why?"

"I need to have a talk with him. Where can I find him?" Turning his head, Ty again swept his gaze over the area.

"He mentioned something earlier about changing the bit on one of the bridles. I imagine he's at the tack shed by the corral. I'll take you there."

When Tara started forward, angling away from the building site, Ty noticed the pole corral that had been erected some distance away, close to the butte. A pair of horses lazed within it. Beyond them, he made out the roof of a small storage shed.

"No need," he told Tara. "I see it." When she continued walking, he caught her arm, drawing her to a halt.
"I said I will find him myself."

"Don't you take that tone of voice with me, Ty Calder,"
Tara chided, but for all the lightness of her voice, there
was a determined set to her chin. "I don't know what
you want with Buck, but I intend to find out."

"It's a private matter, between Buck and myself."

"Buck works for me," Tara stated. "Since you don't
choose to tell me why you want to speak to him, I can
only assume you think he has done something wrong. If
that is the case, I have every right to know about it."

In answer, Ty challenged, "Where was Buck yesterday
afternoon?"

"Yesterday?" Tara stared at him for a blank second
before comprehension dawned. "You surely don't think
he had anything to do with your accident," she protested in disbelief.

"Somebody deliberately shot out the tires. I don't
call that an accident," Ty retorted sharply. Tara recoiled
in shock. Recognizing that her guard was down, Ty took
advantage of it to demand, "Where was he?"

"Repairing one of the windmills," she answered without thinking, then rushed an explanation, "I might buy
some yearling steers and fatten them over the summer—"

"Was he alone?" Ty challenged.

Tara frowned, as if trying to recall. "He must have
been. He rode the gray. That's why he decided to
change the bridle bit." She looked up, her dark eyes
frantically searching his face. "But that doesn't prove
anything, Ty."

"It proves he had opportunity," he fired back.

"But the windmill is fixed," Tara argued.

"Assuming it was ever broken."

"But he wouldn't risk being sent back to prison and leave his father with no one to care for him."

"If you want to believe in his innocence go ahead," Ty growled and struck out for the corral, leaving her standing there. This time Tara didn't attempt to accompany him.

Buck was inside the corral, standing by the head of the gray gelding, making a final adjustment on the fit of the bridle when Ty walked up. Ears pricked, the gray swung its head in Ty's direction.

Buck glanced over his shoulder, then unbuckled the throatlatch and slipped off the bridle. "What can I do for you, Calder?" Bridle in hand, he sauntered toward the rail where Ty stood.

"I understand you were fixing a windmill yesterday afternoon."

Buck's glance traveled past Ty, as if seeking the source of his information. "That's right." Bending down, he stepped between the rails and straightened.

"And I say you're a liar," Ty accused without emotion.

Buck shrugged it off. "It's a free country. You can say anything you want." He turned to face him and casually leaned a shoulder against a post. "Just what is it you seem to think I've done?"

"Shot out the tires on my truck."

Grinning, Buck reached up and scratched the back of his head. "You can't prove it, though, or you wouldn't be here. Your brother-in-law would be standing there instead, ready to haul my ass off to jail. That's just a guess, mind you."

"Here's something you don't have to guess about—don't try it again. I am only going to say that once."

Buck made a show of whistling silently as he pushed his hat to the back of his head. "You sound like a Calder instead of an O'Rourke. Maybe you've got more of your old man in you than I thought."

"I'll do what I say. Remember that," Ty stated and pivoted on his heel, the warning given. And a Calder only issued one.

"You're wastin' your breath," Buck informed. "You'd better start lookin' somewhere else 'cause I'm not after you."

Ty had expected a denial. "I suppose that's why you tried to make it look like an accident—just like the last time when you planned to make it appear like I had been thrown from my horse."

With firm, purposeful strides, Ty retraced his way to the pickup, ignoring Tara when she attempted to speak with him. She was still standing by the steps when he drove away.

Dark eyes ablaze, Tara wasted no time cornering Buck at the corral. "What do you know about this?" she demanded. "Was it an accident?"

"If Calder said it wasn't, he probably knows what he's talkin' about." Bridle in hand, Buck ambled toward the portable tack shed.

"Don't you walk away when I'm talking to you," Tara snapped in icy temper.

Buck paused and squared around to face her with an almost insolent lack of haste. "You bark out orders about as good as a prison guard."

His lazy smile infuriated Tara. Her palm itched to slap it from his face. "Did you have anything to do with it?"

"You've got a suspicious mind, Duchess. About as bad as Calder's."

"I want a straight answer, and I want it now!"

After a full beat of silence, Buck reminded her, "You know I was miles from here fixin' the windmill."

"I know that's what you told me. But I have no way of knowing whether it's true."

Buck easily met the hot, accusing glare of her eyes, his mouth still wearing its lazy curve. "I guess you'll just have to take my word for it."

"So help me God, if you're lying to me, I swear you'll regret the day you were ever released from prison." Tara's voice was low and thick with promise. "I have told you before—you do what I say and *only* what I say."

"Now, that's the second time I've been threatened today." Buck shook his head in mock amazement. "First Ty warns me that he'll bring the wrath of the Calders on my head, and now you."

Her look was hard and cold. "If anything happens to Ty, I wouldn't worry about the wrath of the Calders if I were you. If you think they can make your life hell, you haven't seen what I can do."

Stiff with controlled anger, Tara swung away and marched toward the construction office. Buck watched her, the smile fading from his face.

"It sure looks like you've got trouble ahead of you, Buck," he murmured to himself. "It surely does."

A breeze stirred across The Homestead's front porch. Jessy felt its soft breath move over her face. Like the rest of the rain-starved plains, it carried the scent of dust. From the corral came a flurry of hoofbeats, followed by a protesting squeal. Jessy paid no attention to the dust kicked up by squabbling horses. Her eyes were on the powdery tan cloud tracking along the road to the Triple C headquarters. Some inner sense told her it was Ty long before she had a clear view of the truck. She pushed out of the high-backed rocker and crossed to the top of the steps to wait for him.

When Ty climbed out of the pickup and headed for the steps, Jessy was quick to detect a heaviness in his movements. She studied the look of stoicism that covered his face, hiding the tension beneath its angular surfaces. Below the thick brush of his mustache, a certain grimness had pulled in the corners of his mouth. He made an effort to turn them up in a smile when he saw her.

"What are you doing out here?" The inflection of his voice was light, but his gaze was quick to make a visual examination.

"Waiting for you," Jessy replied easily. Up close she could see the troubled darkness within his hooded eyes. On impulse she reached out to slip an arm around his waist, seeking to draw some of that trouble from him and absorb it into herself. "How'd it go?" she asked, suspecting that was the source of his heavy thoughts but giving the question an air of idle interest. "Did you see Buck?"

"I saw him." Ty draped an arm around her shoulders, fitting her to his side as they moved toward the door. "Naturally he denied he had anything to do with it."

"You expected as much, though."

"I know. So how are you feeling? You are supposed to be resting," he admonished lightly, "not sitting out here waiting for me."

"That was resting. Besides, being home is the best medicine." Jessy was careful not to mention the throbbing pain in her head. Its level was one she could tolerate. "How are your ribs after that rough road?"

His mouth twisted in a wry grimace. "Sore as hell," Ty admitted.

"That's what I thought." But she sensed that wasn't what weighed on his mind.

"We're a banged-up pair, aren't we?" Almost the minute his smiling sideways glance touched her face, Ty halted, his mood turning serious. He angled himself toward her and reached up to brush the blunt tips of his fingers over the gauze bandage. "Ever since the accident, I keep remembering my father's reaction when he learned my mother had been killed in the plane crash." His low-pitched voice vibrated with rawness. "And those moments right before I told him, when he was so wild and frantic. For one stark, cold second, when you were so limp against me, I knew exactly how he felt. I can't bear the thought of losing you, Jessy."

Moved by the dark and tortured look in his eyes, she cupped a hand to the granite line of his jaw. "But you haven't, Ty. It will take more than a knock on the head to get rid of me."

"I know." He managed a brief smile before that somber moodiness returned to claim his expression. "There's something about this business that gives me a bad feeling. I can't seem to shake it."

She wanted to say something to reassure him, but she suddenly felt the cold grip of it, too. It chilled her.

"Whatever comes, we'll make it through, Ty." She grabbed hold of that thought and held on. "It may not be easy. But we'll make it."

It was that rocklike strength that he relied on. It steadied and calmed him, filled him with a high sense of ease. As long as she was at his side, he could face whatever lay ahead. It was the thought of doing it alone that filled him with dread.

Chapter Eighteen

⤳

June was usually the wet month on the vast Montana plains, but nary a drop fell on the Triple C. Day after day, the sun reigned over that big Calder sky, baking the ground to hardpan and fracturing its surface with long cracks. River levels dropped and several of the smaller creeks ran dry, not entirely an unusual occurrence.

Come July, the drought deepened with no relief in sight. The land was now in its second year of receiving rainfall amounts well below average. The effects were visible everywhere.

During his long tenure as head of the Triple C, Chase had lived through many a dry cycle, but he hadn't seen the land this parched. He remembered the stories his father had told him of the Dust Bowl years when everything was tinder-dry and wind whipped the powdery dirt into walls of fast-moving clouds that hugged the ground, pummeling everything in its path.

Although the ranch had yet to experience the dust storms, its overall condition wasn't much better and rapidly getting worse. And all the precautions his father had taken years ago to make sure the ranch didn't suffer as badly again seemed to be failing one by one.

An aging and weary Stumpy Niles slumped in the chair facing the desk, the bearer of more bad news. "That well is drier than a bleached-white bone, Chase. That's the second one on South Branch in two weeks."

"We'll have to move the cattle," Chase concluded.

Stumpy gave a small harrumph and challenged bleakly, "Where?"

Ty studied the framed map on the wall. "What's the range like around Hazard Creek?"

"It's grazed about as low as you dare. If you throw more cattle on it now, you'll risk killing the roots," Stumpy replied. "Until it rains and the grass can grow back, you can write it off."

Water and grass had long been the two most valuable resources on the Triple C. Many a grassland in the West had been turned into a desert by overgrazing. The Calders had managed to keep their land from suffering that fate through careful husbandry and an awareness that grass was a precious and irreplaceable resource.

Dry years were part of nature's cycle. And the tactics to survive them had changed little over time.

"Check out the north range," Chase said. "The best grass is usually there, and Cat mentioned they received a quarter of an inch a couple weeks ago."

"That grass won't last long," Stumpy warned.

"You're right. It won't," Chase agreed and swiveled his chair to glance at Ty. "I think we need to take a long tour of the ranch ourselves and get a firsthand look at the shape it's in. I have a feeling we'll have to start the fall roundup early—like next week."

"The fat cattle market isn't very good right now," Ty reminded him.

"Right now they have weight on them. If we don't get some good soaking rains, they'll walk it off come fall searching for grass and water. We'll take a loss, but if we hold off, hoping for rain, we'll take a bigger one." And possibly do irreparable damage to the land in the process. Chase didn't say that. But it was there in his mind. He swung his chair back toward Stumpy. "You might as well have your boys start the gather at South Branch first thing in the morning."

Stumpy nodded and wearily pushed out of the chair. "It'll be a hot and thirsty one. You better truck over some water to fill the tank at the Connors windmill. It's so low now they can barely reach it."

Engrossed in the map, Ty didn't notice when Stumpy exited the den. A snaking line marked the course of one of two free-flowing rivers that ran through the Triple C, rivers that had never been known to run dry.

"I'll let Sally know we won't be here for lunch, then we can leave." Chase rose from his chair, then paused, quick to notice Ty's absorption with the map. "Is there a problem?"

Pulling in a deep breath, Ty shook his head and made a slow turn away from the old map. "No. I was just thinking."

"About what?" Chase studied him slowly, probing for the cause of his distraction.

"About all the grass and water on the Wolf Meadow range, and how much we need it right now."

"No." The flat, hard statement came out of nowhere.

Ty frowned. "What are you talking about? No, what?"

"No, we are not making any deal with Tara to lease it—just in case your thoughts were headed in that direction," Chase replied in a voice that brooked no opposition. "There will be no Triple C cow on that land until we have free title to it."

"I don't disagree, but that may be a long time from now," Ty warned.

"Maybe. It all depends on how soon Tara tires of flying in and out of it. She has never struck me as a patient woman."

Catching a movement in his side vision, Ty turned just as a black Range Rover pulled up to The Homestead. "Speak of the devil," he murmured to Chase, "Tara's here."

"An apt phrase," Chase concluded, a wry twist to his mouth. "God knows, she's bedeviled us lately."

"I'll see what she wants." Ty moved toward the door.

"Is Buck with her?"

Ty nodded. "It looked like he was driving—as usual." A part of him would have preferred that Tara fire Buck. Another part of him liked the idea that he knew exactly where the man was. He certainly wasn't foolish enough to believe that his warning had scared Buck off.

It was possible, but Ty wasn't counting on it.

When he walked out the front door, Tara came up the steps, her dark hair unbound and swinging about her shoulders. Her lips parted in a smile of pleasure when she saw him.

"Ty, darling, I was just coming to see you."

"You should have called first." His glance skipped briefly past, locating Buck still seated behind the wheel. "I was just leaving."

"This won't take but a minute," she promised with a coy dip of her head and upward glance of her dark-shining eyes.

"A minute is about all you'll have," Ty warned.

"What on earth is so important that you have to rush off?" Tara issued the protest in a chiding tone.

"It's ranch business."

"I should have known. It's always ranch business."

Her smile retained its hint of amusement of mock exasperation.

"What is it you want?"

"I'm here to issue an invitation—one that's much too important to be given over the telephone," she replied.

"An invitation to what?" Ty asked, then glanced over his shoulder when he heard the front door opening behind him.

"Your timing couldn't be better, Chase," Tara declared, quickly drawing him into the circle. "I was about to issue a very special invitation."

"An invitation to what?" he asked, unwittingly echoing Ty's previous question.

"An invitation to dinner," Tara replied, a catlike smile of pure pleasure curving her lips. "A very special dinner in my new home, this Saturday around sevenish. Strictly casual, of course. I want all of you to come—Sally, Jessy, the twins, Cat, Logan, everyone. The interior designer still has a few touches he wants to add, but nearly all of the furnishings have arrived, including a pair of highchairs for the twins to use." She cocked her head at a provocative angle. "Do you see why this wasn't an invitation I wanted to make over the phone? It will be my first time to entertain guests in my new home. You can't possibly know how exciting that is to me. You will come, won't you?"

"Of course we'll come," Chase replied without hesitation, ignoring the slightly elevated eyebrow Ty aimed in his direction. "Around seven on Saturday, right?"

"That's correct," Tara acknowledged, then declared, "This is absolutely fabulous. I can hardly wait until Saturday."

"Neither can I," Chase agreed with a rare display of charm. "Considering the fortune you spent on this house, I'm curious to see it."

Tara released one of her melodic laughs. "And a fortune it is, I suspect, but I have refused to listen when my accountant attempts to tell me the total. Most of my friends in Fort Worth think I'm crazy for doing this, but you can tell they are secretly envious that I have a home in Montana accessible only by air. The phrase has a certain cachet about it that secretly appeals to them."

"It has that ring of exclusivity they tend to like, I imagine," Ty remarked with a trace of censure. He had never cared much for her circle of friends.

"How true," Tara admitted. "I wouldn't be surprised, after they fly in to visit me, if there was a run on property around here."

"Really?" Chase showed his skepticism. "I thought your friends would have preferred vacation homes with mountain views rather than the flatness of the plains."

"Perhaps, but where I built, the country is a bit more rugged and interesting."

Before she could launch into a lengthy description of her location, Ty interrupted, "Sorry, Tara, but your minute is up. We have to get going."

She waved a hand in a calming gesture. "And I won't keep you one second longer either. There will be ample time to talk more at dinner on Saturday."

When Tara turned to leave, Buck stepped out of the Range Rover and onto its running board, his gaze seeking Chase over the vehicle's roof. "I don't mean to butt in, Chase, but I thought you'd wanta know you've got a cow down in that coulee about a quarter mile east of Flat Bush corner. The way the calf was bawlin' over her, I'd say she was dead."

"We'll check it out," Chase stated.

"I thought you would. There were a couple buzzards

floatin' in the air. The coyotes won't be far behind them. No sense in losin' the calf to 'em."

"We'll go there first," Chase said to Ty "Better hitch up a stock trailer and throw a couple horses in. After we catch the calf, we can put it in with them."

"Right away." With long strides, Ty moved off the porch and down the steps.

"I couldn't help noticin' that the south range didn't look in too good a shape," Buck remarked. "It's none of my business, but you might want to give some thought to gettin' an early start on the fall roundup. It 'pears to me you won't gain nothin' by waitin'."

"South Branch starts the gather tomorrow," Chase stated.

Buck's smile widened to a grin. "I shoulda known you'd be two steps ahead of me."

"You're starting fall roundup now?" A puzzled frown claimed Tara's expression. "But it's only July."

"I imagine you have been too busy building your new home to notice, but we happen to be in the middle of a severe drought," Chase informed her, his voice as dry as the dusty Calder soil.

It was the kind of remark that subtly jabbed at her ignorance of the ranching business, the sort Tara had heard often when she was married to Ty. As always, Tara bridled inwardly at this veiled criticism. She had always prided herself on being highly intelligent and hated being made to feel even slightly nescient.

"Clearly I have much to learn about the importance of such things out here. But I know you'll teach me." Tara purred the words like a cat aching to unsheathe its claws, while smiling the whole time. "Now, I promised I wouldn't keep you, and I won't. See you on Saturday."

She tripped lightly down the steps to the Range Rover.

Not until she was inside and they were on their way out of the ranchyard did Tara unleash the temper she had held so tightly in control. It was Buck who felt the brunt of it.

"Don't you ever do that to me again," she said with heat.

A sandy-white eyebrow shot up in surprise. "Do what?"

"I sounded like a fool back there," Tara replied, still fuming over it. "You should have told me the area was going through a drought."

"It struck me as kinda obvious. After all, it hasn't rained more than a drop in months. The grass crunches underfoot, an' dust coats anything that doesn't move regular."

"There have been dry spells before," Tara said in her own defense. "This could have been simply another one. I couldn't possibly know that it had gone on long enough to be considered a drought. It's part of your job to keep me informed about such things. Among other things, you are supposed to teach me all facets of the cattle business. And that includes the impact weather can have on it."

"Lately you've been more interested in that house than ranchin'," Buck pointed out.

"It's taken more of my time, but you could just as easily have pointed out the condition of the range to me—and that dead cow—during the drive over here." Then *she* could have been the one to tell Chase and Ty about them. Instead she had showed her ignorance of such matters—again. "The next time you notice such things, you are to tell me about them *before* you mention them to anyone else. Is that understood?"

"Loud and clear, Duchess."

"And just why did you tell Chase about them anyway?" Tara looked on him with sudden suspicion. "Since when are you interested in insinuating yourself into his good graces?"

"Pointin' out the sad shape his graze is in isn't likely to cause Chase to look on me with favor. Nobody likes bein' told by others they got problems. Or what they should do about 'em," Buck added.

Unable to argue with his reasoning, Tara conceded, "I suppose not." Closing that subject, she moved on to the next. "Let's don't waste this drive back to town. Point out to me all the things that Ty and Chase will be noticing and explain their importance."

Pulling in a deep breath, Buck looked around and proceeded to lecture her on the essentials of grass and water and the fundamentals of ranching—the amount of land required per cow, the preferred walking distance to water, and the repercussions anytime the two didn't jive. It was a lesson in economics and land management, and the fine line that sometimes had to be walked to achieve a profit. Now and then he would interrupt himself to direct her attention to a dry creek, the motionless blades of a windmill that could be an indication of a dry well, or a cow still grazing at a time of day when it would normally be lying down chewing its cud. All were small things, significant only to a rancher.

Always a quick study, Tara absorbed every minute detail, determined not to be embarrassed again.

Ty and Chase saw all those things and more. The course of action was obvious: an immediate ranch-wide roundup and a downsizing of all the herds to a number the land could safely support. That included the horse herds.

That evening the order went out to every corner of the vast ranch to gear up for roundup. Since the situation was at a critical stage in the South Branch section, they would start there.

Come morning, Dick Ballard let himself into The Homestead. Only strangers bothered to knock first. To his knowledge, the front door had never been locked. He seriously doubted that a key existed for it anymore.

As he headed toward the den, a young Trey charged through the living room, giggling with glee, his diapered bottom waddling from side to side and his legs pumping as fast as they could to elude Jessy's grasp. But she was right behind him. When she scooped him up, he squealed in protest, writhing and kicking to break free.

"Looks like you might need to hog-tie that wild one," Ballard observed with an easy grin.

"Believe me, it's a very tempting thought. Unfortunately I don't have a piggin' string handy." Not without effort, Jessy managed to subdue her young son. "Escape seems to be the only thing on his mind these days. I can't imagine how we're going to keep him corralled at Tara's new house."

"You're going over there?" He showed his surprise at this piece of news.

"She's invited us all to dinner on Saturday."

An instant concern swept his expression. "You watch yourself over there."

But Jessy wasn't worried. "She won't try anything— not with the whole Calder clan there, including Cat and Logan."

"Maybe not, but you be careful just the same," he insisted and glanced toward the den's open door. "Is Ty or Chase in there?"

"Chase is. Ty left about an hour ago."

"Thanks." With a nod, he resumed his path to the room. Chase was on the telephone when he walked in.

Ballard wandered over to the window to wait until he was through.

The minute Chase hung up, he was quick to challenge. "Why haven't you left for South Branch?"

"That's what I came to talk to you about," Ballard acknowledged with a small bob of his head. "If it's all the same to you, I'd like to sit out the roundup and stick close to headquarters. Things are always comin' up about the auction that need to be handled and I—"

"—want to keep an eye on Jessy," Chase cut across his words to state the true reason behind the request. Reading the startled question in Ballard's expression, Chase confirmed, "Jessy mentioned the suspicions you have about Tara."

"I should have remembered that Jessy has always been a forthright woman. I probably should have come to you with 'em but I got nothin' to base 'em on but a gut feeling," Ballard admitted. "Still I can't help thinkin' there wouldn't be a better opportunity with everybody off to roundup and hardly anyone around headquarters. If I was gonna pick a time, that would be it. And I sure couldn't look myself in the mirror if anything did happen an' I was off chasin' a bunch of cows."

"I'm not sure I share your concern," Chase answered thoughtfully. "By the same token, I'm not willing to risk being wrong. You stay here and keep an eye on things."

"I appreciate that, Chase." Ballard smiled his relief then sobered with a new thought. "You do know Ty may not like the idea if he finds out. He doesn't understand that me and Jessy go back a long ways. I can see why it wouldn't sit right with him, him bein' married to her an' all."

"I'll square it with him," Chase promised. "Is there anything else?"

The question was a subtle prod to leave. "Nope. That

just about does it," Ballard replied and headed for the door, adding as he went, "You can rest easy that nothin's gonna happen to Jessy. I'll see to that."

Try as he might, Chase couldn't put much stock in Ballard's suspicions. He doubted that he would be able to as long as Buck was in the picture. It was a prejudice he had, one that could blind him. Which was the reason he had agreed to Ballard's request.

The sun sat low in the Saturday evening sky, throwing its strong yellow light over the Wolf Meadow range, intensifying the ochre hues in the stone and stucco exterior of the newly constructed house. During his only other visit to the site, Ty had taken little notice of the low and sprawling, single-story house. This time he ran an inspecting eye over it as they approached the thickly graveled area in front of it.

Its roof was steeply pitched to shed winter snow and shingled in a dusty brown color that blended with the face of the butte behind it. The roof line extended far beyond the exterior walls, shading the south-facing windows from the sun's glare and creating a covered porch along the front, with stone pillars for support.

In the back seat, Sally craned her neck to get a better view of the house. "That's it, isn't it?" she murmured, then added with a touch of surprise, "It isn't quite as grand as I expected. Do you think so, Jessy?"

Jessy was quicker to note how much ground it covered. "It's bigger than you think. But it could have been worse."

"She could have built it on top of the mesa." Dryness rustled through Ty's voice.

Chase reacted with a harrumph. "Thank God for small favors."

Approaching the graveled area, Ty slowed the vehicle and swept his gaze over the rest of the site. A helicopter sat in readiness on a concrete pad a goodly distance from both the house and the bluff, sharing the skyline with windmill eleven. Roughly the same distance from the house to the left stood the horse corral.

"Looks like they're building a stable," Chase remarked, taking note of the construction in progress near the corral. "Isn't that a house trailer back there?" With a frown, Chase peered at some sort of structure near the corral.

"Could be." Catching a movement in the rearview mirror, Ty glanced up to see the reflection of another vehicle behind them. "Here comes Logan and Cat."

Chase checked his watch. "One minute before seven. That's as close to being on time as you can get."

Both vehicles parked on the gravel near the stone walk that led to the house. As Jessy freed Laura from the car seat, Tara emerged from the house to welcome them.

Strictly casual, Tara had said the dress would be. But Tara's definition of casual had always been slightly different from others. This evening she wore a squaw skirt and matching blouse in a rich wine red. The hem of the skirt skimmed her shins, revealing the fashionable boots she wore. A chunky belt, mounted with silver and strung with elongated conchos, showed off the smallness of her waist. Her ebony hair was pulled back in a sleek chignon, the severe style accenting the perfection of her face.

Casual? Jessy supposed it was, but it left her feeling a little underdressed in her sea green slacks and top. Being around Tara, it was something she was used to experiencing. It no longer bothered Jessy that much.

After the usual exchange of greetings with their hostess, Tara clasped her hands together with barely suppressed delight. "I can't believe you all arrived at the same time. This is perfect." With a graceful pivot and a presenting sweep of her hand, she directed their attention to the house. "Here it is. My new home. What do you think?"

"It's beautiful," Cat answered for all of them.

"It is, isn't it?" Tara unabashedly agreed. "Obviously not every little thing is finished yet—like the landscaping. But we are planting only native shrubs. I made it clear to the landscape architect that I wanted the grounds to be an extension of the plains. Perhaps a few flowering plants in containers on the porch, but that is all. And something still has to be done to finish the driveway area, but I haven't decided if I want to do it in stained concrete or pave it with brick or stone."

"I noticed you are building a stable by the corral," Ty remarked.

"Yes. At the moment it will hold six horses, but I have space to expand it to ten if I choose," Tara explained. "And the architect is working on drawings for some sort of hangar shed and fuel storage facility for the helipad area. Once it's finished, we'll extend the driveway to it."

"What about the trailer over by the corral?" Chase asked. "Is someone living there?"

"Buck Haskell and his father, for the time being anyway," Tara replied and smiled with a touch of wry resignation. "That's another thing that has to be built yet—a house for the groundskeeper, but I'm still debating about the exact site for it. I have to decide soon, though. It needs to be finished before winter."

Trey chose that moment to let loose with a protesting shriek as he twisted in Ty's arms, wanting down to run off some of his pent-up energy from the drive. His angry outcry initially startled Tara. But she quickly laughed.

"Bored with standing around, are you, young man?" She playfully tweaked his arm. "I think you are absolutely right. Let's all go inside. You must be thirsty after that dusty ride. We'll have a drink. Then I'll show you around the house before we sit down to dinner."

Without further ado, Tara ushered them into the house and straight to the main living area she identified as the great room. It possessed a comfortable lodge-like atmosphere with slate floors and roughly textured walls painted a soft gold that cast a warm glow over the room. Its decor was a curious blend of Western and Old World, bergère-style chairs upholstered in geometric-patterned fabric reminiscent of Navajo designs, an overstuffed leather sofa scattered with tapestry pillows. A deep red Persian rug covered the floor beneath a sturdy wooden coffee table, and antlered chandeliers hung from a darkly paneled coffered ceiling. Dominating the entire room was a massive fireplace, built of moss stone.

A waiter, dressed in cowboy boots, blue jeans, and a pearl-snapped plaid shirt, moved among the group, first taking their drink orders then returning with them. When all had their drinks in hand, Tara raised her wineglass, signaling a toast.

"A warm welcome to all of you, my first dinner guests at Dunshill." There was a knowing look in Tara's dark-shining eyes as she sought out Ty.

"Dunshill?" Sally repeated in unspoken question.

"Yes. That's what I have decided to call my new home," Tara explained.

"After the mesa outside?" Sally asked, clearly puzzled by the choice.

But Ty had no such problem. He had made the connection immediately. But like his father, he left it to Tara to answer Sally's question.

"Not at all," Tara replied, a deepening of the knowing quality in her smile. "I named it after the wife of the Earl of Crawford, Lady Elaine Dunshill, who was a business partner of sorts with the first Chase Calder years and years ago."

"For heaven's sake," Cat exclaimed, recognition dawning in her expression. "I had forgotten all about her."

"I didn't," Tara replied and lifted her glass again. "To my guests," she repeated the toast and took a sip of wine.

Everyone followed suit. But Sally wasn't about to let the subject drop now that her curiosity was aroused. "If you don't mind me asking, whatever made you decide to name your place after her?"

"That's easy." Tara smiled. "Ever since I began working with Ty on the auction, she has been on my mind. Lady Dunshill has become something of an inspiration to me. Therefore it seemed appropriate to name this estate after her. In a way, it's like history repeating itself."

"Except she never owned any Calder land," Ty inserted the dry reminder.

"No, not to my knowledge she didn't," Tara conceded and swiftly directed the conversation back to its original topic. "But it still wouldn't surprise me one bit to find out she was once a Calder."

"That's right. I remember when you showed me those photographs," Cat recalled. "One was of Lady Elaine and the other was a picture of my great-great-grandmother. You were convinced they were the same person, one as a young girl and the other as a much older woman."

"You must admit the resemblance was amazing—the same coloring, the same features, the same overall look and expression," Tara added.

"It was a little uncanny," Cat remembered, then divided a quick glance between Sally and Logan, suddenly realizing that neither knew what she and Tara were talking about. "Tara has this theory that my great-grandmother Madelaine Calder and Lady Elaine Dunshill were one in the same person. She based it both on their physical similarities and on an old family story. The way I heard the it," she continued, "my great-grandmother ran away with a remittance man when Chase Benteen Calder was just a little boy."

"What on earth is a remittance man?" Sally asked, a slight laugh in her voice.

"As I understand it, the term was usually applied to a younger, ne'er-do-well son of a wealthy European family, usually members of the aristocracy. They often paid him an allowance not to come home," Cat explained.

It was an old story to Ty, one that had interested him little in the past, and even less now. But he remembered how excited Tara had been when she discovered the two photographs. At the time she had been thrilled by the possibility a Calder might be linked, however nefariously, to English aristocracy.

"Obviously you can see the coincidence," Cat said. "Madelaine Calder runs off with a remittance man. Then years later, Lady Elaine Dunshill, the wife of an earl, shows up at the Triple C." Cat lifted her hands, palms up, to indicate she wasn't sure what it meant.

Laura started fussing in Jessy's arms. When Jessy checked, her suspicion was confirmed. After gathering up the bulky diaper bag, she turned to Tara. "Excuse me. Is there someplace I can change Laura's diaper?"

"Of course. Down that hallway, second door on the right." Tara pointed to a wide archway framed in stone that opened off the great room. After a second's hesitation, she offered, "If you like, I can show you the way."

But something in Tara's expression made it obvious that she thought it unnecessary. "I'll find it. Thanks." Toting the diaper bag, Jessy moved toward the stone arch and the hall beyond it.

Tara immediately turned back to Ty. "I still think it would be fascinating to do a little research into Lady Dunshill's background. I would be curious to find out who she was, before she married the Earl of Crawford, and where she was from."

"It's hardly important." He lifted his shoulders in a shrug of disinterest.

"I don't know how important it is, but there is this blank spot in your family history. What happened to the runaway Madelaine Calder? Where did she go? What did she do? When did she die? Where? Your family tree won't be complete without that information," Tara argued lightly.

"Actually it would be interesting to track down more information on the family," Cat said thoughtfully. "Not just Madelaine Calder, but Grandpa's wife Lily, too. And where was Seth Calder born? In Texas?" She glanced at her father for the answer. "Do you know?"

"I can't recall anyone mentioning it to me," Chase admitted.. "And I was never curious enough to ask. I know he had a ranch somewhere outside of Fort Worth called the C Bar. Beyond the fact that he was buried in Fort Worth, that's about all I know."

"We really should document our family's history," Cat decided. "For the sake of future generations, if nothing else."

"I can't disagree with you, Cat. What do you say, Ty?" Chase cast a glance his direction, eyes twinkling. "Shall we put Cat in charge of it?"

"I think she's the perfect choice," he agreed, smiling.

"You two are making a joke of this, but I'm serious." Cat wore a determined look.

"So are we," Chase assured her, fighting back a smile.

"Wonderful. It's all settled." Tara beamed at the three of them. "It will be a fascinating project, Cat. If I can help at all, let me know. In the meantime, though"— she paused and pressed a hand on Ty's arm, claiming his attention—"I have a favor to ask of you."

"What's that?"

"I know the perfect housewarming gift you can give me."

"You're assuming I planned to give you one," Ty countered.

"You wouldn't be so rude, and I know it," she insisted confidently. "Shall I tell you what it is?"

He noted the avid gleam in her eyes. "I think you should before you burst."

Tara tipped back her head and laughed, exposing the slender curve of her throat. "You know me so well, Ty. The mere thought excites me because I know it will be the perfect finishing touch for the house."

"Don't keep us in suspense," Cat protested a trifle impatiently. "What is it?"

"The loan of Lady Dunshill's photograph. Just long enough for me to have a good copy made from it," Tara added in quick assurance. "I know this excellent portrait artist who creates the most stunning works, almost entirely from photographs. And the minute I walked into this room and saw this huge stone fireplace when the masons finished, I knew whose picture I wanted hanging above the mantel. Lady Dunshill, the home's namesake." Tara swung around to face the fireplace and contemplated the empty area above the mantel. "Won't a portrait of her make a perfect focal point for the

room?" She sent an appealing look over her shoulder to
Ty. "Say that you will loan me the photograph. I won't
need it for more than a week."

Without an adequate reason to refuse, Ty replied,
"I'll look for it the first chance I get."

"It's probably still buried in that old trunk in the
attic with all the rest of the photographs. Perhaps one
day next week we can look for it," she said to Cat. "With
roundup starting, Ty will be too busy. And there is an
absolute treasure trove of memorabilia up there, both
of the family and the ranch's early days. It will be an ideal
starting point for your research of the family."

Cat hesitated, no longer quick to agree to any suggestion from Tara as she once might have been. "Actually
Quint and I promised to help with roundup, but maybe
we can slip away for an afternoon. We'll see."

"Wonderful." Tara considered it a firm date.

Jessy had no difficulty locating the guest room. Its
decor was another artful blend of old and new that was
both rustic and elegant. The bed offered the only flat
surface big enough, short of the floor, to lay Laura on.
Jessy took one look at the bed's off-white coverlet and
dug a receiving blanket out of the diaper bag to spread
beneath Laura.

The minute Jessy laid her down, Laura stopped fussing and took immediate interest in her new surround-
ings. Her eye was first caught by an old rocker in the
corner, its wood finished in a distressed white, and its
seat and back cushion covered in a black-and-white
cowhide. Next Laura became fascinated by the gauzy
drapes that swooped from a half-moon canopy to the
end posts of the rusted iron headboard.

All the twisting and turning slowed the diaper changing process, but it was nothing new to Jessy. One more corner to pin and she would be finished.

Laura pointed a finger at the drapes. "P'etty, Mama. P'etty."

"Very pretty." The pin secured, Jessy reached for the ruffled and plastic-lined panties that matched Laura's dress.

As she slipped them on, she became conscious of a prickly sensation along the back of her neck. Jessy suddenly had that uneasy feeling she was being watched. A quick glance assured her there was no one in the hallway.

When she stood Laura up to pull the panties over the bulky diaper, Jessy snuck a look at the sheer-curtained window behind her. Her blood ran cold when she saw the dark silhouette of a slim man in a cowboy hat looking into the room.

Haskell. Who else could it be? Jessy reasoned. A dozen thoughts whipped through her mind at once, Ballard's warning among them. Her first impulse was to walk straight to the window, push back the sheers, and confront him. But having Laura with her made Jessy more cautious than she might have been on her own.

Careful to give no sign she had seen him standing outside, yet alert to any sound or movement, Jessy swung Laura onto her hip, picked up the diaper bag and walked unhurriedly from the guest room.

Approaching the great room, Jessy noticed Chase not far from the archway, standing apart from the others, a drink in his hand. She walked up to his side.

"Just now there was a man outside the window, watching while I changed Laura's diaper." She kept her voice pitched at a level intended for his hearing only. "I think it was Haskell."

Chase didn't bother to ask questions. "Ty." His voice

was hard with command. "Someone was outside. Come on."

He headed for the door, setting his drink on a table. After a startled second, Ty handed Trey to Cat and went after him. Logan was only a half-step behind both men.

"What's going on?" Tara frowned in confusion then whirled on Jessy. "He said someone was outside. What was he talking about?"

"Just that. There was someone outside watching me through the window." She was blunt with her answer, her eyes cold in their regard of Tara.

"Just now?" Sally gaped at her.

"That's ridiculous. You must have imagined it," Tara insisted.

"You mean, while you were changing Laura's diaper?" Cat said, as stunned as Sally.

Ignoring all of them, Jessy headed for the door, as eager as the men to confront the man. Tara, Sally, and Cat were quick to follow her.

Jessy reached the front walk in time to hear Chase bark, "Stop right there, Buck."

As she rounded the corner of the house, Jessy spotted the three men converging on a fourth, dressed in jeans, a blue chambray shirt, and a cowboy hat. Buck swung around to face them with an almost studied nonchalance. Even with the brim of his hat shading his features, there was no doubt in Jessy's mind Buck was the same man she had seen moments ago.

"What's got you in such an uproar, Chase?" Buck drawled with a kind of lazy innocence.

"You were seen looking in the window, Buck," Chase stated, a steely flatness to his voice.

Buck drew his head back in a show of surprise. "What window? What the hell are you talkin' about?"

"Don't try to bluff your way out of this, Buck," Chase warned. "It won't work."

Before Buck had a chance to respond, Tara arrived and inserted herself into the conversation. "Jessy claims there was a man outside the window watching her a few minutes ago."

"Well, she's wrong," Buck declared forcefully.

Ty took an angry step forward, "You were warned—"

Logan laid a restraining hand on his arm and smoothly placed himself between Ty and Buck. "Why don't you tell us what you're doing out here, Buck?"

"I noticed somebody skulkin' around the house." Buck kept his eyes on Ty. "I figured it was probably O'Rourke and came over to take a look-see. For all I know, I could've been standin' in front of a window, but I sure as hell wasn't lookin' in. I was tryin' to spot where O'Rourke had disappeared to."

It was a plausible explanation, one that Jessy found difficult to refute. The many folds of the sheers had prevented her from seeing more than the silhouette of a hatted man. Any other details had been obscured.

"There's your answer." Tara lifted her hand in a presenting gesture. "Obviously Jessy only imagined that he was peering in the window. Isn't that right?" Her dark gaze gleamed with confidence.

"It's possible," Jessy admitted, still searching her memory in an attempt to pinpoint the reason she had been certain the man was looking inside.

"Culley is around here somewhere," Logan inserted quietly. "I caught a glimpse of that bay gelding he always rides grazing in one of the draws as we were driving in."

"You see, it was all a mistake," Tara proclaimed and cast a pitying smile at Jessy. "It's an easy one to make. I know if I saw a man standing outside a bedroom window, I would assume he was looking in. Any woman would." She turned her smile on the others. "I don't know about the rest of you, but I'm relieved this whole fuss was over nothing."

"Just make sure it stays that way," Ty warned, continuing his stare-down of Buck.

Wisely, Buck made no response to that.

But Tara was quick to slide a calming hand over Ty's arm. "Ty Calder, I swear you are just itching for a fight," she chided, all beguiling charm. "This is a special evening for me. Don't you go spoiling my first dinner party." Then, as if to end this confrontation once and for all, she smoothly glanced at Buck. "Go on back to the trailer. And pay no attention if you see Culley about the place. He isn't likely to cause any harm."

"Yes, ma'am." Buck dipped his head in a respectful nod and backed up a few steps before turning to head toward the trailer.

"Let's go inside, shall we?" Tara suggested to all of them. "Dinner will be ready soon, and I still haven't shown you the rest of the house."

The incident was not referred to again that evening, but the memory of it stayed, like an uninvited guest at the table, creating a tension that didn't allow any of them to totally relax.

Later that night back at The Homestead, the twins fell asleep almost before the covers were tucked around them. Bending, Jessy smoothed a dark strand of hair off Trey's forehead.

"They're exhausted," she murmured to Ty.

"It's been a long day for them."

"It was." Jessy nodded in agreement and drifted toward the door along with Ty.

Both paused in the opening to make a final check on the pair. A dim nightlight spilled over the sleeping toddlers and the baby monitor was positioned on a dresser between the cribs, ready to transmit the first cry from either of them.

Satisfied that all was quiet and likely to stay that way, they left the room, closing the door behind them. In a companionable silence, they walked to the master suite next door to the twins' room. Jessy went directly to the closet to change into her nightshirt while Ty crossed to the bed and sat down to pull off his boots.

The first one had thudded to the floor when Jessy called from the closet, "What time are you getting up in the morning?"

Ty held the other boot while he thought about it. "It's a two-hour drive to South Branch. Three-thirty, I guess. I want to be there by first light."

He placed the boot next to its mate then reached over to set the alarm clock as Jessy emerged from the closet, wearing a T-shirt that stopped about midthigh.

"Set it for three, and I'll fix you some breakfast before you go." Tomorrow might be Sunday, but once roundup started, it continued seven days a week until it was finished.

"No, I'll grab a bite at the chuck wagon with the rest of the hands." Ty stood up and tugged his shirttail out from the waistband of his dress jeans.

"I won't argue," Jessy replied, a faintly mischievous gleam in her eyes. "I'll be glad of the extra sleep."

"Keep gloating like that and I'll make sure you're wide awake before I leave," Ty declared in a mock threat, peeling off his shirt and tossing it at her.

She caught it easily and detoured to the clothes hamper. "As soon as the twins wake up from their afternoon nap tomorrow, we'll drive over and have supper with you."

"No, don't."

The firmness in his voice prompted Jessy to pause in the act of depositing his dirty shirt in the hamper. She threw him a startled look. "Why not?"

"Because there is no need for you to drive all the way over there. I'll be home by nine or ten." There was an edge to his voice that puzzled Jessy.

"The twins will be asleep by then." She dropped the shirt in the hamper and closed the lid.

"I expect they will be." Ty emptied the pockets of his jeans and placed their contents atop the tall dresser, his back angled to her. "Just the same, I prefer that you don't come out."

He had left something unsaid, something Jessy had a feeling she wouldn't like at all. But she needed to be certain.

"Don't come out tomorrow—or anytime?" Her demand for clarification was close to a challenge.

After the smallest pause, he turned, his glance bouncing off her. "Anytime," Ty said, a closed-up look to his expression.

The incident with Buck Haskell was behind this; Jessy was certain of it. "Buck Haskell is not going to scare me into hiding," she declared with force, angered that Ty would even suggest that she should.

"Jessy," Ty began in a reasoning tone.

"Don't Jessy me!" she flashed.

As calm and steady as she was by nature, Jessy had a temper that was the match of any man's when aroused. And Ty knew he had triggered it. He moved into her path, catching her by the shoulders and immediately noting her stiffness.

"Cool down and listen for a minute," he said.

"Why? I'm not going to like it any better this time." Jessy glared at him, not backing down an inch.

Ty studied the angry glitter in her eyes, aware that she felt all things passionately—love and hate, joy and grief—but she seldom let it show.

"I don't often ask you to do something for me. But I'm asking now." Ty was careful to word it as a request, not an order. "Stick close to headquarters."

"I won't be any safer here than at roundup. That rebuilt shoulder of yours is proof of that," Jessy stated with heat. "At roundup, I would be surrounded by dozens of hands. Here, it's just me and a bunch of old men."

Ty couldn't explain why he felt so strong about this. There was no logic in it. The request was based purely on a gut feeling that wouldn't stand up under an argument.

"Do you know when you get angry, your eyes flash fire and your lips lay all tight together?" he mused aloud.

"Don't change the subject, Ty." The fire in her eyes leapt a little higher.

"Why not?" He shifted a hand to the side of her neck and stroked his thumb over the clean line of her jaw. "I've made my request. I'm not going to try to talk you into it. You'll either agree to it or you won't."

Ty bent his head and tested the tightness of her lips. When they failed to soften immediately, he shifted his attention to her cheek and the shell of her ear.

"Give me one good reason why I should agree," Jessy challenged, but in a voice that suggested she might be open to reason.

"That's easy," Ty murmured, smiling as he nuzzled her neck. "Because you love me." His arms encircled her, molding her T-shirt-clad body to his length.

"That's not fair." But Jessy smiled the protest and slipped her own arms around him, spreading them over the corded muscles along his back to increase the closeness.

Pretending to misunderstand, Ty drew his head back to look at her. "You mean you don't love me?"

"You know very well I do," Jessy chided, her eyes shining with love as she ran her gaze over his face.

"Good. Because it's becoming more and more obvious to me that there is nothing under this T-shirt but your skin." In a silent reinforcement of his statement, his hands glided down the small of her back and over the womanly shape of her firm buttocks and hips.

"And you are wearing way too much." Her fingers worked to loosen the waist of his jeans.

"We'll have to do something about that." At the moment he was more interested in exploring the giving taste of her mouth. There would be time later for the heat and urgency of skin against skin.

Stretched in a limp sprawl with Ty's warm flank against hers, the bed covers kicked to the foot and a fine sheen of perspiration covering her body, Jessy reveled in the tingling aftermath of their lovemaking. It mellowed the stand she had previously taken.

"I've been thinking," she murmured as an opening.

"So have I." Ty stifled a yawn. "Three-thirty is sounding earlier and earlier."

A smile curved the wide edges of her mouth. "Actually I was thinking about something else." Jessy rolled onto her side to study the craggy male lines of his face. "Roundup will last another two weeks or more. I can't guarantee I'll stay close to headquarters that whole time. But if I do leave, I promise I will be extra cautious."

For a woman who loved open country and the feel of a horse beneath her, it was a major concession, and Ty knew it. Reaching out, he drew her into the hollow of his shoulder.

"I'll rest easier in my mind knowing that," he murmured.

Yet her assurance did little to chase away the shadows that lurked at the edge of his consciousness, without shape or identity.

PART FOUR

The summer grass, it grows brittle and dry.
And heads are hangin' forlorn.
'Cause it turned red
With blood from the dead.
And a Calder has reason to mourn.

Chapter Nineteen

〜

By the end of the first week, the routine had been established. Every morning Ty was up and away at the crack of dawn. Most evenings he returned around ten o'clock. True to her word, Jessy didn't venture from the Triple C headquarters. But being bound by that promise seemed to increase her restlessness.

Friday morning she stood at the kitchen sink and gazed with longing at the big sweep of country beyond the window. Laura sat on the floor, happily playing with one of her dolls while Trey tore around the kitchen in a release of overabundant energy.

With neither child requiring her attention, Jessy let her thoughts roam where she couldn't. The summer roundup had shifted its operation north to the Broken Buttes country, an area she knew well.

"I hope somebody remembers to check that hanging valley." She dipped the oatmeal pan in the rinse water and passed it to Sally to dry. "That old longhorn-cross brindle cow always hangs out there, usually with two or three others."

Sally stared at her as if she had taken leave of her senses. "What does that have to do with chicken salad?"

"Chicken salad?" Now it was Jessy's turn to stare in bewilderment.

"Yes. I just asked what you thought about having chicken salad for lunch today."

"You did?" Jessy said in surprise. "I'm sorry. I guess I was miles away."

"That's obvious." A suppressed smile of amusement carved dimples in Sally's plump cheeks.

Trey chose that moment to pick a fight with his sister by snatching her doll. The theft evoked the expected response, as Laura screamed an angry, "No!"

With the devil gleaming in his dark eyes, Trey taunted his sister with the doll. When Laura clambered to her feet to snatch it back, Trey took off with it, grinning from ear to ear. Laura turned to Jessy for help.

"Mama, Mama, dolly, dolly," she wailed, her hand outstretched toward her brother, fingers clutching and unclutching in that familiar gimme-gimme gesture of a child.

"Trey, you give that back to your sister," Jessy ordered.

With a gleeful giggle, he clutched it tighter and tore out of the kitchen as fast as he could. "Trey Calder, you come back here this minute." Jessy dropped the dishrag in the sink water, hastily dried her hands on a towel, and ran after the fleeing toddler, leaving Sally to comfort the furious Laura. When she entered the living room, she spotted Trey making a beeline for the den. "Trey Calder," she called one last warning.

He threw a look behind him and barreled into Chase, who was on his way out of the den. The collision with Chase's legs knocked Trey to the floor. Seconds after he landed, he broke loose with an ear-splitting shriek.

When Chase crouched down to see how badly the boy was hurt, Trey took one look at him and screamed all the louder. In Jessy's experience, it was a sure sign that his pride was hurt a lot worse than he was, a fact she confirmed when she arrived.

"He came out of nowhere," Chase said in regret.

"I know." Satisfied that Trey had suffered nothing worse than a bruise or two, Jessy picked him up. But he made it clear he wanted nothing to do with her, his whole body stiffening in resistance while he twisted toward the den, screaming for his daddy. "Daddy isn't here, Trey," Jessy told him, which brought a freshened cry of anger. In the age-old response of all mothers, Jessy bounced him up and down in her arms and slid an annoyed glance at Chase. "The poor guy hasn't seen Ty in a week. They are always asleep by the time he comes home."

"It's rough on them," Chase agreed and laid a comforting hand on Trey's head, but Trey batted it away with his fist. "I was just on my way to Broken Butte. I'll make sure Ty comes home early today."

In that split second, Jessy made a decision she would never regret. "I have a better idea. We're going with you. Give me five minutes to get their things together."

Thirty minutes later the headquarters of the Triple C was well behind them, and the ranch road to the Broken Buttes area stretched ahead of them in a long tan line. Jessy glanced in the back seat to check on the twins. The drone of the Suburban's engine had worked its magic, lulling both toddlers to sleep.

"I don't have to worry about them missing their morning nap," she said to Chase.

He threw a look over his shoulder and smiled in agreement. "I thought it was awfully quiet back there."

Facing the front again, Jessy scanned the land on either side of the open road. But one look at the drought-seared earth took any enjoyment from the outing.

"It has to rain soon," she murmured.

"Not according to the thirty-day forecast," Chase replied grimly. "At best, we might see an isolated shower."

"Even that would be better than nothing," Jessy said with feeling.

Shortly after midmorning they arrived at the gather point. A dust fog swirled around the small herd that had already been collected. A thin film of it drifted into the makeshift camp set up by the motorized cookshack. Parked nearby were a half-dozen pickups and stock trailers hitched behind them. Chase parked alongside one of them and gave Jessy a hand with the twins. The minute Trey spotted the spare horses tied in the shade of the trailers, his excitement knew no bounds.

"G'mpa, horsey." Trey pointed to them with a look of pure joy.

"Lots of horses," Chase agreed.

"Trey wide, G'mpa," Trey asserted with a vigorous nod of his head.

Chase shook his head. "We'll ride later. Right now your grandpa wants a cup of coffee."

"Me, too."

"I'm afraid you're not quite old enough to be drinking camp coffee." His mouth crooked in a suppressed smile, but his eyes beamed with a mixture of pride and approval.

He had missed out on being part of Ty's formative years, but Chase intended to be part of his grandson's. He liked the idea of passing on the wisdom and range lore he had learned from his father. Chase didn't fault the way Ty had turned out. Maggie had done a good job of raising him. But Ty didn't have the same understanding of the land and this life that he would have if he had been raised with its legacy from birth the way Trey would be.

"You see that sky, Trey." Chase looked up at the vastness of it. "That's a Calder sky. My daddy told me a long time ago that it takes a big chunk of land to fit under it."

"Horse, G'mpa." Trey pointed instead to a pair of riders, pushing a half-dozen cows with their calves toward the gather site.

Chase recognized the short-coupled bay mare and the small rider on its back. Which made the identity of the second rider obvious. "Looks like that's Quint and your Aunt Cat."

Trey's eyes got big with the news. "Kint."

"Yup. You'll see him in a little bit. How about some coffee, Joe?" he said to the thirty-year-old cook, a new man by the name of Joe Johns, who had taken over the job from Tucker when he retired a year ago.

Johns was a mountain man, born and raised, and looked the part with his stocky build and bushy beard. Although he was a stranger to the plains country, the Triple C riders had gladly overlooked that flaw the first time they tasted his coffee.

"You want a cup, too, Miss Jessy?" He filled a tin mug for Chase and reached for another.

"Are you kidding?" Jessy smiled. "I would never turn down a cup of your coffee."

As they drifted away from the cookshack on wheels, cups in hand, Chase told her, "The men have taken to calling him Coffee Joe. As far as they're concerned, the job is his for life."

"Let's hope he agrees."

Chase sat down on one of the collapsible campstools, but Jessy remained standing, breathing in the familiar roundup smells of horses and cattle, saddle leather, and strong coffee. A scan of the riders holding the gather failed to locate Ty among them, but Jessy was quick to recognize her own father when Stumpy split away to ride into camp with Cat and Quint.

"I saw we had some special visitors this morning." Stumpy chucked a finger under Laura's chin, drawing a giggle from her. "Ty never said anything about you coming by this morning."

"That's because he didn't know." When Laura stretched out her arm to her other grandfather, Jessy handed the child over to him. "Where is he, anyway?"

"He was with me." Cat pulled a kerchief from her pocket and wiped at the dust film on her face. "He sent us back with the cattle and went to make a sweep through the area by Three Fingers butte. I swear I ate a pound of dust that last mile. It is really dry here, Dad."

"It's bad everywhere." Chase let Trey down to play with Quint and stood up to look northward in the direction of Three Fingers, gripped by an unease he couldn't name. "I wonder what's keeping him."

"If he came across any cattle that found some decent graze, he'll have his hands full trying to get them to leave it," Cat replied. "I was just telling Stumpy that if Ty doesn't show up soon, I'll ride back and give him some help."

She had no more than finished her sentence when the distinctive *crack* of a rifle shot sounded in the distance. Chase whipped his head around in instant alertness. After a short pause, it was followed by two more quick shots. On the Triple C, such a spacing of shots meant only one thing—a rider was hurt. It was a sound that chilled Chase all the way to the bone.

"Watch Trey." He threw the words at Cat. Unaware of dropping the full mug of coffee, he headed for the nearest saddled horse.

Fighting a sick feeling in his stomach, Chase jerked the reins loose and swung into the saddle. Both Jessy and Stumpy were right on his heels. But Chase didn't waste time waiting for them, leaving camp at a swift canter. Every inch of him strained in anticipation of the next shot that would guide him. In the meantime, he pointed his horse in the direction of the rock butte Cat had mentioned, hoping against hope that he was wrong.

Hoofbeats pounded the ground behind him as Jessy and Stumpy galloped after him. Two more riders came from the east, abandoning the bunch of cows they had gathered.

The rifle cracked again, the sound coming from somewhere ahead of him, but a little to the east. With a twitch of the reins, Chase altered his course. The other riders did the same. All five riders converged on a high knoll and reined in to make use of the land's vantage point.

"There he is." An out-of-breath Stumpy pointed to a rider, visible against the skyline about a half-mile away, an upraised arm waving the rifle. Behind him was a riderless horse, its head hanging low and a foreleg raised, suggesting an injury.

It was Jobe Garvey who spoke the words Chase dreaded. "Isn't that the big bay Ty was riding?" The minute he finished, he froze and shot a quick glance at Chase.

There was no reaction from Chase. With a nod, he signaled everyone forward and led the way, keeping his mount to a strong lope.

Riders were always getting thrown, even the best of them, and Chase ranked Ty among that group. An accident—that was likely what had happened. His horse spooked or stepped wrong. There were a hundred possible scenarios that might have separated Ty from his horse. It didn't have to be the one that was making his throat go dry.

The waiting rider was another of the Garvey boys. It was the youngest one, Jed, not much more than twenty-four. There was a clear uneasiness about the young man. Chase was quick to identify it in the way the rider had trouble looking him in the eye when Chase pulled up before them.

Instead the Garvey boy focused on his older brother. "I came across Ty's horse back there." He gestured over his shoulder. "It looks like he mighta bowed a tendon."

"Any sign of Ty?" Chase made a scan of the open ground beyond the rider.

"No, sir." Again the Garvey boy failed to meet his gaze. "I didn't really expect to."

Nobody called him "sir," but it was something else in his tone made Chase stiffen. "Why not?"

"One of the reins is broke. I figure the horse was running and stepped on it."

Leather creaked as Chase shifted in his saddle to address the rest of the men. "According to Cat, Ty was headed for the Three Fingers. The horse probably threw him somewhere in that area."

"I don't think he was thrown, sir," Jed Garvey ventured hesitantly.

The "sir" business was beginning to annoy Chase. "Why not?" he asked with impatience.

"Because"—he paused and pulled the lame horse forward, turning it sideways—"there's blood all over the saddle."

The summer sun had already dried it a dark color. Chase reeled slightly. The sight of the big smear shut off the air from his lung and momentarily robbed him of speech.

Somewhere off to his left, Jessy murmured a pained, "Dear God, no."

Soft as it was, her voice cracked over Chase like a whip.

Immediately he sat tall in the saddle, his big shoulders squaring up. "You ride back to camp, Jessy."

The crispness of his order wiped the stricken look from her face. "No, I won't," she replied in a voice equally firm in its defiance. "I am riding with you to look for Ty."

"No, you aren't. You are going back to camp now. And that is an order!" He was deliberately harsh with her. Ignoring the angry glare of her eyes, Chase fired his next order at the young Garvey boy. "You go with her. And get Amy Trumbo here on the double."

Every instinct told Chase there was too much blood on that saddle. If they were lucky enough to find Ty alive, he would need medical attention as fast as they could get it to him. A registered nurse was the closest he could get to that, and Amy was a damned good one.

"Yes, sir." Jed immediately urged his horse forward and gave a tug on the reins to the lame bay. It took a hobbling step forward.

"Leave the horse," Chase ordered as his own mount shifted restively under him, catching the high tension of its rider and the blood smell in the air. "It will make its own way to camp. When it does, make sure no one goes near it. Logan will want to examine it."

"Logan?" Jobe echoed with a puzzled frown. "Why—"

"There's too much blood for this to be an accident." It was a truth Chase had already faced. He spoke it now, with no feeling in his voice. Emotion was a luxury he couldn't allow himself, not until he found his son. "Let's go," he said to the others and reined his dancing horse around the injured bay.

Out of the corner of his eye, he had a glimpse of Jessy as she angrily hauled her horse around and pointed it toward camp. He had a momentary regret that he had been so harsh with her. In his heart, Chase knew she was not a woman who needed to be shielded from the sometimes brutal realities of life. But he had been raised otherwise, and he hadn't wanted her along.

The small band of riders bunched close to Chase as they rode off. Behind them, the bay horse issued a forlorn whinny and limped gamely after the two riders headed for camp.

The Broken Butte range was rugged foothill country, its rough terrain offering a thousand hiding places. Three Fingers was a name given to an area where three brush-choked coulees emptied into a shallow valley.

A half-mile from the entrance to the first, Chase raised his hand, signaling a halt, and reined in his horse. It sidestepped impatiently under him, swinging its rump into the horse on its right.

"We'll fan out here," Chase ordered. "Stumpy, you and Jobe check out the first finger. The rest of us will take the second. If we still haven't found him, we'll all look in the third."

Acknowledging the order with a nod, Stumpy reined his horse to the left and sent it forward at a walk. Jobe swung his mount farther to the left, creating a good twenty feet of space between himself and Stumpy.

"Keep your eyes peeled," Chase called after them. "And not just for Ty. You see anything, you holler."

Stumpy responded with a lift of his hand, signaling that he had heard and understood. Maintaining his position in the center of the small search party, Chase walked his horse forward, resisting its head-tossing tug on the bit. As anxious as he was to find Ty, he knew a slow and thorough sweep was better than a hasty one. On either side of him came the dull *thud* of hooves on the hard ground and the rustling *swish* of dry grass against the horses' legs.

The morning breeze carried to him the high-pitched bark of a prairie dog, alerting the rest of its town to the presence of riders. But Chase had no interest in them. He was intent on the area before him, searching for any sign that a rider had passed this way. But the hard, dry ground held few impressions, and none that resembled a hoofprint.

Periodically he lifted his gaze and scanned the countryside ahead of him, alert for any movement, anything that didn't look as it should. He spotted a buzzard floating in the sky to the north on the lookout for carrion, as always. Its mere presence overhead was enough to twist his stomach into knots.

In a rare burst of impatience, Chase pulled up and bellowed, "Ty! Ty! Can you hear me?"

Startled, the other riders reined in, then waited and listened. The morning breeze whispered through the dry grass, but it was the only sound in the stillness. Chase hadn't expected a response. The shout hadn't been for Ty's benefit. Chase wanted whoever was out there to damn well know he was coming.

Again he started his horse forward, traveling at a walk as before. He was on a straight course to the entrance of the middle coulee. Brush hugged the sides of its floor, their withered leaves showing the effects of the drought.

The last hundred yards to its mouth were long ones, made longer by his reluctance to see what might be waiting for him. At the same time he was pushed by an inner feeling of urgency. Picking up on it, his horse shifted into a jog-trot.

As Chase approached the coulee's wide mouth, the other two riders swung in behind him. Brittle, sun-yellowed grass grew in a thick mat along the mouth floor, leaving not an inch of soil uncovered. Chase pulled up to study it, searching for the telltale gouge of a hoof.

"Yo!" The shout came from Stumpy.

Instantly Chase wheeled his horse in Stumpy's direction. "What have you got?"

"Hoofprints coming out!" Stumpy shouted back. "And they're dug in deep!"

Chase knew with certainty there was no reason to look in the middle coulee. The search would end in the first. With dread in his heart, he rode over to join up with Stumpy and Jobe.

Ten yards inside the mouth of the first wide ravine was a large patch of bare ground where a heavy runoff had at one time scoured away all the grass. Right through the center of it, hooves had gouged out a set of deep tracks. They were the kind of prints a horse left when it was digging for speed.

Chase studied them for no more than a few seconds then swept a hard glance over his men. "All right, we'll go in." All feeling was flattened from his voice. "But we'll keep to the left. If there are any other tracks, we don't want to mess them up."

Taking the lead, he walked his horse into the coulee. The branches of a tall scrub brush raked across his leg. The dry rattle of it sounded unnaturally loud. Ears swiveling, his horse snorted. Chase could feel its muscles bunching under him. There was something up ahead it didn't like. Steeling himself, Chase continued on.

Twenty yards in, the going got rough. Brush and small boulders crowded in from the walls of the coulee, forcing Chase to steer his horse into the center.

Ahead the coulee widened out to make a sweeping turn northward. When Chase rounded its bend, he saw

Ty lying near some brush on the right. Blood soaked the front of his shirt, coloring it a dark scarlet. Braced as Chase had been for the sight, it was still a blow that ripped a deep, guttural moan from his chest.

"Sweet Jesus, no," Stumpy murmured behind him as Chase piled out of the saddle.

Pain and rage welled up together, but Chase knew this was not the time to release either of them. He was a Calder, and there were orders to be given.

He barked them out even as he moved to Ty's side. "Jobe, ride to camp. Tell them we found him. The rest of you, stay where you are."

Already he had noticed the dead calf lying only a couple feet from Ty, half hidden by a bush. He guessed it had been the lure to get Ty on the ground.

Chase had no memory of crossing the space to Ty. One minute he was swinging out of the saddle and the next he was sinking to the ground beside his son, on legs that felt like rubber. Flies swarmed and buzzed all around as he bent over the ashen-faced Ty.

Instinctively he gathered Ty into his arms, never once noticing the limp heaviness of him. The back of Ty's shirt was as wet with blood as the front. Chase's searching hands quickly discovered the broken edge of a knife blade embedded in Ty's chest. His skin was warm to the touch. Whether from the life or the sun, Chase couldn't tell.

"Is he—is he alive?" Jobe had yet to leave. Despite Chase's order, he lingered to learn what word he should carry.

Chase never heard the question. At that moment his only world was the man in his arms. "Ty." Emotion choked his voice as his eyes swam with unshed tears. "Can you hear me, son?"

There was a traitorous quiver to his chin. Squeezing

his eyes shut, Chase fought to get control of himself. When he opened them, his eyes were clear—clear enough to see a fluttering lift of Ty's lashes.

"Ty." Desperation made his voice rough with demand as Chase experienced the first spark of hope.

"Knew . . . you'd . . . come." Ty's voice was soft as a breath, so faint Chase wasn't sure if he heard it or imagined it.

Unconsciously he dug his fingers into the sodden shirtfront, wadding the wet material into a ball in his fist.

"Who did this to you, son? It was Buck, wasn't it?" Chase guessed as rage crowded to the front of his thoughts.

"Jes—" Ty never quite got the word out, but he said enough of it for Chase to know he meant Jessy.

Then he was gone. Chase knew the exact instant he died. It was something he felt in his heart. There was no need to check for breath or pulse. His son was dead.

Slowly, almost woodenly, he laid his son's body back on the ground and remained there, too numbed with grief to move.

"Chase?" Stumpy's questioning voice was slow to penetrate his consciousness.

Chase knew what he was asking. "He's dead."

It was the word Jobe Garvey had been waiting to hear. He reined his horse away from the rest and sank his spurs into him, taking off at a fast gallop for camp.

The discordant jangle of a horse chewing on its bit filled the silence that followed. For a long minute, no one said a word. Then Stumpy cleared his throat.

"Did he say who killed him?" Stumpy's words were stiff with repressed feeling.

"No."

"I thought, maybe . . ." Stumpy let that die unfinished. "Did he say anything?"

It required much effort, but Chase looked Stumpy in the eye and lied, "He was already dead when we got here. Stabbed."

Just as he had once withheld his father's dying words, Chase did the same with his son's. It was better that he lived with the pain of them since he had been the one to order Jessy back to camp. Her grief would be enough to bear without adding such bittersweet knowledge to them.

"You'd better ride back to camp, Stumpy," Chase said with great weariness. "Jessy will need you. The rest of you go, too."

Stumpy hesitated, compassion welling up. His daughter was alive, but Chase had lost his only son. "What about you?"

"I'll stay here with Ty."

One by one the riders turned their horses around and rode out of the coulee, leaving Chase alone on the ground beside the body of his son.

Chapter Twenty

～

Tension hung over the camp with all the thickness of a heavy fog. Only the twins were immune to it. Trey played his own boisterous version of tag with Quint while Laura sat on Jessy's lap and made eyes at the cook. The twins' innocence gave a look of normalcy to the scene that was taken away by Cat's restless pacing. As usual, she made no attempt to conceal the anxiety that gripped everyone.

Cat made a few attempts to occupy herself with the children, but after a short while the edginess took hold and she wandered off, usually to stare in the direction of the Three Fingers, watching for a rider to return with news of Ty.

After another fruitless vigil, she walked back to the cookshack and refilled her coffee mug. It was not the coffee she wanted as much as it was something to do with her hands. Worry clouded her green eyes when she darted a look at Jessy.

"Just because there was blood on the saddle, that

doesn't necessarily mean he is badly hurt. You can bleed a lot just from a nasty cut." Cat seemed to gain some reassurance from voicing the thought aloud. "That's probably all that happened, Jessy."

"I know." Jessy had told herself the same thing, but she had trouble believing it.

A ranch pickup came roaring toward camp, traveling at a reckless speed. Its approach brought Jessy to her feet as Cat hurriedly discarded her cup in the wreck pan and moved toward the oncoming vehicle.

"That must be Amy," Cat murmured.

But it was Ballard who emerged from the cloud of dust that swallowed the truck when it came to a stop. His first few strides toward camp had a frantic quality about them. Then he saw Jessy and relief visibly sagged through him.

"There you are." He walked straight to Jessy, a faint smile lifting the corners of his mouth. "I've been half out of my mind since Sally told me you'd come out here to roundup. How did you manage to sneak away without me seein' you leave?"

"I didn't sneak away. I rode with Chase," Jessy replied, her attention already straying.

"I never gave it a second thought when he left this morning. It never crossed my mind to check and see if you were with him. I'll know better next time." His lazy smile was full of self-reproach.

"When we saw your truck, we were sure you were Amy." Cat glanced toward the road and chewed absently at her lower lip.

"Amy Trumbo?" Ballard asked with a frown. "Why are you expecting her? Is somebody hurt?" His glance made a lightning sweep of the camp area as if searching for an injured rider.

"Ty is missing." Cat's jumbled nerves needed the release of words. "They found his horse."

"Don't tell me he got thrown?" Ballard reacted with a half-smile of disbelief then shook his head. "Naw, his horse probably stepped in a prairie dog hole and took a spill."

"There was blood on the saddle." In Cat's mind that negated any thought that Ty would be found walking back to the roundup site.

After a slight pause, Ballard darted a look of concern at Jessy then insisted, "That doesn't mean anything."

Cat took heart from that. "I said the same thing to Jessy not two minutes ago."

"I guess they're out lookin' for him now," he surmised. "Is Chase with them?"

"Yes." Cat nodded. "He made Jessy come back to camp when they found Ty's horse."

He eyed Jessy with a measuring glance. "Knowin' you, that was bound to gall a little. But I wouldn't hold it against him. It was the way he was raised."

"I know that," Jessy confirmed.

"It's the waitin', though, isn't it?" Ballard guessed. "It would be a lot easier to take if you were out there with them."

The answer to that was too obvious to be spoken. Idleness had never suited Jessy. The circumstances only made it worse.

"Don't worry. Chase will find him," Ballard stated. "He'll move heaven an' earth until he does. Isn't that right, dark eyes?" He grinned at Laura and tickled her under the chin. She giggled with delight. He held out his hands to her. "Wanta come with me while I fetch myself a cup of coffee? I'll bet your momma's arm is about broke from holdin' a big girl like you."

Without hesitation, Laura stretched out her arms to him. At a year-and-a-half, she was already eager to make a new conquest. Jessy passed her into Ballard's arms.

"You're a Calder, that's for sure," Ballard told her as he headed toward the cookshack. "I remember when your aunt used to flirt with all the cowboys at roundup. She wasn't but a few years older than you are then." Laura made a grab for something in his shirt pocket, but he stopped her. "Don't you go stealin' my makings. In case you don't know it, you're too young to smoke."

"Mine," Laura stated.

"Nope, it's mine. I'll tell ya' what, as soon as I get my coffee, you can sit on my lap and watch while I roll me a smoke. How's that? Okay?"

" 'kay."

"He's good with children." Cat watched the pair, almost glad of the distraction. But it didn't last. Turning, she dragged in a worried breath and gazed toward the Three Fingers. "Surely they have found him by now."

"It's rough country." Jessy visualized it in her mind, trying to recall all the hard-to-see places.

"And if he's unconscious—" Cat bit down on her lip, shutting off the rest of that thought.

An engine droned behind them. Turning, Jessy saw another pickup traveling across the open ground, but at a sensible pace. "Here comes Amy."

"Thank God." Cat's voice vibrated with feeling.

With brisk efficiency, Amy Trumbo stepped out of the truck, carrying her medical emergency kit. Her sharp glance searched both their faces.

"They haven't found him yet, have they?" Amy guessed, empathy softening her expression.

Before Cat could confirm that, the cook Joe Johns hollered, "Riders coming in."

Her heart in her throat, Jessy swung around and immediately saw a handful of riders in the distance, approaching camp at a slow lope. Exhibiting a rare show of emotion, she gripped Cat's arm.

"Do you see Ty with them?" She strained forward, her gaze scouring the riders in search of Ty's familiar high and wide shape.

Mutely Cat shook her head. "I don't understand," she murmured. "If they haven't found him, why are they coming back?"

Jessy had a feeling she knew the answer, but she refused to say it. She picked out her father's short, stocky shape and fixed her gaze on him.

It was an unwritten rule of ranch etiquette that a man didn't ride his horse into camp and possibly foul the ground where other men were to eat and drink. But this was one time when the rule wasn't observed. Instead of swinging away to the picket area, the band rode straight into camp.

"Where's Ty?" Cat's voice had a trace of panic in it. "Didn't you find him?"

The other riders glanced at Stumpy. Jessy knew at once he had been the one chosen to break the news. When he ducked his head, avoiding her gaze, and climbed out of the saddle before answering, Jessy took a step backward, going cold all over.

"We found him all right." There was such utter sadness in his eyes when he finally met her look. "I'm sorry, Jessy, but—" Stumpy tried, but he couldn't get the words out.

"He's dead, isn't he?" She said them for her father.

Stumpy nodded, his mouth tightly compressed, a kind of pain in his eyes.

."That's a lie!" Cat screamed, an underlying sob to her voice. "He isn't dead. Not Ty. Not my brother!" Amy Trumbo stepped up and attempted to wrap her arms around Cat in comfort, but she was rigid in them. "It can't be true," Cat protested. "It can't be."

"We don't want it to be," Amy murmured. "But we both know Stumpy wouldn't lie."

A horrible moan of pain came from Cat as she sagged against Amy and sobbed brokenly. All the while Jessy stood beneath the heat of the sun's full glare, cold to the bone. A hand moved onto her shoulder, but she barely felt it. It was almost as though the person behind her were touching someone else.

"You're white as a sheet, Jessy." It was Ballard's soft voice that came from somewhere near her shoulder. "You'd better sit down."

"No." She rejected that suggestion out of hand and looked straight at her father. "How? How did he die?"

Stumpy knew better than to pull any punches with his daughter. "Chase thinks he might have been stabbed." He passed the reins to one of the other riders and moved to Jessy's side, wrapping a fatherly arm around her. "Ballard's right. You need to sit down."

Making no objection this time, Jessy let him guide her to a campstool. Somebody put a cup in her hand.

"Drink this," the cook ordered.

Almost trancelike, she took a sip then drew back in distaste. "It has sugar in it."

"It's good for shock," the cook told her. "Drink it."

Shock, was that what she was feeling? It felt like a great raging emptiness—with a giant ache where her heart should be.

"Where's Chase?" The sudden and sharp question came from Ballard.

"He stayed with the body," Stumpy replied.

The body. It was a cold and final phrase. Pain closed around her throat, briefly shutting off her air. In desperation Jessy gulped down more of the disgustingly sweet coffee.

"You left Chase out there by himself!" Ballard thundered. "That was a fool thing do. What if Haskell's still out there?"

Jessy's head came up, his question slicing through her own emotional haze. "You have to go back," she said to her father. "You can't let Chase stay out there alone. It might not be safe."

When Stumpy wavered, equally concerned for her well-being, Ballard spoke up, "You stay here, Stumpy. I'll take some of the boys and ride back."

"You do that." There was deep-felt gratitude in the look Stumpy sent him. Turning, he called to the others, "Jobe, Hank, Ben, you ride with Ballard back to the Three Fingers and keep an eye on Chase."

Ballard hesitated, watching as Trey toddled up to Jessy and patted her knee for attention. "Mama?" Young though he was, Trey sensed the change in atmosphere. It showed in the uneasy worry in his expression.

His eyes were the dark brown of a Calder. For an instant, Jessy saw Ty in them and gathered Trey into her arms. Here was the tragedy—that Trey would grow up without ever knowing his father. She hugged him close. For once, Trey didn't object.

"You might want to take Jessy and the twins back to The Homestead," Ballard suggested. "There is really no reason for them to stay here. It'll be another hour or more before Logan shows up. Once he's here, it's probably gonna take him a long time to check everything out."

There was truth in what he said, and more in what he had left unsaid. The investigation into Ty's death had yet to begin. Which meant it would be hours before the body would be taken away. Jessy would accomplish nothing by staying. And she had two very good reasons for leaving—their children.

Rising to her feet, she shifted Trey to her hip. "Come on. Let's find your sister and go home." Her voice was thick with the tears she hadn't allowed herself to shed.

Trey scowled. "See Daddy."

His innocent demand ripped through her. Jessy struggled to find her voice, at last managing to utter a choked, "Not today, sweetheart."

Not ever again.

A purpling dusk pressed against the windows of The Homestead, something bleak in its darkness. Chase stood in front of the fireplace, a booted foot propped on its raised hearth, a hand gripping the mantel. He stared into the blackened opening, the heaviness of his loss weighing on him, his mind turning back.

"Chase?" Logan's questioning voice penetrated his reverie.

Rousing himself with an effort, Chase threw a glance at his son-in-law. "Sorry," he said and dragged in a long breath. "My mind drifted."

"You were thinking about Ty, weren't you?" Logan guessed.

Chase nodded. "I was remembering the night Ty showed up in Blue Moon and informed me I was his father. I brought him back here." He lifted his gaze to the sweeping set of horns mounted above the mantel. "He asked about the horns, wanted to know if they were real. I told him the story of the brindle Longhorn steer called Captain that led the first cattle drive to this site. The same story my father told me." After a long pause, full of memory, his big chest lifted on a deep breath and Chase turned from the fireplace. "I feel old, Logan, older than this land." Grief haunted the darkness of his eyes. "A man shouldn't outlive his children."

"There can't be many things harder to bear." Logan's glance slid to the dried bloodstains on the front of Chase's shirt. It made for a poignant image of this powerful man.

During his years in law enforcement, Logan had observed similar things before. But it had more impact on him this time. He had come to know and respect both Ty and Chase Calder as more than just his in-laws.

Avoiding the desk, Chase walked over to the drink cart and poured a shot of whiskey into a glass. "What was it you were saying earlier?" he asked crisply, making it clear the time to reminisce was over. That he had made any expression of grief to Logan was a measure of the trust Chase had in him. Logan was counting on that, heavily.

"The autopsy is scheduled for tomorrow afternoon. The body will be released for burial either late in the evening or the next morning." He kept his answer factual, sensing it was what Chase wanted.

"Good. We'll be able to finalize the funeral arrangements." Chase studied the whiskey in his glass. He gave it a quick swirl then bolted down half of it. "Have you spoken with Culley yet? With Cat there, he was bound to be somewhere around."

"I talked to him," Logan confirmed with a nod. "He said he didn't see anything. He shadowed Cat and Quint when they drove the cattle back to camp." Like Chase, he avoided any direct reference to Ty.

"What about that piece of a knife blade that was still embedded in the wound? Were you able to learn anything from it?"

Logan briefly toyed with the idea of keeping that information to himself. But it came back to that issue of maintaining Chase's trust in him.

"We're still checking on it, but it appears to have been homemade."

"Like the kind you might confiscate from an inmate in prison," Chase suggested.

Logan didn't like the cold, steely look in Chase's eyes. Since coming to Montana, he had heard a few whispers about Calder justice. At that moment, Logan knew he needed to make it clear he would brook no interference.

"I'll handle this, Chase, just like I did the last time there was trouble," he stated firmly. Even though Buck Haskell hadn't been mentioned by name, they both knew he was the prime suspect. "Don't do anything on your own that you'll come to regret."

"I won't. You have my word on that." The corners of his mouth lifted in a smile that was as cold as his eyes, which made Logan all the more uneasy. "By the way," Chase continued, much too casually, "have you learned where Haskell was this morning?"

"It's being done now." Logan had nothing confirmed and refused to pass on any speculation that had been heard.

Chase didn't have an opportunity to question him further on the subject as footsteps approached the den. Recognizing the familiar light tread of them, Logan rose from the chair. When Cat entered the den, her green eyes were without their usual sparkle. Grief had dulled them and given her a faintly sunken and hollow look. It was a sight that ripped at him. Cat felt all things deeply; this time it was her brother's death.

She stopped when she saw him, her gaze clinging to his face. "I didn't hear you drive in."

Sensing the tight control she was exerting on herself,

Logan crossed the room and gathered her loosely in his arms. "I've only been here a few minutes." He felt her shudder then relax against him, her arms circling to clutch him close. "Chase said you were upstairs helping Jessy get the twins in bed. Are they asleep?"

"Finally," she mumbled against his shirt then drew back, tilting her head to look at him, a stark pain in her expression. "It was awful, Logan. Three times Trey asked for his daddy. I know he's too young to understand, but he must sense something." With a sudden flicker of concern, Cat looked quickly around the room. "Where's Quint?"

"In the living room," Chase told her. "Sound asleep on the couch."

"Poor guy." She managed a wan smile. "It's past his bedtime, too. We're ready to go home whenever you are."

"Sorry, but I'm going to be tied up awhile longer." Logan didn't say with what, but she knew he meant with the ongoing investigation into her brother's murder.

On other occasions when he had to work late, she had usually made some joke about being married to a sheriff. This time, though, she drew away from him, bright tears welling in her eyes.

"Cat." Logan took a step after her.

"I'm fine," she insisted with a quick, high lift of her head. "Honestly. This Calder is tougher than she looks."

He looked at his petite wife and smiled, knowing it was true. "I stopped by the ranch and picked up a few things for you and Quint. I thought it might be better if you spent the night here. That way you won't have to drive back over first thing in the morning. If there's anything I forgot, you can let me know and I'll drop it by tomorrow."

"It's probably best that I stay here," Cat agreed on a

thoughtful note. "All the arrangements still need to be finalized, and—" She paused and glanced at Chase. "What will you do about roundup?"

"Nothing. I'll pull the boys off long enough to attend the funeral then send them back out 'til we finish. We can't stop now that we've started. You know that," Chase replied with a trace of impatience.

Cat knew it wasn't directed at her, but at the fact that it had to be that way. "Of course I do."

He threw a look beyond her. "Is Jessy coming down?"

"In a few minutes, she said," Cat replied.

"Good. I—" Chase broke off the sentence, catching the muffled roar of a fast-traveling vehicle outside.

He turned with a frown as headlight beams slewed across the windows. This was not a night when people would call to offer their sympathies. Tonight was a time for the family to grieve in private.

As the bright beams swung away from the windows, brakes squealed and tires skidded. In all of it, there was a sense of alarm. Chase headed for the front door as racing feet pounded up the porch steps.

"Dear God, what's happened now?" Cat picked up the same vibrations and darted a worried look at Logan, but he had already followed Chase into the wide hall.

The front door burst open with a force that slammed it against the doorstop. A wild-eyed Tara rushed in and halted briefly when she saw Chase, wet streaks of black mascara running down her cheeks.

"Chase, thank God." She launched herself at him, desperate fingers clutching at his shirtfront. "They just told me—" Tara broke off the sentence with a denying shake of her head. "It's not true. It can't be true. Ty is here, isn't he?" Emotion sobbed in her voice. Frantic, she looked past him. "I need to see him."

"Tara." Chase gripped her shoulders. "Tara, it's true. Ty is—"

"No!" she screamed to silence him and twisted in a wild frenzy to pull away, fear giving her a man's strength. "That's a lie! He isn't dead. He's here. I know he is."

In a frenzy, Tara charged toward the living room. Logan made a grab for her, but she jerked free from him as easily as she had from Chase.

"You aren't going to keep me from him. None of you!" Tara hurled the warning, a half-crazed glare in her eyes. "I'll find him. Ty!" she called then saw Jessy coming down the stairs, her outer calm in direct contrast to Tara's hysteria. Tara froze for a split second then ran for the steps. "He's up there, isn't he? Ty! Ty?"

At the landing, Jessy blocked Tara's path. "You can't go up there. You'll wake the twins."

"Get out of my way!" Tara shrieked and reached to push Jessy aside. "Ty's up there! I have to see him. Ty! Ty!"

As always, she had met her match in Jessy. Jessy shoved her back. "Stop it, Tara! He's dead."

Wild with denial, Tara threw herself at Jessy again. "You're lying," she sobbed hoarsely. "You're all lying."

Reinforcements arrived in the form of Logan as he grabbed Tara from behind and pulled her off Jessy. When Tara started to fight him, Jessy slapped her hard across the face.

"I have wanted to do that for a long time." Jessy glared at Tara with a kind of cold, controlled anger. "Now, get it through your head—Ty is dead. All the ranting and raving in the world won't change it."

With a horrible cry of pain, Tara collapsed into Logan's suddenly supporting arms. He managed, with some difficulty, to scoop her up and carry her down the short flight of stairs, her arms, legs, and head dangling in limpness.

"I think she fainted," he said to Cat and Chase.

"I'll see if Sally has any smelling salts." Cat moved toward the kitchen.

"Ordinary household ammonia will work just as well," Logan told her as he carried Tara into the living room.

Awakened by the commotion, a sleepy-eyed Quint looked on in confusion. "What's wrong, Dad?"

"Nothing, son. Tara fainted, that's all." With Quint on the couch, Logan deposited the unconscious Tara in the overstuffed armchair.

Jessy followed them into the living room and looked at Tara with dispassion. "I don't care what you do with her, but she isn't staying here."

"Don't worry. She won't," Chase stated.

Busy propping Tara in the chair, Logan made no comment. When Cat returned to the living room, Sally was right behind her. Revived by a couple of whiffs of ammonia, Tara coughed and choked into wakefulness. She looked around wildly for a second. Then her eyes focused on Sally.

"He's gone, Sally," she blubbered. "What am I going to do?"

She immediately began to sob and wail hysterically. When Sally took over the job of attempting to console her, Logan left her to it and turned to Chase.

"See if you can raise somebody at Tara's place. Have them fly a doctor there right away. She'll likely need to be sedated." He made a grim study of the distraught woman. "As soon as we can get her to settle down, I'll put her in the back of my squad car and take her there. Maybe Sally can ride along and keep an eye on her tonight. She is in no condition to be left alone, that's for sure."

After twenty minutes, Tara's hysterical sobbing finally subsided to an incessant weeping and moaning. Logan half carried and half walked her to his vehicle and installed Tara in its back seat. Sally crawled in after her and gathered the sobbing woman into her arms.

With The Homestead quiet once more, Cat retrieved their overnight case, took Quint by the hand, and led him upstairs to bed. Jessy watched the pair until they disappeared from view.

"Poor guy," she murmured to Chase, observing, "he is so tired."

"Are you?" His gaze made a thoughtful study of her face.

Jessy reacted with a sharp shake of her head, her glance sliding upward in the direction of the master bedroom. "I can't sleep. Not yet."

"Good. We need to talk." He started toward the den. But Jessy was quick to reject it. "I'd rather not, Chase."

His glance was full of understanding, yet insistent. "I don't want to any more than you do, but these next few days will be hectic and there are things that need to be said. Right now may be the only time we have."

Jessy didn't renew her objection when he placed a guiding hand on her back and steered her into the den. She sat down in one of the wing-backed chairs, but she didn't relax in it, tension showing in the line of her body. Chase paused at the drink cart, poured some whiskey into two glasses and carried one to her, then reluctantly made his way to the swivel chair behind the desk.

"It doesn't seem real, does it?" he guessed astutely.

Her mouth twisted in a wry grimace of acknowledgment. "A part of me keeps expecting him to walk through the door." Head down, Jessy stared at the glass in her hand. "I have to be honest, Chase. I'm not sure I can stand to live in this house."

"Why?" He rocked back in his chair. "Because it's nothing but a bunch of rooms, filled with familiar things yet empty and lifeless? Because it doesn't feel like a home anymore?"

Jessy lifted her head, stunned that Chase could describe it so accurately. Until that moment it hadn't occurred to her that the house might feel the same way to him. Why should it when he had lived in it all his life while it had been her home for only a few years?

"It's a feeling that won't go away anytime soon, take my word for it," Chase told her, and Jessy immediately thought of Maggie and how difficult it must have been for Chase to live here after she died. "Eventually Trey and Laura will breathe life into it and make it feel like a home again. In the meantime, you have to hang on and wait."

"I suppose." She felt much too empty inside to care.

"You are a strong woman, Jessy. And a smart one, too. I'm counting on that," he stated. "Take a good look at that map on the wall behind me."

Responding to the authority in his voice, Jessy did as she was told even though she had looked at it a thousand times before. Every mark and line on its aged surface was as familiar as her own face in the mirror.

"There is no way any man can know if he will live two more days or twenty years. But we both know it isn't likely that I will live to see Trey take over the reins of the Triple C. That means it will be in your hands."

Jessy stared at the map, the length and breadth of its boundaries making a new impact on her. The possibility that she might one day shoulder the responsibility of its operation was not one she had ever imagined. But the truth in Chase's words couldn't be ignored, however much she might want to deny them.

As if reading her mind, Chase said, "Neither one of us expected this to happen, but it has. Maybe I should have waited a few days before telling you, but it has to be faced. You might as well know the Triple C won't give us time to mourn. There is work to be done, Jessy. And it's up to you and me to do it."

Everything he said rang true. "I have a lot of learning to do," she realized.

A small smile of approval edged the corners of his mouth. "Not as much as you think." He nodded at the glass in her hand. "Drink that whiskey and go to bed. It's going to be a long full day tomorrow."

She bolted down the liquor and shuddered at that searing burn that banished the coldness within. She met Chase's gaze, feeling closer to him than she ever had. Rising, she set the empty glass on his desk and crossed to the door.

Pausing there, Jessy glanced back. "When are you going after Buck?"

He studied her for a long measuring second. "You'll have no part of that, Jessy."

Calm as could be, she replied, "Yes, I will."

Chapter Twenty-One

~~

By 6 A.M. the following morning, Jessy had a hearty breakfast of steak, eggs, hash browns, toast, and oatmeal on the table, taking over the duty that would normally have been Sally's province. When Chase walked into the dining room, his hair still damp from a shower, she was already seated at the table, spooning homemade strawberry jam onto her toast.

Chase glanced at the empty chairs before crossing to the chafing dishes on the sideboard. "Isn't Cat up yet?"

"She and Quint are getting the twins dressed. They will be down shortly, I imagine."

"Good. I just saw Logan drive in." He lifted the lid on one of the dishes, releasing a fresh wave of steam, scented with the aroma of seasoned beef.

It was a tantalizing aroma, but it failed to stir Jessy's appetite. She ate because the day would be long and she would need the energy food could give her.

"Maybe he'll have some news for us," she said as the front door opened. Seconds later Logan entered the dining room. "There's plenty of food over there. Help yourself," Jessy told him.

"Thanks, but I'll just have coffee. I ate about an hour ago." He poured a cup from the coffee urn and carried it to the table. "Is Cat up?"

"She should be down shortly." Chase sliced into his steak.

"I spoke to Sally this morning. She should be home in a few hours. One of the household staff in Fort Worth is flying up to stay with Tara," Logan said.

"Probably Brownsmith. He's been with the family for years," Chase said, then paused, his gaze searching Logan's face. "Anything new with the investigation?"

"Not yet."

Logan's voice and expression were a bit too bland for Chase's liking. It made him suspicious. "What about Buck? He's been questioned by now, hasn't he?"

"No."

As good as Logan was at his job, Chase could think of only one reason for that. "Buck has disappeared, hasn't he?"

"It looks that way," Logan admitted. "A couple workers remember seeing him yesterday morning, but they aren't sure of the time—early or late. Virgil claims they had lunch together. Obviously I haven't been able to verify that."

"Virgil would swear the sky was green if he thought it would help Buck," Chase scoffed. "Where did he say Buck was going?"

"He said he didn't know, and the helicopter never left the ground at all yesterday. Plus the construction foreman was able to account for all the vehicles."

"What about the horses?"

"According to Garcia," Logan replied, referring to one of the deputies, "the gray was the only horse in the corral when he arrived yesterday afternoon. Around five o'clock, he noticed a chestnut gelding drinking from the tank, grabbed a bucket of oats, and caught it."

"No saddle or bridle?" Chase guessed.

"None," Logan confirmed. "Virgil said it probably jumped the corral fence then wandered back when it got thirsty."

"Possible but not likely." Chase speared the bite of steak with his fork. "The chestnut was too flashy, too easily recognized. Buck probably switched to another horse. Did Garcia check the tack room to see if any saddles were missing?"

Logan nodded and took a sip of his coffee. "None of the saddle racks were empty, but no one seems to know how many saddles were there. Garcia tried to get a number from Tara. Before she answered, she insisted on knowing why he was asking—and you know what happened after that."

"There really is no doubt that Buck did it, is there?" There was a hint of anger in the grim set of Jessy's features. "He wouldn't have taken off before Garcia got there unless he was guilty. He wouldn't have even known about it."

"That's not quite true. He might have," Logan said. "Garcia said there was a police scanner in the trailer. I plan to find out today whether Virgil had it turned on yesterday. If he did, then Buck could have heard something before Garcia arrived."

Cat's arrival with Quint and the twins signaled an end to the subject. The conversation quickly turned general with heavy emphasis on the demands of the twins.

After a second cup of coffee, Logan rose from the table, kissed Cat goodbye, rumpled Quint's hair, and headed for the door. Finished with his breakfast, Chase walked with him.

Trey, as usual, was more interested in playing with Quint than in eating his breakfast. Judging by the amount of cereal smeared on his face, in his hair, and on his clothes, Jessy suspected Trey had more food on him than in him. The bowl had three bites left when Trey began splatting his spoon in it.

"That's enough, young man." She took the sticky spoon from his equally sticky fingers, grabbed the wet washcloth she always kept handy, and wiped his face and hands with it before freeing him from his highchair. "You definitely need a bath before your grandma gets here."

"Gamma come?" Trey cocked his head at an inquiring angle.

"That's right." Jessy noticed a glob of cereal on the sleeve of his T-shirt and picked it off. "The brave woman is going to watch you two today."

"Kint?" He stretched out a hand to him in question.

"She's brave, not foolish." Jessy turned, her attention caught by the sound of the front door opening. "Sounds like Grandpa is headed off to roundup. Let's go say goodbye to him."

With Trey straddling her hip, Jessy reached the front hall in time to see Ballard enter the den. Curiosity drew her forward to within earshot of the conversation inside the room.

"Is there a problem, Ballard?" Chase asked.

"The problem is me," Ballard replied on a grim note. "I would've bet my life Jessy was the target, but we both know I was dead wrong. I feel like it's my fault. If I hadn't opened my mouth, none of us would have been distracted with worrying about Jessy."

"That's something we'll never know."

"I recognize that," Ballard admitted. "I know I wasn't raised on Triple C, but when you go after Haskell, I want to come along."

After a slight pause, Chase said, "I'll remember that."

"I hope you do. It's the only way I'm gonna feel right about any of this. Anyway, that's what I came to say. I know there's a lot you've gotta do today, so I won't keep you from it."

As his footsteps approached the hall, Jessy quietly backed up a few steps to make it less obvious she had been eavesdropping. Ballard halted when he saw her, his achingly gentle eyes making a quick and thorough study of her face.

"Are you holdin' up all right, Jess?"

Unconsciously she folded both arms around Trey, drawing a measure of comfort from the child Ty had given her. "I am."

"Good." The look of empathy in his eyes managed to convey that he knew the deep pain she felt. " 'Cause them kids are gonna need you, little though they may be. I guess you know if there's anything I can ever do . . ." He let the sentence trail off, unfinished.

"Thanks." The corners of her mouth lifted in a semblance of a smile.

He responded with a nod and a bolstering smile of his own. Then, without another word, he moved past her and out the front door. Jessy lingered in the hall a moment then continued to the den, entering as Chase stood up and reached for his work Stetson, a clear indication he was preparing to leave.

"I guess you're heading to Broken Butte," Jessy observed.

Chase nodded and pushed his hat on. "I'll be there until late."

"I listened in on your conversation with Ballard," Jessy admitted. "Will you take him with you?"

Chase ran his gaze over her face. "Would you?"

In that instant, Jessy knew this was to be her first lesson in leadership. She thought it over for several seconds. "I'm not sure why—I certainly don't question his loyalty, but—I wouldn't."

"You have good instincts," he told her. "Remember that and go with them, regardless of what your head says."

Late that afternoon, Chase took his own advice. With the roundup well in hand at Broken Butte, he left Stumpy in charge, climbed in his pickup, and headed southeast, but not toward The Homestead. The route he traveled took him straight to Wolf Meadow.

Bypassing the house, he drove directly to the mobile home, set back in the shade of the bluff. He climbed out of the cab and made a slow scan of the area, taking special note of the workers moving about, especially the idle ones. He saw what he expected to see, and climbed the metal steps to the trailer door. Chase rapped twice on it and walked in.

It took a second for his eyes to adjust to the relative dimness of the trailer's interior. He swept his glance over the narrow living room and brought it to a stop on Virgil Haskell, seated in a corner recliner, an afghan bundled around his legs despite the trailer's stuffy warmth. Virgil sat forward, his bony fingers gripping the ends of the chair's armrests, his eyes glaring his hostility.

"I had a feeling you'd show up," Virgil said, a slight smirk to his mouth. "But I didn't figure you'd come alone. You took quite a chance, Calder. What if Buck had been here?"

"Then my search would have been over," Chase replied smoothly. "Where is he, Virgil?"

"I can't say." Virgil leaned back against the recliner

and folded his hands on his lap. "For all I know, he could be in Canada by now."

Bowing his head briefly, Chase glanced at the floor then back at the old man. "I imagine that's what you told Logan so he would switch his focus away from here. But I don't buy it. He's still around, isn't he?"

Avoiding any comment on that, Virgil settled a little deeper in the chair, his expression taking on a look of malicious satisfaction. "You're mad clean through, ain't ya? I guess now you know how it feels to have your son taken away from you."

"I always knew there was a bitterness in you, Virgil. But I never realized how deeply it had eaten into you. You even poisoned your own son with it." After throwing the old man a look mixed with pity and disgust, Chase struck out for the kitchen area.

Startled, Virgil demanded, "Hey, where are you goin'?" Then he grinned. "You don't really think Buck's hidin' in here somewheres. The cops already searched every nook and cranny in it. But you go ahead and look."

"I'm not looking for Buck." Upon reaching the kitchen, Chase began going through the cupboards.

"What are you doing in there?" Puzzled and a little worried, Virgil stretched forward to peer into the kitchen.

"Checking to see what he might have taken with him in the way of supplies."

"You've got no business snooping through them cupboards." Virgil groped for his cane, found it, and struggled out of the recliner.

"He didn't leave much for you to eat," Chase observed.

"I don't need much." Virgil entered the kitchen, the cane giving his shuffling footsteps a three-beat sound. " 'Sides, mostly we eat what's left from the meals over at the main house. I ain't much for cookin' and neither is Buck."

"It shows." Chase closed the door on the last cupboard and made a final scan of the kitchen.

Gripping the cane with both hands, Virgil leaned his weight on it. "You aren't gonna' quit snooping now, are you?" he challenged. "Go ahead. Check out the rest of the rooms. Maybe you'll find him hiding in a closet."

"No. Buck isn't here."

"What makes you so sure of that?"

"Buck is a lot of things, but he isn't a fool. As long as there is someone watching this place, he won't try sneaking back here." Chase paused, noting the surprise that briefly registered in the old man's face. "You didn't know there was a man posted outside, did you?"

"Don't matter." Virgil dismissed the subject with a shrug of his bony shoulders. "Like you said, Buck's no fool. You can have people watch 'til the snow flies and they ain't gonna see him. He's far from here, way beyond your reach, long as it is." He shot Chase a look of pure loathing and shifted in place, turning to head back into the living room.

"No, he's holed up somewhere." It was a gut feeling Chase had, and it was a strong one. "Somewhere on the Triple C. Somewhere right under my nose. That's the way he thinks."

Halting, Virgil pounded his cane on the floor in a fit of anger. "Why can't you let him be? You drove him off. Ain't that enough for you? Why do you have to hunt him down?"

"We both know why I'm doing it. So does Buck," Chase fired back, his voice cold and hard.

Virgil looked at him with bitter resentment. "The minute he heard Ty was killed, he knew you'd be comin' after him."

"I suppose you're going to tell me that you heard about it on the police scanner," Chase guessed.

"I did," Virgil insisted forcefully.

"And you, of course, told Buck. But that's not to say he didn't already know about it." He watched the old man closely and got his answer when Virgil had difficulty meeting his gaze.

"Grief, that's all you Calders have been to my family," Virgil grumbled and shuffled into the living room. "It's past time you had some grief of your own."

During the long drive back to the Triple C headquarters, Chase made a mental list of anyplace on the ranch that might afford Buck an out-of-the-way hiding place, both the obvious and the not-so-obvious ones. The size of the ranch made for a long list.

The doors of The Homestead opened to a steady stream of callers that evening as townspeople and neighboring ranchers stopped by to express their sympathy. It was close to eleven o'clock before the last one left and the family had the house to themselves once more.

With the silence pressing on him from all sides, Chase retreated to the den. Aware that sleep would be a long time coming to him this night, he went through the telephone messages that had come in for him. The stack was a tall one. About halfway through them, he became conscious that he was being watched. Glancing up, he saw Jessy in the doorway.

"Turning in?" he asked.

"Soon." She ran her gaze over the fireplace. "Every time I go by this door, I keep expecting to see Ty standing by the fireplace. It's always such a shock not to see him."

"I know." Chase rarely looked in its direction.

"Sorry." Jessy knew it was not the way of the Calders to talk about the loved ones they had lost. Tonight it had been unavoidable.

"I understand."

Restless and reluctant to go upstairs to an empty bedroom, she wandered into the den. "Did you have a chance to talk to Logan tonight?"

"Just for a few minutes. Long enough to learn he had nothing new to report," Chase admitted.

"He mentioned that he alerted all the border guards to be on the lookout for Buck. He seems to think he might try to slip into Canada."

Chase shook his head. "I don't think so. I'm certain Buck is hiding out somewhere on the Triple C. He knows everybody will expect him to make a run for the border. He'll lie low for a while until some of the heat is off. Then he'll make his move." But Chase didn't think it would be north to Canada.

Caught by surprise, Jessy said, "You don't really think he's here on the ranch, do you?"

"I do," he stated. "It's the kind of clever plan he would come up with. But this time he has outsmarted himself."

"But where?" Jessy looked at the yellow map on the wall for answers.

"*That* I don't know," Chase admitted. "But I intend to scour every inch of this ranch until I find him."

"When?"

"After the funeral."

On Sunday, private aircraft crowded the hangar area of the Triple C landing strip. The ranchyard itself was a parking lot for the multitude of vehicles that had brought a host of mourners to the graveside service. The huge turnout spoke both to the far-reaching power of the Calder name and to the esteem in which Ty was held by those who had known him.

It was standing room only in the small cemetery near the river. Folding chairs were provided only for the immediate family and the more distinguished mourners. Wearing a dress of unrelieved black, Jessy sat next to Chase, her tawny head bared to the sun. Laura sat quietly on her lap, fingering the petals of the red rose in her hand, entranced by their velvety texture. Chase held Trey, who had yet to fidget restlessly as if sensing the solemnness of the occasion.

When the last murmured "Amen" faded to silence, Jessy lifted her head. Grief was locked deep inside, too private and too painful to share. Cat and her family were the first to rise and step to the bronze casket, gleaming in the sunlight. One by one, each of them laid a single red rose atop it. Chase touched a hand to her elbow, signaling it was their turn.

Her legs felt wooden beneath her when she stood, but Jessy managed to step up and laid her rose on it. Wordlessly she let her fingers trail over the casket in a farewell caress.

"Leave your rose for Daddy," she murmured to Laura and held her forward, watching as she carefully placed it with the others.

Moving to the side, Jessy waited for Chase. Tight-lipped with pain but otherwise without expression, he deposited his rose with the rest. Without being told, Trey stretched forward and dropped his flower onto the casket.

"Bye-bye, Daddy." His innocent voice rang out, clear and poignant.

For the first time in two days, Jessy choked up. Fighting back tears, she turned away and allowed Logan to draw her into their circle.

Other mourners filed past the gravesite. Those who had yet to speak personally to the family continued on to pay their respects. It was a moment before Jessy could no more than nod in a response.

Tara was among the last to approach the grave. Wearing a black hat, black veil, black dress, black gloves, and supported by her houseman Brownsmith, she made a tragic figure. Recalling Tara's last display of hysteria, Jessy braced herself for another such exhibition of it. But it didn't come.

Without a single audible sob, Tara placed something on the casket, but Jessy wasn't able to see it until Tara moved out of the way. There, atop the bright red roses left by the family, lay a single Texas-yellow rose. In many ways, it was a galling sight, but Jessy refused to give rise to the anger she felt.

Just the same there was a bitter taste in her mouth when Tara paused before her. The black veil's thick screen failed to conceal the haunted flatness of Tara's eyes. The absence of their lively black gleam was a kind of shock.

"I know how deeply you grieve, Jessy," Tara said in a lifeless voice that revealed her own pain. "I don't know what role I played in his death, but I will wonder until the day I die whether Ty might still be alive if I hadn't come back. I wanted him to hurt just as I hurt. But I didn't want this. I swear I didn't." Giving Jessy no opportunity to reply, she turned to Chase. "I will use every means I have to see that his murderer is found."

Then she was moving away, her place taken by the lieutenant governor and his wife. Others were lined up behind them. Jessy understood that this was all part of death's ritual, but she was eager for it to be over even though it would almost be worse to be alone with her memories.

The line was still long when Jessy caught splashing sounds coming from the river, followed by the telltale pound and scrape of hooves climbing the bank. Curious, she glanced toward the deep shade of the cottonwoods along the bank as a slender rider scrambled out of the saddle and moved swiftly through the trees toward the cemetery. Jessy recognized Culley at once and wondered at his haste.

Although distracted by the next in line, she kept darting glances to keep track of Culley as he made his way toward Cat. Jessy knew instinctively that something was wrong or the shy man wouldn't come anywhere near such a large gathering.

But it was Logan that Culley drew aside, said something to him, and pointed west. Jessy automatically glanced in the same direction. At first she saw nothing. Then she noticed the dark cloud band that hugged the far horizon. For a split second, she froze in alarm.

Turning, she reached to claim Chase's attention. But she was too late. "Chase!" Ballard pushed his way to the front of the line. "Look! That's smoke."

It took only one look for Chase to confirm the sighting. He didn't have to see the flames to know they were dealing with a grassfire, and a big one at that.

Immediately Chase began snapping out orders. "Stumpy, get the pumper truck manned. The rest of you, load up your trucks with every rake, shovel, and blanket you can lay your hands on, and fill up anything that can hold water." He pushed Trey into Cat's arms. "Notify the county, Logan. We're going to need help."

Ballard paused long enough to warn Jessy, "Get the kids to the house as quick as you can. It's gonna get crazy around here."

Jessy could already see the beginnings of it. Fire was a word that spread through the throng of mourners like a contagion. Those who knew what to do were already moving into action. The rest had stopped to gawk, unaware of the very real danger it presented. The drought had turned the grass plains into a vast tinderbox. Any fire that took hold would be hard to stop. And the wide swath of dark smoke warned of the fire's momentum. Worst of all, the prevailing wind was blowing it straight toward the Triple C headquarters.

Pushed by the urgency of the moment, Jessy handed Laura to her mother. "Look after the twins for me, Mom."

Grateful for the flats she had elected to wear, Jessy ran toward The Homestead, weaving in and out of the people and vehicles in her path. Once inside the house, she didn't pause but raced upstairs, stripped out of her dress, and pulled on jeans, boots, and a shirt. Then she was running back outside.

It was a chaotic scene that greeted her. Vehicles clogged the yard, some attempting to leave, more trying to get to the fire. Already three pickups had broken free from the traffic jam and were speeding over a ranch road toward the ominous wall of smoke.

Not far behind them was the pumper truck. Jessy knew instinctively that Chase was in one of the pickups.

A horse whinnied near the barn area, drawing her attention to a cowboy in his Sunday suit leading two saddled horses to the ramp of a stock trailer. With a slap on the rump, he loaded them into the trailer and disappeared back inside the barn.

Launching herself off the steps, Jessy headed for the stock trailer and a certain ride to the fire. Along the way she passed her mother and Sally, each with a twin in her arms and Quint herded between them.

"Be careful," her mother called. "And remind your father he isn't as young as he used to be."

Jessy didn't bother to reply. But none was expected.

* * *

At the head of the ranch pickups, Chase sat on the passenger side, one arm braced against the dashboard to absorb the jolts of the rough ride. His gaze was fixed on the smoke wall still some distance ahead of them. Stumpy was behind the wheel, his short leg stretched stiff to keep his foot hard on the accelerator.

"What about Six Mile Road?" Stumpy said. "Maybe we can use it for a firebreak."

"I don't think so. It looks like it's already on this side of it," Chase said grimly. "We'll have to make a stand along that big dry wash. It's the only natural barrier left between here and the river. God help us if it gets that far."

Stumpy muttered a few choice expletives under his breath. A half-mile farther, he slowed the truck and made the turn into the fence gate. Chase hopped out of the cab, threw the gate open wide, signaled for the rest of the vehicles to follow them, and climbed back in.

As the pickup rolled through the gate, Stumpy pointed its nose in the direction of the wash and took off cross-country. When they topped a hillock, Chase had his first glimpse of the long red line of flames that underscored the smoke clouds.

Stumpy saw it, too. "Jeez, Chase, it's close to a half-mile wide already."

"And spreading fast."

When they reached the dry wash, Stumpy traveled along its bank until they reached a spot that would be roughly the midway point of the advancing flames. The minute the truck rolled to a halt, Chase piled out of it. The smoke from the grassfire had yet to reach them, but the smell of it was in the air.

"Spread out in both directions," he shouted to the

others. "We'll start a backfire on the other side of the wash. Don't let it get away from you."

The dry washbed ran wide for a good distance then narrowed dangerously. Coulees emptied into the wash in three other places along this stretch, two of them overgrown with brush. All were critical points, but Chase was more concerned about the south end of the wash. He dispatched the pumper truck to that area where water would be their best weapon, maybe their only one.

By the time Jessy had arrived on the scene, flames from the first backfires were crackling through the dry grass along the opposite bank. At intervals all up and down the wash, men in suits and white shirts worked to keep the backfire contained. Most were Triple C hands, but Jessy noticed a few from neighboring ranches plus some longtime residents of Blue Moon among them. A smoke haze hung over the entire scene, scratching her throat with each breath she took.

"What's the plan?" she asked.

"With any luck, the backfire will slow it down and give the fire trucks a chance to get here. At best, we'll force it south, away from headquarters," Chase replied.

A half-dozen pronghorn antelope bounded out of the smoke, saw the men on the fire line, and veered off. "We have got livestock trapped over there," Jessy realized.

"It can't be helped." Chase threw a look over his shoulder. "I told Ballard to load up some horses."

"He's parked over there." Jessy hooked a thumb in the direction of the stock trailer. "I rode with him."

"Get yourself some riders and start making a sweep. Push any cattle you find toward the river. I don't want to lose any more than we have to."

"Right."

Aware that it was a job that didn't require an experienced hand, Jessy made her pick from among the teenagers on the fire line. All were young enough to be glad that a different task had been found for them, one that would take them away from the heat and choking smoke.

Ballard had all the horses unloaded when Jessy returned with her four young riders. She gave each of them a specific area to cover and climbed into the saddle herself. As she reined her horse away from the trailer, she noticed Ballard was still on the ground just putting a foot in the stirrup.

"When you make your sweep north, don't forget to check that big coulee," she told him.

"I won't." Ballard swung into the saddle.

Satisfied, Jessy rode away. Not thirty yards from the wash, she came across a half-dozen cows. Already snuffy from the pungent smoke smell in the air, they spooked immediately at her approach. But they were headed in the right direction and Jessy let them go and continued along her parallel course with the wash.

She hadn't traveled far when she was surprised by a trio of young steers that bolted across her path. Not far behind them was a cowboy on a bay horse. A faded blue bandanna sat high on his nose, filtering out the ever-thickening smoke.

The minute he caught sight of her, he pulled up and shouted, "Seen Chase?"

"Back on the fire line," she answered. Unable to recognize him, Jessy assumed he was from a neighboring ranch.

The man sketched her a salute and loped off in the direction she indicated. Still puzzled, Jessy watched him a moment then started her horse forward. Yet she felt uneasy without knowing why. A little frisson of alarm shot through at the possibility the man had been Buck Haskell.

In a flash she wheeled her horse around and set out after him.

Smoke hung over the dry wash like a fog, burning eyes and scratching throats, but there was a blackened stretch of fire-scorched ground five feet wide on the other side. It was a good start on a firebreak, but that was all.

Like most of the men, Chase had shed his suit jacket and loosened his collar. Already the flying ash and cinders had grayed his white shirt and deposited a coating of soot along the brim of his cream-colored dress Stetson. Those with large kerchiefs had tied them across their faces, but not Chase.

He moved along the bank of the dry wash, constantly checking on the main fire, measuring its speed and distance. He knew if he could stop its advance here, the road to the north could contain it with only a handful of men, allowing him to shift the bulk of his manpower to the south.

When he paused to wipe the sweat from his face, Chase noticed a tiny tongue of flame licking through the dry grass on this side of the wash. Moving quickly, he stomped it out with the heel of his boot then slid down the bank to the floor of the dry wash, scooped some sand and gravel into his hat, carried it back up, and dumped it on the blackened patch to smother any remaining embers. Worried now, he made a quick scan for more such hot spots.

"Chase! Chase, over here!" The shouted call came

from somewhere behind him and to his right. Turning, Chase saw someone wave an arm then cup his hands to his mouth and call, "My horse is down! Can you give me a hand!"

The swirling smoke made it difficult for Chase to make a visual identification, but the voice sounded like Ballard's. Unwilling to pull anyone off the backfire to help him, Chase went himself.

When he was closer, Ballard yelled, "He's down here." Then he turned and half walked and half slid down an embankment. Almost immediately Chase heard the panicked whinny of a horse.

The minute he reached the gully's edge, Chase saw the problem. The horse was lying on its side, its legs tangled in a length of the rope and thrashing wildly despite Ballard's attempts to calm it.

"What happened?" Chase slithered down the bank a safe distance from the horse's flailing legs.

"He stepped wrong or somethin' comin' down the bank. We took a tumble," Ballard explained. "How the hell he got his legs tangled in the rope, I'll never know. I tried to cut him loose but he damned near kicked me to death. Straddle his neck for me, will ya? And hold him down. Maybe he'll stop fighting long enough that I can cut him loose."

Obligingly Chase circled around to the horse's head. "Easy, boy. Easy," he murmured to the wild-eyed gelding, then swung a leg over its neck and carefully lowered himself onto the animal.

The horse made one frightened attempt to throw him off then subsided into shudders. "If you're ready, I'm gonna work on the rope," Ballard said, knife in hand.

"Go ahead." Chase gave a sharp nod and glanced back as Ballard lowered himself onto the saddle skirt and cautiously swung a leg over the horse's belly. Then he was out of sight.

"Look out, Chase!"

Startled by the sudden shout from atop the gully, Chase turned, catching sight of a horse and rider above him. Then something hot stabbed his side. It took Chase a split second to realize it was the knife.

The overwhelming instinct for survival numbed him to the agonizing pain in his side. He threw himself around and grappled to seize Ballard's knife hand.

Suddenly a shot rang out. Ballard grunted, his expression freezing in shock, his back arching stiffly. Then he sagged against Chase, fingers clutching at him for support.

Chase pushed him off, pain stabbing at his side. He put a hand to it, felt the warm wetness of blood, and looked up. Buck Haskell stood at the edge of the embankment, a blue kerchief down around his neck and a rifle in his hands, a faint trail of smoke curling from the barrel.

"Any debt I owed you, Chase, is squared now." Buck's mouth crooked in a near smile.

Chase was too stunned to reply. In the next breath, a rope sailed out of nowhere, its noose falling around Buck. It was tightened in a flash, and Buck was jerked off his feet, the rifle falling from his grip.

"No!" Chase shouted and scrambled up the bank of the gully.

There was Jessy, wrapping the rope around the saddle horn and backing her horse to keep it stretched taut. "Chase, you're alive," she cried in relief when she saw him climb out of the gully. "I heard the shot and—"

"Let him up," he ordered. "He just saved my life."

"Haskell," Jessy repeated in disbelief and belatedly

urged her horse forward, putting slack in the rope. "But the gunshot?"

"He wasn't shooting at me." Chase crouched beside Buck, clutching his side with one hand and tugging the encircling rope loose with the other one. Eyes shut in pain and mouth open, Buck strained to get air into his lungs, a sure sign the wind had been knocked out of him. "He was shooting at Ballard."

"Ballard?" Jessy peeled out of the saddle, dropping the reins to hurry over to them.

"Yes, Ballard. He tried to kill me." With Jessy's help, Chase propped Buck into a sitting position. "Just like he probably killed Ty."

Buck choked down a couple gulps of air and murmured hoarsely, "That's the way I figure it."

Shocked and confused, Jessy stared at Chase. "But—why? I don't understand."

"You'll have to ask him," Chase replied and jerked his head toward the gully, "if he's still alive."

In a daze, Jessy moved toward the gully. A sudden surge of caution made her pick up the rifle. She paused at the gully's edge and looked down, seeing first the horse, then the prone figure of Ballard, lying facedown. Unwillingly she recalled all the times Ty had expressed his lack of trust in Ballard. That made the pain of losing him all the worse and the anger all the deeper until she shook with it, her fingers tightening their grip on the rifle, knuckles showing white.

Why? The question screamed in her mind.

Then she saw the slight, small movement of Ballard's fingers digging into the gravel. He was alive. Jessy threw herself into the gully, determined to have her answer.

Falling to her knees beside him, she grabbed his shoulder and rolled him onto his back, indifferent to his sharp groan of pain and the big smear of blood on his shirt-front from the bullet's exit wound.

"Ballard, can you hear me?" She gave him a hard shake. "Ballard."

His eyelids fluttered open, those blue eyes that she had always thought of as kind slowly focusing on her. "Jessy." His voice was faint, the corners of his mouth lifting in a smile before a grimace of pain twisted his features. "I . . . failed . . . didn't I?"

"Chase is alive, if that's what you mean," she answered tightly. "Why did you kill Ty? Dammit, I have to know!"

His mouth moved, but Jessy could only catch snatches of his answer. "Tara . . . clutches on . . . him . . . hurt you . . . 'gain."

"And Chase?"

". . . old. You . . . 'n me . . . ranch together . . . swear . . . didn't know you . . . in truck." He coughed spasmodically, blood pouring from his mouth. Then he was limp and silent.

She had her answers, but they didn't explain what made Ballard think she would turn to him after Ty was gone. But it was obvious the thought had gotten into his mind. It only made Ty's death seem all the more tragic and senseless.

With a knot in her throat as big as a fist, Jessy pushed to her feet and climbed out of the gully into the smoke haze. Buck was on his feet, but hunched over, still struggling to fill his lungs with air. Chase had a hand on his back.

"How did you know about Ballard?" Chase asked him.

"I saw him settin' the fire," Buck replied then twisted his head to peer up at Chase, a trace of his cocky grin showing. "I was holed up over in that old buffalo wallow by the west road. I figured you would never look for me in plain sight. I heard this vehicle stop, travel a little ways then stop again. I got curious and took a look-see. There Ballard was, crouched by the roadside, using his hat to fan a wisp of smoke into flames." Buck straightened and dragged in a good, deep breath. "It was easy to put two and two together at that point. I knew I hadn't killed Ty. I just couldn't prove it. And I knew he wouldn't have started the fire if he didn't have a plan. I decided to see if I could figure out what it was. I got lucky."

"I think I'm the one who was lucky." Chase hesitated, then held out his hand to the man who had once been his best friend.

Epilogue

৵

The bright September sun looked down from its perch in the never-ending sky and spread its light over the Triple C headquarters. Autumn's crispness was in the air, invigorating the senses and bringing a sharpness to the scene.

Chase stood outside the open doors of the old barn. Garbed in a Western-cut suit, string tie, and a new Stetson, he looked every inch the patriarch of the Calder Cattle Company. He gazed at the collection of vehicles parked in orderly rows a short distance from the barn and smiled when he caught sight of two dusty pickups among the Cadillacs, Mercedes, and BMWs.

The ranch's first livestock auction was scheduled to begin in twenty minutes, and the turnout for it was huge, bigger than Chase had expected. A steady hum of voices came from inside the barn, where most had already gathered, but a few continued to stroll past him. Chase recognized few of them by name although there were many faces he recalled seeing before at some function of the cattlemen's association. And in his opinion, few of those qualified as "cattle ranchers."

Ben Parker wasn't one of them. Chase eyed the Wyoming rancher now approaching him, the same man who had unwittingly sparked the idea of this livestock auction with his purchase of a young Triple C bull. The man with Parker, however, was definitely a stranger.

"Good to see you again, Chase." Parker greeted Chase with a typically hearty handshake. "Judging from this turnout, I won't be getting a bargain on any of your young bulls this trip."

"You can't win every time, Ben," Chase replied.

"But you can try," the rancher countered with a grin then gestured to the man at his side. "I thought your auction could use a little international flavor so I brought along a friend of mine. Chase, I'd like you to meet John Montgomery Markham, brother to the Earl of Stanfield in England. This is Chase Calder. I don't think I would be wrong in calling him one of the last of the cattle barons."

"I have heard of you by reputation, of course, Mr. Calder." His handshake was firm. "A pleasure."

"Welcome to the Triple C, Mr. Markham," Chase said with a nod.

"My friends call me Monte," the Englishman replied with an easy smile. "Ben tells me this is exceptional cattle country."

"Monte's looking to buy some land. I've been trying to talk him into buying that spread I've got over in the Wind River range."

"Going into the cattle business, are you?" Chase surmised.

"Nothing the scale of your operation," the Englishman replied. "I don't imagine there are many ranches like it still left these days."

"I guess not," Chase replied, although he suspected there were few if any that still encompassed their original boundaries. The Triple C did—thanks to the woman approaching the barn with Buck Haskell at her side. "Enjoy the auction, gentlemen," he said to the two and turned to await Tara's arrival.

He touched his hat to her when she paused before him, resplendent in a sparkling Western jacket, embroidered with stone-encrusted yellow roses. A month ago Tara had presented him with a free and clear title to the entire ten thousand acres of Wolf Meadow with the provision that she retained a life estate to the home she had built on it, Dunshill.

"I had to come, Chase," Tara said. "We worked so hard on this." She paused, pain flickering in her eyes. "I wish Ty could be here to see what a huge success it is."

"He knows."

"Of course," Tara murmured and glanced around. "Where is Jessy?"

"She'll be here shortly."

"I guess I'll see her later." She turned to Buck. "We had better go inside and find ourselves a seat."

With a lift of his hand, Buck gestured for Tara to precede him, then nodded to Chase. They exchanged no more than a glance, but there was no longer any animosity or distrust in it.

After the fire Chase had offered Buck a job, but Buck had refused, saying, "I think that would be pushin' it for both of us. Let's just take what we got for now."

The relief that Chase felt at his answer only confirmed the wisdom of Buck's decision. Maybe they would never be as close as they once were, but at least they were no longer enemies.

Moments later Chase saw Jessy coming across the yard, tall and strong and straight. His head lifted, a faintly stunned look to his expression at the sight of his daughter-in-law. There was nothing eye-catching about the suede shirt and pants she wore, both the same tawny gold as her hair, with matching boots and hat. But Jessy was eye-catching in her outfit, a slender column of gold, tall and lithe, moving with that long, free-swinging stride that was so natural to her. She emanated strength and steadiness and something else he hadn't noticed before, a trace of authority.

Chase smiled. When the day came for him to hand over the reins, they would be in good hands. And he strongly suspected that when they walked in that barn together, everyone else would see it, too.

Please turn the page for a preview of

SHIFTING CALDER WIND

by Janet Dailey.

A November paperback
from Zebra Books.

A blackness roared around him. He struggled to surface from it, somehow knowing that if he didn't, he would die. Sounds reached him as if coming from a great distance—a shout, the scrape of shoes on pavement, the metallic slam of a car door and the sharp clap of a gunshot.

Someone was trying to kill him.

He had to get out of there. The instant he tried to move the blackness swept over him with dizzying force. He heard the revving rumble of a car engine starting up. Unable to rise, he rolled away from the sound as spinning tires burned rubber and another shot rang out.

Lights flashed in a bright glare. There was danger in them, he knew. He had to reach the shadows. Fighting the weakness that swam through his limbs, he crawled away from the light.

He felt dirt beneath his hand and dug his fingers into it. His strength sapped, he lay there a moment, trying to orient himself, and to determine the location of the man trying to kill him. But the searing pain in his head made it hard to think logically. He reached up and felt the warm wetness on his face. That's when he knew he had been shot. Briefly his fingers touched the deep crease the bullet had ripped along the side of his head. Pain instantly washed over him in black waves.

Aware that he could lose consciousness at any second, either from the head wound or the blood loss, he summoned the last vestiges of his strength and threw himself deeper into the darkness. With blood blurring his vision, he made out the shadowy outlines of a post and railing. It looked to be a corral of some sort. He pushed himself toward it, wanting any kind of barrier, no matter how flimsy, between himself and his killer.

There was a whisper of movement just to his left. Alarm shot through him, but he couldn't seem to make his muscles react. He was too damned weak. He knew it even as he listed sideways and saw the low-crouching man in a cowboy hat with a pistol in his hand.

Instead of shooting, the cowboy grabbed for him with his free arm. "Come on. Let's get outa here, old man," the cowboy whispered with urgency. "He's up on the catwalk working himself into a better position."

He latched onto the cowboy's arm and staggered drunkenly to his feet, his mind still trying to wrap itself around that phrase "old man." Leaning heavily on his rescuer, he stumbled forward, battling the woodenness of his legs.

After an eternity of seconds, the cowboy pushed him into the cab of a pickup and closed the door. He sagged against the seat back and closed his eyes, unable to summon another ounce of strength. Dimly he was aware of the cowboy slipping behind the wheel and the engine starting up. It was followed by the vibrations of movement.

Through slitted eyes, he glanced in the side mirror

but saw nothing to indicate they were being followed. They were out of danger now. Unbidden came the warning that it was only temporary; whoever had tried to kill him would try again.

Who had it been? And why? He searched for the answers and failed to come up with any.

Thinking required too much effort. Choosing to conserve the remnants of his strength, he glanced out the window at the unfamiliar buildings that flanked the street.

"Where are we?" His voice had a throaty rasp to it.

"According to the signs, there should be a hospital somewhere ahead of us," the cowboy replied. "I'll drop you off close to the emergency entrance."

"No." It was a purely instinctual reply.

"Mister, that head wound needs tending. You've lost a bunch of blood—"

"No." He started to shake his head in emphasis, but at the first movement, the world started spinning.

The pickup's speed slowed perceptibly. "Don't tell me you're wanted by the law?" The cowboy turned a sharp, speculating glance on him.

Was he? For the second time, he came up against a wall of blankness. It was another answer he didn't know, so he avoided the question.

"He's bound to know I was hit, so he'll expect me to get medical attention. The nearest hospital will be the first place he would check."

"You're probably right about that," the cowboy agreed. "So where do you want to go?"

Where? Where? Where? The question hammered at him. But it was impossible to answer because he didn't know what the hell town they were in. That discovery brought a wave of panic, one that intensified when he realized he didn't know his own name.

He clamped down tightly on the panic and said, "I don't know yet. Let me think."

He closed his eyes and strained to dredge up some scrap of a memory. But he was empty of any. Who was he? What was he? Where was he? Every question bounced around in the void. His head pounded anew. He felt himself slipping deeper into the blackness and lacked the strength to fight against it.

*   *   *